# Wandering Warrior: Book 3

# Executioner

Michael Head

Copyright © 2024 by The Legion Publishers Ltd
Editing by James Kelly
Cover by Paganus
Typography by Paganus
Formatting by Christine Cajiao

## <u>TABLE OF CONTENTS</u>

## PROLOGUE 1

"Have there been any changes, Shōen?"

The man leaning against the stone railing seemed larger than his physical form, as if his internal power was barely contained by his corporeal being. He exuded a pressure that weighed on both the mind and body of anyone who entered his presence. It was something the person standing next to him had long since gotten used to experiencing.

"No, Milord. The structure's all there, but we can't get it to move without the key. Once we have it, I'm sure the new power source we installed will work far more efficiently than anything they had all those years ago. We won't know for sure without that key, though."

"And the key is lost with the princess, somewhere to the south, amongst the remains of the failure of our latest defeat and her destroyed army."

"As you say, Milord."

The two dropped into an uneasy silence, looking out over the vast cavern that held the airship that once carried the hope of an entire kingdom on its polished decks. Now, centuries later, its new intended purpose held even more importance than mere kingdoms could contain.

"You know the stakes. Don't stop trying to bypass the ancient security systems. If you can get this aloft, we can still stop the incursion before it spreads too far."

"It will be as you order, Destitute." The Duergar, or Gray Dwarf, turned away from the ancient vampire and shouted directions in his guttural language down to the swarm of workers crawling over the airship. Their frantic activity sped up by a fraction, and the two went to the other side of the overlook to observe the other structure in the underground cavern.

Another work crew was working on a second, sleeker version of an airship in a separate dock alongside the first. The sounds from the hammering and shouts coming from its narrow deck were blocked by the glowing runes that lined the perimeter of the area it was stored in. No one except those allowed by magic could enter the exclusion zone, and the guards placed intermittently around the construction site ensured no one working on the secondary airship left without permission.

"How much longer until this one is ready?" The ancient vampire's nails scraped along the stone railing, absentmindedly carving dusty grooves in the polished granite. "If we can have both of them ready, it would make our plans for the dragon much easier to make a reality."

"Not long, Milord. It's missing a power source, and we don't have the weapons installed, but everything else is nearly finished." Shōen leaned over the railing to get a closer look at the work being done. "The final set of masts are being secured in place now, and the balloons are being tested for leaks by the teams tonight."

"Good. It won't be long until at least one of these will be required to fly." The Destitute reached into a pocket and pulled out a small figurine of glass, shaped like an upraised fist. "We're going to have guests soon, and I want to greet them from a position of undeniable strength, not questionable authority. Owning the skies would go far toward convincing them, without having to resort to outright violence."

"You don't want to kill them? After everything they've done, I'd think you'd want to crush them the moment they got close enough for you to reach out and touch them." Shōen picked up a pebble from the ground and crushed it to dust between his fingers. "Keeping enemies running around isn't a smart move, especially with the demons pushing further into the caves."

"Don't forget our true mission. While the interloper is an annoyance, they aren't the focus. Besides, the enemy of my enemy can be a tool used to my advantage." The ancient vampire curled his perfectly manicured fingers around the symbol, flickers of blue flames dancing across his knuckles. "The demons won't care who they are, or which side they're on. They're only here to consume, and placing them in the path of the interloper will certainly end in my advantage. We'll have to ensure the two sides meet one another before we introduce ourselves."

"As you say, Destitute." The Duergar turned to leave, taking one last look over the railing before walking carefully down the steep set of steps. "I've got to report to the Council. I'll be back before sunrise."

"Tell them another team would make a lot of difference." The Destitute frowned, causing the flames dancing along his knuckles to flare in intensity. "I know it isn't likely, but it never hurts to ask."

Shōen shrugged, stopping to look back at his leader. "It's not their world to save, so they don't care like you do. For them, it's an investment, and they've already lost too much on this gamble."

"They're short-sighted fools." The Destitute took a deep breath, giving up the burst of frustration that passed over him. "If this world falls to the demon's corruption, what does the Council think will be their next target? Where will the demon lords open a portal to when there is nothing left of this one but bare rock and brimstone?"

"You don't have to convince me, Milord. That's why I'm here, remember?" Shōen waved at the construction going on below. "I know how hard it is to close a gate. These ships are our only chance."

"Thank you, old friend. Do what you can with the Council. That's all I can ask." The Destitute turned his back on Shōen, once again looking at the figurine in his hand. "They're not our last hope, but they are our best one. We've got to have help from somewhere, otherwise, this world is lost."

## PROLOGUE 2

"Have there been any changes, Lieutenant?" Commandant Beck stood on the tallest of the surviving gate towers with his arms crossed, looking over the city of Greendown. Below him, the process of rebuilding was in full swing, with several improvements implemented by both the Wardens and the guilds. At least, they were *trying* to implement them. Not every guild was happy about losing their power and control over the populace with the changes wrought by the new 'Constitution' they had been forced to sign, but enough were willing to see how the new plans could benefit *all* of Greendown. Which, of course, included the guilds.

Several districts had been outright flattened, along with several sections of the city walls. New ideas had been introduced by documents found in the Sailor's Guild, which made this the perfect time for the renovations the city would need to undergo. A new age was coming for the northernmost city in the kingdom, and nothing would be the same if they were successful.

"No, Commandant. The same problems still slow down construction, with new ones cropping up every day." Lieutenant Lucente was still recovering from the battle that happened three weeks ago, even with the healers helping her when they could. There weren't enough of them to go around, so she made sure they prioritized others before herself. It meant she was still wrapped in bandages, and her arm was in a splint, making it impossible for her to give a proper salute. That didn't stop her from trying. "The airship facility worksite is being hindered by lack of materials, like everything else. Crews are doing their best to build the actual airship, but the shipwrights keep complaining about the wrong kind of lumber, while the Leatherworker's and Weaver's Guilds are in competition with one another over who can make the better balloon. The leather version would be tougher, but heavier, while the fabric version would be lighter, but far easier to puncture. At least we've got the final selection of volunteer crews training for a test run once the first ship is ready, but there's no telling when it will finally be ready to fly."

9

"Did the Sailor's Guild give any kind of timeline for when it might be done? Our people's lives are depending on that ship getting to the mountains before they do. Without those supplies, they're going to freeze and starve to death the moment they get above the treeline." Beck looked off toward the east, where the construction of the airship was supposed to be progressing. "I don't want to do it, but we *could* ask the witches for help. They're certain to have some kind of spells to help speed things along."

"Sir, I can tell you right now, there is absolutely no way the coven would be willing to assist us. I don't even know of anyone who would be willing to go and ask them!" Lucente looked around at the destroyed city, her gaze lingering on the charred section that had served as the burning fields where the bodies of the fallen had been disposed of. "Too much blood has been spilled, on both sides."

"I'm fully aware of the lives lost, Lieutenant. Once you get to be my age, you begin to realize that yesterday's enemy can quickly become today's ally. It only requires the two sides to set aside their egos, and embrace the new reality." Beck took a long moment to gaze into the forest bordering the fields that surrounded the city, his eyes seeing into the past. He shook himself free of the memories plaguing his aging mind, and spun back to his subordinate. "Is there no one in our group willing to at least try? Someone with enough strength to travel the forest alone, while still presentable enough to represent our interests. We don't have the personnel to provide an escort for something like this. It's a longshot at best, and we need our Wardens here to assist in the building efforts."

"There… might be one." Lucente shifted her injured arm so it pointed toward one of the groups training on a skeletal mock-up version of the airship that was still being built. There were three separate teams trying to work out the inevitable issues that something so new and experimental was bound to produce. "It's the first mate of our primary crew. The brother-in-law of the new Sailor's Guild leader. You can see him from here. He's the exceedingly large man currently smacking the men out of the rigging with a mop." She squinted at the ludicrous scene, trying to figure out what was happening without being able to hear the shouts traded back and forth. "I think he's trying to teach them the importance of hanging on, even if you get hit by a bird when in the air. Either that, or they are running from him, and he's trying to get them down."

"And he can fight well enough to make his way to the witches' stronghold?" The Commandant suppressed a chuckle as a man in the very top of the makeshift rigging was knocked out of the ropes by a well-thrown mop handle. The large man on the decking of the training ship did his best to catch the man, keeping the wayward sailor from breaking his neck from the fall. He then started beating the man with the mop head, berating him for his failure to hold on. "I can see he has fire but the man seems… volatile. Can he negotiate without bringing more problems down on our heads?"

"He's a former mayor of one of the nearby villages, and he is fiercely loyal to the Judge. Apparently, James Holden healed his family, and the man is now one of his most vocal supporters. He's also a werebear, so he can easily defend himself." Lucente shrugged, wincing in pain at the motion. "I don't think we can do better on such short notice."

"A werebear, you say? I think I remember hearing something about his situation. It's interesting that he and Holden managed to become friends." Beck sighed, then pulled out a scroll and quill from a nearby pack so he could start writing. "I'll have the orders prepared shortly. Make sure he understands the importance of this mission. If he can convince the witches to join our side and help with the construction of the airships, it could make all the difference. He might be directly saving Holden's life."

"I'll let him know, Commandant. I have no doubt the former mayor will do everything he can to convince them." The Lieutenant turned to leave, but she paused before walking down the stairs. "Do you think we can do it, sir? Finish in time, I mean."

"Let's hope so, Lucente. While I still don't fully understand the dire rush Holden was in to hurry north, it doesn't change the situation." Commandant Beck turned to the north, where the normally beautiful peaks of the distant mountain range sat brooding under a cloudy sky. "I'm afraid too much of our future rides on the shoulders of too few. Those shoulders are capable enough to handle the load, but if we can't get at least one airship in the skies soon, all is lost. They can't eat air, and there's little enough of even that on those mountain slopes."

## PROLOGUE 3

The cavern had probably started as a natural formation, long before the dragon had turned it into its lair. Broken sections of stone stuck out of the ground and ceiling, where its nearly impenetrable scales had snapped off the rock formations that had formed over centuries of isolation. A clear pool of water sat in the center, fed by some unseen hot spring from deep in the earth. Its surface steamed faintly, causing a thin layer of condensation to form over every surface before it froze in layers of ice across the distant ceiling. Giant icicles replaced the shattered remains of stalactites, nearly touching the ground in thick columns near the edges of the underground chamber. Piles of ice-entombed treasure formed miniature hills of glittering gold, while mounds of frozen diamonds and gemstones cast rainbows of color that lit the room in a cascade of glowing beauty. It was a true wonderland that would steal the breath of any person that might stumble across it.

Now, the cavern deep in the mountain served as both the dragon's home, and prison. Long claw marks lined the walls, carved deep into the layers of ice and stone. Both the entrance and exit tunnel showed signs of amateurish excavation, widening them into archways that were still too small for the creature that lay curled along the banks of the steaming pool to fit through. The blue and silvered dragon had grown too large for its chosen home, becoming fat on the invaders that wandered into its lair. It waited patiently for the next wave of its chosen food to present itself, sleeping lightly enough that the slightest sound would quickly wake it. The scales that covered its thick hide seemed stretched to their limit, only underscoring how bulbous and rotund the dragon had become. It had been eating well, for a *very* long time.

Above the pool floated a long jagged line that hovered in the air, a piece of broken glass in the fabric of the world no larger than a single claw on the dragon's oversized paw. It glowed with a faint, steady yellow light, reflecting endlessly over the water and ice of the oversized cave. The false daylight it created lacked any warmth, but the hot spring was more than enough to keep the dragon alive in the frigid temperatures and high elevation where the cave was located.

Time passed, and the light gradually began to change. Its sunlight-like yellow slowly turned amber, before fading to a burnt orange. A high-pitched whine, barely on the edge of being audible, started to cause ripples across the smooth surface of the hot spring. Like the sound of two pieces of broken glass rubbing against one another, the jagged line started to grow.

Being a creature of powerful, ancient magics, the dragon was already awake and waiting when the change started. It could feel when the tear between dimensions was ready to disgorge its latest group of invaders, and readied itself to pounce, hunched down and trembling like an overly excited–and overweight–barnyard cat, its tail whipping back and forth in excitement. An outside observer unaware of the danger such a creature could pose might find it 'cute', but anyone who had experience in the realm of dragons knew the giant creature should only be described with words such as 'monstrous' and 'deadly'.

The final change came nearly instantaneously. With a burst of fiery red light and blue-hot flames, the jagged line burst open with the sound of a thousand shattered panes of glass, throwing solid shards of reality across the cave in a blizzard of chaotic violence. If anything other than the magical scales of the dragon were in the way of the crystal-like pieces of time and space made corporeal, it would have been ripped apart, shredded by the magical forces wrought upon flesh that was unable to withstand such devastating forces. Since the dragon's scales were part of a creature more ancient than the magics used to develop such things as a tear in reality, they simply fizzled out against the permanence of the creature's existence.

As the portal took shape, a flood of trespassers into this realm poured out, splashing heavily into the roiling waters of the hot spring. They were twisted, unnatural things, not of a place where the laws of creation were remotely the same. Most would recognize them instantly, despite their lack of natural presence in this dimension.

Demons of all sorts and sizes poured free, some with horns and wings, likened to imps and gargoyles, tried to take flight above the water. They were the first to be snatched from the air by the dragon, its mighty jaws snapping down on them like the crack of a whip as they disappeared down its hungry maw.

Larger, more dangerous demons struggled to stay afloat in their heavy armor of black metal that seemed to drink in the light cast by the jagged edges of the portal. Both skeletally thin casters and thick, burly demon knights fell prey to the supernaturally sharp teeth of the dragon. Insect-like demonic spiders the size of horses and even larger giant scorpions with stingers filled to bursting with caustic poisons meant to burn the soul were crushed as they merely got in the way. Their blood–all of the demon blood–somehow both red and black, sank to the bottom of the hot spring, not dissipating into it. Like oil and water, the two didn't mix, but instead stayed separate despite the waves caused by the thrashing of those few still struggling to stay afloat. It was both a massacre for one side, and a buffet for the other, one that carried on for many long minutes.

Finally, with a deafening explosion of broken reality, red light, and blue fire hot enough to cause the outermost layer of ice to melt throughout the cave, a demon lord burst through. Its tentacle-covered form lashed against the dragon, pounding on the creature's thick scales of silver and azure as it was slowly ripped to more manageable pieces by sharpened claws harder than diamond. A floating eyeball with a hundred tentacles was no match for the ancient beast, and its silent screams fell on deaf ears. No dragon had a shred of mercy in any of their five hearts, most especially for a delicious outsider like this one. Or, for the thousands that had come before it.

The dragon ate its prize with relish, too absorbed in its victory to notice the dozens of demons that managed to escape. While it was only a fraction of what came through the portal, there were still enough invaders to crowd both tunnels of the cavern as they rushed toward freedom. Enough that the outside world, without the nigh-invincible power of a dragon, might face an insurmountable problem.

None of that was the dragon's concern. It finished its meal, and curled back up on the bank of the spring as the waters settled back into a state of calm peacefulness. Soon, there would be another meal, and it wanted to rest before it came. There might be the most delicious of invaders this portal could contain in the next wave–a demon prince–and it had to be ready. They were exceptionally fast, and it didn't want another one to get away.

## CHAPTER 1

I don't care who you are, or how tough you think you might be. Getting punched in the nose *always* hurts.

"Hah! Got you that time, James!" Jess danced back, avoiding my return swing and resetting her stance for another attack. "You're getting slow in your old age. Maybe I should take it easy on you."

Cross snorted on the sidelines, where he sat next to the fire stirring a pot of stew. "Old? Look at him. I bet he hasn't seen thirty winters. Just wait until you get old enough you start to hurt because you slept wrong. Nobody really warns you there's a way to sleep wrong, but believe me, there is. That's when you know you're getting old." He took a small sip of the broth with the ladle and winced. "Needs more blackfrond."

I winced with him. Blackfrond was a lot like if cinnamon and cayenne peppers had a baby, and that baby was angry at the world for ever being born. And with Cross cooking, we had an even chance of enjoying dysentery-like symptoms that burned like fire because of the spice. Cross serving as chef always ended up like this, but our good cook, Murphy, was off scouting with Leedy.

They were looking for signs of the small hunter and trapper village that was supposed to be somewhere in the foothills of these mountains. It had been two days, and we still hadn't found anything, spending most of our time dodging groups of orcs and goblins that infested the area. I would have bypassed the village entirely, but we were hoping to find a guide to the mountain pass we knew had to exist somewhere to our north. Without that guide, it could take weeks of searching the rugged terrain before we would find it on our own. That meant spending a few extra days looking for a guide was the better choice. So, we took turns with the cookpot, and today Cross was cooking, while Jess and I got extra training time in.

Somehow, I was losing all the way around.

"I don't care what he *looks* like, Cross. It's pretty obvious James is much older than what's on the outside." Jess snapped a couple of kicks at my waist, but it was my turn to dance out of the way. She huffed in frustration before resetting herself for another combination. Her increased speed as a shifter hybrid negated the weight of the armor she was wearing, but it wasn't quite enough to keep up with me in just a simple shirt and pants. "Call it a woman's intuition, but I know he's *not* younger than thirty winters."

The fact she was correct didn't seem to sway Cross. He waved away her words with a flick of his curse-blackened hand, concentrating on the cast-iron cauldron of stew. His chiseled features and swollen muscles had served him well as a captain in the Wardens, but now that he was an apprentice Judge he was starting to grow a beard. It suited him annoyingly well, and the fading light of day only seemed to improve his features. I definitely didn't want to punch him in the face for general purposes. Definitely.

"Sure, whatever you say." He scoffed to himself, trying to keep his voice down. "Woman's intuition. What a load of rotten toenails."

She obviously heard him, and now two people wanted to punch him in the face. Unfortunately, Jess decided to take her frustrations out on her sparring partner. Me.

A sweeping kick swept my legs at the knees, causing the leading leg to buckle. As I fell to the side, Jess drove the heel of her left hand into my floating rib on the right side, followed by a hard knee into my hip. She used the momentum to flip me over onto my head and shoulders, where a normal person might suffer a dislocated shoulder, or even a broken neck. I was not a normal person, so nothing happened to me beyond getting some dirt on my clothes, but it was annoying getting manhandled so roughly by one of my apprentices. The small grin on her face was the last straw, so I decided to stop sandbagging. I couldn't have them thinking I was weak. Or old. Even if I *was* getting a little long in the tooth.

I pushed off the ground, throwing my weight forward into a flip that allowed me to slam an elbow on the side of Jess's head. I still pulled it, since I didn't want to hurt her, but it was enough to ring her bell a bit. She was trying to shake it off when I hooked her ankle with my foot and pushed her to the side, bouncing her off the dirt with enough momentum to kick her clear of the circle that marked our training boundary.

"Good try, Jess, but you got cocky. Talking during a fight instead of concentrating on your opponent is a good way to lose." I walked over and helped her up, quickly casting a healing spell over the both of us to take care of any bruises. "Calling me old, smack-talking, that kind of thing is fine, but you don't want to involve a non-combatant to distract you."

"I'm right though, aren't I?" Jess brushed herself off, trying to get the worst of the dirt and pine needles out of her clothes and armor. "You're older than you look."

"Yes. And no. You're both right, and we can leave it at that." Explaining how I was physically reset to a guy younger than thirty every year, while simultaneously being forced to hop between worlds against my will, was more than I wanted to get into at the moment.

This was my twentieth world, and I had learned a long time ago that trying to tell others about my situation seldom ended well. They either didn't believe me, or they did, and neither option was helpful. There was nothing anyone could do to help me, beyond assistance with completing the missions given to me by whatever mysterious and nebulous god, pantheon, or system was responsible for my situation.

"How can we both be right? That doesn't make any sense." Cross took another sip of the broth, and started having a coughing fit. "Whoo! Maybe too much blackfrond."

Jess and I shared a grimace. Dinner was going to be exceptionally rough tonight.

"It doesn't really matter how you're both right. This isn't 'find out about my mysterious past' hour. It's 'training and eating food' hour. Besides, what *does* matter is that we find the trail to the mountain pass within the next couple of days. We don't have time to scour the whole mountain range for the Destitutes base of operations. This whole world could depend on how quickly we find it." The invisible weight of the literal timer counting down on my status sheet was a constant pressure I didn't enjoy thinking about.

"Yeah, yeah, we get it." Jess stepped out of the training circle and picked up a staff leaning against her pack. It had formerly belonged to an ancient vampire princess, but I had broken it, then fixed it–with some upgrades–and now it was on loan to her. She still hadn't mastered how to use it, which is why practice and training were so important. If she could figure it out, I might let her keep it.

19

Otherwise, the ancient artifact of immense power would probably be better served *not* in the hands of an amateur mage. "You somehow *know* something very bad is going to happen, and you can't properly explain why or how, but we've got to stop it. We know, James. We've probably heard this a thousand times by now."

"Hey, I didn't force you to come along." I scooted around to where my pack leaned against a log, being careful to stay upwind of the smells coming from the cookpot. "You could have stayed in Greendown and helped with the airship."

"Oh, it isn't that we don't believe you." Cross sliced a root vegetable into pieces over the cauldron, hopefully in an attempt to mellow out the flavors. The vapors were making even *his* eyes water. "If you say there is a serious threat that we need to hurry and stop, I'm sure it's real."

"Then why–?" I didn't get to finish my question, because a ridiculously oversized arrow slammed into my chest, knocking me over the back of the log I was sitting on as it punched into my body like a hammerblow.

"Ambush!" Cross shouted, jumping to his feet as another arrow flew through where he had been sitting. He took a step toward the place where his armor and weapons were stacked, but gave up on the idea when another arrow thunked into a tree next to him. He charged at someone out of my line of sight, the knife he had been using to cut vegetables raised over his head.

Jess had already disappeared, blending into the shadows cast by the trees surrounding our campsite. She was the only one of us fully armored, and with the staff she carried, I almost felt bad for whoever was attacking us. Almost.

The arrow sticking out of my chest diminished any feelings of empathy I might have developed. With my inflated stats, it meant the non-magical tip didn't puncture very far into my pectoral muscle, but I had still absorbed all the inertia from the hit in a very not-fun way. I grabbed the arrow and ripped it out, causing a chunk of skin and muscle to tear free with the barbed tip. It didn't feel very nice.

A quick glance at the roughly smelted metal broadhead was enough to tell me who was ambushing us. Orcs.

We had been dodging groups and small encampments of the oversized greenskins for several days. Wiping out a few scouting parties had been unavoidable, but we had dodged as many of them as we could. None of us wanted to let them know we were in the area, especially if they decided to band together and start hunting us.

Now, it seemed like they had found us, and somehow they had snuck up on our camp without setting off any of the alarm wards guarding the perimeter. That meant they were either the luckiest orcs in history, or they had a magic caster with them. Considering Jess didn't smell them with her cat shifter nose, it basically confirmed a magic user. Probably a shaman, priest, priestess, or whatever they called themselves on this world. I hadn't bothered to learn the specifics of orc culture for this world, much less for this region, especially since it was all just different words for the same thing.

I used another healing spell to close up the hole in my chest, then crawled to the end of the log I was taking cover behind to get a better idea of how many we were fighting. The healing spell had clued in their magic user that I wasn't dead, and an impressive bolt of lightning shot out of the trees to rip apart the ground near where I was crouched behind cover. It wasn't accurate or widespread, but the power behind the lightning told me the orc who cast it had some juice to back up their spells.

Since I could still reach my rucksack, I grabbed it and dug out two glass orbs from a pouch on the top. The green and red liquid inside each of them swirled as I popped the tabs on the top that separated the two alchemical ingredients. I had about five seconds before the two inert substances decided they didn't like one another very much and I would need to throw them as far away as possible, which was enough time for me to cast an *Identify* spell to ensure they were functioning properly.

---

**Item: Grenade**
**Type: Explosive/Concussive/Fire**
**Grade: 4/5**
**Description: An alchemical mixture of Hearthwart and Pestilnine in a specially prepared glass bottle demijohn that explodes upon combining the two ingredients, or upon sharp impact with a solid surface. Purity level is advanced. Initial explosion causes blast damage to soft tissues. Concussion**

---

> **causes enhanced damage to cognitive function in entities that have functioning organs. Fire will stick to all surfaces until it burns through its contents. Effects are variable based on environment and resistances of target. Area of effect is three paces for explosion radius, six paces for concussion, and unpredictable for fire.**

They were new mixtures I had been working on since we had moved into the colder biome of the mountain region. New places meant new herbs, and new herbs meant new chances for alchemical surprises when giant dickbags decided to shoot you with arrows. Like right now.

My toss wasn't perfect, but it was close enough. Just as the saying goes, close only counts in horseshoes and handgrenades, and I was basically using the latter. When the pressure from the mixture combining became too much for the structure of the glass to hold, they exploded.

Now, the description I had just looked at told me exactly how large the radius *should* be for each explosion. That didn't mean it was *accurate*. I had a Title specifically intended to enhance the effects of any explosion I caused, and it most definitely worked on at least one of the two grenades.

> **Title: Send Them into Orbit III**
> **-Your ability to cause more destruction and chaos is guaranteed to help you find new paths to glory!**
> **Skill Imparted: Primary explosions are 60% more powerful. Secondary explosions carry a 10% chance to also carry the same bonus as the primary explosion. This chance applies to each secondary explosion individually, not cumulatively. Can be used at any time, up to four times in any thirty day period. Explosions are still dangerous to both friends and enemies.**

I activated my shield bracelet the moment the grenades went off, and I was still thrown a good twenty feet back. The bracelet seriously needed an upgrade, but I hadn't come across any materials that would hold the runes safely enough for me to do so. The barely visible energy bubble shattered like broken glass as I slammed against a tree trunk, causing a shower of pine needles to rain down around me.

While it definitely hurt to get thrown against a tree at roughly half the speed of boom, it had hurt our ambushers *far* worse. The clearing where we had set up camp had grown a little larger on the side where I had thrown the grenades. Over a dozen orc archers had been tossed around like broken toys at a defunct daycare where the children had taken over and thrown a violent, pyrotechnic tantrum. Screams and groans of the wounded were almost drowned out by the crackling of fire as the undergrowth quickly went up in flames. A full-blown forest fire was going to break out if I didn't act quickly to stop it.

I wasn't sure that was going to be possible with the fresh wave of orcs that came storming in to attack us.

## CHAPTER 2

Leading the orc charge was a caster that was surely the one who had been targeting me. I knew it was the one who was trying to kill me, mostly because it was the only magic-wielder in the group, but also because I had thrown a fire-causing bomb in its general direction, and currently the shaman-looking orc's hair was on fire. It was scrawny compared to the other eight-foot-tall hulking orcs swinging around clubs and cleavers the size of small trees, and the bone fetishes and feather-bedazzled clothing only enhanced the protruding potbelly that jiggled as it ran.

While it might not win any fashion competitions, the lightning spell forming between the shaman's upraised hands wasn't any less deadly as it aimed in my direction. I shook my head, trying to clear out the cobwebs as the attackers drew closer. My back felt funny, and it was hard to get my left leg to listen as I tried to get to my feet. Probably a concussion, along with nerve damage to my spine. The fact that my body's outline was imprinted in the tree like a freaking cartoon was a good indicator of how hard the impact had been.

I blinked, and Cross was by my side, helping me up. He'd somehow managed to snag the spear I had loaned him, and green-tinged shadows danced along its paper-thin blade as he held the weapon in his curse-blackened hand. Healing energy came from his non-cursed hand where he steadied me by the shoulder. It wasn't targeted, so the healing didn't patch me up instantly, but it did help clear my head enough that I could cast my own spell to finish the job.

"You good?" Cross let me go as he saw my legs steady beneath me. "That was quite the hit you took."

"I'll be fine." I flicked my wrist with my index and ring fingers curled inward, causing a wave of wind-powered force to launch across the clearing at the orcs quickly closing in on us. The shaman used their lightning spell to cut it in half, keeping them from aiming it at either of us. "Don't overuse your own magic. It isn't worth it to let the curse grow."

Cross had been infected by a lich-curse, and it had settled in the hand he used primarily to cast magic. A hand I had cut off as a punishment and later regrown when he showed he had decided to become a force for good, but that wasn't important right now. What was important is that when he used magic, it somehow fed the curse and allowed it to spread deeper into his body. If it went too far, he would risk losing himself to whatever the curse was ultimately intended to do. We didn't know what that was, or how to stop it. All I had managed to do was delay the expansion, and enabling it was a terrible idea. Unfortunately, our enemies weren't getting any easier to fight, and for a mostly-vanilla human, magic was the only way to even the playing field.

"Don't worry about me. I've got it under control." Cross immediately disregarded what I said and fired a bolt of green shadow at the shaman from the tip of the spear he was holding. The shaman deflected it to the side, where it hit an orc warrior near the back of the pack in the thigh. It tumbled to the ground with a garbled scream, its leg withering away into a desiccated husk with a flash. Cross didn't notice as the blacked fingers of the hand holding the spear seemed to twist and writhe in place with happiness at the screams of the orc where they gripped the shaft of the weapon.

"Yeah, sure you do." I didn't have any of my weapons nearby, so I needed to improvise. I held up a closed fist and rolled my wrist, pushing power into the spellform that my hand helped to shape. My thumb lifted as a pointed rod of clear solid quartz about the same size as my spear erupted from the earth in front of me. It would be ridiculously heavy to use, and brittle against a sideways strike, but it would work just fine as a temporary weapon. "Let's try doing this, *without* magic."

He didn't have time to reply, as the orcs finally reached the two of us.

Standing against the edge of the trees made it harder for them to surround us, so we only had to face two or three at a time. The first orc to close with me was holding a shoddy-looking sword that was barely more than a giant, dull meat cleaver. It was obviously used to taking advantage of its greater size and strength to overpower any opponent it went up against. That's not how it went down this time.

I slapped aside the thick iron blade intended for my head, and thrust forward with the heavy quartz rod. The needle-sharp point had no problem punching through the orc's thick hide, and I kicked it off the end of my makeshift spear as it bled out from a puncture to the heart.

Cross wasn't wearing the enchanted armor that enhanced his speed and strength, but years of battle had left their mark. The spear he was using had a lethally sharp blade that sliced through any exposed skin with almost no resistance. His movements were smooth and methodical, cutting down the orcs that got close to him before they could do more than raise their crude weapons to attack.

For some reason, none of the orcs wore leg armor. There were plenty of roughly forged breastplates along with the occasional bracer or pauldron, but not a single greave or cuisse covered a shin or thigh in the whole bunch. It was probably a cultural thing for this specific tribe, or maybe they thought leg armor would slow them down too much. What it *really* did was make it easy for Cross and I to rip through them like a chainsaw at a banana factory. There were a lot of messy splits.

Both of us had to continually retreat deeper into the forest, especially since we didn't have time to finish off the orcs we dropped. They were still feisty enough to try and hack at us as they crawled forward, growling in rage as we danced out of range.

The shaman had held back on casting any spells once its own tribe members were in the way, and instead managed to put out the smoldering flames on top of its head. I caught the occasional glimpse of it working on something in the middle of the clearing, shaking and stomping around in a circle. Energy was slowly building as it powered a ritual from scratch, calling on its gods to provide aid. A sickly yellow and brown spellform was already faintly visible to the naked eye, meaning it already contained enough power to be a genuine threat.

Ritual magic was a dangerous field of study. The right ritual had the potential to create wondrous things, or unleash devastation on a wide scale. It could also target extremely specific enemies, if you had a way to focus the spell on them. It was normally the kind of magic wizards focused on, which made the shaman–more of a druid, or nature-type caster–a definite oddity.

While ritual magic had plenty of reasons for a caster to use it, there were huge downsides. Downsides nasty enough that I had never bothered to learn more than the simplest of rituals, and I had seldom used them in all the years I had traversed the universe. The need for hard-to-find materials, precise timing, and a dedicated location were all huge limitations I hadn't wanted to deal with on a regular basis. But, none of those were the biggest issue. As the shaman found out, getting interrupted in the middle of creating one was by far the worst thing that could happen to someone.

"Surprise, dumpster fire!" Jess popped out of nowhere and blasted the orc caster off his feet with a magically thrown boulder, twirling her staff with a flourish. Recently, she had been working on copying some of my idioms, but it wasn't translating well most of the time. Calling someone a dumpster fire was actually far better than some of the other phrases she had tried out.

The shaman had some kind of magical shield to keep him from being crushed by the boulder, but it hadn't stopped the kinetic impact from knocking him halfway across the clearing. It also didn't stop him from losing concentration, and the ritual spellform he was building collapsed with a knee-shaking *whump*.

I don't know what the ritual was initially intended to do. What I *did* know was the returning rush of power popped the orc like an overinflated water balloon.

Jess wasn't prepared for the explosive results, and it was her turn to get knocked off her feet, coated in a waterfall of blood and gore. She sat up with a rather shocked look on her face, and immediately began spitting dead shaman out of her mouth.

"Well, that was disgusting." Cross dodged behind a tree limb to avoid an orc club before spearing his attacker in the foot. It fell back with a howl of pain, and was immediately replaced by another orc that pushed its injured clan member to the side. "What happened?"

"That was the best proof I've ever seen to show you why we leave ritual magic to wizards and ritualists, while we concentrate on battle magic and our job as Judges." I spun my crystal staff upward into a sharp uppercut that caught an orc in the elbow, shattering the joint and forcing it to drop its sword. Continuing the spinning motion, I slashed the incredibly sharp tip across the stunned enemy's face, tearing through skin and bone. It fell to the side, fouling the approach of another orc trying to flank me. "Watch yourself, they're starting to spread out."

Cross started huffing and puffing from the extended exertion of the fight. Without his magic or Warden armor on to help boost his physical abilities and endurance, he was slowing down quickly. It was only a matter of time before he made a mistake, and got himself hurt. Not that Cross wasn't already giving an impressive showing. Fighting for even a short period of time was exhausting, and I could vividly remember what it was like when my physical stats were still in the range of a normal human. We had been fighting for over ten minutes by this point, and he was still going strong. I just knew it wouldn't be much longer before he hit the invisible cliff of exhaustion, and tipped over the edge.

Even with a handful of orcs breaking off to chase down Jess, we were facing too many for Cross and I to fight by regular means. It was time for me to change the game before Cross got hurt, or he decided it was time to use his magic and cause damage to himself in a different way.

The mana in the air around us was stirred up by the failed ritual, making it difficult for me to do anything that would target several enemies at once. That left me with an area of effect attack as my best option, which usually meant fire. We were in a bunch of trees, so fire was probably bad, too. I had a quickly-developing forest fire on the opposite side of the clearing already, and I didn't need one on this side making it worse.

Water magic without a nearby source to draw from was hard to manifest for me most of the time, and the stream we had been using for our camp was on the other side of the forest fire. There were storms nearly every day on this planet, but of course, there wasn't one right now. It always worked that way. When I don't want to get soaking wet, it won't stop raining, and the moment I want rain, it's gone.

The only options remaining I could use quickly without additional tools were earth and wind. Since I didn't want to cause an earthquake–I'd done that recently, and it wasn't a good idea–I decided on wind.

A steady cool breeze was coming off the mountains to the north, so I used what was already there to help boost what I was doing. I held my hand out to the side like I was asking for a fist bump, except both my pinky and index fingers were pointed straight down. A series of transparent swirling miniature tornadoes started to drag leaves and dirt into their bases as their spellforms started to take hold, and swirling winds started to tug on my loose clothing. The drain on my mana reserves with so many spellforms was sharp, forcing me to fight back a wave of vertigo.

While I was trying to quick-cast a series of major spells, the orcs weren't giving me a break. Three orcs wearing a higher quality of armor that were obviously used to working together still tried their best to crack me across the skull with their clubs, but I managed to stay out of range by weaving between trees and forcing them to nearly trip over one another as they repositioned around me.

My makeshift crystal spear was too unwieldy to use effectively one-handed against so many skilled enemies at once. They still couldn't disregard it completely, and I managed to draw blood on one of the orcs that got a little too brave with one of his swings. Not enough to put it down, but the trio certainly pulled back a bit and gave me some room to power my spells.

Our group had fought together enough that it was easy to recognize when something out of the ordinary was about to happen. That meant I didn't even need to shout a warning to Cross and Jess to take cover when the spells finally finished forming. I could sense as two quick bursts of mana signaled they had done something to protect themselves. I just anchored myself to the nearest tree by wrapping an arm around the trunk.

I initially tried to control the tornadoes, but with so many in one space, it wasn't possible. The push and pull of twisting wind currents rapidly escalated from several small twisters into two that were much larger than I had ever intended. They repelled one another, like two magnets trying to be forced together, which forced one tornado toward the fires that had been quickly building this whole time.

Thankfully, the other one went where I had initially intended. The remaining orcs–along with their wounded clanmates–

were swept away, along with all the loose debris of the forest. Their bodies were slammed against tree limbs, scoured by rocks and dirt, and carried away from us as the tornado drifted south, following the natural path of the northern wind currents. It would quickly die off once it got to a region with less turbulent mana flows to fuel it. Probably in another mile or two, at the most.

As for the second tornado, which was now a giant column of fire that speared up into the sky a good hundred feet, it already seemed to be dying off. Its rapid heating of the air into the upper atmosphere must have destabilized the natural wind current the spellform was using to supply its momentum, so there wasn't enough focused power to hold its shape. The sudden influx of extra oxygen had caused the fires on the ground to flare up hot and fast, which burnt them out. Once the fire column finally fell apart, we would only have to put out a few spots that still faintly smoldered along the edges of the initial forest fire. Pure luck, but I'd take it. We were due some good luck.

"Well, that was exciting." Jess popped up next to my elbow, causing me to jump. I swear, she was bound and determined to give me a heart attack. "I'm surprised you went with something so flashy. I thought you were trying to keep a low profile out here, so the Destitute doesn't know we're coming."

"I *am* trying to keep a low profile. That was supposed to be a bunch of powerful little dust-devils, not two ginormous tornadoes. It kinda got away from me there." I stabbed the crystal spear into the dirt in front of me, then forced it to disappear back underground. "It's a good lesson for you to remember. Even someone as experienced as I am can have unexpected things happen with magic. The ritual the orc shaman tried to do messed with the mana flows more than I thought, and the results were… dramatic."

"Dramatic? That's putting it lightly." Jess shook her head as she looked around at the devastation around us. The forest had certainly seen better days. "We should go check on Cross. I think I smell him closer to our campsite."

A sudden shout of pain caused us both to look at each other in surprise. Did an orc manage to hide from the tornado, and sneak up on Cross? We both sprinted for the camp, fearing the worst. As we broke through the trees into the clearing, I saw Cross down on his knees, hunched over something black, and an eye-watering smoke filled the air.

"Cross, are you okay? What happened?" Jess coughed a few times as she got closer to where Cross was kneeling on the ground. "Are you hurt?"

"No, but a great injustice was done." Cross moved to the side, revealing the tipped-over cookpot. Orc bootprints told the tale of a single attacker kicking his stew into the fire, ruining his hard work. "My food is ruined!"

Jess and I shared a guilty look of relief. Not everything about the ambush had been a bad thing.

## CHAPTER 3

Putting out the fires and tracking down our scattered gear took up most of the rest of the day. Most of our things, like our personal packs and such, had been protected by Jess when she had rushed to take cover, forming an earthen dome over the area that she had dismissed once the tornadoes swept through. Unfortunately, that still left things on the outskirts, like our packaged food supplies and the clothing we'd recently hung on lines to dry, tossed and scattered all over the place.

One of the alchemical mixtures I had been experimenting with was a total loss. Shattered glass containers and burnt scraps of my notes were all that remained of hours, if not days worth of work. Tomorrow, I'd have to gather more of the mushrooms and vines that showed signs of having the necessary reaction to create a physical fortification potion. If I could finish it, the potion would be very useful when coming up against hordes of undead. Zombies never got tired, so having a potion to help my team's stamina might be the thing to tip the scales.

"Oh, for Trinity's sake. This is ridiculous." Cross tossed down a broken crate and stomped off toward the stream at the edge of the clearing. "I'm going to get cleaned up, and try and salvage some of our spices they stomped into the dirt. Stupid orcs! I can't believe they did this!"

I looked back at Jess, noticing the very careful neutral expression on her face. I wouldn't have been surprised to hear it was mostly the blackfrond that was ruined, and the other spices were just fine. She was much closer to our camp throughout the fight, and a 'misplaced' spell would easily explain the destruction of a certain item she was very tired of dealing with on a regular basis. She didn't need to worry about me saying anything. My guts could use a break, too. Besides, snitches get stitches.

Once we had everything gathered up, and we'd all had a chance to clean up as best we could, the three of us moved camp. It wasn't a good idea to stick around the same spot where a giant fire column had shot into the air like a beacon to the rest of the forest. We left a few subtle markers that Leedy and Murphy could use to follow our trail, and moved farther north into the foothills.

Finding a suitable place to stay on such short notice was all but impossible, so we decided to make one. All we needed was an energy-rich location, and a hill or cliff that could give good sight lines for our surroundings. Since most of the region seemed dense with mana, that just left us with finding a place to start building. Before coming to this world, it would have taken me several hours to carve a hollow into the side of a solid granite hill. I'd recently received a Title that helped with earth magic, so it wasn't nearly as much of a struggle to move large amounts of stone.

---

**Title: Crack Kills**
**-Your unique use of earth spells has managed to crush enemies in vast quantities. This pleases the gods that enjoy observing things getting squished. Don't use your Judge powers to look at that too closely. It isn't polite.**
**Skill Imparted: Large-scale earth magic uses 3% less mana per minute. An additional 2% will be applied if the earth magic being used is outside of combat, including construction, training, and enchanting.**

---

The five percent boost might not sound like a lot, but it really added up over time the longer I used a spell. Having Jess there to assist me also made things easier, especially with how good she was at reinforcement spells.

After finding a hill that was more rock than dirt, I started by leveling out an entrance and creating an overhang to keep out any rain. Then, I made sure it had proper drainage, because it was already starting to rain. Like I said before, exactly when I didn't want it, there would be rain. A few boulders helped hide where I was going to put the entrance, along with providing a wind break if the storm got worse.

I added a few traps on the outside, along with my normal set of alarm wards. A small pit trap with a thin layer of stone over it that would hold up the weight of a single human walking between the boulders, but anything heavier, like a monster or orc, would break through and fall a few feet onto thin granite spikes hidden below.

Another simple trap was to pull several lumps of rock to the surface, which created great tripping hazards. Paired with some knee-deep holes placed randomly throughout the area, any large group trying to sneak up on us would certainly make a lot of noise when they started spraining ankles and twisting knees.

By the time I was done with all of that, Jess was done reinforcing the interior of the hill. I used both hands to push the earth and granite back, creating a narrow tunnel with a short zig-zag to keep any of the light coming from inside from escaping to the outside and giving our position away. After a few paces of tunnel, I spread my arms apart and started making an artificial cavern. Compacting everything into the ceiling, walls, and floor gave me a space that was roughly the same size as a taproom in a small inn or tavern. I added a chimney at the back, angling the flue at the back to have several small exhaust holes that curved to the surface instead of one large hole that went straight upward. It would require smaller fires, but the smoke would be more dispersed, and no light would escape during the night.

Setting up a stone table and benches only took another minute or two. I then pulled some walls up along one side to give each of us a semblance of privacy. Some raised stone benches would have to work for beds, but we'd all slept on worse.

My next addition was a small restroom near the fireplace. I dropped a stone tube straight down until I hit ground water. Then I made a rock seat and set up a sealed stone chamber under it with a flap and lever system to use as a toilet so we wouldn't contaminate our water supply. A few raised walls of stone made a bathtub, and a cistern against the same wall as the fireplace with a stone pipe created a way for us to take a hot bath without using magic. The heat from the fireplace would heat the water, and it didn't require anyone to recharge or refill it with the pressure differential I created in the underground well.

I took a break to let my mana generator refill before I finished up. The final step was to add an emergency exit. On the side of the fireplace opposite the bathroom, I created a tunnel narrow enough that I would have to walk sideways down it. I added the same zig-zag pattern, and stopped short a few feet of punching through the back side of the hill. A few air holes went all the way through, but they were low to the ground, and should be hidden by the foliage on the outside.

Overall, it wasn't exactly a palace, but it was a solid, defensible base of operations for us to use while we found the pass to the north. While it might be overkill for a short stay, it was worth it. I didn't want to face another ambush without a better way to face a large group, and the narrow entrance would allow a single person to hold back hundreds of attackers for as long as their stamina–and skill–held out.

"Wow. Quite the place you built here, James. I'm surprised you bothered." Cross tossed his heavy pack down in the nearest sleeping room before walking over to inspect the bathroom. "I thought we weren't slowing down for anything."

I shrugged, moving my stuff into the room nearest the emergency exit. "I've come to realize we need a place that isn't so dependent on mobility for security. Moving camp every day is great and all, but it doesn't do us any good if we have to keep circling the same area." I thumbed the doorway. "We know the pass is somewhere within a few days' walk from here. So does everything else that lives around here. They can find us too easily. We might as well get some quality rest, and stay out of the rain for once. I'm sure Leedy and Murphy will show up soon with news, and we can move on in a better condition than we would if we had stayed sleeping outside."

"That, and cold baths in mountain streams get old really, really fast." Jess didn't even bother tossing her things in a room. Instead, she used a snap of her fingers to get a fire going, and was already moving to the bathroom. "Ladies first, gentlemen. I'll try to save some hot water for you." She disappeared into the room, leaving Cross and I to finish unpacking the rest of our gear.

Cross let out a long sigh. "Why do I get the feeling we're not going to get a hot bath until tomorrow?" He started stacking supplies on the table, while I shaped a few shelves to come out of the wall so we could organize the spices and foodstuffs that had survived the ambush.

"Because you're a smart man, who knows which battles are worth fighting." I thought about my experiences on world seven, where a white witch named Lizbeth had seemed to always take all the hot water, no matter what time I went to take a bath. It had been a while before I figured out that if you couldn't beat them, you should join them. I still hadn't gotten over her. She was an amazing woman, who sacrificed herself to save an entire continent of innocent people from a black coven. "That's one battle you shouldn't worry about. We washed back at the campsite, anyway. It's not like we stink."

"Yeah, but it isn't the same." Cross pulled out the cooking cauldron and sniffed it. "Ugh. Do you think you could add a sink or kitchen or something? This didn't get cleaned out well, and it's starting to stink."

"Sure, give me a second." I went back to work, doing some more renovations while Cross finished unpacking. I had to get rid of one of the rooms to create a kitchen area, but I figured it wouldn't be a problem. Jess and Murphy would probably share a room anyway, so this only made it a necessity instead of an option.

I turned the bed pedestal into a dry sink with a countertop, and pulled out more shelves. Another pedestal of stone became a second workstation, and I ran a stone pipe down to the well so it would have a wet sink. There wasn't enough hot water in the cistern for me to add a pipe for hot water in this sink, but it was too easy to heat water over the fire if we needed some. Another lever and valve system led to the same waterproof waste tank, and a small imperfect shield spell worked like a lightbulb in the ceiling. I could have made an actual glowstone or light spell, but the shield spell used less power, and I liked the more natural yellow tones it gave off, instead of a harsh blue or orange that a more conventional spell would create.

"That's perfect, thank you." Cross immediately started filling the pot with water. He'd already finished organizing the shelves, and stacked what wouldn't fit in neat piles on the floor. "So, now that we have a more secure location, what do you want to do next?"

I didn't want to, but I checked my full stat sheet, looking specifically at the timer at the bottom.

> **Name: James Holden (Earth v7.4)**
> **Title: Chief Justice/Arbiter/Justicar/Executioner/etc...**
> **Level: 100/MAX**
> **Rank: 4.8/10**
> **Age: 27 (Physical) 47 (Actual)**
> **Class: Warrior/Soldier/Knight/Paladin/Mage (5/5)**
> **Profession: Healer/Alchemist/Blacksmith/Runesmith/Judge (5/5)**
>
> **Status:**
> **Strength- 97**
> **Flexibility- 97**
> **Vigor- 102**
> **Mind- 113**
> **Mission:**
> **Mythical Quest: Deliver Justice - World Count 20/???**
> **Legendary Quest: Return Home - Requirements not met**
> **Epic Quest: Find out why - Requirements not met**
> **Rare Quest: Track down Silver Star - Ongoing [Time remaining: 39 days]**
> **-Sub-quests:**
> **-Find the Key to the Silver Star**
> **-Close the Demon Gate [56,128 minutes]**
> **Unique Upgrade Quest: Find ten places of power - 3/10**

My stats had all gone up a point or two from training, but that wasn't the important part. It had already been three weeks since the timer had started counting down, and I had no idea where the Demon Gate even was, what kind it might be, or how to close it. Gathering the materials necessary to shut it down could take months. At this rate, I would be lucky to have a week or two. The sense of impending doom made the underground chamber feel claustrophobic. I was busy *building* underground bases, when I should have been assaulting *other* bases. Three weeks of taking it slow and easy had to end. I was running out of time.

"What do I want to do next? Try to take over–I mean–save the world."

## CHAPTER 4

A quick inventory of our remaining supplies showed we had about a week's worth of food remaining, if we kept eating full rations and didn't supplement any of our supplies with things we hunted or foraged. There was supposed to be a resupply headed our way at some point from Greendown using an airship, but I wasn't holding my breath. We'd have to start spreading our efforts as we searched, getting meat and whatever else we could scrounge as we traveled. It would only slow our travel even further, but it couldn't be helped.

I volunteered to take the first watch while the other two got some rest. The mana generator that sat in my lower abdomen had already refilled my reserves from the exertion of building our bunker, so I didn't worry about meditating. Instead, I sat in the entrance of our bunker and worked on beefing up the runes in my new armor.

This set was much heavier than the scout armor I'd had before. It was meant for a soldier, and was mostly steel plate and leather, with no mana added during its creation whatsoever. The thick metal allowed for more robust enchantments, unlike the more flexible wooden armor that had been destroyed in the fight for Greendown. Robust didn't mean varied, though. The non-magical base materials meant I was limited on the number of enchantments the steel and leather could hold. It was still tough, so it could handle bursts of power effectively, or store power if the runes weren't deformed too badly. After adding some baseline heating and reinforcement runes that interlocked with one another across the entire set, I was left with only the large pieces of armor that could handle extra runes. That meant one-use effects that would take time to recharge for the steel parts, and longer, slower effects for the leather were my best options.

A lot of the leather backing still had the dense fur from the animal that supplied the skin, which would help with the frigid temperatures of the high elevations we were marching toward. I still had to use a good portion of the leather armor's surface area for heating runes, and staying warm was a necessity for extra protection against the elements. I might have been able to add something else to the chain of runes, but I left it until I knew the fur wouldn't catch fire the first time I walked through snow. Better safe than sorry, especially when it comes to underwear that could potentially spontaneously combust.

Each of the steel pieces for my arms, called vambraces, got an extra set of shielding runes. They were weaker than my shield bracelet since the plain base material couldn't handle anything too complex, but they would both stop a single arrow, or deflect the damage from a weak spell. Every little bit helped, especially when you really needed it.

I had a feeling I would need it.

The leg pieces, or greaves, got an extra set of speed-boosting runes. I didn't want the imperfect steel armor to blow apart when I dumped a bunch of energy into it–dodging a spear or spell wasn't the time to think about mana management–which limited me on how strong I could craft the rune chains. Too many symbols chained together in a row would be potentially catastrophic, so keeping it to simple three-rune repeating strands was the best I could do. Getting a quick burst at the right moment during a fight felt like the right choice, especially with my limited options. And, I wouldn't have to worry about accidentally overloading them in the heat of battle.

My back and chest plates were the last pieces to get extra attention, beyond the basic heat and reinforcement runes everything else had. I made sure to give the metal extra strength, as well as a light and flare function. You never know when a sudden burst of light could come in handy. Unless your enemy didn't have eyes. I hated it when they didn't have eyes. It was usually worms. Giant worms. The kind that liked to sneak up from below and eat people by surprise. Creepy bastards.

Once I was done carving the runes into my own armor, I started looking over the pieces Cross and Jess had left in the main room. Cross had a heavily enchanted breastplate from his time in the Wardens, but there wasn't anything to help him with the extreme cold we would be facing. Since I didn't want to mess up the breastplate, I added a few heating runes to his belt and boots, which would keep him from freezing to death. He'd have to dress warmly, and try to keep out of the wind, but that was something all of us needed to do anyway.

Jess was still using the scout armor she'd found before we'd fought in Greendown, and it was looking a little worn. I did my best to repair what I could, and added a more extensive heating rune chain to her armor. Since I'd been the person who'd added all of her runes, it was easy to avoid any power cascades or frying out rune chains. She would have to personally provide mana to heat the runes if it got too cold, as well as manage the power levels to everything else the armor did, like providing minor camouflaging and speed enhancements. Luckily, that's what training was for.

The sound of a thick tree branch snapping came from somewhere to the north, causing me to freeze in place. Our entrance faced the south, meaning I couldn't see what had made the noise. A gust of wind stirred the branches of the trees surrounding us, drowning out any other sound for a long moment. I gently placed the armor down, and carefully grabbed the spear leaning against the stone entrance to our hideout, taking great care to be as quiet as possible. Whatever was approaching would soon regret it.

"I'm telling you, they have to be around here somewhere!" The hushed whisper was much louder than the speaker surely intended, but I wasn't surprised. Considering how loud Leedy tended to get when he was upset, it was a miracle he wasn't outright shouting. "The trail leads right over there, but where it cuts off means–"

"Means you two should get in here before you bring every beast within twenty miles down on our heads." I deactivated the wards on their side of the hill with a wave of my hand as I leapt to the top of the rise. "It took you long enough to find us. I was starting to wonder if we were going to need a search party to bring you back."

"Good to see you, James. It looked to me like you had quite the party back at the old campsite. Sorry we missed it." Murphy was the first to reach the top, clasping forearms with me in a warrior's handshake. "We'd have been here sooner, but the survivors asked us to lay down a few false trails before we left them. It was impossible to say no."

"Survivors? I take it you found the village we've been looking for, then?" Even in the faint light of the moon barely poking through the cloudy skies, I could see his grimace. "And it seems things weren't going well for them."

"You could say that again." Leedy walked up, looking a little ragged around the edges. I gave him a warrior's handshake as well. "They've had it rough. Dealing with undead moving through the area, stirring up the orc tribes, and all the game getting run off. It's a miracle they're still alive."

"If it weren't for the size of the trees farther into the forest, they wouldn't be." Murphy motioned to the north and a little farther east than we had been searching. "There's a place where the trees grow taller than the walls of Greendown. The hunters set up a bunch of platforms that connect the branches together, and that's where they run and hide when armies of undead pass by their huts."

"We only found them because they've been up there long enough, they've started to wear walking trails through the underbrush." Leedy dropped his pack with a groan of relief and pulled out a ridiculously long wooden arrow with an oversized flint arrowhead. It could have been a reasonably-sized stone spear tip from my original world's caveman era. To see it on the shaft of an arrow made it a struggle to imagine the size of the bow that could handle something so large. "They almost killed us with a pair of these as warning shots. Those hunters… they're not normal. It's like they're ghosts. And their strength is at least as much as a Black Warden, maybe higher. I don't know if we can convince them to take us where we need to go, but they can certainly manage to hold their own in a fight."

I took the arrow from him, carefully looking it over. The Black Wardens were basically this region's version of firemen, government inspectors, and guards for special locations. Their armor and training wasn't as strenuous as a Blue, White, or Green Warden, but it still put them far above the average human running around the area. It especially put them at a higher level than what the average half-starved hunter eking out a living in the cold northern forests should be at.

After a basic visual inspection of the arrow, I tried using my *Inspect* spell on it. The results were surprising.

> **Item: Greater Arrow of Bleeding**
> **Type: Armor Penetrating**
> **(Damage Enhancement)**
> **Grade: 5/7**
> **Description: An arrow crafted by expert artisans meant to bring down large targets with superior protection. Can be used for both game animals with thick hide and enemies with chain or leather armor. Arrowhead is magically toughened due to extended exposure to high mana, making the relatively mundane weapon effective against greater undead. Durability is enhanced, allowing it to be used several times before breaking.**

I barely had time to finish reading the description when another box popped into my vision, flashing a vibrant blue with silver borders.

> **Quest Update!**
> **Unique Upgrade Quest: Find ten places of power - 3/10**
> **-You have found an object that was crafted in an area with high mana concentration. Perhaps you should investigate further?**

If that wasn't a softball pitch of a quest update, I was a monkey's uncle. Apparently, the reason why the hunters were so strong, and had such effective weapons, was because they were sitting on a place of power. Finding the hunting village for a guide suddenly became more than just a way to get through the mountains. It was necessary for me to gain stats, and boost my chances against whatever the Destitute had in store for us. Having another stepping stone in my Quest was huge, and I couldn't help but be happy about it.

"We need to go back and talk to them. Even if they say no, I need to figure out where they're getting the materials to make these." I handed the arrow back to Leedy, who put it back in his pack. "Did you see anything else while you were scouting?"

"Just the usual." Murphy shrugged, grinding the base of his halbert into the dirt. "Orc bands, a few loosely-controlled packs of undead, and a big cave where goblins or giant spiders are probably hiding." He looked back toward the south, in the vague direction of Greendown. "Any sign of the resupply?"

Leedy leaned forward, excitement dancing across his features. "Or better yet, have the Green Wardens returned? Or maybe you heard something from Oriana?"

"Nothing yet." I waved my hand, reactivating the wards behind them. "It's probably going to be another week or two until the airship is even finished being built, and then it has to travel to us. As for the Green Wardens... I'm not holding my breath."

Tew and Oriana, the two extremely powerful Green Wardens that had helped us save Greendown, had left for their home in the south the moment ships had started returning to the city. Tew had gone to see what he could do about a book they called *The Oracle* that spoke directly to the gods. It had been subverted and used to manipulate their organization, and he wanted to put a stop to it before he retired. I wished him well, and definitely expected him to fail miserably, especially considering how reverently the Wardens viewed the holy object. People didn't like to hear their super-special-whatchamacallit wasn't so special anymore, even if it was the truth.

Oriana was still a Warden-in-Training, and Greendown had been her first large-scale battle. She had performed well enough that Tew was almost ready to consider her a full-fledged Green Warden, and no longer a Warden-in-Training. She was going to try and raise a larger group of elite warriors and return to help us fight, but that would require explaining why they had let me live. Their holy book had sent orders for me to be killed, and they obviously hadn't done it. Tew would have to win his fight before Oriana even had a chance.

"Ah well, I guess you can't have everything." Leedy let loose the sigh of a man deep in the throes of unrequited love. "A man can dream, though."

"You and Oriana?" I couldn't hold back a smile. "I'm sure the mixture of the venerable Corporal Leedy and the always perfectly-stable and reasonable Oriana would create a match made in heaven. Nothing bad could *ever* happen with the two of you as a couple."

"Yeah, yeah, laugh it up, funny man." Leedy fought back a yawn before giving my shoulder a playful shove. "You just wait and see. I'll win her over, and our kids will be true powers in the kingdom one day."

Instead of answering, I took a closer look at how tired both of the former Blue Wardens looked. The two of them were practically falling over with exhaustion, their bleary eyes squinting at me in the dim light of the stars. I was asking them questions instead of letting them get some rest. While it might be necessary to run with little to no sleep in the coming days, right now there was no reason to keep them from their beds.

"Okay, guys. I think it might be time for you to get some rest. Tomorrow's a big day. We'll keep this place as our base of operations while we deal with the locals, and head north once we've secured a guide." I started back down the hill, leading them to the entrance. "Oh, and leave me a piece of gear you want inscribed with heating runes. It's going to get *really* cold the higher we go, so I want to prepare for it now."

They both gave me grunts of agreement, the thought of a bed causing their tired minds to already begin focusing on nothing but sleep. As they got settled into their respective bunks–and Murphy had to fight for sleeping space with Jess–I looked over the boots and belts they'd given me to inscribe. Since neither could do magic, it required working in ambient mana collection runes to power them, as well as a way to manually turn them on and off. It was more work, but I could pull it off.

As I picked up one of Leedy's boots, one thing became immediately obvious. "Bleh. Leedy most *definitely* needed to wash his socks. Those things smelled like rotten cheese soaked in vinegar. I wish I knew some anti-smell runes…"

## CHAPTER 5

"Why do all of you smell so bad?" Gleason did his best to ignore the cloying stench that clung to his nostrils, but the orcs surrounding him made the only living member of the self-proclaimed Blood Wardens toss away the roasted rabbit leg in disgust. "Centurion! Where are you, you mangy mutt?" He stood from his place by the campfire, looking for the largest and most heavily-muscled orc under his command.

The orcs immediately surrounding Gleason mostly ignored his shouts, focusing on the bowls of food in front of them. They had learned it wasn't a good idea to make eye contact with the violently unstable man. Most carried at least a few scars across their backs from his whip, and all of them universally understood the risks associated with becoming the focus of his ire.

"Here, Primus." The lumbering brute of an orc stomped his way into the firelight, the thick furs covering him only enhancing his bulky appearance. "What want from me?"

"I thought I told you to start enforcing bathing routines for the entire century each time we stopped for the day. Was I unclear with my instructions?"

Gleason had begun instituting the ranks and discipline of the ancient military traditions almost immediately upon gathering what was left of his current forces.

As he had grown his army, the idea had proven itself to be almost genius. There was no better way to incorporate the small bands and groups of orcs he collected along the way, despite the outdated form of command and control. It was a military structure that had ceased to be implemented hundreds of years before even his grandfather was born, but the old ways had allowed the founders to form the kingdom into what it was today. He felt it was only proper to revert to them when saving the kingdom was his mission. Given the uneven rows of hide tents and irregular groupings of orcs around the dozens of campfires spread throughout the ruins of the small village, it was still a work in progress.

"Not unclear, Primus. It cold outside. Men tired, and hungry. Men want food and fire before wash in creek." The muscular orc motioned to a section of the ruined village where a handful of orcs were trudging their way outside the edges of the firelight. They picked their way carefully over the remains of a broken-down wall, none of them wanting to turn an ankle. "See? They go now, wash off dirt and stink real good."

Gleason ground his teeth in frustration, already picturing in his mind the different ways he could flay the skin from the orc's bones. He took a deep breath before letting it out slowly. Now wasn't the time. It had taken him an exceedingly long time to find an orc with enough brawn and brain to effectively serve as his second, and the struggle to replace him wasn't worth the effort. For now. "Tomorrow, don't give them the option of what they *want*. No one eats until they've washed, and *you* don't eat until everyone else has a bowl of food in their hands. Understood?"

"Every orc wash first. Me eat last. Me understand, Primus." The large orc didn't look happy about the orders, but he was smart enough not to argue. A glimmer of intelligence in the orc's eyes was proof of why there wasn't an angry outburst, and showed that it wasn't just his muscles that caused him to serve as the de facto second for Gleason.

"Since you're here, did the scouts report on that column of fire we saw in the distance? It's been hours since they were sent to check." Gleason knew not to expect much from the cumbersome oafs that served as scouts, but he hadn't gathered any goblins yet, and they were who usually served in the more subtle roles of the greenskin forces. "Surely you've heard *something* by now."

"No, Primus. No hear nothing." The orc tucked his thumbs in his belt, relaxing the tension in his shoulders now that he knew he wasn't going to be whipped. "Orcs look for fire in forest. No more smoke to show where to go, so take long time to find."

Gleason ground his teeth, doing his best not to take the whip from his belt to show the extent of his displeasure. Now wasn't the time, even if it would be satisfying. He was almost out of the concoction he laced the cook pots with to control the orcs, and soon he would have to rely on fear alone to guide them. That, or attempt using his own blessed blood without the addition of the mixture created by the alchemist he'd enslaved back in Greendown. With the number of orcs he'd collected, there might not be enough blood in his body to accomplish such a task. He was certainly fine with leading by fear, but it had to be properly measured and controlled. The kind of fear he needed to induce had an order to it, one he was well experienced at cultivating.

"Useless. They're all useless." Gleason knew the column of fire had been created by magic, but it had been too far away for him to feel what kind of powerful creature had made such a thing. If he could somehow capture it, Gleason would have a mighty source of power under his command. He started pacing back and forth, imagining the things he could accomplish with such a monster. "What of the pass to the north? Surely the scouts have found a way through by now."

"All dead. They eaten by big spiders, Primus. Cave spiders very hungry right now." The orc swept his arm to the north, encompassing a wide area. "Whole place covered in caves. Eight scouts go out. One scout come back. He die from poison bite after tell what happened."

That information caused Gleason to actually stop in his tracks. He'd never heard of a spider big enough to overpower an orc, or one that carried venom powerful enough to outright kill one of the tough greenskins. For *eight* to be brought down, this constituted a genuine threat. If it was true, of course. "The whole squad was wiped out? Are you sure they didn't get lost, and only the one who managed to find his way back was actually killed?"

Shrugging, the orc absentmindedly picked at his teeth with a broken section of an arrow shaft. There wasn't much of a point to his actions, given how much space there was between each of his yellowed teeth, but Gleason didn't bother trying to understand how an orc's mind worked. "Scouts not lie about things. Want tribe to not die. Want tribe to revenge his death. They lie, wants not happen."

"As convoluted as that thought process might be, it does make a certain kind of sense." Gleason looked around at the dozens of fires around him. With the number of orcs he had gathered, a frontal assault was most likely the best option. Overwhelming a nest of gigantic cave spiders in one headlong rush would cause some casualties, but he could afford them. That, and any kind of complicated plan was certainly beyond the mental prowess of his forces. With that in mind, he gave his orders. "At dawn, we clear out those caves. Then we'll find the way that allows us to venture deeper into the mountain range."

Nodding in agreement, his subordinate wandered off. The oversized orc didn't immediately begin to issue any commands, which bothered Gleason, but he once again fought off the urge to unlimber his whip and begin punishing the lazy creatures around him. Now wasn't the time. The moment he took his hand off his enchanted weapon, the voices in his head spoke to him.

*Come to us.*
*Come to us, chosen one.*
*Come to us, and finish your task...*

Gleason knew the Holy Trinity spoke to him, and their insistent calls for him to travel north hadn't stopped since he'd destroyed the town of sinners and villains called Greendown. His great victory had assuredly proven to the Trinity that they had selected the right person, and he was nearly ecstatic at the idea of finishing whatever mission they had for him. Gleason had no doubt the rewards would be great. He'd already been rewarded with the deaths of his enemies, and the increased power of his magic. Whatever they had in store for him next was certainly going to be glorious.

The black veins that ran under his skin swelled to the surface like writhing worms, squirming and shifting across one another in unnatural twists and turns. Before he could get lost in the sensation, he rested his hand on his whip once more. The voices disappeared, and his body calmed.

"Soon. I'll be there soon, and the world will remember my name."

# CHAPTER 6

The hideout in the trees was less impressive than my imagination had made it out to be, yet somehow better than I'd hoped. After all, I'd lived and trained with elves on my eighth world, and half their time was spent in the trees. They'd built intricate interlocking cities, with branches painstakingly shaped into open-air cathedrals, bridges, and houses as beautiful and enchanting as anything I'd ever seen, before or since. You could tell at a glance the elves' living spaces had been created and crafted by artisans over generations, with a special care and love for nature.

This place was more like a bunch of middle school kids with a handful of nail guns, no advanced planning, a complete lack of safety standards, and zero supervision built the whole thing over a long weekend. To say I liked it would be an understatement of epic proportions.

"When you told me the people in the hunting village had a bunch of platforms in the trees, I didn't expect... this." I glanced back at Leedy, who was busy looking carefully up at the branches immediately surrounding us. The last time he was here the hunters had easily ambushed him, so I understood why he was being watchful. We were on the edge of the clearing surrounding the tiny village, scouting the best way to approach. "How do you get up there to talk to them?"

The miniature tree city was built in a cluster of trees that were basically redwoods. Not *exactly* redwoods, but close enough. I wasn't an arborist or anything, but the gray bark was definitely not the same as the trees I'd seen on my home world. They looked out of place next to the mixture of oak, elm, and pine analogs that made up the rest of the forest, making me think they were planted here on purpose a long time ago. I hadn't seen them anywhere else I'd been on this journey, so it was likely they came from some other continent on this planet.

Whoever planted them hadn't understood how big the trees would eventually grow, and placed them entirely too close to one another. Their branches were tangled together in a snarled mess, and

I didn't even want to imagine how the root systems looked underground. It had certainly choked out any other plant life nearby, creating a muddy clearing that surrounded the giant trees for dozens of yards in all directions.

There was certainly an upside to all the snarled limbs. They provided the stable foundation for the rough twig huts that perched high off the ground, and the few single planks of wood that served as bridges and walkways between trees. From the ground, it appeared that no hut was tall enough that I would be able to stand upright inside of them, but their short and squat shapes were certainly large enough to fit a bed or two. A communal kitchen area was visible on the ground through gaps in the trunks, letting me know they didn't risk fires among the tinterboxes that were their living spaces. That meant they didn't have any enchantments to protect from fires, and someone in charge was smart enough not to make simple mistakes. Even if they would have given a safety inspector from my world a brain aneurysm with everything else they had going on.

"I don't actually know how to get up there. Murphy and I were wearing hoods when they brought us up last time. It definitely wasn't rope ladders, that's for sure." Leedy was still looking up, so he was completely surprised when a fern stood up behind him and tapped him on the shoulder.

"Hello!"

"Braafragalaaa!" Leedy's shout, while exceedingly loud, was somewhat lacking in any ability to effectively communicate with our new friends.

"Quite the jumpy one, aren't ya?"

"Don't do that! By the Trinity, I think I lost two years of my life." Leedy was hunched over, hands on his knees as he struggled to get his breathing under control.

"Not so funny when it happens to you, huh?" I ignored the evil glare Leedy gave me. He'd laughed every time Jess had snuck up on me, finding it to be quite the source of enjoyment. Now that the turns had tabled, I didn't feel bad for him at all. I looked over at the person wearing several ferns as camouflage. Their clothing and face paint made it hard to tell, but the walking vegetation's voice sounded young. And feminine. I held up the arrow that had given me a quest update and pointed to the stone tip. "We're here to make a trade."

"A trade? Well, that's something we haven't heard in a long time." A second hunter stepped away from a tree, his camouflage making him blend perfectly into the bark of the trunk he was leaning against. Even his longbow was painted to match, which had allowed him to stand less than twenty feet away while fully armed. There was no doubt this one was the leader of the pair. He was big enough to have thews. Actual *thews* of muscle. "Why don't you two come with us, and we'll get the Senior Huntmasters to sort things out."

The way he asked didn't make it a question.

"Where's the other guy? You know, the handsome one that was with you yesterday?" The smaller hunter–who I was now convinced was a huntr*ess*–slung her bow over her shoulder as she led the way into the clearing.

Leedy cleared his throat before answering, obviously uncomfortable about *not* being described as the 'handsome one'. "He's back at our camp, on cooking duty to replace our hardtack and jerky. The other two in our group are patrolling near him, looking for fresh meat while they make sure there aren't any more orcs nearby."

"Any more? I take it you had a run-in with a war band, then?" The larger hunter, who was wiping face paint off with a rag while we walked, motioned with an elbow toward where we had fought the day before. "That column of fire we all saw was your group's doing? You must have a mighty sorcerer in your group."

"Mage, not sorcerer." I couldn't hold back the correction. Sorcerers were either too lazy, or too stupid, to gain power the old-fashioned ways. They were almost universally evil, especially after making a contract with some kind of extraplanar entity. In my experience, beings that lived outside the dimension or world they belonged in, didn't normally do nice things when they managed to find their way to a different one. Except for me, of course. "Guilty as charged, though. I caused the fire tornado. A couple of spells combined, and it got away from me a bit. Killed all the orcs, anyway."

"Exterminating a war band of orcs is a good way to introduce yourself." He swiped at the brown paint on his chin and held out a hand for me to shake. "The name is Jaeger." He pointed with his paint-smeared hand at the huntress. "That's Hilda. We're in charge of protecting the tree homes while the others are out hunting."

I grasped his wrist in a warrior's handshake. "I'm James, and you've apparently already met Leedy. It's a pleasure to meet you."

Hilda perked up and came over to shake my hand as well. "So, what do you have to trade? I didn't see any wagons as you approached, or even a cart. It's hard to trade when you don't have goods, and your pack doesn't look very big."

Jaeger grimaced at the forwardness of his partner, but he didn't correct her. Instead, he motioned for us to follow him, and led the way toward the trees. "While it's none of her business, Hilda has the right of things. If all you have is shiny metal in your pack, you won't get much out of our people. Coins don't fill bellies, keep out the cold, or kill greenskins and the undead."

I nodded in agreement. I'd seen plenty of villages–even entire worlds–where money was all but useless. Holding in the shudder from my memories of world fourteen, I tried not to remember all the off-key singing everyone constantly did to keep out the mind flayers. Almost the entire planet had bartered in new song lyrics, instruments, and enchanted weapons. While I'd been absolute garbage at creating instruments, I had created whole new waves of music genres. Unfortunately for me, the Spice Girls had been a big hit for some reason. Even the weapons I had made were worth almost nothing compared to the words 'So, tell me what you want, what you really really want.' I had *really* wanted to kill everyone around me with a machete, but that was a long time ago, and I needed to let it go.

Thankfully, 'Let It Go' had *not* become popular.

Anyway, the point was, when every day was about survival, it made things like gold all but useless. "No, I'm mostly offering a trade of services. I know runescript, and I have a feeling your living situation would benefit quite a bit from what I can do."

Both Jaeger and Hilda gave me guarded looks. Their reaction surprised me. It meant either a distrust of magic, or they didn't understand the different ways enchanted items could help in their daily lives.

We didn't have time to talk more about it because we had already made it to the inner sanctuary of the trees. There was a wooden platform barely big enough for Jaeger, Leedy, and me to stand on. Once Jaeger guided us into the positions he wanted, he let out a piercing whistle. A thick log that served as a counterweight fell from the branches high above, causing hidden ropes to fly up from each corner and we slowly started to rise on the makeshift elevator.

Leedy stumbled, almost going over the edge before I caught him. He gave me an absentminded nod of thanks as he looked wide-eyed over the edge. "I'm almost glad I was blindfolded the last time I was here. This is crazy."

Both Jaeger and I hadn't stumbled, and shared a look between us that conveyed both our humor, and our silent agreement. Fighting an enemy was one thing, but you can't fight gravity. Well, I was powerful enough now I *might* be able to tank a fall this high, or even manage a spell before I hit the ground. There was no guarantee.

I saw Hilda scampering up the side of a tree like a monkey, using the rough bark like the handholds at a rock climbing park. She'd probably run and tell their leadership about our intentions, given that our slow rise would provide plenty of time for the people waiting above us to talk. Hopefully, they weren't as close-minded about enchantments as the two hunters seemed to be.

Once we finished our silent and somewhat awkward rise through the branches, the platform gently came to a stop next to a tree branch wide enough we could walk on it. Jaeger led us toward the more narrow end, where the branch we were standing on had been tied to its mirror on a different redwood.

The entire village seemed to be contained on this level, except for a few small platforms a level or two higher up the tree. Those were probably for lookouts, or maybe just a place for people to get away from the overcrowding on the single layer. Every twig hut and wooden platform I could see on the main level were bursting with villagers. If a single person got sick with something dangerous and contagious in these conditions, the outcome would be devastating. I was genuinely surprised it hadn't happened already. It was a time bomb that most forward-thinking leaders would already know about, and I didn't envy their blood pressure.

Jaeger led us through the maze of connected branches, each section falling silent as we passed through their portion of the miniature tree village. They burst back into conversation as we left, and I did my best to ignore the distrustful glares and furious whispers. And the camouflaged archers that tried to hide their presence higher above us, their bows not quite pointed at us, but ready to do so in an instant. This was clearly not a community that got a lot of visitors.

The three of us eventually made it around to a woven stick hut with a roof of layered hides. It was almost twice the size of the other huts, stretching across several thick branches that provided support.

As we approached, Hilda came out of the narrow entrance, pushing aside the hide flap they were using as a door. "They're ready to see you. Please remove your boots as you come inside, and leave your weapons by the door."

While I normally wouldn't leave my mace and sword out of reach in an unknown place, I didn't want to start off the negotiations with their elders in a standoff. I still had my magic, wrist cannon, and shield bracelet on if I really needed to fight, and I was fast enough that I could get back to my pack and heavier weapons in just a few seconds.

Leedy didn't try to argue when he saw me dropping my pack, sword, and mace on a shelf by the entrance. We both piled our things before taking off our boots, and followed Hilda and Jaeger into the hut.

Inside, there were three people waiting for us, sitting on the floor around several platters of food. All of them were dressed in deer hide clothing, with long gray hair and weathered skin that showed they had spent most of their lives outdoors. The center position was taken by a man that looked downright ancient. His scraggly white beard was longer than the thin hair that remained on his head, and his smile had more than a few gaps from missing teeth. I'd put his age at somewhere close to ninety, but it was hard to tell with the kind of hard living the hunters probably dealt with. Despite his age, his grip still felt like iron when we shook hands.

The two on either side were at least a decade younger, and looked like they were brother and sister. Both had a lot more hair than their older counterpart. They also had a lot more teeth. Neither of them seemed to be happy to see us, unlike the older man. Their smiles didn't reach their eyes, and both shook hands like a merchant, not a warrior.

"Welcome. Please take a seat, and share a meal with us." The oldest member waved his hand, motioning at a pair of cushions placed across from the trio. "We're interested in learning what you could offer our little outpost."

I sat first, with Leedy scooting his cushion to the side to give us more room. Jaeger and Hilda stood near the entrance, serving as both guards and keeping away any eavesdroppers. Jaeger's 'thews' nearly blocked the whole door, so their job was pretty easy.

"My name is James, and I believe you've already met Leedy." I made a motion to him, and all three of them gave Leedy a nod of greeting. "What I'm offering is a trade. I'm skilled at rune enchantments, healing, and blacksmithing. In return for my services, I'd require a–"

None of them reacted to enchantments, but the woman perked up at the mention of healing, and their leader leaned forward a bit when I mentioned blacksmithing. The brother of the woman seemed skeptical, and interrupted me before I could finish what I was saying.

"You trying to feed us a pile of rotten snapfish, boy?" He scoffed, and waved a hand like he was brushing me away. "You don't look old enough to know anything about anything. We ain't a bunch of brainless bumpkins you city dwellers can swindle out of our britches. It might be best for you to go on back where you came from, and leave us decent folk alone."

"Ah, you're one of 'those' kinds of people." I used air quotes to emphasize the word 'those.' I could tell he didn't like it very much, even if he had no idea what it meant. The intent was still conveyed nicely by my tone. "Don't let my appearance fool you. I'm not as young as I look. And I'm not trying to take your britches. I only need a guide to the quickest way out of the foothills and broken cliffs into the mountains, and I'd like to see the place where

55

you get the stone for your arrowheads. I'm offering long-term benefits for a pittance of the value your community would be getting."

"While my nephew might be harsh with his words, it does seem rather suspicious that you would know so many skills." The oldest of the hunters stuck his tongue out to the side, clearly thinking over the situation. "How about a demonstration, so we know what you mean when you say 'skilled.' There could be a canyon wide enough to separate one person's view of a good blacksmith from another's opinion."

The smirk on the face of the guy who doubted me was a key indicator that I didn't want him judging whatever I did. I had a feeling whatever it was, it wouldn't ever be good enough to make him admit he was wrong.

"Fine. What did you have in mind?" I tapped at the exposed runes on my chest armor. "I can enchant an existing object, or make something from scratch if you have a forge available. Although, if I make it, I'm going to keep it unless it's included in our trading agreement."

The younger of the two men opened his mouth to argue, but it was his turn to have to wait to finish a sentence. The woman interrupted her brother's impending outburst, and instead told Jaeger and Hilda to wait outside. Once they were gone, she turned back to me.

"James, you mentioned you were good at healing. What kind of healing are you offering? Are we talking herbs, poultices, and tinctures? Or is it something else?" Before I could answer, she kept talking. "What about old injuries and illnesses? Can you heal something that happened years ago, or just new problems?"

"I can handle almost anything you toss my way, and I use magic to heal. While I might have some knowledge of herbs and medicines, I'm not an expert at the plants available to me in this location. I'm from… somewhere with different herbal remedies." It was hard for me to miss her grimace at the mention of magic. This whole village must have something against magic use. "While I understand most people are afraid of magic, I assure you the magic I'm talking about isn't bad, or evil."

"That's exactly what an evil warlock would say." Jaeger, who was obviously listening in, mumbled loud enough to himself that the whole hut could hear what he said. When he realized everyone was looking at him, he ducked his head in embarrassment. "Sorry. I was just thinking out loud." He gave me a suspicious glare that lacked any anger. I was pretty sure he didn't mind me personally. It was only a general distrust of all magic users. "All I'm saying is, how can we be sure you're telling the truth?"

"First off, I'm not a warlock. I don't get my power from sacrificing living things and harnessing the power of their death. I'm a mage, and we get our power through manipulating the magic that exists all around us." I held back the sigh that wanted to escape. This was getting old. On my next planet, I was going to have pamphlets printed out that explained the differences in magic users. I'd make sure to include a lot of pretty colors and pictures, so it kept the attention of all the smooth-brains that didn't like to read. Maybe some pop-ups to keep it interactive. "As for if I'm telling the truth or not, that's exactly why I'm offering to perform a test. You guys just have to pick which area I'm going to prove myself in. That should be enough to show I'm telling the truth, and trading in good faith."

The woman leaned forward and whispered a few words into the oldest man's ear before clearing her throat and looking back at me. "Allow us to discuss this for a moment. You must be hungry. Please, eat while we take some time to decide what to do." I nodded in agreement, and they stepped away.

While the three elders shuffled to the back of the hut to furiously argue with one another in hushed tones, Leedy and I tried the various plates of food they'd laid out for us. It was mostly an assortment of jerky, with a few different kinds of pickled vegetables. I'd had worse. One of the kinds of jerky had a crumbly texture with a sweet and sour flavor. Finding out what it was made from would be nice, because it was delicious.

"Do you think they'll agree?" Leedy had honed in on the same kind I liked, and was doing his best to pocket some while no one was looking. "What are we going to do if they don't?"

"Nothing. We'll have to either figure out what they *do* need, or move on and find the way forward by ourselves." I didn't mention how I'd have to sneak my way into their hidden place of power and tap the energy there before we left. That was a 'me' thing, and not something he needed to worry about. "It's not worth having a disagreement with anyone. This is just meant to help speed things along."

"That's good to hear." The old man sat back down across from us. "We have agreed on a task for you to complete."

"Just to clarify, you won't undo any healing you perform, right?" The woman arched an eyebrow at me, almost daring me to say I would do something so monstrous.

"I'd only remove healing if I found the person I helped was a very, very bad person." I thought about it for a second. "Actually, I still wouldn't take back the healing. I'd just kill them instead. That's much more humane."

The old man nodded in agreement, while the other two seemed shocked at my casual statement about taking a life. Apparently, the old man was more used to death than his niece and nephew.

"Your task is to heal my grandson." The woman shouted some orders to Jaeger and Hilda, who poked their heads back inside before leaving to bring my new patient. "He was injured in the last raid we suffered from the undead, when we decided to make the move up here more permanent. If you can help him, we'll discuss trading whatever you want. Our herbalist has done what she can, but he's only getting worse."

"James will have no problem healing an injury." Leedy finally spoke up, after finishing off a plate of what looked to me like pickled asparagus. "He can handle almost anything. You'll see."

A few seconds later, Jaeger and Hilda came back into the hut carrying a makeshift stretcher. While I was expecting a child when the woman said 'grandson,' I should have known that someone her age would have *adult* grandchildren. Laid out on the rough canvas was a naked man that looked a whole lot like what I would expect Jaeger to look like in about twenty years. The man had similar facial features, skeletal structure, and even more mighty thews than Jaeger. His hair color was the same, except for the gray at the temples. This was either his father, or a much older brother. It spoke to the levels of nepotism this village favored that so many important figures were all related in some way, but that was how things worked on my home planet for hundreds of years, so I wasn't too surprised.

They laid the cot down next to me, and I immediately saw the problem. A bite mark on his neck was badly infected, with veins of red and black radiating from the wound. A bite mark from an undead. One I was supposed to heal, without any problems, according to Leedy.

Fantastic.

## CHAPTER 7

"Well, this sucks." Leedy nicely voiced my internal dialog. "How is he supposed to heal an infected bite from an undead? You should've put this poor man out of his misery." He poked at the man's wound, causing the unconscious patient to twitch in his sleep. "If this was from a vampire, he's going to turn, and be a threat to everyone in your little tree town."

"We're not sure it was a vampire. No one was there to witness what happened. My father stood as rearguard while we got the children to safety." Jaeger clenched his fists in anger, his mind replaying the events of the past. "By the time he caught up to us, he was already feverish and talking to himself."

"My grandson is a hero, and he deserves a chance at survival. Even if that means using *magic*." The old woman's tone told me everything I needed to know about how she truly felt about me using my powers. She walked over and laid a hand on the man's feverish forehead, then looked over at Leedy with a hard glare. "Not only that, but we can't *kill* the man who saved the lives of dozens of children. Have you never led a group of people before?"

Leedy, who had been a corporal in the Blue Wardens, blushed hard. He had definitely led others before, and he understood how demoralizing it would be to kill the hero of the moment. For the huntmasters, it would amount to political suicide, even in a place as tiny and isolated as this one.

I stepped in before Leedy could answer. "Let me take a look at him. I'll do my best to fix his injury, but I can't promise anything if this is a vampire bite." Everyone backed away, and I moved into a comfortable position next to him. "This may take some time, so don't interrupt me, no matter what you see or hear."

The rest of the room faded away as I laid one hand on his chest, and the other on the top of his head. I pushed a bit of healing energy into his chest, and monitored how his body reacted with the other hand.

Instead of feeling any kind of healing, or even a negative reaction, it was like pushing power into a black hole. It was sucked away into nothingness, and my patient was completely unresponsive. I tried it a second time to confirm my suspicions, but the same thing happened.

Healer had been my very first profession. The one I'd picked on my first world, when I'd been a naïve young twenty-something who still believed in the inherent good of humanity. While I quickly learned how wrong I was about the ratio of good people to bad people–it's much closer to fifty-fifty than ninety-ten, like I had been led to believe–I got plenty of practice exploring and expanding my healing abilities.

The ruler of the region I'd first arrived in even tried forcing me to become his own personal healer, serving at his beck-and-call like a slave. He'd quickly learned that messing with someone who you depend on to keep you alive was a *very* bad idea. Ensuring the fatty deposits around his heart got a little nudge to block even more blood flow had freed me from his clutches within a month. Hiding and running from the authorities quickly became my focus, while the local peasants gladly fed me and helped me avoid their patrols in return for free healing.

It had been a trial by fire, fixing all kinds of maladies and injuries that I'd never seen before. The few levels it gained me were enough to keep me alive, especially when I got to my second world and gained my warrior class. The combination of a healer profession with a warrior class was perfect for a guy that had never used medieval weaponry in a fight. If I had gone with any other kind of combination, I had no doubt I would have died to the demonically-possessed dead raised by the dark cultist on that war-torn planet.

After twenty years of being a healer, I'd seen and cured more kinds of sickness and injuries than any one person could ever believe. And somehow, I was still occasionally surprised. I couldn't remember a time when this had ever happened. It was similar to the curse Cross was dealing with, but completely different in that it lacked any perceived sentience. And, it seemed like it absorbed my healing energy instead of trying to manipulate or avoid it.

I had no doubt this was a vampire bite. I'd seen them before on other worlds, but no two planets had exactly the same kinds of undead infections. On world two, it had been caused by demons inhabiting bodies. World eleven–the worst world I'd ever been on, even if this one was giving it a run for its money–had featured an actual viral infection, much like the zombie movies I'd had on my home world. Sixteen had more of a religious bent, and bodies that weren't blessed properly before burial would rise from the grave to track down and eat the nearest human or animal it could find. I'd never truly understood that one, but the gods and their religious shenanigans were always a mystery to me.

From what Jess had told me when I first arrived on world twenty, zombie bites were contagious, and vampires had to bite you and swap blood to complete the transformation. Her casual comments made it seem like curing a zombie bite was commonplace, even if it wasn't exactly easy. The many ghouls I'd interacted with were made and controlled by magic, but it was possible they were an entirely different species from regular zombies and vampires. To me, that said this planet had a blend of magical curse and zombie virus. Possibly even a magical virus, which only reinforced how much this planet sucked giant goat balls.

A pulse from my internal mana generator reminded me that this time was different. In the past, power was always a limitation I could never get over. Healing someone immediately after they had been bitten on world eleven meant I could usually stop them from turning. If it had been too long, and the infection was allowed to spread, my only option was to put them out of their misery. I'd never had the juice to pour into their bodies to completely clean the virus from them, and they would eventually change into a raving, brain-craving beast when least expected, even if their visible injuries were healed. A few bad experiences had taught me that lesson quickly.

This time, I had an energy source inside me that I'd never had before. This time, things could be different. I had a genuine chance to heal the man who had knowingly sacrificed his own life for the children of his village. While I didn't know this man personally, a warrior who was willing to make that kind of decision was the kind of person that deserved my full and complete effort.

Looking inward at my mana generator, I was once again surprised at how different it appeared from when I first formed it. The mana scales that made up its walls flexed and shifted like a beating heart, and the gold and silver lightning that pulsed along its surface traced unknowable patterns that teased at hidden secrets of the universe in the back of my mind. The condensed liquid that swirled on the inside still resembled the blue and purple sheen my old mana generator's walls had been, but the lack of crystalized mana in its interior told me I was a long way from my next upgrade.

At least, I suspected I was. There weren't any manuals or ancient scrolls to help guide me on this new path. If I could find more places of power, I had no doubt I could skip forward in the next steps much faster than my current rate of absorbing the misty mana around me, and allowing my mana generator to condense it into a liquid.

Considering I was dealing with a disease that caused death, I tried focusing on pushing the golden lightning that formed my life mana into my patient. At first, there was no reaction. The black hole that was his body absorbed every bit of what I put into him, and any onlooker would think I was only meditating next to a naked dying man.

That wasn't exactly a hobby I was into, so I tried adding in some of the more generic liquid mana to fortify the golden lightning. Once again, there was no change. I tried cutting off the life mana lightning to see if there would be any change, but it only continued to swallow the energy like a bottomless pit.

I opened my eyes and didn't see any changes to his wound, or the infection that was actively spreading from it. The only thing that *might* have happened was a slight increase in his heart rate. Whether that was from me, or the fact that his body was moved recently, it was impossible to know.

Either way, I decided to find out if the bottomless pit truly was bottomless. I unleashed the proverbial floodgates, dumping every bit of mana my body could sustain into his body. Even the silvery lightning of death mana got thrown in, linked together with the golden lightning of life mana.

Maintaining a slight hint of healing energy was all I could manage. It wasn't targeted or formed into a proper spell, only with the purpose and intent to improve the body and condition of the bitten man.

I lost track of time sitting there, all of my focus going into nothing but maintaining the constant flow of power. Despite the improved mana channels that ran through my body, the extended period of time they were forced to endure such massive amounts of energy was making them ache. It wasn't all that long ago that my mana system had been nearly crippled, and here I was again pushing myself to my limits.

Any doubts about stopping or slowing down were pushed away. You didn't improve yourself by playing it safe. Not at the speeds I needed to increase my power, anyway. Being the most powerful human meant little against the strength of ancient undead, or the greater monsters that hid in the darkest of places. The world's most powerful mouse wouldn't fare well against an average-strength dragon. I didn't know who or what the Destitute was, but I had no doubt it was incredibly strong if it commanded ancient vampires and liches.

I could feel sweat dripping down my back from exertion, and through my closed eyelids I could see a vibrant green and yellow glow. The throbbing ache from my limbs faded to the background as my mana channels slowly adjusted to the heavy amounts of mana I pushed into my patient. A ding from my system alerted me to some sort of update, but I mentally brushed it aside. Now wasn't the time to break my concentration.

Something was starting to change. The black hole that took everything I could give it seemed… smaller. It was hard to describe what I was mentally seeing. While it still absorbed every bit of mana, the edges appeared more ragged. As if the bottomless pit was wearing out, the same way my own mana channels were.

If this was an endurance competition, I wasn't about to lose. It was time to speed things up, because I couldn't run the risk of the disease adapting like I had.

After seeing a sign of weakness from the undead infection, I redoubled my efforts. I pushed even harder, squeezing everything I could get out of my mana generator. Before, it hadn't strained at the pace I had set. Now, it was finally emptying faster than it could absorb and create more mana. The strain on my mana channels worsened to the point that it felt similar to when a muscle or ligament was about to snap from being stretched too far. Luckily, nothing ruptured, and I kept on going. The light I could see through my closed eyelids was growing in intensity, but I didn't feel any negative side effects, like heat or smoke, so I ignored it as well.

Now that my mana generator wasn't keeping up with the flow of power anymore, it was a race to see who would last longer. The disease, or my mana reserves.

The edges of the pit frayed more and more, as if it was a cloth tapestry someone was slowly picking apart with a jagged set of tweezers. As it shrank, I was forced to put a spin on my mana to keep it from backing up. Like a drain in a bathtub, it poured into the diminishing hole without clogging.

When I was down to the dregs of liquid mana, and most of what I was pushing out was only a condensed mist that barely had a single swirl inside my generator, something changed. The black pit that had taken everything I threw at it seemed to almost hiccup. Energy backed up at the entrance, and as if it was a clogged sink, mana started to back up and swirl on the surface.

Following my instincts, I grabbed hold of the pool of mana and shoved it as hard as I could into the small gap that still remained in my patient. It fought against me, not wanting the healing energy to invade what little space remained. I continued to push back, not relenting. It cracked, then shattered like a piece of black marble, before getting washed away in the healing energy I'd been forcing into this man for who knows how long.

A flash of golden and emerald light blinded me despite my eyes being closed, and I fell away from the stretcher holding the naked man. I tried to cast a healing spell on my eyes to help them recover, but I had nothing left in the tank to give.

"James! James, are you okay?" Leedy's voice was right next to my head as I felt him grab at my shirt. The rest of my senses came flooding back to me, and I could smell a rotten stink, like burnt decayed flesh mixed with dead fish. I was also hungry, thirsty, and tired.

"Is he alive? Did I heal him, or did I kill him?" It wasn't until just now that I realized how dangerous it was to push that much energy into a person. I wouldn't be surprised if he was little more than a chunk of human-shaped charcoal. "I still can't see anything."

"He's alive. He really needs a bath after you pushed all that gunk out of him, but he's definitely alive." I could hear the scrape of boots on rough wood as Leedy got to his feet. "I'll go see what's taking the others so long. Jaeger should have been back with them by now. Everyone went to rest when it got late, but he hasn't left your side since you started."

"Bring food and water when you come back." I gave up trying to blink the giant spots in my vision away, and laid my head back on the wooden planks as his footsteps faded away. "I'm going to take a little nap."

The explosion that rocked the hut disagreed with me.

## CHAPTER 8

"You have *got* to be kidding me." I tried to sit up, but a heavy hand on my chest easily pushed me back down.

"Don't worry, my friend. Let the hunters handle this. You've done enough this day." The sound of naked feet slapping against the wooden floor faded away, and I felt that I was alone in the hut. Truly alone, meaning the person who had just spoken to me had been my patient, and my nose agreed with that assumption. He needed a shower worse than a high school boy after football practice. If that football practice was being held on a pile of rotten fish guts.

More sounds of fighting drifted up from the forest floor, but there weren't any new big explosions or spells mighty enough to rock the hut I was laid out in. As much as I wanted to sleep, instead I focused on drawing in as much of the ambient mana around me as I could. I knew I had to be close to a place of power, because the density of mana in the area was much higher than the average I'd come to expect on this world, which was already pretty high.

Once I recovered enough to cast a healing spell on my eyes, I was finally able to get some idea of how long I'd been unconscious. It was fully dark outside, and rain fell in dense sheets that limited visibility to almost nothing. As a courtesy to my hosts, I made sure to drag the soiled stretcher out into the rain so it could rinse off some. I did the same, looking up into the starless sky to try and catch as many raindrops as I could in my mouth to lessen my thirst.

My pack and weapons had been moved, so I had no access to food besides the few pieces of jerky I'd squirreled away. I ate those quickly, and already started feeling better. The minor amounts of mana, water, and food I'd gotten in my system were making a world of difference. Cool rain on my hot forehead also helped, and I felt more clear-headed than I had since starting the healing procedure. If you can call 'overload the illness with mana' a healing procedure, anyway.

The sounds of battle finally died down as I finally felt like I could contribute. I was mad at myself for being so weak, especially since my stats were so high. My body had become so dependent on

67

mana to function properly that it was now a weakness. Now that I knew how weak I felt when I was extremely low on mana, I could start focusing on training it out of me. Just because my body *wanted* the extra mana to function didn't mean it *needed* the extra mana. It got bumped to the top of my to-do list, right behind tapping the nearby place of power. That still took priority.

While I was still standing in the rain and waiting for someone to come and let me know what was going on, I decided to check and see the update my system had given me while healing the naked guy.

---

**New Title Earned: Jaw Cracker**
**-From the jaws of defeat, the cusp of death, the very brink of darkness, you pulled back a heroic man destined for a fate filled with a demeaning and inglorious end. Some would say you righted a great wrong in the universe, and punched those jaws of defeat in the face! Congratulations on being the first person of this world in over a thousand years to heal a greater undead affliction!**
 **\*Note - Your feat may have angered a faction from the Greater Cosmos. This is not yet a warning, but continued actions of this type could lead to steps being taken against you.**
**Skill Imparted: Healing abilities are 25% more effective against undead afflictions, curses, and infections. Does not apply to those already deceased. Cannot be combined with Paladin skills or Light mana for area of effect healing techniques.**

---

My immediate thought was how important it was to try and heal Cross again. The boost of twenty-five percent was huge, and could help me push the lich curse straight out of his body entirely. Then the note about a greater cosmos faction sunk in, and I had to stop and think for a moment. I'd gotten plenty of warnings over the years about local and planetary deities being upset with me. Hell, this planet had already sent more than one dinosaur-sized representative to convey how angry they'd been about some minor deforestation

This one was entirely different. I could somehow feel through the simple blue and silver screen that this 'note' held far more weight than any warning I'd received in the past. Like the difference between a city cop being mad at you, and the federal government targeting you, there were definitely levels of trouble you could be in in my home world. This felt a whole lot like my system was trying to tell me I was on thin ice with someone, and that *someone* wasn't the type to send a note when they finally decided I'd crossed enough arbitrary lines with them.

Without consciously drawing on it, the mantle of Judge settled on my shoulders and I dismissed the screen. My concerns about greater powers and hidden factions in the cosmos went away. The mantle didn't care about such things. It was primordial, from a time long before these cloak-and-dagger games the gods played at. Judgment eventually came to all, no matter their level or station, an implacable force that was as inevitable as the heat death of the universe.

The scales would be balanced, no matter the wishes and whims of some fickle and far-away pantheon. Their anger at me had no bearing on what was right and wrong, and the fate they had tried to bestow on that man had been wrong. He'd stood when no others would, to save those who couldn't save themselves. The mantle bestowed upon me agreed that the healing was just, and anyone trying to interfere with it could take a long walk off a short pier. Twice. I'd deal with any fallout as it came, and I knew whatever the thing was that gave me my mantle would stand with me. So, as they say in my homeland… fuck 'em.

Before I could check my stat sheet for any upgrades, Leedy came stumbling out of the rain to lean on the wall of the hut next to me, water dripping off of him in steady streams. He had my pack in his hands, and passed it over.

"Glad to see you up and about, James. Sorry it took me so long. A bunch of giant spiders attacked while I was walking over here, and things got a little crazy. Let's just say, those arrows they carry pack a real punch. If it weren't for the goblins riding the really big ones helping, none of the nasty things would have gotten out of the clearing. Jaeger and Hilda are leading their hunters on a chase through the woods for the rest of them right now." Leedy wrinkled up his nose a bit, and leaned away from me. "Speaking of nasty, you smell a bit like the guy you healed. I know it's cold, but you might want to wash up a bit before anyone gets here."

"Thanks." I grabbed a brick of scented lye soap out of my rucksack and started scrubbing myself down, clothes and all. The rain was heavy enough it was basically a shower, so I took advantage of it as best as I could. "Tell me about what happened, from your perspective. All I know is I closed my eyes, and the next time I opened them it was dark outside and things were blowing up. I have no idea how the elders of this place were feeling when they left, or how long I've been under."

"Sure." Leedy took a look at what I was doing, and decided to wash up a bit himself as well. He pulled out a much smaller piece of soap from his own pack and started washing his hair, stepping under a particularly heavy stream of water falling off a cluster of tree leaves. "First off, it's still the same day. Well, it might be close to morning of the next day by now, but you weren't in your trance for a really long time or anything. The Senior Huntmasters–that's the title of their elders, in case you forgot–weren't happy when your little light show started up, but they calmed down once the bite mark started to look better. It took a bit, but it was impressive when those lines of infection started to reverse. Very emotional moment for Jaeger, especially."

I grunted in approval as I washed my face. It was hard to talk when you didn't want to get soap in your mouth.

"Once they realized you were the real deal, they went off to discuss what they wanted to do next. From what I could tell, the old lady basically wants you to heal the whole village, while her brother wants you to make a bunch of metal weapons so they can fight better." Leedy finished rinsing out his hair and sat down to pull off his boots. Thank the gods, he was going to wash his feet. "The really old guy didn't say much. I'm not sure what he wants from you, but I get the feeling he agrees with his nephew about blacksmithing, just not in the same way. My guess is he wants armor. Their arrows are good enough as far as weapons go, but they don't have anything beyond basic hides for protection."

"Agreed. I got the same sense when I talked about what I can do." I started peeling off my clothes so I could rinse them off better and also wash my skin under them. Thankfully, the rain wasn't letting up yet, so I wasn't stuck being all soapy with no water. That was the worst. "While I understand, that's not what they *really* need. If they'll listen to reason, I can improve their living conditions, and help all of them more than they realize. A few runes could make all the difference in the world to this village."

"Maybe they'll be more open to your ideas once everyone gets back from their hunt." Leedy was scrubbing between his toes, really going after it.

I approved. Greatly.

He shrugged, not bothering to look up from what he was doing. "Anyway, after nothing exciting happened beyond the gradual improvement, the Senior Huntmasters decided they were too busy to spend their whole day watching you, so they left. Hilda went back down to guard the village, and Jaeger stayed with me to keep an eye on you and the sick guy. It got late, and I nodded off for a bit. Jaeger sat there the whole time, watching the infection getting pushed out, little by little, without a break. It was impressive."

"He really cares about the guy. I think it's his father." I gave up any last shred of modesty and stripped off my underwear. Leedy and I had traveled together long enough that we didn't have many secrets from one another anymore, so it didn't bother him. As for anyone else seeing me, it was night, and the rain was heavy enough that even someone approaching the hut would only perceive shadows until they were almost all the way across the connecting branch. "Tell me about the attack. I didn't know goblins rode giant spiders."

"It's not common. Cave spiders don't normally get big enough for goblins to ride them, unless they're bred for it. Something has to provide enough food to keep a bunch of monsters like that from starving to death, or eating each other." Leedy finally finished with his feet and started washing his socks.

I would have done a happy dance if I wasn't naked. And the rain wasn't so cold. If there were angels on this planet, they'd probably be singing 'hallelujah'.

He scrubbed the socks together to make more suds while looking off to the north, fighting off a shiver. If the temperature dropped a few more degrees, we'd be getting snow instead of rain. "The fact they're bold enough to attack this far from the nearest cave entrance is concerning. Either they're starving, or their numbers are large enough to push south in force. Probably both. The orc and undead armies moving through must have pushed out the game animals they normally feed on, so now the goblins are switching to raids to make up the difference. It means trouble for us when we travel through their area."

"We'll have to use a show of force. Goblins won't try us if we prove how strong we are at the start." I finally finished rinsing off and stepped into the doorway of the hut, out of the rain. I dried myself off using a small towel from my ruck, laying out my wet clothes to dry at the same time. "I have a lot of experience with goblins. It doesn't matter where I am, or what I'm doing. If I prove how bad of an idea it is to fight me, they usually leave me alone."

As I was digging through my ruck for a spare set of clothes, Leedy stepped into the hut, dripping water everywhere. He laid his wet socks out next to mine to dry, and I silently hoped he got them clean enough that they didn't infect my own socks somehow. "You say that, but never underestimate the power of stupid in large groups."

I didn't disagree with him about that one bit.

## CHAPTER 9

We ended up having to wait until sunrise before anyone came to see how we were doing. The temperature had finally dropped those final few degrees, and the heavy rains had quickly turned into a thick blanket of snow by the time the sun had risen. One positive thing about it getting so cold was that our wet clothing had frozen solid, so we were able to shake out the ice crystals, allowing them to dry faster.

They were still damp when we put them on, but it was far better than the sopping wet mess it could have been. The warmth enchantments I'd added to Leedy's equipment had kept him from being too uncomfortable, and my own high stats and warmth runes made the frigid hut perfectly acceptable to me.

I was a little surprised to see it was the oldest of the Senior Huntmasters that asked us to follow him back down the elevator, but everyone else seemed to be too busy to play errand boy, and they probably didn't want to offend us by sending someone we might see as ranked too low in their society. Leedy and the old man made small talk while I ate the bowl of porridge and dried fruit the man had brought with him. We ate while we walked, and I paid more attention to our surroundings than to the conversation.

Signs of the fight from last night had mostly been covered up by the blanket of snow layering everything, but it hadn't successfully hidden everything. Broken tree limbs, sections of damaged tree bark, and splatters of blue, green, and red blood were sprinkled throughout the village. A few huts looked as if something large had tried to crack them open like wooden eggs. People were already out starting repairs, clearing away the debris and using what pieces they could scrounge to patch the broken homes. The nearby scorch marks and various pieces of spider and goblin bits proved the prowess of the defenders. Whatever was in those arrows the hunters used, it packed a serious punch.

It only reinforced how much I needed to find the place of power where their arrowheads were sourced. Ever since I'd learned the places of power were influenced by different kinds of mana–and when I absorbed that mana it permanently changed me–I was eagerly anticipating the new opportunities it could bring. There was no telling what kinds of advantages a new mana type might give, or how I could pack more punch against the enemies we were bound to face in the mountains.

As the elevator settled onto the ground, the other two wandered off, somehow deep in conversation about the pros and cons of canned beets. At least, I think that's what they were talking about. I wasn't really paying much attention.

Instead of following them right away, I turned around and saw a man wearing a nice set of hardened leather armor getting treated like a human playground set by a whole gaggle of toddlers. The man was enjoying every minute of it, his booming laughter echoing amongst the trees as he was nearly depantsed by a kid using the buckles on the side of his leg armor as a ladder. When he bent down to pick up a little girl reaching up for him, I realized it was my former patient. I hadn't recognized him at first. Probably because he didn't look dead. And he had clothes on now.

The laughter tapped something inside my brain. A memory I hadn't thought about in a long time tried to bubble to the surface. Then, I wasn't seeing what was in front of me. My mind brought me back to a place that was a long time ago, on a planet that might as well not even exist anymore.

*"You keep this up, and you'll never get out of here. The tots will hold a revolt."*

*I pulled a screaming kid off my back, their shouts of delight only drowned out by the happy sounds of the nearby children trying out the swing set I had just finished building. Healing their bodies was only part of the equation. Getting them some fresh air and exercise would do them wonders.*

*Building playgrounds across most of the southern coastline might have made it easy for the trackers following me initially, but the new idea was starting to spread like wildfire, and soon every town and village would have happy children with designated and safe places to play. It was worth the extra few months of scared and hurried harassment.*

*"We both know I can't stay long, Trenis. There will be men here searching for me soon enough. The Crown Prince will never*

*stop looking for me."* I let out a long sigh, wishing things were different. Wishing I was stronger. *"Maybe one day, people in power won't be able to push me around like a pawn on their chessboard. Until then, I'll either have to keep running, or be willing to stay captive in some tower."*

*"Chessboard? You say the strangest things. Anyway, after all the good you've done for the citizens of the kingdom, it's hard to believe the nobility hates you so much."* Trenis shook his head, still disbelieving the situation I was in. *"Don't they understand that without us, they wouldn't have food to eat? Taxes to collect? People to tell what to do?"*

*"I think some of them understand that, but far too many have convinced themselves that their world of intrigue and silks is the only world that matters. That's why they take whatever they want–whoever they want–and don't think about the consequences."* I had been kidnapped at swordpoint by the king, who forced me to be his personal healer while thousands of his people died by what I was sure was cholera.

The old bastard had ignored everything I'd said about getting clean water to the sick. He'd regretted it when I'd figured out how to move fatty deposits around in his bloodstream. The Crown Prince would be the new king as soon as his father passed away, but the stroke he'd suffered from hadn't killed him yet. It only left him partially paralyzed, and now all he could say was one word, over and over again. 'Bottles.'

*"Be that as it may, we'll never forget what you've done for us."* Trenis brushed his hands against his salt-stained pants before reaching over to grab a brand new rucksack that was sitting on a nearby table. It was a thing of beauty, with a frame made from the same lumber they used in the fishing boats that sailed the nearby harbor. The mixture of canvas and leather was meant to last, with more pockets than I'd probably ever use. *"This is something we put together for you, as payment for saving our little ones. It's nothing compared to what you've given us, but we hope it will serve you well in your travels."*

The weather-worn fisherman held it out to me, and I took it carefully from him. It was a fantastic gift, and tears that had nothing

75

*to do with the salt from the nearby sea stung my eyes. "I–it's great. Thank you."*

*I shifted the few meager belongings I carried into my new ruck and looked east, where I knew more seaside towns were in need of help from a traveling healer. It was time to move on, before these people were hurt because of him.*

"James?"

Blinking back into reality, I pushed back memories from the past. World one was a *long* time ago. All the recent healing must have brought back old memories. I'd spent an entire year on the run, healing where I could, not doing much fighting at all. The only positives from that place had been getting my Healer profession, my rucksack, and the realization that I needed to get physically stronger as fast as possible. On world two, I'd gained my Warrior class, and never looked back.

Remembering that a voice had pulled me out of my musings, I looked around for the person who had called for me. At first, I didn't see anyone. Then, the thew-bedecked form of a hunter materialized out of the winterscape.

"I'll never be able to repay you for bringing him back to us. To me." Jaeger stepped up next to me, doing his viking-ninja-hybrid-thing. He was wearing a snow-themed camouflage that blended in perfectly with our surroundings. "I thought I'd lost my father, but you brought him back to me."

"Healing him was part of a trade with your village. You don't have to repay me." I nodded my head toward the man playing with the kids. "Although, a guy like that? I'd have healed him for free. Kids can usually tell if someone is a good person or not, and they seem to think he's a pretty good guy."

"While I was able to lead the hunters in my father's stead, I'm not yet ready to fill his boots." Jaeger looked down at his hands, clenching them into fists. "One day, I'll be the kind of man to make him proud."

"Give yourself more credit than that, Jaeger." Hilda popped out from behind him, her much smaller frame hiding behind the large hunter easily. "You did a fine job. You're not as good with the kids, but you don't have any of your own yet, so that's normal, I'd say. Once you have a herd of cubs running around, you won't have any problems."

Once again, I was impressed by how well these hunters could make themselves disappear. If I didn't know any better, I'd say they were using magic. Maybe it was a side-effect of the mana in the region?

"Thanks for saying that Hilda, but I think it's time we got our healer friend where he needs to be. There are people waiting for him." Jaeger motioned with his hand, and we started crunching our way through the snow toward an area on the edge of the redwood trees where a small stone-paved platform had been cleared of snow, and several tables had been set up.

Several villagers were using it as a location to clean and separate the kills their hunters had made during the recent battle. Chunks of dead giant spiders were being sorted and organized as others packed them in snow and stacked them against specific tree trunks. It was controlled chaos, and I was impressed by how well the entire village came together to get the messy job done. It also explained why the big guy I saved had to play babysitter and jungle gym. All the parents were over here, working.

Jaeger pointed out where the elders were standing, and held out a hand for me to shake. "After what you've done for us, be sure to bargain hard with them."

"Oh, don't worry. I will. And Jaeger." He turned to look at me over his shoulder, his boots crunching in the snow. "Try talking to your dad. I have a feeling he's already proud of you." He gave me a nod as he walked away, once again disappearing into the snow and trees.

I joined Leedy and the trio of village leadership already in a heated debate about something. I'd only been separated from the former Warden for a few minutes, so I was surprised to see him already stirring up trouble in such a short amount of time. None of them even noticed when I walked over, so I cleared my throat to try and see if my arrival would calm the situation. It didn't work.

"–don't care! We're not going to throw away our hunters' lives because you saved one." The younger of the two old men was up in Leedy's face, shaking a finger under his nose in anger. "Even if nothing went wrong, when they part ways with your group and return home, they could lead another group of these things straight back here, and risk all of us!"

"Hey!" My shout finally caught their attention, causing them to turn and look at me. Leedy gave me a look of relief, while the one who had been yelling looked at me with resentment. "First off, if I know anything about goblins, it's that they're good at retreating, so your argument is already invalid. There were certainly at least one or two that got back to their caves last night to tell the rest where you live."

"You doubt the abilities of our hunters?" The frustrated man moved his angry pointer finger in my direction. "Do you have any idea the size of the insult you heap upon our most lethal citizens? It sounds to me like you should leave."

"No, I properly estimate the cowardice of goblins. If you don't think there were some waiting on the fringes to commit to the attack, and they ran at the first sign of trouble, you're out of your mind." I looked over his shoulder at all of the people sorting sections of tough spider hide to be used as armor who were obviously listening in on our conversation. "And, more importantly, are you willing to risk the lives of your people to plan as if there *weren't* any that got away?"

That shut him right up. He was aware enough to realize I'd gotten the best of him, even if I wasn't completely sure what game he was playing. Why he was trying to sabotage any future deals with me was confusing. There was no upside I could see, and only negatives for his people.

I'd already proven myself, and they could only gain more by trading with me. Unless, of course, the villagers staying weak and dependent on certain factions which favored him was his true goal. Which, unfortunately, was the only thing that made sense, besides him hating me for no reason. Politics were everywhere, even in the most remote locations with a bunch of people so poor and destitute they were living in freaking *trees*.

Sometimes, those bumper stickers back on my home world wishing for a meteor to hit the planet were completely understandable.

"How about we all take a deep breath, and let the healer explain *exactly* what he's requesting?" The old woman spoke, grabbing her brother's shoulder, sharply pulling him back. "I'm certain we can all be reasonable adults about this."

Her brother, despite being old enough to know better, wasn't very good at hiding his emotions. It was plain to everyone watching that he was upset about his sister calling him childish in a roundabout manner. He brushed her hand off before turning his glare on her. "I don't need you to calm me down. You wait and see, you'll regret dealing with these outsiders!"

With his final threat directed at everyone, including the onlookers, he stomped his way through the snow toward the distant elevator. A few of the people dealing with the legs of the dead spiders got up from their work stations and joined him, not meeting the eyes of their fellow craftsmen and laborers. They appeared to represent a specific job or faction within the village, but I couldn't tell by looking at them which one it was.

I had no idea what them leaving meant for the future of the little community, and I genuinely didn't care. The details of a political landscape in such a small location were so far down my list of concerns, I couldn't even see it. If I didn't make it to the Demon Gate in time, none of their ridiculous little games mattered anyway. They'd probably all end up dead.

"Well, that could have gone better." At least the man's sister looked a little embarrassed at her sibling's actions. "Let's move past that unpleasantness, and focus on the future, yes?"

"At least tell me this much. Who were those people that left with him?" Why had I asked that? I mentally kicked myself, knowing there was no good answer. I always managed to put my foot in my own mouth at the worst possible times. Knowing the details of how badly things could go for these people would only make things worse.

"That was the remainder of our Bowyer's Guild. My brother is their de facto leader, ever since our real village got overrun." The old woman shivered as a gust of wind blew loose snow into her face. "Most of the members, including the original guild leader and vice leader, were some of the first to die when the attack came over our walls."

Leedy let out a dramatic groan, and rubbed his face with both hands. "And since your people need bows to hunt food, and fight, it gives him an unreasonable amount of sway over everyone."

"Don't worry too much about him." She patted at the air, as if trying to calm us down. "I promise, the Healer's Guild, Blacksmithing Guild, and Fletcher's Guild can get more done when they work together toward a common goal."

Considering how the oldest elder had reacted when I had mentioned blacksmithing yesterday, he probably represented their interests. His niece, the old woman we were talking to, was most likely in place for the healers. That only left out the Fletcher's Guild, which were the people who had direct contact with the place of power. They probably trusted the combined council to look out for their interests.

"What about the Hunter's Guild? Wouldn't they be the most powerful guild in the village, considering they're the ones who actually *do* the hunting?" Leedy seemed genuinely confused, and started looking around the small platform. "Where is their representative? Wouldn't they be interested in trade with us, especially if they're the ones that have to escort us north?"

"I'm the highest of the Senior Huntmasters, and represent them." The nearly toothless old man bobbed his head, and gave both Leedy and me a smile. "It says a lot about you, to care about the men involved."

"Well, if we might end up fighting next to them, it figures we should do our best by them." Leedy glanced my way for approval, and I gave him a subtle thumbs up. We were on the same page. "So, now that we're finally in agreement about doing business together, how about we discuss terms?"

The old man nodded and stepped forward, while his niece behind him pulled out a rolled up parchment and unfurled it with a long list written down its entire length. "As we understand it, you wish to visit the hidden location where our arrowheads are made, and then receive guides through the mountain passes to the north. In return, the Blacksmithing Guild was interested in what runes you were willing to engrave in bulk, while the Healer's Guild wanted to–"

As he kept rambling on, I was suddenly able to predict the future.

It was going to be a long day.

## CHAPTER 10

Gleason took off his spiked helmet to wipe the mixture of venom, blue spider blood, and green goblin gore from his forehead before it could drip down into his eyes. He needed to be able to see clearly if he was going to avoid all the damnable traps the nefarious little greenskins and their cave spider friends left littered throughout the maze of caverns his stupid underlings had lost him in. It was their fault he was in this situation, and now the treacherous orcs were nowhere to be found! He should have known better than to trust the brutes, but letting them lead the assault into the goblin stronghold was his only option. Letting them be at his back, where he couldn't see them, was even worse.

The splashes of darker green and occasionally red orc blood that coated the dirty spiderwebs along the cave walls showed one of his teams had fled this way. The lack of bodies meant they were either doing well for themselves, or the hungry cave spiders had already been through here to clean up behind them.

After making sure his armor was as clean as he could make it, Gleason started picking his way carefully down the tunnel, ignoring the smaller offshoots that he occasionally passed by. Most of them were covered in webs anyway, meaning no one but spiders had been down here in a long time. He had the strong urge to burn out all the webs, and the mutated bugs that certainly hid among them, but the air was too thin for him to vent his rage. Even though his rage was reaching new highs, he wasn't suicidal. Maybe one fireball would be okay. He would only risk it if his life was in danger.

While he walked, Gleason cursed his luck, and ruminated on how it had all gone so wrong. His day had started out so well, with all of his forces mustering in the early dawn hours at the edge of the forest, across from the caves that his Centurion had said were the source of the goblins and their cave spider threat.

There had been three visible entrances, so Gleason had divided their century into three equal groups, and sent them in to kill everything they could find. A fourth, much smaller group of elites stayed with him outside to ensure no goblins would get away. Any survivors they could scrounge up after the initial battle were to be added to his century, and integrated into his new and improved scouts.

Unfortunately, there hadn't been *three* entrances. There had been far, far more, and when his orcs had disappeared inside the caves, the goblins had erupted forth in an overwhelming mass, riding their cave spider calvary as if they were some conquering horde from a bygone era. Gleason had ordered his elite orcs to provide a ring of protection around him as they fought their way to reunite with the rest of the century, but even the strongest of his orcs were no match for the paralyzing venom the spiders carried within their razor fangs.

The fight on the surface had raged for what felt like hours, but had probably been no more than thirty minutes. Still, it was enough time for Gleason's whip to savage the goblins that dared to threaten his life, and extinguish the spiders that attempted to turn him into their next meal. He'd had to teach an orc what would happen if they tried to run, but only the one. Once the others saw what happened, no others dared to try. There were plenty of things worse than death.

It had been a near thing, but Gleason had managed to make it into one of the cave entrances, and he'd been hiding, fighting, and casting spells in his own defense ever since. It could have been days since the last time he'd seen the sun. There was no way for him to know, down here in the depths.

While he wasn't concerned about the goblins and spiders in small groups, the battle on the surface had proven that even his existence could be threatened if they swarmed him in large enough numbers. That was why he was forced to scurry about like a mouse, and only bring his formidable force to bear when he was sure of victory. Risking his own life was foolish, of course, especially since the Trinity had a task that was greater than himself. He needed to guard his future in order to complete their mission.

The sounds of scuttling came from up ahead, and Gleason hurried to crouch behind a recently created pile of rubble. A few pebbles came tumbling down as his shoulder brushed against the broken pile of rocks, causing them to clatter against the stone floor and make enough noise that whatever was approaching fell silent.

The only sound Gleason could hear afterward was the pounding of his own heart in his ears.

In the underworld rules of caves, the predator with the most patience was more often the one who lived to see another day. Of course, that didn't apply when one of the predators could cast a smoking ball of red fire that seemed to contain the screaming faces of tortured souls, normally trapped in the depths of hell and only released for a brief moment to inhabit the spells of a man more heinous than the demon who tortured them throughout eternity. Which, as specific as a circumstance that might be, Gleason managed to fit.

Tired of acting the part of a scared mouse for untold hours, the self-proclaimed Blood Warden leapt from behind his hiding place and unleashed a blistering ball of fire that sounded as if it was filled with the screeching wails of the damned. A cluster of tiny cave spiders went up in a mighty conflagration that reached the tunnel ceiling, creating a wall of flame that quickly spread up and down the webs that lined everything Gleason could see farther down the tunnel. Now, everything deeper into the caves would know he was coming, and the few spiders he had used the spell on were barely a threat. Gleason could have stomped on them in only a few seconds, and no one would have been the wiser.

"*Damn.*" Gleason's curse was quiet, but filled with more venom than any cave spider could hope to hold. Unlike normal smoke, the cloying smog that his red flames produced sank to the ground, allowing him to continue to stand as it swirled around his feet like a fog that was eager to hide threats to the unwary. The level slowly started to rise as the flammable webs deeper in the tunnels continued to burn, and just like a sinking ship filling with water, the air would eventually run out.

After a few hurried steps, Gleason realized he had another problem. The flames had burned away any traces left behind by his orcs. "Now what am I supposed to do? Stupid *orcs!*"

Deep down, Gleason was sure the Centurion that led his orcs into the caves had done this on purpose. There was no other excuse for such an oversight. "What kind of leader doesn't ensure there's a plan to mark the direction of travel for their forces that follow behind the main attack? A bad leader, that's who. And it was that Trinity-cursed Centurion that led my orcs into these caves!"

Feeling better after voicing his feelings, Gleason decided to continue onward, despite the rising tide of deadly smoke. It wouldn't be much longer before it was up to his knees, and since he was walking deeper underground, it only accelerated the problem. If he didn't find a way out soon, Gleason would be forced to turn around and try battling his way through the horde of goblins and cave spiders that he knew waited for him on the surface.

One positive thing about his situation was the abrupt lack of enemies. Either they were running from the smoke and flames, or the many collapsed side tunnels he suddenly started seeing were their way of cutting off the spreading destruction before it could consume them. The end result was it left him with a clear path deeper into the warren of the goblin stronghold, without opposition or clues to his whereabouts.

Just as the smoke was starting to reach his thighs, there was a major junction that went in five directions. Six, if you counted the tunnel he came in from. At some point his flames had died off since there were still webs in this chamber, however, the smoke wasn't dissipating. It was settling into the lowest portions of the tunnels like a thick oil, sticking to the floor in a heavy coating that swirled with a hot, dark menace.

For Gleason, it was the perfect tool to show him how to get back to the surface. The second tunnel to his right had no smoke pouring into it, meaning it angled upward, which was the direction he wanted to go. For any creatures that were in the lower levels unaware of the danger sinking down on their heads, only a silent death with no chance for escape hunted for them.

Now that he'd discovered a path that might lead out, Gleason's mood rapidly improved. Despite the need to stay quiet, he couldn't help making some noise as he tromped up the web-lined tunnel. He'd once again proven his superior intellect and survivor skills, and he was on his way to complete his mission from the gods. Even incompetent orc underlings wouldn't be able to stop Gleason now.

The occasional signs of goblins sharing the caves with the spiders were absent in this area, but that was of no concern to him. Also of no concern was the gradual change in webbing as he ascended. He was too busy to notice the coloring of the webs going from an off-white, barely sticky, and thin material, to a pristine white that nearly glowed blue, made from much thicker strands, and sticky enough that Gleason would have been in serious trouble if he'd been in anything other than plate metal armor. No, instead of picking up on any of that, he was focused on the steadily improving air quality that his nose and lungs detected.

As he approached another intersection with several tunnels, Gleason stopped to take a drink from his canteen and try to get a better sense of which direction he should take. That was when he heard the sounds of something he'd long since given up on. The battle cry of orcs.

"Some of those useless mongrels are still alive? Good. I'll show them what happens when you disappoint me." He caressed his whip, imagining all the things he was soon going to be able to do with it. "After they help me get out of this maze first, of course."

Hurrying down the tunnel that echoed with the sounds of battle, Gleason didn't notice the trio of spiders emerge from one of the tunnels he hadn't taken. They were larger than any of the ones the goblins had been riding, and the only spots of color on their pitch black bodies were the cluster of glowing red eyes on the front and an equally bright spot of red on their abdomens in the shape of a twisted butterfly. The mutant spiders, instead of following the human, started closing off the tunnel, using their webs to create a thick wall of impenetrable silk.

Gleason, still blissfully unaware of what went on behind him, charged toward the flickering light of torches, clashing of metal, and screams of the wounded and dying. He rounded a sharp turn at full speed, eager to fight, and almost tripped over the bodies of an orc and spider clasped together in a final embrace. Looking down, he was briefly shocked at what he saw.

The venom that caused the foam frothing from the orc's mouth could have been what killed it, or it could have been the pair of spear-like limbs that pierced its abdomen, but either way, the orc must have known it was dying. A broken sword hilt was still clasped in the orc's grip, with the other end thrust through the bottom of the giant spider's head. Several wounds littered the spider, but only the final blow had been lethal.

From what Gleason could tell, the orc had sacrificed itself in its final moments to ensure the monster it was facing would die. He hadn't known the orcs in his century could seek such a noble death. It was so far outside his understanding of their abilities and culture, it had created a sense of dichotomy so strong he fought back a bout of vertigo.

Then, his personal reality reasserted itself. "Huh. The spider must have fallen on the orc, and it killed it before they could pull themselves apart. Just a fluke of war." His view of the world once again in the right, Gleason finally worked his way into the chamber where the battle raged.

As soon as he got a good view of what was going on, Gleason froze. Today truly was cursed. Instead of rushing into battle, he started looking for the nearest escape. There was no way he wanted anything to do with *that* monstrosity.

## CHAPTER 11

Negotiations had gone well into the afternoon hours before an agreement was finally made with the council. They'd wanted several things that were outright impossible, and even more things that would have taken months, if not years, to accomplish. Once we'd gotten through the differences between fantasy and reality–believe me, I get the irony–the deal finally started to come together. I'd left the majority of the details up to Leedy, who thankfully had no qualms with making the fiddly bits work.

He worked through the logistics of another group joining our own for an unknown length of time, the minimum amount of aid required to give in the event someone was captured, loot distribution, even what would happen if a member of our party fell in love and wanted to marry a member of our escort group.

It was quite the document, and after the basics were covered it felt more like an excuse for the old man to mess with Leedy than to actually cover every eventuality. I guess when you get to be that age, fighting boredom and messing with people are pretty much your main hobbies.

While the old man had put Leedy through the wringer, the woman had taken me around to start knocking out the tasks I could complete right away.

First up on the list had been giving everyone in the village a quick health examination. Once they'd organized everyone into neat, orderly lines, I'd been able to get through all the adults and babies in no time. The children who could actually walk and run on their own were a different story. Those little buggers were more elusive than a capuchin monkey on a pound of cocaine, and nobody was actually sure if we'd gotten all of them yet. I'd leave it up to the parents to figure it out.

After clearing up a few old injuries, healing the occasional lack of nutrients, and taking care of a few nasty communicable diseases that were just waiting for their hosts to weaken before they came out to play, I shifted over to rune work and enchanting. Considering the village had been moved to a bunch of tree huts, the Blacksmithing Guild was now only four guys that shared a makeshift forge and anvil. They had plenty of ore from the nearby mountains to work with, but not much in the way of tools or equipment. There also wasn't much of a need for metal in their current circumstances, so there weren't any expeditions to restock their ore on the council's calendar anytime soon. That didn't mean I couldn't make things better.

To help them out, I did what I could to improve their forge first. It didn't take much to draw up some stone from below for an extra layer of insulation and strength, and then I added some runes to improve airflow that would run off the ambient mana in the area. They would still need to use bellows for precise temperature control, but there wouldn't be any cold or hot spots to worry about any more.

Next, the anvil needed a friend, so I shaped a block of dark quartz crystal that was roughly anvil-sized and etched a repeating trio of runes that I'd learned on world twelve–where I gained my Runesmith profession–around the base. The quartz wouldn't last as long as a real iron or steel anvil, but anything with an enchantment wouldn't explode when you worked on it. While one rune suppressed the item being worked on, another rune strengthened the anvil, and the last rune made sure the other two were powered and liked each other. Runes that didn't get along could go boom, and as much as I loved them, not all booms were good booms.

After making a set of tools to go with the anvil, I wrote out the instructions necessary for the blacksmiths to use them, along with detailed drawings of the runes I'd agreed to give them. One rune for adding fire to a weapon, another to add light, and a ring of five runes to create a medium-sized stationary shield that would stop several arrows, a few heavy hits, or disrupt a single big spell.

It was one of the safer shield spells I knew, since it was stationary, and it only started drawing power once all the runes were properly connected. If it didn't require such long charge times and it wasn't a constant drain on the ambient mana where it was placed, I'd probably use it more often myself. Unfortunately, on the ground, another magic user would notice the blank spots of mana, and it was easy to spot and destroy. Up in the trees, where the villagers were? It was perfect for them.

While I had use of the facilities, I took a little time for myself. My wrist gun had three barrels, and right now all three of them were loaded with what was basically a fifty caliber solid silver slug. That was great and all–especially against undead–but I had been thinking of ways to increase my versatility, what I could do to reload faster, and what I might need when facing other kinds of monsters in the mountain caves and passes.

During a high school history class, I vaguely remembered that paper cartridges were used for hundreds of years before modern firearms were invented, and I thought it was worth a shot to try it as a way to improve my current form of reloading. It would also give me a way to rapidly prepare and swap out ammunition types based on the kind of enemy I was fighting.

First, I cut some strips of parchment that were roughly the size and shape I needed. Then, I rolled them into tubes the size of my wrist gun barrels and dipped them into some melted wax so they would hold their shape and be waterproof. I capped one end with a piece of parchment and dipped it one more time, giving the outer layer an extra bit of protection from the nearly constant rain and dampness of this world.

Next, I measured a healthy amount of boom-boom dust into each tube, and then dropped another disk of parchment into the tube. Just to be safe, I put a little piece of cloth on top of the parchment, and then another disk of parchment on the other side, and finally a little bit of wax to seal the gunpowder into its own chamber. I gave each of them a shake to make sure the wax hadn't leaked through and ruined the gunpowder. Satisfied with the end result, I set them to the side.

Before going crazy with all kinds of different bullet types, I started off with several basic rounds, using up the remainder of the solid bullets I'd already made. After seating the fifty caliber rounds into the paper tubes and sealing them with wax to waterproof them, I test-fired a single shot and had no problems. Seeing the proof of concept was a success, it was time to get started on the more interesting ideas I had bouncing around in my head.

Since I wanted a variety of options, I started off with the nastiest of rounds I could think of. That meant creating two equally sized balls of lead, and then connecting the two with a thin chain of a silver and steel alloy that I hoped would hold together when it was fired. In theory, the chain would be able to cut through any organic material like a hot knife through butter, and wrap around anything harder than itself, hopefully still doing damage. A bolo round, if it worked, would be a flying razor of whirling destruction. If it didn't work, I still had two heavy balls of lead that wouldn't feel good when they hit something.

I made several of the rounds, using different amounts of steel in the chain alloy. Hopefully at least a few of them would work. Once I fit them neatly into the ends of my paper shells and sealed it into place with more disks of paper, cloth, and wax, the whole thing barely fit in the barrel of my wrist gun. Accuracy wouldn't be great, but it would certainly fire.

Basic buckshot rounds were next, but they were anything but basic. Normally, a buckshot round was a shotgun round that has somewhere between eight and twelve metal balls that all come out in a tight cone of hate that erases whatever is in front of the barrel.

Mine were going to have a little more oomph.

The special arrowheads from the nearby place of power broke apart nicely on the new anvil without blowing up in my face, and I sprinkled in several large chunks of the explosive and sharp flint pieces with an even mix of lead and silver balls. They should provide a good smack to the face to anything I generally didn't approve of, or wanted to delete from existence.

The next experiment was something I'd always wanted to try. Now that my Mind stat was over one hundred and ten, I could do it. Before now, carving and etching dozens of miniscule runes would have taken weeks, if I could have even pulled it off in the first place. That wouldn't be a problem for me anymore.

Flechette rounds were basically just shotgun rounds filled with needles instead of metal balls. The idea was horrifying, but in real life the application was useless. Needles were so light, they didn't penetrate much of anything when fired from a gun. Luckily for me, I had something people on my homeworld didn't. Magic.

Instead of using needles, I used dozens of thin rods of mixed metals. Whatever I could find, I included it. Copper, tin, brass, silver, iron, gold, nickel, bronze, lead, and steel, all of it got thrown in. On the flat tip of one end of every rod, I used magic to etch one rune. Heavier. On the opposite end, I etched 'faster'. There wasn't enough space for anything else, like the rune for them to absorb ambient mana, so I would have to power them myself before I fired it. Considering their size, they would only hold a charge for a few seconds. Realistically, that's probably all I would need, so it should work out fine.

My *Identify* spell wasn't working on any of the rounds, which was concerning, but that could have been because they were too new or untested for the system to quantify. It wouldn't be the first time a brand new thing I made had to be used in combat before it could be quantified by hard numbers. Either that, or they were a complete failure. I was pretty sure it was the former because the basic round I test fired had functioned. It would just need to hit an enemy to gauge the amount of damage it could do.

Even with my advanced Mind stat, the time it took to make the flechette rounds was extensive, so it was starting to get dark when Leedy came to find me for supper.

"You done playing with tiny pieces of paper and metal, James?" Leedy looked exhausted, but happy. He'd done well today and he knew it. "The group of hunters that's supposed to lead our team through the foothills is meeting us for the evening meal. They wanted to talk with you before we head out tomorrow morning."

"I'm finishing up now." I sealed the final flechette round closed, and gave it one last dunk in the hot wax. I would need to set up a better way to store my ammunition now that I had different types, but for now I dropped them in my pouch with the others. "What about the guide to where they make their arrowheads? When does that happen?"

"After we eat, and full dark hits. The hunters prefer to go when there's no sunlight. It's supposed to be safer." Leedy shrugged, and bent down to grab his pack. I'd been holding on to it for him while he was dealing with the negotiations. "I don't know if the trip is safer, or if the location is safer. They weren't exactly happy about giving me details."

"Once I leave, make sure you go straight to our camp and bring the others here. It doesn't matter that the hunters know where we're staying. We'll head north from this location, and maybe even thin out some of the goblins causing these people problems." I thought for a moment about our usual procedures, and decided to make a change. "Tell Jess to leave our base open instead of collapsing it or closing it up. The people here can use it as an outpost, or a place to stash emergency supplies. They can use any advantages they can get, especially since those waystations the Wardens maintain don't extend this far north."

Leedy looked up from his things and gave me a sharp nod of approval. "I think that's a great idea. While that one council guy might have been a real troublemaker, everyone else I've met deserves as much help as we can spare."

"I couldn't agree more." I turned to leave, going toward the elevator.

"Hey, James? Do you have any idea what happened to my socks?" Leedy held them up to the light of the setting sun, showing rows of very distinct holes that were definitely not exactly the right size for my new paper rounds cut out of them. They were more holes than socks at this point, with only ragged bits of fabric holding them together. My pouch was *very* full of new rounds, and it had taken a lot of cloth to help make all of them. "It looks like some kind of giant bug, or maybe a mutant moth chewed them to pieces?"

"That's crazy, Leedy. I have no clue how that could have happened." Maybe because I wasn't going to use my own socks, and I was tired of smelling his. The world would never know for sure. "You're right, though. Probably some weird moth native to the area we need to keep an eye out for, otherwise we won't have any socks left."

I hurried away while he quickly searched the rest of his clothing for damage. I didn't want to be standing there when he found out all his boxers were now briefs.

## CHAPTER 12

Our evening meal with the hunters was quite the celebration, with more than a few drunken speeches given by the time things wound down. The whole village was celebrating both the victory over the goblin attack, and the return of the hero they had thought lost when retreating to their tree homes. A clean bill of health and the new runes we'd traded for only added to the merriment.

Leedy spent his supper questioning the people around him about unique insects in the region, but he was too embarrassed to get specific. That meant he spent most of the time hearing about all of the weird and nasty creepy-crawlies that frequented the forest around us instead of enjoying his meal. Oddly enough, there were several examples of bugs that could have damaged his clothing in a similar manner to what he saw, so he now was on a mission to find and kill any bug hives and colonies he could find that met the description of the ones the hunters gave.

I almost felt bad about everything, but the memory of all the times he'd encouraged Cross to add more blackfrond to our food when he *knew* I didn't like the strong spice eased my guilt. I'd buy him newer, nicer items the next time we were in a city that sold them. Until then, he'd be okay with one fewer pair of socks and smaller underwear than he was used to. If we were lucky, maybe he'd start doing his laundry more often.

The team of hunters assigned to us was led by a gray-haired man by the name of Lighter. Pronounced Lig-hit-er, he was supposed to be the man with the most experience getting through the foothills and into the actual mountains. According to him, there were several ways to get close to the mountains, but a narrow band of steep canyons that separated the two regions made it necessary to finish the crossing in only two places. Both were dangerous, and he didn't know which was worse.

Joining Lighter were seven other hunters. They weren't supposed to stay with us the whole time, but serve as scouts, relay supplies, and report all the way back to the village about the conditions to the north. This was a major expedition for their people, and they were treating it as such. Information on enemy movements, possible loot from defeated monsters, and even future hunting and mining locations were all up for grabs. That meant the council wanted the best available, so they were sending everyone the defense could spare.

Unsurprisingly, two of those seven were Jaeger and Hilda. They were the pair that were meant to stay with us the longest, and escorting Lighter back to their village after we made it through the pass was their responsibility. Their advanced camouflage tricks would make sneaking through hostile territory much easier for a smaller group, so it made sense for them to be the last out. They were also the two who were escorting me to the place of power.

"Are we ready to go?" I already had my rucksack on my back, and I was standing by the elevator, waiting for it to take us down. "I'd like to get this over with as quickly as possible."

"Sure, just hold on for a minute. It's not like the flint hills are going to run away or something." Hilda was fastening an extra quiver to her belt, but she was having problems getting the buckle to fasten while she was wearing gloves. "Stupid thing, doesn't want to get in–"

"Let me help." Jaeger dropped from the branches above, landing with only a quiet thud against the wooden planks of the elevator flooring. "New quivers are always the worst."

"No, the worst is having to deal with weird hillbilly-ninja hybrids that suddenly act like drop-bears. Next thing you know, I'll have to start doing puma checks." I quickly looked all around me, making sure I didn't have to worry about the exceedingly dangerous creatures. Thankfully, I was in the clear. "Anyway, how far do we have to go?"

"It's close. We're pretty sure the reason these trees were planted is because of the magic in the flint hills. Our ancestors have been watching over them for generations, and using the tools they provide to help protect their families. It's a beneficial relationship for both sides." Jaeger motioned for someone out of sight to start the elevator, and we quickly went down, our descent matching the disappearance of the sun. "By the way, what's a ninja?"

"A poorly educated person might call a ninja a type of spicy samurai. Does that clear things up some?" The stoic look on his face was enough to tell me it most definitely did not, and I was perfectly okay with that. Confusing people was one of the only simple pleasures left to me in life. As the platform settled onto the ground, we stepped off, and it quickly lifted out of sight. "Well, I guess that means there's no going back, huh?"

"If we want to return to the heights before sunrise, we'll have to climb. It's a new measure the council decided to take ever since the goblin attack." Hilda finally seemed happy with her equipment situation, and passed me to take the lead. "It's supposed to make the village safer."

"Not to nitpick or anything, but weren't the goblins riding spiders that could simply climb the trees?" I looked up at the faint scars on the tree trunks around us, still fresh from the recent battle. Plenty of them were obviously left by the sharp tips of cave spider limbs as they vertically ascended the thick trunks. "In fact, did any of the goblins ride the lift?"

"You and I both know they didn't." Jaeger fell in step next to me, his eyes diligently scouting the quickly deepening darkness for threats. "It's about putting forth the appearance of safety. If the council is seen taking action to help reduce the threat, even if that action is only a symbolic one, it makes the people feel better."

"See? I told you." Hilda glanced over her shoulder and gave Jaeger a wink. "You'll be ready to take your father's place in no time. Then he can finally take his seat on the council."

Jaeger blushed at the praise, which looked funny on the muscle-bound hunter. It made me wonder about his actual age. I'd initially guessed late twenties, but now I was thinking it might be closer to barely twenty.

Even though I'd been away from my home world for two decades now, it was still difficult for me to tell how old someone was once they hit maturity under the more medieval conditions of the planets I traveled. Frontier life was hard, and it aged people quickly. A person in their forties could look nearly twice that, or possibly appear exactly like they were forty. There was no logical way for someone to walk up and accurately know someone's age just by looking. It was one of the little things that still bugged the crap out of me.

"Let's get moving. We need to get there quickly, before the weather turns on us." Jaeger waved Hilda forward, rushing us onward instead of responding to her earlier comment.

When we reached the gap between the giant redwood-like trees and the regular forest, I got a good look at the sky and realized Jaeger wasn't hurrying us along to deflect the conversation. As per the norm for this planet, a heavy cloudbank was blotting out the sky to our north. It swallowed the last few dregs of light from the sunset, and blasted me in the face with a bitterly cold wind that tried to steal my breath.

After getting her bearings, Hilda took off at a steady jog through the first few flakes of falling snow. The three of us were able to maintain a steady pace through the forest for almost an hour while the edge of the storm seemed to hover in place over our heads.

What had started out as a normal-looking snowstorm was quickly developing into something far more serious. Even by the light of the stars that were yet to be covered, it was easy to see how heavy and ominous the clouds were becoming. Wind whipped treetops in unforgiving bursts, swirling the few flakes of snow that managed to fall into dizzying designs that vanished amongst the forest's branches.

We came upon a small clearing that surrounded a pond as the snow started coming down in heavier amounts. During the warmer months, the pond was probably an ideal fishing spot. Right now, it only gave the wind an easier opportunity to slap us in the face without the forest there to slow it down.

"This might be a bad one." Hilda had slowed down to walk between Jaeger and I, the three of us all stepping carefully over the icy ground as we circled the edge of the pond. The clearing had gotten enough sun to allow the snow to melt into a slush, which had refrozen into a hard layer of slick ice. It was great for not leaving tracks, but not so great for everything else. Hilda was handling it the easiest out of our little group. "If a thunder blizzard hits while we're between the sites, no one will find our bodies until the spring thaw."

"I don't think it's going to be bad enough to be considered a thunder blizzard, Hilda." Jaeger's words were a lot more confident than his tone of voice. A flicker of lightning danced between clouds high over our heads. We all waited with baited breath for the boom of thunder, but none came. "See? It's only a regular storm. A bad one, but not too bad. If we hurry, we'll be fine. The first—"

97

Thunder shook the ground so hard it cracked the ice under our feet.

I grabbed both of them by the collar and pulled them away from the edge of the pond, just in case. I didn't want anyone falling into the water and disappearing under the ice. That was a nasty way to go.

"Okay, so it's a thunder blizzard. I take it they're really bad." Both of them looked at me with wide eyes, either from the shock of getting yanked so quickly or because they thought my question was exceptionally dumb. Probably both. "What's closer, the village, or the site?"

It took them a few heartbeats to pull themselves together, but Jaeger managed to be the first to answer. "We're about halfway between both places. Maybe a little closer to the village, but not by much. If I had to come up with the worst place to get hit by a freak storm, this might be it."

Even with the danger of the storm, I needed to reach the place of power. It helped that it was also the best choice. All I needed to do was convince the hunters. "With the lift no longer on the ground, and the storm certain to cut visibility down to nothing, there won't be a way to signal anyone to lower it and get back into the trees at the village." A strong gust of wind hit us, and I helped steady the other two. A rumble of thunder that was far less dramatic than the first one we experienced came from the north, signaling we were out of time. "Not that riding that thing in a blizzard would be a good idea in the first place. I say we tie ourselves together so no one gets lost, and push hard for the other site. If it gets too bad, I can raise an earthen shelter to protect us."

They communicated with a series of quick hand gestures and facial movements that were indecipherable before Hilda started pulling some rope out of her pack. She pointed to the northwest while she worked, where a small gap in the clearing was barely visible. "That's the path we need to take. Normally, we'd take outsiders on a longer loop to make it harder for them to find their way back on their own, but now isn't the time for games." Holding up a loop, she dropped it over Jaeger's wide shoulders and tightened it around his waist. "I'll take point, Jaeger in the rear. We'll go single file so the rope doesn't tangle in the trees."

She dropped another loop over my head, and I took off my rucksack for a moment so I could tightened it diagonally across my chest. I didn't want it accidentally messing up my weapon belt. The end by my hip went toward Jaeger, while the end on my shoulder went toward Hilda. It was uncomfortable when I put my heavy ruck back on over it, but there was no way it was coming off now.

Jaeger double-checked Hilda's knots on her own loop and handed her a large brass oil lantern before stepping back. "If you get tired, let me know and we'll switch places."

"You'll wear out before I will, muscle-boy." Hilda gave him a shoulder bump and lit the lantern with a flint firestarter. "Keep a sharp eye out. Just because there's a thunder blizzard doesn't mean there can't be undead, or monsters. Anything could use the weather to hide."

And with those cheery words, we stepped back into the forest.

Just as the thunder blizzard unleashed its fury.

## CHAPTER 13

*"How much farther?!"* I gasped for breath, the wind sucking the air out of my lungs after shouting. Jaeger only shook his head, his eyes mostly glazed over. I wasn't even sure if he was seeing me anymore, let alone hearing me. The last time I had gotten a verbal response from him, his lips weren't nearly as blue as they were now.

His entire focus was putting one foot in front of the other, and not letting go of the rope he gripped in one hand and the lantern in the other. Hilda was even worse, her feet dragging through the snow drifts, with both hands tightened on her rope. She was trying desperately to use Jaeger's bulk as a windbreak, unfortunately that meant she wasn't getting the benefit of the heat from the periodic bursts of white-hot fire I blasted in front of us to keep the trail visible.

I'd been forced to take the lead position almost an hour ago. That was a long time for the other two to endure the sub-zero temperatures and biting winds. If it weren't for the insane amounts of magic I was throwing around to keep us going, there was no doubt in my mind they would have died from hypothermia. I wouldn't have been much better off if I hadn't already added the warmth runes to my kit, and I was already thinking about how to add more.

Snow was coming down so hard it was impossible to see anything past ten or fifteen feet. The lantern Jaeger was holding up for us provided just enough light to illuminate a dome of swirling whiteness, with the occasional tree limb that reached out for us like the demonic claws of some withered and frozen creature. My blasts of fire ensured we didn't drift off course, but that was all.

To make matters worse, the ground wasn't as nice and flat as it had been, so now we were stumbling and falling when a snowdrift wasn't actually a snowdrift, but a natural rock formation. Getting back up was getting harder and harder each time, and the extra effort was sapping what little strength everyone had left.

After another minute or two of walking, in which I was pretty much dragging the other two, I knew I'd already pushed us too far. It was beyond the time I should have stopped and set up a shelter, but the timer ticking away on my stat sheet was forcing me to make decisions I didn't want to make. The risk of frostbite that I could quickly heal was nothing compared to the death of a planet. That, I didn't know how to heal.

I started to look for a likely place to set up a shelter, and let loose a trio of fireballs to clear out the snow around us. As if to answer my magic, a bright flash of lightning similar to the first one we experienced lit up the forest around us.

Thunder and lightning had still raged overhead, but the snow fell so thick that most of the light was barely more than a faint glow, and the sounds of thunder were only muffled thumps. This one was different. It gave me a glimpse of our surroundings, before shaking the ground hard enough to nearly knock me off my feet.

In that brief moment, I thought I'd seen something. A chimney.

"*Almost there*! *Keep going*!" I tugged on the ropes, getting the other two moving. They didn't respond, and I glanced back to see the lantern on its side in the snow.

Jaeger had fallen, and Hilda had landed on his back. Both of them were unresponsive, and cold to the touch. The wind was so intense, and so filled with moisture, it was almost impossible for them to breathe. I got a steady pulse from both of them, but I knew time was short. Healing them wouldn't solve the problem, so instead I gave each a quick burst of unfocused healing mana to help stabilize them and struggled back to my feet.

*Damn*, it was cold.

I made sure I had a good grip on the ropes tied to them in one hand, and picked up the lantern in the other. A few seconds of focus and I was able to activate my shield bracelet, and form it into a kind of sled to help drag the two hunters behind me. It started rapidly draining my mana to maintain it, but my mana generator was doing its best to keep up with the demand. The dense, wild storm mana certainly helped with how fast it could absorb the ambient energy in the area.

The next hundred yards were the hardest of the whole trip. It was like the storm was angry that I neared my goal, and tried everything in its power to stop me. I fought for every step, dragging the two young hunters behind me, fighting the snow and wind with fire and shield.

101

When I went to take another step forward, I bounced my head off a vertical wall of stacked rocks. I stumbled back a bit and looked around, realizing I'd found my destination. Shelter.

A few bursts of fire cleared away enough snow to reveal a long, low building of stacked shale and flint. The thin sheets of rock were stacked haphazardly, with pebbles and muddy chink filling in the many gaps. A deerskin stretched over a wooden frame that served as a door was on the opposite side from the trail, so it took me longer than I would have liked to finally get us all inside and out of the wind.

The inside was as simple as the outside, and was clearly used as a workshop for making stone arrowheads most of the time. The tools for doing so were spread out everywhere along tables that lined the walls, and sharp rock chips layered the entire floor several inches deep. You couldn't even see the dirt, except in the bottom of the fireplace. It was the only gauge to tell how deep the flint chips went. The proof that this represented generations of work was right here, and I felt the weight of the dedication that went into the labor the men and women put into this place to feed and protect their families. To say that it was impressive was an understatement.

I built a fire with some dry wood left in a corner, and got Jaeger and Hilda set up on two tables under some blankets. Another quick round of healing for each of them fixed the damage they had suffered, and both settled into the deep sleep of exhaustion. I was about to do the same, when I felt an echo of power after my mana generator finished refilling and my system gave me an alert.

---

**Quest Update!**
**Place of Power Detected**
**Unique Upgrade Quest: Find ten places of power - 3/10-Absorb the power built up at the location to increase your level.**

**\*Note - This place of power is currently in flux with a natural meteorological event, potentially affecting its mana absorption rates and percentages (Earth Mana Aspect 60%/Nature Mana Aspect 13%/Storm Mana Aspect 10%/Lightning Mana Aspect 7%/Ice Mana Aspect 5%/Light Mana Aspect 3%/Darkness Mana Aspect**

> **1%/Friction Mana Aspect 1%). Disturbing it may lead to unexpected consequences. Proceed with caution.**

Looking over the aspects of the place of power, I knew I couldn't wait for the storm to end. Getting storm, lightning, and ice mana was too important to pass up. I also now knew how the arrowheads were so explosive. Flint made sparks by creating friction with iron or steel. The one percent friction mana must be enough, when combined with the earth mana, to create the same effect.

Pushing aside my exhaustion, I got ready to go back outside and face the thunder blizzard once more. I gave myself a quick healing spell, and dropped my rucksack by the door, along with a note for the other two in case they woke up while I was gone. Grabbing the lantern, I lifted the latch and took several deep breaths before stepping outside.

Opening the door was like getting punched in the face by the abominable snowman, if the abominable snowman was also driving a freight train going about 'I hate your face' miles an hour. I forced myself forward, and closed the door to the already warm building behind me. Sometimes, I really hated my life.

At least the place of power was close. I could feel it as soon as I started drawing in more mana. It was almost straight north, and a row of low pillars were barely visible through the snow drifts to mark my path. A second set of pillars that looked a little newer probably marked the path for a newer hut a little farther to the east, but the blizzard was still too intense for me to see it in the distance. If I had more time, I would've checked it, but I was already noticing a change in the environment. The storm had leveled off in intensity, which meant it would hopefully start to die off in the next few hours. That gave me a time limit to absorb what I could, before the place of power went back to its normal percentages.

The trail led to a cleft between two hills, where some past earthquake–or maybe a meteor strike, or magic spell, or the Jolly Green Giant with a huge freaking axe, I don't know–had opened a crack in the earth's surface. A set of rickety scaffolding led down to a series of ledges. They looked like knife cuts in the side of the tiny canyon-shaped crater, and each showed signs of mining. And of course, the *entire crater* was the place of power. It wasn't so deep that I couldn't see the bottom with a quick fireball spell, but I definitely didn't want to fall that far, even with my enhanced stats. My best guess put it at around sixty or seventy feet deep, with razor sharp flint rocks at the bottom. It was probably double that in length, with the hills on either side helping to partially protect it from the fierce winds.

Considering the size difference of what I was dealing with compared to what I'd absorbed in the past, I didn't think there was any way I could drain the whole thing like the last three. All of those had overwhelmed my abilities, and I would have died at the last place of power if it hadn't been so strongly aspected toward life mana. Controlling how much I took was the number one priority this time. I'd simply absorb what I could, be happy for the benefits it provided me, and move on.

Not trusting the scaffolding, I decided to get comfortable along the edge of the miniature canyon and just lean down to touch the nearest edge of the place of power. It was far enough back that I would be safe from falling in, and I wouldn't have to worry about the old wood and rope contraption the people had made several generations ago breaking under me.

Once I was settled and in place, I closed my eyes and started spinning the dense liquid inside my mana generator as fast as it would go. The centrifugal force pushed it out into the channels that ran throughout my body, filling me with a buzzing energy that was similar to the blizzard's rampaging power.

Almost against my will, the connection between the place of power and my mana generator formed, and it snapped into place with the crackling sound of a high power line coming to life. I barely managed to catch it in time, and I throttled down on what I allowed to pass through into my body with all the willpower I could muster. The outside world faded away as all my concentration and focus was taken, every bit required to keep me alive. For the first time, it actually worked.

I managed to squeeze down on my channels, letting in a firehose of mana instead of a flood. It was still an incredible amount of power, but my upgraded abilities were able to handle it. The dragonscale-heart mana generator in my center flexed and beat as it compressed and assimilated the new power, growing in size as it grew new scales that added to its density and variety.

The cage of life and death mana that formed the outermost shell of gold and silver lightning grew more distinct, increasing in luster and strength. Even the channels the mana traveled along were reinforced as they were stretched to their limit, deepening in both length and width.

Any overflow was released as a fine mist into my body, increasing the baseline power each cell contained. My muscles, organs, bones, blood, and finally skin were suffused with a slow heat that quickly built into a burning intensity. Even my brain felt as if it was cooking inside my skull, but there was no pain to go along with it, only a sense that I was building up to something greater.

I felt almost euphoric, knowing I was on the cusp of advancing into a new realm of potential, and in perfect control of the mana storming through my body.

Which was precisely when someone pushed me into the crater.

# CHAPTER 14

It felt like I was falling in slow motion. The smooth edges of the razor-sharp rocks waited at the bottom of the crater like the world's most patient predator. All it had to do was hold still, and prey would fall victim to its deadly grasp. I knew from my home world that the edge of a flint rock could be sharper than a steel scalpel, and even cut a molecule in half. Falling head-first six or seven stories into the crater was a death sentence. My brain was going to be shredded on a cellular level before I could have a chance to heal myself.

There was nothing I could do to slow myself, because casting magic became impossible the moment I'd felt those hands push me. I'd already lost my grip on the mana flooding into me, and in only a few heartbeats I was going to be destroyed from the inside out as the power from both the thunder blizzard and the ancient place of power ripped through my body like wet tissue paper. No matter what I did, the person at the top of the crater had ended me.

In one final bit of nonsense, my vision flashed with a silver-bordered blue message from my system, as if it needed to mock me in the final heartbeat of my life. It had been doing that for two decades, so I guess it was only fitting to see it as the last thing before I finally met my end.

> **Title Upgraded: Crack Kills II**
> -**Your rapid increase of earth mana containment and control inside your body has drastically improved the spell structure and potential of all earth magic cast by you. Absorbing a place of power which holds sixty percent earth mana was a good idea, huh? Keep it up, and you'll turn into a human-shaped rock golem in no time!**
> **Skill Imparted: Large-scale earth magic uses 3% → 15% less mana per minute. An additional 2% → 10% will be applied if the earth magic being used is outside of combat, including construction, training, and enchanting. In addition, all earth magic will become easier to perform, and require less focus from the caster.**

> **\*\*Warning\*\***
> Instinctive casting can be detrimental if the caster is inexperienced in its use. Serious injuries, including death, can result from wandering thoughts, misplaced musings, and violent dreams.
>
> **\*\*Warning\*\***
> Friction mana containment and control detected. Use of friction mana combined with certain types of earth mana can cause unexpected explosions.
>
> **\*Note - Title: Crack Kills II has potential synergy with Title: Send Them into Orbit III. Ensure synergistic titles have the same upgrade level for the chance of possible title fusion. Remember, any explosion, whether unexpected or planned, has a chance of activating Send Them into Orbit III, increasing the size of the blast by sixty percent. For more precise details, please check the full description in your Titles menu.**

I was able to absorb the information at the speed of thought. There was a chance. Depending on how reactive the ground beneath me was, and how effective my new title actually turned out to be, I might be able to save myself from getting sliced and diced. It wouldn't save me from the mana already starting to melt my insides, but one thing at a time.

The words disappeared from in front of my eyes as I fell the last few feet. Despite the lack of control I had over anything going on inside my body, the ground seemed to crumble into dust right before I hit.

Don't get me wrong, it still felt like falling on my face from on top of a six story building. But the cloud of fine powder that flew up from the ground was like a pillow compared to the alternative. With my stats, a six story fall was easily survivable, but right now wasn't the time to jump for joy in celebration and thank my lucky stars that I'd made it. As I felt my own feet kick me in the back of the head, I had to return all my focus to what was going on inside me.

In the few seconds it had taken for me to get pushed, fall, get my new title, and hit the ground, everything had gone to shit. The carefully controlled scales of power that were forming around my mana generator were all misshapen and out of place, and the energy flooding into my body was running out of control. My mana channels were bulging and rupturing almost everywhere I looked, and the gentle mist that had been steadily rejuvenating and strengthening my body was now a gritty liquid that was drowning my cells instead of helping them.

Throttling down on the mana coming in was impossible. Ruptures along my mana channels made the pain excruciating, and I couldn't concentrate enough to close every new inlet the connection now had with my mana system. I tried to break the connection entirely, but now that I was in the center of the place of power, it wasn't happening.

I tried to think of ways people dealt with rivers that went out of control, because that's what it felt like I was experiencing. They built dams, levees, irrigation control, and dug out new paths for the water to follow. By reducing the amount of water in the main path the floodwaters were flowing, they could spread out the damage done over a wider area, reducing its severity.

Creating a whole new set of mana channels in my body without any planning or forethought would take an incredible amount of power, and it sounded absolutely insane. So, basically, something I would do.

There was no way I could manage something that precise and demanding while still being ripped apart from the inside. That left me with shunting as much of the power as I could somewhere else, just like someone would do if they were in charge of controlling a flood. Luckily, there was a thunder blizzard slowly losing power hanging right over my head. All I had to do was survive the process of being the conduit between the place of power and the mana-hungry storm. Considering I was hoping to make new conduits, hopefully I could manage it.

Reaching out for the clouds above me as my insides were being simultaneously drowned and cooked was an exercise in sheer willpower that I only got through by concentrating on the mission I had waiting for me once this was over. The entire world depended on me closing the Demon Gate, and dying here wasn't an option. I stretched out a billowing cloud of mana from the top of my head, trying to push it as high as I could. The flow of energy from the place of power wasn't happy about the mana moving away from the path it had chosen, and stripped away everything it could. The remaining wisps of power floated up, gradually gaining altitude as I grew closer to death.

To add fuel to the fire, I was vaguely aware of an arrow that thunked into the dusty ground next to me. Whoever had pushed me off the edge was trying to finish the job. Thankfully, the storm was ruining visibility too much for them to get a good shot. I'd square up accounts with them as soon as I could, but first I had to survive.

I think it was the storm mana I was already absorbing that finally allowed me to connect with the thunder blizzard. The place of power must have only been able to reabsorb the earth and nature mana, allowing what remained to flow free. It felt like it had taken hours for the faint trails to reach the low-hanging clouds, but the still-vibrating arrow shaft next to my arm meant only moments had passed.

Once the connection formed, I stopped trying to restrict anything. The influx of mana from the place of power tore through my abused and rupturing channels and made its way out the top of my head into the thunder blizzard. As the amount of mana grew, the faint connections to the clouds above strengthened. And so did the blizzard.

Temperatures plummeted, the wind screamed in a mighty downburst, and lightning crackled above the crater in a flashing crown of destruction. Shrapnel rained down as night turned to day, and I thought I heard two people screaming from where I'd been attacked. Maybe one problem had sorted itself out on its own.

Now that the force of nature and the locus of magic were connected–which I'm sure wouldn't have *any* long-lasting negative effects–I focused entirely on easing the path it had through my body. Just like a river would follow the natural contours of the land, mana was trying to follow certain paths through my anatomy. Most of those channels already existed with my current mana system, but I saw plenty of places where I could add more, or improve what was already there, especially in and around my skeleton and major organs.

Making new mana channels felt like burning holes through my body from the inside. Right now, it was like turning on a loud fan while there was a room full of televisions blasting static noise at full volume. A little more pain didn't really amount to much. With the mana already pushing through me, actually making the channels turned out to be relatively fast. It wasn't easy, and took an incredible amount of focus and concentration, but each one seemed to want to be formed as soon as I started lining them up and forcing them into place.

New primary channels took shape along the long bones in my arms, legs, pelvis, and both sides of my spine, reinforcing my entire body in a mirror of the channels that were already in place. Several secondary tributaries encircled my brain, stomach, pancreas, esophagus, lungs, heart, liver, intestines, and kidneys. Once those settled into place, branching feeder channels, like smaller canals, or capillaries, stretched into all the other parts of my body, reinforcing the rest of my skeleton, less important organs, and muscles. They all connected to my mana generator through the existing mana system, ensuring the misshapen dragonscale heart wasn't deformed even more by my meddling.

By creating the new pathways, it relieved some of the pressure on my original primary channels. Not enough for them to recover, but there was definitely a difference. The ruptures weren't bleeding loose mana into my body in an unmanageable torrent anymore. Just a manageable one. The biggest change was what happened to the rest of my body. By giving the mana an outlet, and allowing it better ways to pass through, it stopped drowning and burning me up.

Enough time had gone by that the thunder blizzard was really starting to build up some momentum from all the new mana. There was some rotation in the clouds directly above the place of power, and the tiny part of me that was aware of the connection with the storm was beginning to wonder if thunder blizzards could form tornadoes. Because if they could, I was starting to think I was going to see one soon.

Deciding to ignore the dangers of a thunder blizzard twister, I looked at what I could do for my malformed mana generator. The thing that stood out the most was how much the earth mana scales had grown, with none of the other scales growing to match the new dimensions. They made the dragonheart look as if it had some kind of disease, or a bunch of tumors that bulged out in random places. At first, I thought about forcefully breaking apart the oversized scales and reshaping them into smaller pieces, but a sense of danger told me that would be a mistake. Shattering the thing maintaining the power flow I could barely manage was probably a bad idea in the first place.

My next thought was to somehow forcefully grow all the other scales to meet the new size the earth mana scales had created. While that would be fantastic, I didn't have a source of mana for all the various elements to do such a huge task. Not only that, the scales had never all been exactly the same size. They'd been close, but definitely not the same.

The best idea I could think of was to provide order to the madness. By moving and restructuring the scales, I could layer them in a way that made more sense both by their size, and elements. Since the earth mana scales were now the largest and most numerous, they would become the outermost ring, like an equator for the generator.

Moving the scales was a tedious and time-consuming struggle. They were slippery, and mentally grabbing one to move into a new position was a genuine tribulation. I couldn't move just one, either. Once I lifted a scale out of position, all the others wanted to start shifting. It was like doing one of those brain puzzles, where you have to get everything in order in a certain number of moves before everything resets. And the cage of life and death mana lightning that held it all together fought me the entire time. A rubix cube from hell, that electrocuted you with life and death lightning every time you messed up. It went on my list of favorite hobbies, right under repeatedly stepping on Legos while barefoot, but above juggling rabid raccoons.

Eventually, I got the ring of earth mana scales in place. After that, everything went much smoother. Nature mana went next, then

111

water, light, fire, and so on, with various mana types that meshed well and coexisted alongside one another until the last two rows, where the new friction mana made a thin row of tiny scales, followed by a thick cap of darkness mana that capped the top and bottom, or poles of the heart-shaped generator.

The moment I let go of the final scale, a heavy thrum went through me. The new harmony that ran through my entire mana system was a clean musical note cutting through the chaotic dissonance of cracked bells that had never had the chance to ring true. Clean, pure energy erupted from my center, calming the raging flood that still rampaged through me. Ruptures in my primary channels slowly started to close as the crystalline walls were given the chance to heal.

I'd never realized how dirty my mana was before now. As it poured in from the place of power, swirled through my generator, and came back out again, the difference was staggering. What I thought of as clear only moments earlier, I now saw as clouded and heavily contaminated with aspects of past uses the mana held. It was a whole new experience, and something I didn't know even existed.

For a single heartbeat, I held on to a portion of the nature mana from the wave of power that pushed up from below me. Somehow, I could tell it had recently been used by a beast to grow the plants outside its shelter to help it camouflage the entrance to its home. Then it returned to the nearest world artery, or what I was now understanding was a ley line, where it got caught in the whirlpool of power created by the intersection with another ley line. A place of power. There it waited, until I came along and poked it with a proverbial stick, unclogging the intersection and gaining the upgrades I could manage to glean from the backlog of power without getting burnt to a crispy critter.

If all mana was like this, there was no telling what spells I could learn, or what secrets I could uncover. A series of dings from my system told me I'd discovered something important. I'd have to check it once I wasn't playing the part of an overstressed fuse box.

After letting go of the nature mana, I redoubled my efforts on fixing what issues I had left. Repairing the rest of my body was a slow process, considering I was still fighting back damage from the power actively flowing through me. It wouldn't have been possible at all without everything that had happened. My tolerance for the higher levels of energy had increased with the secondary and tertiary mana systems in place, and the restructured mana generator gave me a far greater boost in control and influence.

There was no way for me to tell how much time had gone by during all of my struggles. For me, it had felt like days, maybe longer. In reality, it had probably been hours, but how many I didn't know. The clouds overhead were too thick to see if the sun had started to come up. It could be noon, and the blizzard still ensured it stayed dark outside.

Once I was finally put back together, I again tried to disconnect myself from the place of power and thunder blizzard. With my newfound sense of control, I thought I could manage it.

I was wrong.

Like a person who'd grabbed onto a live electrical wire, no matter how strong I was, there wasn't a way to let go until the power was shut off. In what seemed to me to be a direct response to my attempts to cut it off, the thunder blizzard appeared to get angry. The clouds that had been swirling for what felt like hours finally let loose, unleashing another round of lightning that shattered the lip of the crater and blasting more razor-sharp rocks everywhere I could see.

And then it dropped a tornado on my head.

## CHAPTER 15

Gleason hid under the rocky outcropping next to the piled bodies of dead orcs, unwilling to move despite the growing puddle of blood and offal that was about to reach his refuge. Moving meant a sudden and immediate end. The stacks of bodies already in cocoons along the opposite wall, waiting to be hung from the ceiling, were all the proof he needed of that glaring truth.

Pairs of pitch black spiders the size of horses were working in teams, cleaning up the battlefield using an organized efficiency that was terrifying in a way Gleason couldn't describe. Their glowing red eyes burned with a malevolent intelligence, showing these were nothing like the cave spiders the goblins used as cavalry. The way in which they communicated, with sharp taps on the ground mixed with high-pitched whining noises when their fangs rubbed together, even hinted at signs of a rank structure or hierarchy.

Lording above them all, and most certainly the reason why Gleason had refused to enter the battle with the orcs, was the monstrosity hanging from the ceiling of the cavern. It was easily ten times the size of the other spiders, and had two rows of eyes that ran along the sides of its head, all the way to its back, in the shape of an arrowhead. It exuded the presence of a lethal predator, giving off a low hum of danger to Gleason's senses.

The way it had torn through the ranks of armed and armored orcs had immediately convinced him that there was no possible way he could fight it. Their weapons had simply bounced off its thick chiton, or missed entirely when it moved faster than even his enhanced vision could see. Slaughter was the only way to describe what had happened to the nearly hundred warriors who had made their way into the chamber. None would make it out.

James Holden had been the most formidable opponent Gleason had ever seen, and that was counting all the Green Wardens the Hunter's Guild had in their ranks. After seeing what the giant spider was capable of, even if James Holden and every Warden currently in uniform joined forces, they'd still be crushed into nothing more than meat meant to feed the spider young. If the spider ever made it south, to the more populous regions, it would be classified as a kingdom-level threat by all the guilds.

As far as he could see, the only hope Gleason had of surviving to see the surface was to wait for the spider to leave, or possibly create a cave-in large enough to separate himself from the unbelievably fast monster. There was no chance of him simply making a run for it.

When he'd entered the cavern, there had been over fifty orcs still alive and fighting. Dozens of smaller, dog-sized spiders had fought against the orcs in an actual phalanx formation. An actual, honest-to-Trinity, fighting formation. The horse-sized spiders had acted as cavalry, moving in on the flanks when the orcs rushed the spider lines. While Gleason's orcs acted as an unorganized mob, using nothing better than horde tactics, the monstrous spiders had fought like the more thinking, advanced species.

Still, even with the superior tactics and maneuvers the spiders were using, they weren't easily able to overcome the heavy armor and weapons of the orcs. None of the orcs in Gleason's Century had been new to warfare, and they accounted well for themselves against the larger force. All that experience meant nothing when the creature hanging from the ceiling entered the battle.

There was nothing they could do to stop it. Weapons bounced off its hardened exoskeleton. Arrows deflected off its hateful eyes. Breastplates and shields were no better than wet parchment against the tips of its many limbs. Worst of all, it could cast *spells*. Magic that stank of brimstone and damnation burned both orc and spider alike, the evil creature uncaring of who or what it destroyed in the sweeping waves of fire it cast throughout the cavern. The flames burned black, with a green and purple smoke that was poison to the touch.

Once the great spider started casting demonic magic, the orcs broke. They scattered, running in all directions, and making themselves easy prey for the more mundane spiders that waited to bring them down.

Gleason had seen his Centurion amongst the fighters for a brief moment, the foolish creature leading a charge through the smaller, dog-sized spiders. Their escape had looked almost assured for a time, until it became clear that their destination was a death trap. The tunnel they had run toward was marked by a unique set of emerald outcroppings, but the entrance was choked with webbing, and it had been no surprise to Gleason when it had erupted with thousands of fist-sized baby spiders, with needle-like limbs and fangs. Their ravenous hunger had made short work of the handful of orcs, before returning to their tunnel of horrors.

Now, the dead were being sorted by size, stripped of their gear, cocooned in webbing, and strung up on the ceiling. There was no chance of escape for Gleason, and all he could do was lay still in his hiding place and wait for an opportunity to make his move.

When a ram-horned figure that looked like a blend of goat and man came tromping into the cave, it was so unexpected that Gleason nearly gave himself away in surprise. When the cavern full of spiders didn't immediately pounce on the interloper, it was even more of a shock. After a few minutes of carefully watching the creature make its way toward the center of the cavern, Gleason became even more concerned. There was something going on that he didn't understand, and perhaps this was part of what the Trinity had sent him here to do. That thought might have been the most unsettling of all.

Firstly, he'd never seen such a creature before. It was like a lycan or shifter race, but he'd never heard of a goat shifter twice the size of a bear, with red and black fur dense enough to almost be considered armor. He'd also never seen a goat that had claws the size of daggers. Its features were more twisted and cruel looking than any lycan he'd ever seen, and coming from someone who abhorred shifters, it was shocking to see one that lacked even the faint hints of humanity those abominable creatures still managed to maintain.

Second, its eyes glowed the same kind of red that the spiders did. That feature alone showed they were related in some way. How magic-using spiders and goat men were related was a mystery he couldn't wrap his mind around, but the evidence was right in front of him. As the new creature passed by his hiding place under the rocky outcropping, Gleason got a better look at it.

The goat man looked almost exactly like the images of demons carved in the ancient pillars of the old churches in the south, like the building where *The Oracle*–the book that the Trinity used to speak with mankind–was kept. Supposedly, warriors and heroes from long before the founding of the Wardens, long before even the founding of the kingdoms that would one day become the Empire, had fought true demons straight from the depths of hell. Only through the assistance and grace of the Trinity did they conquer the interlopers, sending them back to the burning dimension of damnation where they belonged.

When the demon spoke, it made all the hair on the back of Gleason's neck stand on end.

"My Prince, we require more reinforcements from your offspring." The goat man dropped to one knee as he spoke, looking up at the giant spider hanging from the ceiling. "The meddling undead have managed to collapse another of the primary tunnels, and none of the drones pushing to the south were able to be salvaged from the wreckage." The demon flinched as the spider moved, shifting itself to have a better view of the demon below it. When nothing else happened, the goat man continued speaking. "Your brother, Prince Sunar, thinks we're getting close, despite the setbacks. Soon, we'll have a tunnel that will allow us to bypass the undead armies, the freezing cold, and the lack of air that weakens our brethren. Then we'll gather our strength, kill the dragon, sweep across this world, and nothing will stand in our–"

"*Enough.*"

Both Gleason and the demon clutched their ears when the giant spider finally spoke. The dry rasp was somehow both achingly loud and barely at the range of what a human could hear. If it weren't for the distraction of the demon thrashing on the ground in pain, Gleason's own movements would have certainly given him away.

"*I am no brother to a giant mole rat. Sunar only carries the title of Demon Prince because he's not worth the trouble to hunt down and eat. His kind only tastes like dust, and disappointment.*" The giant spider, apparently a Demon Prince, slowly dropped from the ceiling to crouch above the goat man. "*I will not send more of my offspring to be massacred under the command of an inept leader like Sunar.*" It gave a few sharp taps on the ground, sending out orders to the other spiders in the cavern. "*However, I do understand the need to end the dragon menace that stands guard over our entrance to this world. I will send most of my offspring to assist, but*

117

*they will work independently from the mole rat and his forces. Understood?"*

"Yes, of course, Prince Makadee!" The goat man slammed his head into the ground so hard that Gleason heard the stone crack. "I'll explain everything to Prince Sunar. With the assistance of so many of your mighty offspring, I have no doubt victory will come swiftly."

The giant spider didn't bother answering, instead scuttling back up to the ceiling in a flash of rumbling power. Its angry red eyes glared down upon the thousands of spiders that came pouring out of the tunnels that led into the cavern. In only a few moments, the walls, floor, and ceiling were covered in the squirming black bodies and glowing red eyes of demonic spiders.

Gleason was only able to stay hidden by wedging himself into the crevasse of the outcropping and the wall. Some of the smallest spiders in the horde, roughly the size of a large rat, were only feet away from him, but they seemed to be so engrossed in the excitement of the moment that they paid no attention to their surroundings.

A few sharp clicks and squealing sounds from the largest of the brood were barely heard over the rustling sound of all the clattering limbs and rubbing bodies. Still, the orders were passed along the evil horde, and the mass of nightmarish horror and venomous fang started moving. Like a tub that was suddenly unclogged, they disappeared into a far tunnel, swirling away into the distance and sweeping clean the cavern to a polished, spotless sheen with their many clattering limbs and smooth underbellies.

"I guess I'll take my leave, then." The goat man was staring wide-eyed at the tunnel where the spider army had gone, clearly terrified at what he'd seen.

Gleason felt exactly the same way, but he wasn't stupid enough to say something out loud right after such a display of power. Even if it had been the perfect time to escape, he wouldn't have taken it. There was something about respecting such overt symbols of dominance, and as one predator acknowledges another, greater power than itself. The demon goat man must have missed the lesson on respect, and paid the price for it.

Without warning, the Demon Prince silently dropped from the ceiling, spearing the messenger through the chest with two of its many limbs. As the goat man gasped silently for a breath that would never come, the giant spider turned to go into a smaller cavern close to the tunnel where all the terrible baby spiders were hiding.

*"There is no need to warn my brother of what comes. You and your kind have proven to be useless as warriors. At least you can serve as food for the next generation of my brood."* The giant spider disappeared, leaving Gleason alone in the cavern.

A few spiders were still hanging corpses from the orc battle, but Gleason knew this was his chance. He crept his way along the cavern wall, staying close to the piles of corpses. There was no way for him to fight his way free and survive. Stealth was his only option.

Hours went by as he zigzagged his way across the cavern. While the space wasn't very large, he only moved an inch at a time. More than once, a spider walked right by his prone form laying on the ground to deal with the remains around him. How he was undiscovered must have been by the grace of the gods.

Eventually, he made it to the tunnel that had been rubbed smooth by the thousands of spiders that used it to leave. When there was a moment where Gleason didn't see any red eyes looking in his direction, he took his chance and sprinted for freedom. After long minutes of frantic running, he stopped to catch his breath, hunched over and panting. In front of him, the faintest hint of true sunlight was barely visible around a slight bend in the tunnel.

He'd done it. Gleason had made it out. A few steps further confirmed it. He was no longer in the foothills. This was the true north, where mountains reached so high that mortal man would die from simply climbing beyond the level the gods deemed them worthy.

Nothing but monsters, undead, and ancient mysterious ruins inhabited this region. Few lived to tell the tale of traveling the slopes of the unforgiving cliffs, snow capped ridges, and twisting caves of the empty quarter of the continent. Entire expeditions had been lost time and time again, with no sign of survivors beyond the occasional scrap of cloth or broken weapon.

Suddenly, Gleason understood the true magnitude of the mission the gods had sent him on. He alone was meant to stand against the evil incursion of the demonic hordes. He alone was righteous enough to represent the Trinity in all their glory, cleansing the land of the unclean corruption, just like he'd done in the cesspit of a city in Greendown. Entire empires couldn't enter the north and survive, but *he* could do so, with the Trinity's blessings.

While he didn't understand the minutiae of the conversation the demons had been having about undead, dragons, princes, and entrances to worlds, he knew one thing for sure. Demons, undead, and dragons were all unclean, nasty creatures. And somehow, he was going to find a way to wipe them out.

## CHAPTER 16

As the tornado dropped from the sky like a ton of bricks, I did my best to use what storm mana I'd gained to take control of the massive twister. I was like a toddler trying to walk a full-grown bull with a dog leash. My attempt wasn't successful.

Since I was in the bottom of a crater, it didn't actually drop *directly* on my head. It touched down on the rim sixty feet above me. Then it sucked me into the base of the tornado like it was the world's strongest vacuum cleaner, and I was the most offensive dust bunny it had ever laid eyes on.

While it was definitely bad to get sucked up by a tornado, it did manage to sever the connection between me and the place of power. Or, as I had just learned, the more properly named intersection of ley lines. Getting instantly ripped out of the flow between the thunder blizzard and the place of power was more than a little uncomfortable. It was similar to the sensation of getting my skin ripped off by rusty fish hooks, being slapped everywhere at once by stinging jellyfish, and having peanut butter stuck to the roof of my mouth, all at one time. Casting a spell to control my fall was definitely out of the question.

To add insult to injury, the arrow that had been shot at me earlier was scooped up by the wind–along with the dust I'd created– and somehow it ended up stabbing me in the back of the neck. Which sucked almost as hard as the tornado.

Then, it spit me out into the forest, where I got introduced to several trees in a manner that none of us probably would've appreciated, especially considering they were mostly firewood now, and I was going to have to spend a ridiculous amount of time repairing my armor. It wasn't until I stood up that I realized I only needed a healing spell for the arrow lodged in my neck, and nothing for the impacts with the tree. My toughness had gone up quite a bit from this upgrade.

A quick check of my stats only confirmed it.

**Name: James Holden (Earth v7.4 → v7.6)**
**Title: Chief Justice/Arbiter/Justicar/Executioner/etc…**
**Level: 100/MAX**
**Rank: 4.8 → 6/10**
**Age: 27 (Physical) 47 (Actual)**
**Class: Warrior/Soldier/Knight/Paladin/Mage (5/5)**
**Profession: Healer/Alchemist/Blacksmith/Runesmith/Judge (5/5)**
**Status:**
**Strength- 97 → 126**
**Flexibility- 96 → 125**
**Vigor- 102 → 136**
**Mind- 113 → 145**
**Mission:**
**Mythical Quest: Deliver Justice - World Count 20/???**
**Legendary Quest: Return Home - Requirements not met**
**Epic Quest: Find out why - Requirements not met**
**Rare Quest: Track down Silver Star - Ongoing [Time remaining: 33 days]**
**-Sub-quests:**
**-Find the Key to the Silver Star**
**-Close the Demon Gate [47,520 minutes]**
**Unique Upgrade Quest: Find ten places of power - 4/10**

The version number, rank, and individual stats had all increased by an incredible amount. I was almost thirty percent stronger across every measure. If I could find a few more places of power before I ran into the Destitute, the mollywhopping he'd get would be so epic, I *almost* felt bad for the guy. The new channels in my body made moving the cleaner mana feel so smooth and easy, and only the sharper-than-steel flint arrowhead had managed to hurt me. Right now, I felt like I could fight a tyrannosaurus rex without breaking a sweat. As long as I had some watermelons, of course.

The countdown had also dropped by six days since the last time I'd checked it, meaning time was going by faster than I'd thought. I must have been stuck in the connection between the storm and place of power for a lot longer than I could afford. Leedy and the others were probably going nuts wondering where I was by now.

With the mana from the ley lines no longer feeding the thunder blizzard, the storm died out rapidly. Within minutes, I could see daylight fighting to get through the clouds, and in less than half an hour it was no more than light flurries. Finding my way back to the crater wasn't hard after that.

Once I got there, I checked the area for signs of the people who'd attacked me. After looking around a bit there was a large patch of bloody snow I was able to uncover, probably caused by flying stone shrapnel from the lightning striking the rim of the crater. A smaller smattering of blood a little farther back meant there was an accomplice, or at the very least a witness. Any trail had been covered up by the heavy snows, and I was forced to give up after a cursory search of the surrounding area. They were unsuccessful, and I didn't have time to worry about them any more.

I'd kept the arrow, just in case there were any distinguishing markers on it that Jaeger or Hilda could use to identify the wannabe assassin. It had a few small marks and dings that might mean something, or they could be from simple wear and tear. It was impossible for an outsider like me to know. Checking on those two was a priority, anyway. After all, I hadn't left them in the best of conditions.

Moving anywhere outside the forest was a struggle. The thunder blizzard had been in place for so long, and dumped so much snow, that open areas had created snow drifts a good ten or fifteen feet high in some spots. I eventually resorted to trying out my ice mana as a way to tunnel through them, creating a straight path from the crater to the ancient flint outpost.

There was a faint trail of smoke coming from the jagged tip of the stone building's chimney at the end of the trail, but I couldn't get inside because it was buried up to its roof in snow. I quickly cleared a path to the door, anxious to see how Jaeger and Hilda were doing. When I stepped in the room, it was to the shocked faces of more than just Jaeger and Hilda.

"You-you're alive!" The councilman who'd stormed off in anger during the trade negotiations was warming his hands by the fire. He was staring at me with open-mouthed shock, pure disbelief on his face. "How? How are you not dead?"

On either side of the grumpy older man stood two of the men that had left with him when he'd disappeared from the clearing. One guy had a large bandage wrapped around his head, and he was leaning heavily against the nearest table. The other had a bandage wrapped around his calf, and he was holding a nasty-looking pistol crossbow that I was surprised to see in such a remote location like this. It was more of an urban combat weapon, and the villagers lived in a place that no one would ever describe as urban.

Backed against the far wall, farthest from the heat, were Jaeger and Hilda. Neither had their hands and arms tied or anything, but their items and weapons were on the tables next to the councilman and his men. Jaeger had positioned himself to stand in front of Hilda, and it looked like I had interrupted some kind of negotiations between Jaeger and the three men.

Hilda was using my rucksack as a chair, which I appreciated. It meant she was trying to keep their grubby mitts out of my stuff. If I remembered correctly, Jaeger was some kind of distant blood relation to the councilman, which certainly protected him from most shenanigans the councilman might get up to, but that protection probably wouldn't extend to Hilda.

It was pretty obvious to me who my attackers had been. The two injured men had snuck up on me when I'd been distracted with the place of power. Their group had probably left for the crater the moment negotiations for the councilman went sour, and they were probably waiting in the other, newer hut I'd seen signs of earlier. The sudden storm meant we ended up here, in the older building, foiling their initial ambush plan. They almost succeeded on their second attempt, but luck had been on my side.

"Sorry to interrupt the party. It looks like you're having a bunch of fun in here." I closed the door behind me, dropping the bone peg in the slot that locked it in place. "I've got to ask, does this belong to one of you? Because I'd really love to return it." I held up the arrow that had been shot at my prone form, and a lot of things happened all at once.

The guy with the heavy ring of bandages on his head visibly flinched when I held up the arrow, giving himself away.

Hilda, being the quick one that she was, tried using the distraction to her advantage. She pulled a hidden knife from her boot and threw it at the man holding the crossbow.

In response, the man holding the crossbow shifted and fired at Hilda in a practiced motion that showed he had lots of experience using the weapon.

Jaeger, seeing the flash of motion, dove in front of Hilda, protecting her from the deadly crossbow bolt, willingly sacrificing himself for her.

The old man, seeing his underling shooting at his blood relative, reached out a hand to stop him but was shoved back into the fireplace by his own man.

None of that mattered when the bonus from my new Title, *Crack Kills II,* kicked in. Instinctive casting was something I would need to practice with, because it did far more than I wanted.

At first glance, the floor of the building looked like simple gravel. As I'd discovered earlier, it was more than that. The floor was covered by layers of incredibly sharp flint chips and shards, built up over generations of men and women making arrowheads and flint tools inside the building. When I wanted to rip the crossbow out of the bad guy's hands, swat the bolt out of the air, stop the knife, and yank the old man out of the fireplace, instinctive casting did all those things, all at the same time.

Unfortunately, it did those things using the flint chips.

Shredding the bolt wasn't a bad thing, of course. It was turned into sawdust in an instant, and both Jaeger and Hilda were completely unharmed. Hilda's knife was swatted to the ground by her feet, and she had it back in her hands in the blink of an eye.

No, the unfortunate thing was what happened to the man holding the crossbow. Instead of ripping it out of his hands, the swirl of rock chips shredded flesh from bone almost instantly. He fainted dead away when he looked down and saw that on both arms from the elbow down, all that remained was his radius and ulna.

The old man was a little better off, but not by much. A ragged band of flint shards had ripped him out of the fireplace, and ripped open the skin on his back at the same time. It was as if he'd suffered dozens of lashes, laying his flesh bare.

While I knew these men needed to be Judged, this wasn't something I was comfortable with. It wasn't measured and purposeful. This was an accident, and I needed to fix it.

"By the Trinity!" Jaeger was standing there patting his chest, making sure he was still alive. "That was… how did…" He shook his head, looking around the suddenly bloody room. "Remind me to never make you angry. You're certainly more than a simple healer, or blacksmith."

"What he meant to say was, 'Thank you for saving our lives'. It's good to see you alive and well, James." Hilda walked over to shake my hand, and passed over my pack, along with a waterskin. "I'm sure you have a tale to tell, but drink some water first. You look a little… worn."

"Thank you." I took a deep drink, not realizing how thirsty I'd been. Next time, I wouldn't leave my pack so far behind, even if the place of power seemed too dangerous. "Mind telling me what was going on? How long have those three been holding you here? I'll need to heal them before they bleed out, but I've got a minute or two."

"Oh, it felt like *forever*." Hilda pointed a thumb back toward the trio, where only one remained standing. "You wouldn't believe how full of themselves they were, especially Councilman Drunn. He's–"

"You killed him!"

We turned to see the bandaged man pointing another crossbow at us. This one was of the heavy variety, and used across the universe to punch through thick armor. The reinforced steel tip was pointed right at me, and I could see the flicker of the firelight reflected from its sharpened point.

"Don't do that. I can save him, if you just put that down and give me a–"

The dry snap of the trigger mechanism was all the warning I had. Instinctive casting raised another swirl of flint chips, destroying the bolt before it got more than a few feet from the man who shot it.

---

**Congratulations! Title: Crack Kills II and Title: Send Them into Orbit III have achieved simultaneous activation! A one-time bonus is applied. Primary explosions are 60% → 180% more powerful. You truly do have the best luck.**

---

"Shit."

We were all engulfed in a massive fireball as the explosion blew the roof straight off the building.

## CHAPTER 17

To be fair, the system had warned me several times about the risks involved. There had even been a steel-tipped bolt I had plenty of time to look straight at, and I knew flint against steel created sparks. That didn't mean I *appreciated* the system for its encouraging words, or for applying the stupid bonus.

"I swear, one day, when I find out who you are…" I sat up with a groan, pushing the heavy table off of me. "Is everyone okay?"

"What happened?" Jaeger was holding his head, with blood leaking from his ears. "Did he have some kind of destructive crossbow?"

"*Meeeep*! *Meeeeep*! I can't hear anything but ringing! *Meep*!" Hilda came stumbling around the edge of the building, holding her ears. She must have been blown completely outside when the roof came apart.

Only three walls were still standing, with the end that held the chimney where the men were standing spread out over the snowy hills. I looked for the councilman and his two henchmen, but there wasn't much left to be found. The mantle of Judge found the punishment of death for two counts of kidnapping and attempted murder to be acceptable, but I'd wanted more from them.

Answers, for one thing. None of it made any sense to me. Forced labor for the betterment of their village for the rest of their lives was going to be my second idea, but considering the size of their population, it probably wasn't a practical choice. They didn't have the resources to watch them constantly, or to ensure they didn't escape and cause problems elsewhere. I suppose, ultimately, they'd made their own choices–and created their own punishments–through their actions, and there was no going back and changing things now.

"Hold still. Let me help." I managed to grab Hilda, who was still 'meeping' around, and quickly healed her blown eardrums. She also had a few cracked ribs I fixed, along with one last surprise. "Oh. Um, Hilda. I don't know how to say this, so I'm just going to say it. You're going to have a baby."

"*What*?" Jaeger was suddenly there, like he'd teleported. "How can you know already? It's only been…" He trailed off, blushing furiously.

"I think what the big oaf means to say is, are you sure? There haven't been many opportunities for such a thing to occur. Only very, very recently, in fact." Hilda was blushing as well, but she wasn't nearly as red as Jaeger. "It's almost unheard of for a healer to be able to know something like that so soon."

"Oh, I'm sure." I sent another wave of mana through Hilda, this time helping to reinforce both the mom and the little zygote. It was barely more than a bundle of cells, but I did my best to ensure it would grow to be healthy. Both Hilda and Jaeger were outright glowing with joy, and it had nothing to do with my healing magic. I gave each of them one last dose of mana, just to be sure I hadn't missed anything. "It's too early to know what it's going to be, but you're definitely going to have a baby in about thirty-nine weeks, give or take a few days."

If I could close the Demon Gate in time. Suddenly, that quest and its timer felt a whole lot heavier. Jaeger and Hilda deserved to have that joy, to bring that life into this world. Despite my cynicism, my own struggles and pain, this was so much bigger than just me. It was time to get moving.

Filled with a new sense of purpose, I gathered my things, letting the two hunters have a private moment together. That's all I could afford to give them, though. I found what I could of their scattered belongings, and stacked everything next to the remains of the building.

One of the tables was still in good shape, so I flipped it upside down and used some earth magic to shape three sharp skis on the bottom. A few pieces of rope and some holes through the wood made rough seat belts, and suddenly we had a crude yet effective sled.

"What's that thing supposed to be?" Jaeger watched as I carefully tied down the last of our items in the center, making sure my pack was on top. It was the heaviest thing we had, so I hoped it would help hold down everything else. If the balance was off by too much, it would also make steering terrible.

"It's the fast way back to the village." I pushed it along the ground, showing how easily it moved. "See? We can move much faster this way."

"How do we steer?" Hilda hopped up in front, from the look on her face already liking my new creation. "More importantly, can I sit in front?"

Jaeger moved to pull her off, a concerned look in his eyes. "Are you sure it's safe? Hilda, in your condition, you should sit in the middle, where we can protect you."

Fire filled her eyes, and she hopped down from the sled, ready to fight. "Protect me? Are you saying I can't take care of myself? Are you saying I'm not just as good of a hunter as you?"

"Whoa, hold on, both of you. If you'd let me talk, none of this would be a problem." I held up three table legs, handing one to each of them. "Think of this like a canoe. One person sits in the front, one in the back, and they use these to provide motion by pushing these against the ground. They can also help steer by pushing on opposite sides, the same side, or alternating back and forth to keep it straight. The person sitting in the very back is the one who steers by being a kind of rudder, and helping push on one specific side when needed. They're also the brakes, like the friction lever on a wagon, and they slow us down when we're going too fast. So, our safety is in their hands. Got it?"

Both of them gave each other a sheepish glance. Jaeger was the first to break the silence. "I wasn't saying you're a bad hunter. I only want to protect you and our child, like a provider and father is supposed to do. You can understand that, can't you?"

Hilda sighed, placing her hand on his shoulder. "Yes. And you can understand that I'm not suddenly made of glass. I'm still the same hunter you trusted to guard the village, watch your back, and stand beside you in battle. You're a good man, Jaeger, and only want to do right by me, so remember what I'm capable of."

"As long as you remember that you're responsible for more than just yourself." When she gave him a nod of agreement, Jaeger made a sweeping motion with his arm at the sled. "Well then, where would you like to sit?"

She looked carefully at the sled, then at me, and finally at Jaeger. "In the back, of course. You think I should let you boys steer this thing? We'd be lost in no time."

Laughing, the two hopped in the back of the sled, leaving me by myself in the front. I was okay with it. They still had plenty to talk about.

Once we got moving back toward the village–and a few minor kinks were worked out with the sled, like stopping to put in a clear quartz windshield–I finally got the chance to hear more about what the two had been through while I was trapped in the place of power.

Apparently, the councilman's big issue with me was that he was convinced I was holding great wealth in my rucksack, and by only trading healing and runes, I was cheating the village somehow. He wasn't specific with them on what *kind* of wealth or treasure I might be hiding, but he was convinced of it. He'd also been sure that the healing I'd performed was some kind of trick, and it was only a matter of time before Jaeger's father fell ill once again. A person as young as I looked could never be a master of any subject, except being a charlatan and liar.

Their group had been sure they'd killed me when I fell into the crater, and after getting wounded, they decided it wasn't worth it to find my body. When they went looking for my pack and discovered Jaeger and Hilda, the two had only been up and about for a single day after the healing I'd given them, and weren't prepared to fight off the three men, even though they were in rough shape from the storm.

Jaeger and Hilda had stubbornly been negotiating the terms on when and where to turn over my pack once they understood it was what the men were after. The trio had wanted it then and there, but Jaeger and Hilda had said it made more sense to turn it over to the members of my party back at the village. Of course, the councilman had said he would be willing to do so for them, as the highest ranked representative of the people. Jaeger was able to counter, saying that he was responsible as the guide that allowed his charge to perish under his care. Then, I walked through the door, and the rest was history.

At least I was able to finally get some answers, even if they weren't good ones. Greed and pride, two of the most common reasons for bad decisions the history of mankind had ever seen. I could write a whole book series on the pitfalls of what happens when people make decisions based on the seven deadly sins. Add in a touch of stupidity, and it would probably be a best-seller.

The three of us discussed how the news of the councilman's death would be received, especially by his sister, and unanimously decided that their demise should be announced by Jaeger. He was a blood relative, and they were more likely to listen to him.

Jaeger was going to blame the explosion that killed the men on a combination of the storm and the two hunters that had been with the councilman. They had gathered some lightning-charged rock from the crater, and tried to make arrowheads out of it. The resulting explosion is what destroyed the ancient building, and killed the councilman. Since the flint from the region was known to be explosive, there was no reason to doubt a sudden interaction with a thunder blizzard wouldn't cause a catastrophic accident. As to why they were there in the first place, we'd have to let others speculate on the reason.

My mantle of Judge wasn't happy about the deception, but the reality of needing to keep the peace with the villagers won out. Not everyone would understand someone holding the position of a Senior Huntsman was in the wrong, especially when an outsider was involved. Ultimately, the guilty had been punished, and no one else needed to get hurt over their actions.

By some miracle, we didn't run into any trouble on the way back to the village. The whole trip only took a couple of hours, as opposed to the much longer version we'd had when going to the hills and crater. My instinctive earth magic helped smooth out the path in some of the rougher places, and we had to take it especially slow around the pond, but otherwise we managed to travel at about the same speed as a horse at full gallop. Still, even with the much shorter version, it was cold enough that we were all very happy to see the towering trees of their village when they came into view.

Hilda angled the sled so we would come into the clearing in plain view of the guards, that way there wouldn't be any accidents or confusion about mistaken identity with the new mode of transportation. As we came to a slow stop, we could hear shouts and the running footsteps from the people above, and the clattering of the lift started before we could even get out of the sled.

"James! Finally, it's about time you showed up." Cross shouted down at me, his head poking over the side of the wooden platform. Beside him, Jess, Murphy, and Leedy were taking up most of the remaining space.

It felt good to see all of them, and I couldn't help the smile that stretched the corners of my mouth. Until I noticed none of them were smiling back. "What's wrong?"

"Besides you going missing? Oh, nothing much." Jess tossed me a scroll of rough parchment over the edge, held shut with a twist of simple twine. "Only *that* being spotted, by two different hunting parties, patrolling the only clear pass into the mountains."

I opened it, holding it up to the light. It was drawings of an airship, and not the one Greendown was sending to us. It was a sleek, double-ballooned zeppelin, with enough black sails tacked on to make the most tacky pirate in history green with envy. If the little stick figure drawings on board were to scale, it was large enough to carry enough of a force to be a serious threat.

As the lift settled to the ground, my group gathered around me, waiting to see what I would say about the news. I thought over our options, knowing what it would mean to risk the lives of the hunters that would be traveling with us to the north. To risk the underground route might delay us with unknowns, while the overland pass was a sure battle with a potentially overwhelming opponent. It would be faster if we went overland, but there was almost a guarantee of it costing lives.

Jaeger and Hilda grabbed their things off the sled and headed up on the lift, already on their way to deliver the news about the councilman. They would be two of the people forced to fight the airship. Their unborn child would be put at risk.

Damn it.

"It's not just our lives we'd be putting at risk fighting this thing. We'll take the underground route."

133

## CHAPTER 18

The first order of business was setting up a watch for the airship we knew would eventually be coming from Greendown. While we had no idea when it was arriving, it could be any day now, and it was supposed to fly right through the general area of where we'd built our outpost. That meant someone from the village needed to stay there, watching the skies at all times. They needed to be warned about the Destitute's airship running around, or it could end up flying straight into an ambush. If the drawing was anything close to accurate, our airship didn't stand a chance in a fight against the sleeker, meaner-looking vessel, even if they saw it coming and had time to prepare.

Naturally, that led to a new round of arguments, because Jaeger had the perfect candidate for the person in charge of the brand new, very exciting and important job, with tons of upward movement and potential. At least, that's what he made it sound like when he was trying to convince Hilda to stay behind instead of journeying underground with us. It wasn't going well for him.

"Don't you see? You would have your own hunting team, and a position to command. It's a promotion most of the other huntmasters won't see for years!" Jaeger was making wild gestures with his arms, trying to really sell the idea.

Cross, Leedy, and I shared a look before we took a few steps back. We didn't want to get caught in the crossfire.

"If you think I'm going to stay in some damp, dingy, disgusting hill hut, looking for some crazy flying ship to come crashing down on my head, while you get to go play the hero galavanting through the mountains and killing goblins and zombies, you've got another thing coming!" Hilda wasn't a cat shifter, but I could have sworn her eyes flashed. "I'm going with you, and that's final!"

Jess, who actually *was* a cat shifter, stood behind her in solidarity. The staff she held burned with power, lending weight to her presence. "For the life of me, why wouldn't you want one of your best hunters to go with you underground? Watching the skies is a job for the old, or very young. Not for the capable and deadly."

"Because saving the lives of your entire airship's crew is not something to be taken lightly. And because she's carrying my *child*!" Jaeger's shout caught the attention of several bystanders, but they thankfully only heard the last word. A heated glare from the riled up muscle-man made even the bravest onlookers scurry away.

Flustered, Jess looked between the two. "Oh. Um, maybe I should go see what's going on over there, with that... thing." She darted away, disappearing between two huts.

I think she might have learned a valuable lesson today. Hopefully, she remembered it. Poking your nose in where it doesn't belong can be a very, very bad thing.

Not wanting to repeat her mistake, the rest of us decided to let the two settle things between themselves. We would abide by whatever decision they came up with, but I had a few ideas for a compromise if there wasn't a peaceful solution in the next hour or so.

If this kept up, maybe I could get a Title for relationship counselor or something.

Our second order of business was arranging what time to leave with Lighter and his team. At least, I thought that was our second order of business. The others had different ideas.

"So, are you just going to stand there all quiet and brooding, or are you going to tell us what in the seven outer and thirteen inner purgatories happened to you? Where have you been?" Cross sternly folded his arms, unconsciously covering up his blackened fist. "Leedy told us you were only supposed to be gone for a few hours. It's been a lot longer than that, James. We all know bad weather wouldn't have slowed you down *that* long."

Murphy nodded along with him, clutching his halberd in both hands. "We were worried about you. As soon as that crazy storm stopped, we were trying to convince the people here to take us where you'd gone. No one was willing to take us, but they were going to send their own people." He leaned in a little closer, looking around to make sure no locals were within earshot. "Jess and I were going to follow them when they left, and double-check they weren't holding you somewhere."

"I told them it was a bad idea, but they didn't believe me." Leedy didn't bother looking around. We were up in a bunch of trees, and it wasn't easy to hide, even if someone had 'spicy samurai' camouflage abilities. "The hunters would have known they were being followed. There was no way that plan ended well."

"There was no way we could trust them to tell the truth about James. It was a lose-lose situation. Besides, I think you're underestimating Jess and me." Murphy lifted his chin toward Leedy, hinting that he should turn around. "We're more sneaky than you think."

Leedy glanced behind him and jumped, seeing Jess standing right behind him. "Bah! Okay, I'm with James now. We need to put a bell on you or something."

Jess laughed, giving him a playful shove. "Don't worry. I only use my powers for good, not evil." She scanned the trees around us, and turned back to me. "Do you have a place we can go and talk in private? I have a feeling what those two told their leadership wasn't the whole story, and we'd like to hear all of it."

Smiling, I waved for the four to follow me. I knew where the large hut that I healed Jaeger's dad in was located, and it was as good a place as any to set up at for the time being. "Come on. I'll fill you in on everything that happened, and we can send some runners to track down the people we need to make the plans for tomorrow. That airship was a sign of things to come. We have to keep up, or we'll be left behind."

Relaying the true events of the past few days didn't take long, and all of them were excited to hear about the new way of traveling I'd used to get back. Jess, especially, wanted to learn the trick of instinctive casting. I reminded her about the importance of mastering her new staff before she moved on to something else. Jess, Murphy, and Cross then got together and decided they would make enough sleds for us to use to get to the caves. Both to get to the cave entrance quickly, and so the hunters could use them as a quick way to shuttle supplies back and forth for as long as they were staying with us.

Leedy volunteered to take my beaten and abused armor down to the village blacksmiths. They could get it back into the shape it was supposed to be in, which would save me a lot of time. Then he wanted to start coordinating with Lighter and his team for the trip to the cave. Now that there were going to be sleds to put supplies and packs on, we could arrange our travel to be more front heavy, with only one sled in reserve to bring in resupply and swap out the scouting information for the village.

They all got up and started to leave, so I went to follow them.

"What do you think you're doing?" Cross stopped me at the doorway, putting a hand on the center of my chest. "We don't need your help for any of this."

"I was going to help make the–"

"You were *going* to get some sleep. Have you seen yourself lately? You look like you got smacked around by a pack of hungry wendigos." Cross waved at his nose, and took a step back. "Smell like it, too."

"I know for a *fact* that's not true. You can ask Jess. We had a run-in with some wendigos once. I looked much worse than this afterward." I sniffed myself, trying not to wince. "No comment on the smell, though. At least there's no garlic this time." Stretching, I took stock of how I genuinely felt after all I'd been through the past few days. "Honestly, it has been a while since I slept."

"See? What did I tell you? Seriously James, we've got this part handled. You can take the time to get cleaned up, and then get some rest. You'll need it if we run into something nasty down in those caves." Cross thumped me on the shoulder and left, herding everyone out in front of him. "We'll come get you when it's time to go."

Looking around at the empty room, I realized I needed a few things if I was going to be able to rest and recharge. I flagged down a passing runner for a bucket of water and some rags. I also asked for a cot or stretcher to be brought up so I could use it for a bed, but he told me I might have to make due with a few blankets on the floor.

While I waited, I dropped my pack and pulled out fresh clothes before I started cleaning all my weapons. We were going to be in some serious fights with tough enemies, and I wanted to make sure they were good to go.

My magic-eating ninjatō was as sharp as ever, and only needed a quick coat of oil to ensure it wouldn't bind in its sheath.

The starmetal mace had a few dents and dings, but the heavy chunk of metal didn't need much beyond a quick polish. It was a beast of a weapon, and no matter how much mana I pushed through it, there was never a hint that it was going to fail or explode.

Ammo for my wrist gun finally got properly sorted and arranged in a way that made it easier to find and load, and the actual tri-cannon barrels got scrubbed and oiled. My shield bracelet was looking a little worn, but there was nothing I could do about it. I didn't even know if this world had the proper materials to replace the pieces that were wearing out. I still gave it a good cleaning, and made sure the runes were clear of debris. Even my pocket knife got cleaned and oiled. Just in case.

The last weapon I had was something I'd only recently started using, and I was still working through the kinks. My Knight class had an ability called *Shield Bash* that I'd seldom thought about because I wasn't much of a shield user. When I put a tiny shield on a ring to see if the ability would still work, I was happy to discover that it did. It worked so well that it had allowed me to defeat an elder vampire princess–who'd been kicking the crap out of me–by basically super-punching her jaw clean off her face. There was a cooldown on the ability, but it was crazy not to have it ready and waiting in my back pocket, just in case I had another jaw to blast into oblivion.

My first version had been a simple and cheap ring that broke my finger when I used it. The new version I pulled out of my pack to try on was one I'd had made in Greendown before we left. It resembled a set of brass knuckles, if the brass knuckles were made of silvered steel, and the face was made up to look like a narrow four-pointed shield that reminded me of a compass rose. I could wear it while still swinging my mace, and a few tests proved I could activate the skill without breaking my fingers. It had still hurt to punch solid objects, but hopefully with my new stats that would be diminished some. The only real downside was how clunky it felt to have on all the time. Considering what we were walking into, now wasn't the time to be worried about discomfort.

Once all of my weapons were settled, some people showed up with a bucket of hot water and enough blankets to make the floor comfortable. I got cleaned up quickly, then laid down to try and sleep. It wouldn't come.

All I could think about was the airship, and what it really meant. How much had the Destitute advanced beyond us? Could I defeat him? What were his true goals? What did he have to do with the Demon Gate? How was I supposed to do all of this in one month?

I looked at my ruck, and at the one item that might be considered a weapon that I hadn't pulled out. It was too dangerous, even for me. *Especially* for me. Then, I thought about Jaeger and Hilda, and their unborn child.

Damn it. I got up and grabbed my ruck one more time.

## CHAPTER 19

My hands almost shook as I pulled open the thick leather pouch. Inside, the runes meant to hide the power of the object it contained were glowing with a faint amber tint. I'd probably need to replace the leather in a few days, since it wasn't a material that could hold mana for long periods of time without special treatments and additives I didn't have.

The heavy diamond I dumped into my hand flared with power the instant it touched my skin, and almost without thinking its status screen jumped into my vision.

---

**Item: Enhancing Gem**
**Type: Power Magnification**
**Grade: 1/1**
**Owner: James Holden (by conquest)**
**Description: A diamond of unmatched purity, mined and cut from the Cloudless Realm eons ago by the extinct race of Angelis Angeli. Once common, these gems are now all but lost to time due to the inability of descendent races to duplicate the creation process. This unique, one-of-a-kind artifact doubles any effect when used as a focus. Not limited to any type of energy. Can only be used by the current owner or their direct descendant. New owner can only be designated upon the death of the current owner, or if current owner is separated by more than one dimension from the item. Cannot be gifted or given away.**

**\*\*Warning\*\***
**This is a Greater Object of Power not native to this plane of reality. Handle with care.**

**\*\*Mandatory System Warning for Users of Any Level, including All Supreme, Divine, or Celestial Beings\*\***
**As per the Accords Regulation 29546, any Enhancing Gem using the directed energy of a star, brown dwarf, or similar stellar body with the intent to cause harm shall be**

> **summarily executed by the nearest representative of the Court. Injecting an Enhancing Gem into the heart of an active fusion process or gravity well carries an immediate death sentence, and perpetrators shall be ejected from the System without warning. There are no appeals to this process, as you will be deceased.**

The Enhancing Gem was the diamond that had fallen off the end of the staff the elder vampire princess had been using when I killed her. How the old kingdom had gotten the gem, I didn't know. There were no detailed records that survived that far back beyond a ship's log I'd found in the Sailor's Guild, and it only mentioned they used it as a power source for their airship, the Silver Star. The fact they were crazy enough to use it to power their airship spoke to either how crazy they were back then, or how desperate. The Silver Star's mission was to close the Demon Gate, the same mission as my own. A vampire outbreak had sabotaged their efforts. Finding it had been one of my Quests, which had morphed into my current problem.

For me, touching the diamond had started the timer for the Demon Gate I had hanging over my head. I didn't know if the timer was always there and I only became aware of it when I touched it, or taking possession of the item had started the countdown. Ultimately, it didn't matter. What did matter was dealing with it.

Obviously, the thing that made me not want to use the dangerous item was the warning at the end. I'd never seen anything like it. It hinted at so many truly frightening things, *confirmed* so many things, I wasn't sure what to do with it.

There was some kind of governing body, somewhere, that made rules even gods had to follow. If I could appeal to that governing body about basically getting kidnapped and being forced to world hop all over the universe, maybe I could get home. It was a longshot, and I didn't know how to contact them, but just knowing it existed was huge. Maybe they would even punish whoever took me. Unless, of course, they were the ones responsible. Which put me right back where I was right now.

Also, it confirmed the system I used wasn't unique to me. I'd certainly suspected that one, especially since other worlds I'd been to had systems of their own. But mine had always been separate from theirs, as if it was on a different frequency, or it was run by a different set of higher powers. It was also scientifically advanced, if they knew what fusion meant. Or, the way my brain translated the message turned that part into the word fusion. From all the other stuff in the message, they were probably so advanced and I was so far behind, I was basically a slug and they were the humans wondering if they should pour salt on me or not.

The last bit, about getting kicked from the System and the immediate death sentence, sounded a little confusing to me. Was getting kicked from the System what killed them, or were they kicked from the System, which weakened them so much it became very easy for the Court representative to kill them? It felt like a different warning from the first part, because they wouldn't be kicked from the system if they only *used* the energy from a star. To me, it almost sounded like they would at least get a chance to fight. 'Summarily executed' made it seem as if the fight would be all but pointless, but you could still go down swinging. Immediate death sentence wasn't playing around. It meant I didn't want to have my System removed, even if I hated it, because I would most likely die if that happened.

Which brought my thoughts full circle, back to why I didn't want to mess with this thing in the first place. If I was understanding it right, this diamond, if thrown into a star or black hole, would cause some serious mayhem and destruction, on a scale I'd never even dreamed of messing around with. Doubling the power of something like that could delete entire solar systems. Maybe entire galaxies. Using it to double the power of something simple, even a mundane spell I thought I had under control, could quickly become an unmanageable disaster.

But, if the Destitute was up here with airships that could hold dozens–maybe hundreds–of troops, then perhaps an unmanageable disaster was exactly what was needed. I fixed a few of the runes on the leather bag that were looking a little suspect, and then tied it onto my weapon belt next to my ammo pouch. It was better to have it in a place where I could quickly access it, just in case. Even if I hoped I never had to touch it again.

After everything was in its place and repacked, I was finally able to lay down and get some sleep. At least, I think that's what happened, because it felt like all I did was close my eyes for a second before Cross was there next to me, shaking me awake.

"Hey. Everything's ready to go." Cross looked like he'd taken the time to get cleaned up as well, and his gear was polished enough to be parade-ground ready. He was carrying a jute sack with my roughly repaired armor inside. "The hunting team leader, Lighter, sent out the advance scouts a few minutes ago. We've got about an hour before we're supposed to follow."

"Thanks." I sat up, rubbing my eyes. "Did everything go okay? No problems building more sleds?"

"We figured it out pretty quickly. That couple you came back with figured out a compromise, too." Cross sat down next to the bag with my armor and pulled out a box I hadn't noticed before. Inside, it was insulated, and there was a small pot that held sweetened oatmeal. He dished us each a bowl while I got dressed. "The pregnant lady is in charge of the sled that shuttles supplies and information reports, but she won't be in the advance or main party, or do any scouting. It keeps her safe, and still lets her be a part of the mission."

"A good compromise." I started strapping on armor pieces between bites of food, not wanting to eat it cold. "How about you? How are you doing?"

We both knew I was talking about the lich curse bleeding into his arm. Cross held up the arm in question and flexed it, showing he still had control over the limb. "It's acting normally at the moment. I've gotten plenty of practice pushing it down." He paused while he took a slow bite of food, thinking about how to word what he wanted to say. "The voices I hear sometimes… they're getting louder. I don't know if that's because we're getting closer to the lich's boss, or if it's getting stronger… settling deeper into my head."

I waited a little before saying anything, letting his statement settle into the room a bit. "That couldn't have been easy to admit. Thank you for being honest with me." I quickly finished with my armor and the last few bites of my food. Before he could stand up, I

143

put a hand on his shoulder. "I recently healed someone with an undead curse in this village, and it upgraded some of my skills. I'd like to give healing you another try, if you don't mind."

"Are you sure? We've done this countless times by now, and I don't know if it's worth it anymore." Cross looked out the door, where the first signs of sunrise were starting to show. A few clouds in the distance probably signaled another storm on the way, but we should have several hours before it hit. "There isn't a lot of time left before we have to go."

"Humor me. Please." I really wanted to try the twenty-five percent boost to healing undead afflictions on him. "It shouldn't take long to know if it works or not."

"Fine, but don't take too long." Cross unbuckled his armor so I could see his shoulder. There were a few blackened veins that had spread to his upper arm again, meaning he'd been using magic, allowing the curse to spread. Knowing what was coming, he turned his face toward the door, averting his eyes. Even he didn't want to look at it if he didn't have to. "I meant it when I said we're leaving soon."

Grabbing his shoulder, I concentrated on creating a connection between us. The moment it formed, the mana generator and new channels in my mana system practically leapt at the chance to take on the curse. In the past, the worm-like strands of the blackened tissue were slippery and almost impossible for me to grab. With the boost from my Jaw Cracker title, they were still hard to grab, but it wasn't anything like before. Now, I could use healing and light mana to push the strands of the curse out of his clean, unblemished flesh.

Some instinct told me to add in nature mana, along with touches of earth and water. The new mana types were enhanced by the light mana, which only reinforced the healing mana. It created a resonance that seemed anathema to the cursed tissue in his shoulder, and even a few hidden bits that had snaked their way into his chest. They retreated into his arm, backing down his biceps and triceps, even leaving his humerus bone and the bone marrow inside it. Once it hit the elbow, my progress slowed. The density of the curse had been increasing the entire time, and as it grew in strength, I was unable to push it any harder without risking the connection between us deepening to a point where I wouldn't be able to pull myself out quickly.

For a moment, I was tempted by the gem that sat like a lump of lead on my belt. It would be so easy to use it right now to blast the curse straight out of Cross. It might also blast Cross into oblivion, or he could start growing extra arms. I barely understood the resonance I was taking advantage of to push out the curse, and suddenly doubling it could have some very nasty results. Getting it down to the middle of his forearm was a massive improvement, and it would have to do for now. Cross would also be able to use some of his magic again, without risking being taken over at any moment.

I healed the damaged tissue that was left behind, reinforcing it so the curse would have a harder time advancing. Cross was sweating, the pain from the procedure obviously getting to him. I did my best to calm the irritated nerves. Finally, I tried to put some runes that were supposed to ward against the undead directly on his arm bones. They started to blacken and bubble the moment I added mana, so I healed the bone and removed them immediately. It was wishful thinking on my part.

Once I thought I was done doing everything I could, I let go of the connection and took a step back. "How do you feel?"

Cross stood up on shaky legs, already fixing his armor. "That hurt, but right now I feel better than I have in weeks. Thank you." He inspected the new black line on his skin that marked where the curse was, shaking out his arm as he did so. "I think I can do a lot more in a fight now, too."

"That's what I thought as well." I picked up my ruck and settled it on my back. My mana levels were already returning to their maximum point with my mana generator pulling in the ambient power around me, and even though I still felt tired, I was as prepared as I was going to get. "Ready to show the undead who's boss, and close a demon gate?"

"Oh, I'm so ready."

So, the two of us, both Judges, went to join our band of warriors and hunters, the most deadly group this part of the world had probably seen in centuries.

And we went sledding.

## CHAPTER 20

The mountains held a stark, lethal beauty that Gleason could appreciate, even as they did their best to kill him. Frigid winds sharper than a knife cut at any exposed flesh. Temperatures dropped to such extremes that it felt as if he was breathing in razorblades. Touching the exposed face of his metal armor with bare skin was agony. Even the ground beneath his feet couldn't be trusted.

Once, as he was close to the summit of a minor peak, the snow gave way and swallowed him up as it slid down the rocky mountain face for hundreds of feet. If Gleason had been without magic, he surely would have suffocated under the heavy weight of the compressed snow. Digging and melting himself free had still taken hours, and only the memory of the horrifying demonic threat the Trinity tasked him with wiping out kept him going.

"I will not be defeated by something as banal as snow, or cold, or even demons that can kill a hundred orcs with nothing but an angry glare!" His angry shout echoed amongst the empty peaks, threatening another avalanche. Realizing the mistake, Gleason had focused on digging himself out of his hole and shut up. While he made his way out, it gave him plenty of time to think.

Introspection was not something Gleason had experience with. In fact, accurate self-analysis might be one of the things the men in the entire history of his particular bloodline had been poor at accomplishing ever since they'd moved out of caves and started building cities. No matter their position in society, personal strength or power, his ancestors had become nobility not by asking how they could become better men, but how they could best capitalize on the opportunities life provided them. Like most nobles, the costs others might bear for those opportunities seldom entered their thoughts.

Now, forced to think of the need to cleanse the world of a *genuine* threat, Gleason was having some difficulties adjusting. Instead of the biased and bigoted thoughts about perceived sinners, shifters, unbelievers, and basically anyone and everyone he didn't like, the Blood Warden saw what a true monster was. An actual demon. The true enemy of his faith.

Admitting that he was wrong about his life choices, the hatred he held in his heart, meant invalidating everything he stood for up to this point. It meant the reasons the Trinity chose him as their champion were also invalidated, and the sheer dichotomy had Gleason almost dizzy with spinning thoughts and circular, offsetting ideas. The one anchor he could hold on to, the one constant that still confirmed he wasn't going crazy, were the voices in his head.

*Come to us. Hurry. Inside the King of the Mountains.*
*Time runs short. The end is near.*
*You are the chosen one. The only one.*
*We need you with us, or all is lost.*
*There is no ending without you to prove yourself as the hero.*

The voices kept repeating themselves, saying different versions of the same thing, over and over again. He was the chosen one. He was the hero. He had to prove himself. Time was running out. The tug in his chest pulling him northward was almost constant, throbbing in time with the cadence of the voices. It all meant the same thing. No matter his confusion and inner turmoil, Gleason wasn't being abandoned by the gods. He was still the one they wanted. All he had to do was prove their faith in him was well-placed, and not a mistake.

At any time, Gleason could have touched his enchanted whip and stopped the voices from invading his thoughts. That wasn't something he wanted at the moment. It wasn't only because he needed confirmation that he still had the favor of the Trinity. Everyone knew they weren't fickle gods, and weren't likely to pass the status of champion off to someone else on a whim. No, it was something more… mundane.

Throughout his entire life, Gleason had nearly always had subordinates there to follow his commands. He'd never truly been alone for any extended period of time. Even as a child, there were servants and house guards to look after him or train with. As a White Warden, he'd lived in the barracks with his men, as a true leader should. No trip, training exercise, scouting journey, or ranking tournament had ever been taken solo. Even after he abandoned the White Wardens and became a Blood Warden, he'd never been by himself.

It had settled onto Gleason's shoulders like a lead cloak the moment he stepped out of the caves and into the northern range. He was–for the first time in his life–completely and totally alone. As silly as it sounded, hearing the voices of the gods speak in his head made him feel less lonely.

They didn't answer back when he tried talking to them, or acknowledge his questions when he asked them, but he felt comfort just the same. Still, it wasn't as if he was in a group of people, or even with only one other person. Being alone with his thoughts and the voices in his head wasn't something he enjoyed at all.

"Next time, I'm going to keep at least one underling alive, no matter what it takes. One who knows how to cook." He'd taken several lessons in his family estate on proper cooking techniques, and did a fair job at it. He just hated doing such mundane tasks, especially when he could be doing more important things, like planning his next steps, or practicing to advance his magic.

Gleason cast one last spell with the wave of his hand, finishing the ramp to freedom out of the snow. Veins of blackened flesh wormed throughout his entire body, writhing like living things barely contained by his skin. He sighed in pleasure as they twisted and contracted, eventually curling down out of sight and leaving him looking completely normal on the surface.

"Finally. Now, to get to this 'King of the Mountains' so I can prove myself." Gleason trudged his way back up to the peak, and quickly saw his goal in the light of the setting sun. There, in the distance, was a mountain taller than any of the others around it. Its peak was a shattered tip, as if a giant had snapped off the smooth end of an otherwise perfect cone. As the last rays of sunlight shot across its surface, the jagged snow-covered top became a golden crown wreathed in wisps of amber clouds.

"If that isn't the King of the Mountains, I don't know what else could be." Gleason, overcome for a moment by the evidence in front of him of the favor given to him by the Trinity, raised his hands to the sky in supplication. "Thank you, great and mighty gods above, for this opportunity. I won't let you down."

The fading sunlight caught his shining armor as well, lighting it up like a beacon where he stood on top of the smaller mountain peak. Like an echo of the crown dozens of miles away, it was visible to any and all who might be looking in his direction to see his unfettered glory. It warmed him for a brief moment, and Gleason took it as confirmation from the Trinity that they heard his prayer.

Renewed by the sight of his goal, Gleason decided he wasn't tired enough to stop and make camp for the evening. He pushed onward, deep into the night, ignoring the steadily dropping temperatures in favor of getting closer to his goal. The lack of any type of life, both plant and animal, lulled him into a false sense of security. If there was no place for something to hide, or for that matter, nothing to hide in the first place, why did he need to stay on guard? Gleason kept himself from freezing to death through continuous movement and by casting the occasional fire spell, keeping them small enough not to outright ruin his night vision. He still needed to be able to see where to walk.

Pushing onward turned out to be a mistake. The cold quickly started to seep into his bones, and his mana seemed sluggish to react when he cast his spells to warm himself. His feet were dragging trails through the white powder that covered the side of the mountain, and more than once he stumbled to his hands and knees as a hidden rock or dip in the ground tripped him.

The only thing saving him from frostbite was the blackened veins that ran through his body. They swirled about under his skin, keeping the blood flowing evenly and stopping Gleason's extremities from freezing. He didn't understand how it worked, or how to actively control it. He only counted himself lucky that it was doing what it did. It was still hard to fight the urge to use larger fire spells for more heat, but he held himself back. Gleason knew maintaining his night vision had to be the priority until he was able to set up a campsite.

Despite his precautions, night vision didn't help him see attacks from above. When the looming monstrosity of wood, canvas, and steel came swooping out of the sky, his only warning was the faint creaking sound of strained ropes and a blank spot in the field of stars above him.

Gleason managed to dive into a snowbank at the last second, right as the heavy thuds of iron anchors fell on the rocky mountain all around him, shattered stones and dislodged rocks barely missing him. He wasn't sure why he knew to hide, but those same instincts had saved his life many times, and he wasn't going to ignore them now. He stared, amazed, at the hunks of rusty metal that embedded themselves in the mountain.

The anchors looked exactly like the kinds of anchors you would see on a barge or ship, but he couldn't understand how something like that would end up here, falling from the night sky. Attached to them were heavy hemp ropes that trailed up to the shadowy bulk that hovered above him. He couldn't believe what he was seeing. It was impossible for it to be here, but it was right in front of him. An airship. Had Gleason found the long-lost Silver Star? And if so, who was piloting it now?

He'd heard stories about it growing up, the same as everyone else. Legends of the treasures and magic weapons aboard the missing ship had been the bedtime stories for boys and girls over generations. The secret to making airships had been lost long before the Wardens had been created, but the fact they were once real was never in dispute. If he could capture it, Gleason might have a chance at killing the demons he'd seen masacre all his orcs. The Trinity had delivered him this opportunity for victory, and a way for him to get to the mountain even faster.

As he peeked out from his snowy hiding place, Gleason saw figures sliding down the anchor ropes. They moved too fluidly, too quietly to be human. Either shifters, or greater undead. Those were both enemies he knew how to deal with. He thought it even made sense that it would be undead aboard the ancient airship. Who else would still be flying something so old? Only an immortal being that existed beyond the borders of death could manage such a feat.

Before he could stand up from hiding and start laying waste to the filthy creatures, he realized they hadn't finished coming down the ropes. What had started as a bare dozen was now at least quadruple that number. Even with his powerful magic and blessings from the Trinity, fifty greater undead were too many for him to take on his own. Gleason decided he would be better off waiting to see what they would do. If the undead split up, he could kill them in smaller groups.

Before they separated into teams, two vampires in exquisite chainmail over fur-lined clothing stepped close enough to Gleason to allow him to overhear their conversation.

"Are you sure the gray dwarves saw a human? This is far outside our patrol route, and I don't want to be the one explaining why we let the interloper and his group through the pass."

"They seemed convinced. It wasn't only one lookout, either. Two others saw a figure standing close to tunnel entrance six, right on top of the peak. The sun lit them up like a light spell. If we weren't hiding in the hold from the sun's destructive rays, I'm sure our better vision would have seen them in an instant."

"Well, the trail ends here, but it's impossible to tell if it was an animal or not, the way it was dragging itself through the snow. If those Duergar have us chasing an injured mountain goat, or one of those stupid snow yak creatures they like to eat so much, I'm reporting this directly to Shōen."

"He won't do anything to his fellow dwarves. You know that better than anyone. It's better to report it directly to The Destitute."

"Oh, and do *you* want to disturb him? Because the last time I saw The Destitute, he was preparing another attack on a Demon Prince. *After* he got done winning the *last* fight with it. He would have killed it, too, until the Demon Prince ran away with its tail tucked between its legs as it sacrificed all its underlings to cover its escape."

"Maybe you have a point. Let's search the area, and then decide what to do."

"Good plan."

The two walked off, shouting orders to the rest of the undead that were milling around. Gleason wasn't sure how to take their conversation. He'd never heard of 'gray dwarves' before, and he especially didn't know what to think about this 'Destitute'–which was obviously some kind of leader to the undead–fighting Demon Princes, but none of that mattered right now. His priority needed to be taking the airship. And he knew he couldn't do that on the ground.

Once the search party had spread out, Gleason saw his chance. The anchor nearest his hiding place didn't have a guard, so he sprinted for it as fast as his stiff and frozen limbs would allow. If he could climb aboard the airship, he might be able to take control and fly off, leaving the overwhelming number of advanced undead behind.

Climbing the rough hemp rope was harder than he expected. There were no knots to use as handholds, and the sharp winds whipped him about the higher he got. It didn't take long for him to understand that the airship was much larger than he first thought, and it was hovering a lot higher overhead than he first realized.

It was too late for him to turn back. When Gleason looked down, the vampires, ghouls, and other unsightly undead were already regrouping, most likely so they could climb back up and leave after failing to find him. He had to hurry if he was going to make it with enough time to leave them behind. Seeing how many there were under him, and how many he would have to fight, Gleason knew he didn't have much of a chance of winning. He was pretty sure he could get away from them, given his greater magical abilities. It was winning, *and* taking the airship, that was going to be next to impossible.

The thought of failing, of missing out on the opportunity this chance provided him, gave Gleason the burst of energy his frozen limbs needed. He pulled himself up the rope, hand over hand, without a single pause to rest. The only thing that stopped him was when his gauntlet-covered fist thunked into the wooden keel of the ship above him.

"Finally! Thank the Trinity." Gleason was pretty sure he felt the rope start to twist and shake as someone underneath him started to climb. He was running out of time.

Above him, where the rope came out of the ship, was a dark hole in the side of the wooden planks that were otherwise perfectly smooth. It was the only way he saw in, so Gleason grabbed the lip of the entrance and pulled himself up, his arms shaking with the strain. The long climb, coupled with his heavy plate armor, had managed to wear through both his mana reserves and the black veins that reinforced his body. He flopped to the floor, gasping for breath. He'd made it.

"Oy! What do we 'ave 'ere?"

Looking up, Gleason was stunned to see a short, heavily muscled man standing there holding a section of decking, with a hammer and pouch of nails dangling from a toolbelt. The short man cocked his head to the side, looking Gleason up and down. "You the shiny one, aye?"

Instead of answering, Gleason grabbed for his weapon.

The last thing he saw was a heavy plank of wood as it filled his helmet's visor, at a speed much faster than he thought the short man could have ever moved.

## CHAPTER 21

We made it to the caves with thirty days left on my timer. Lighter, the hunter team leader, hadn't appreciated how hard I was rushing us, but I genuinely didn't care. There were all kinds of opportunities he had in the future to scout the area between his tree village and the caves. *If* we closed the Demon Gate in time.

There were signs a massive battle had recently taken place in the area. Jess was the first of us to notice the mana was still stirred up, and it felt seriously unsettled especially close to the main cave entrance. The most disturbing thing we were seeing though, was actually the *lack* of enemies.

Jess, Lighter, and I all stood on a slight rise overlooking the series of cave entrances, trying to work out our best plan of action while the others were spread out around the various openings. Several were poorly hidden, but the watchful scouts had easily spotted the additional underground tunnels. It was likely the last battle had been a full frontal assault, because those entrances didn't have the same amount of damage and scarring around them, and only a complete idiot would miss such obvious holes in the ground. I mean, they were so noticeable a blind squirrel could have seen them from space.

"I don't get it. This close to their base, we should have been attacked a dozen times. If the goblin overpopulation problem was bad enough to force them into attacking the village, they should be chomping at the bit to come after a group that gift wrapped themselves practically on their front door." Jess had the least amount of experience fighting goblins in our group, but she held a certain amount of dislike for them after almost being left out as a sacrificial meal in front of a goblin cave. It was as good a reason as any to hate them. Goblins sucked on just about every world I'd ever been on. "Do you think they moved after the battle with whoever attacked them?"

Lighter shook his head, the white camouflage hat he was wearing flopping in the wind with the exaggerated motion. "Moved? It's possible, but I wouldn't bet on it none. I'd say there's a better chance the fight helped the gobs with their overpopulation problem.

Now the gobs are deeper underground, licking their wounds. Probably a few hidden ones keepin' an eye on us right now, too."

"What if they were wiped out?" Jess looked around at the broken pieces of weapons, torn up ground, and shattered armor. "They could have all been killed, right?"

"No." I knelt down and picked up a piece of rusted leg armor. "There are no bodies. Goblins never leave any meat behind if they win a fight, even their own kind. They enjoy meat too much to let it go to waste. We know they were at least the last ones here because there's not a single severed limb left behind. Only broken scraps and things they can't use."

Jess winced, turning a little pale. It was clear by the look on her face that she understood how grisly the field in front of us truly was. The scope of the battlefield laid bare the number of bodies it most likely produced. She turned her attention to the armor I was holding.

"Any clues about who attacked them? It couldn't have been undead. Even goblins don't eat zombies and ghouls." Jess shuddered at the thought.

"Right. They probably would have burned the bodies of the undead." I passed her the piece of armor. "Considering the craftsmanship, I think it was orcs. Why goblins and orcs are fighting each other instead of teaming up, I don't know, but I'll be sure to stay out of the way."

"My team reported the same thing." Lighter turned around and started walking back toward our sleds. "All signs point toward orcs and gobs pokin' each other with pointy bits. Personally, I'm all for it. I ain't one to look a gift alpacaoose in the mouth, if you know what I mean."

I nodded, knowing exactly what he meant. I had no idea what an alpacaoose was, but I had no doubt I didn't want to look in its mouth.

Lighter looked up at the sky, gauging the time. "Resupply sleds should be here soon. After we unload, we go in." He waited to see if I would argue, considering I'd been the person pushing us the entire trip. When I didn't, he let out a little sigh of relief. "We'll spread the word. Now's the time for hot food. Might be the last chance for a long stretch."

"As long as it isn't Cross or Leedy doing the cooking, I'm all for it." Jess practically skipped down the rise, already searching for people to tell. She was using her staff to mold the ground under each foot to be more level, simultaneously training her affinity with the tool and pushing toward the new benchmark of instinctive casting.

It was a long road, maybe an impossible one, but constantly improving your abilities every day was never a waste of time. That was a lesson I needed to keep in mind as well. While I walked, the hunter team leader fell into step next to me.

"When we get in those caves, I'm gonna hold my people back." Lighter continued to look straight in front, not turning his head to meet my eyes. "You and your folks can take the lead. I don't care one whit what no deal says between the council and you. We both know who's gonna be in better shape if a fight kicks off, and it ain't my people."

"I've got no problem with that. All I need is someone to point the way if we get lost or turned around." I saw him relax, which made me feel a little frustrated. Maybe it was time to tell him what was at stake. "Look, Lighter, I'm not out to hurt you or your people. I'm trying to *help* them. It may seem like I've been pushing you hard, and rushing your scouts, but there's a reason for that. If we don't stop what's hiding in those mountains in time, everything is dead. *Everything*." I let the passion and stress of the moment bleed into my voice. "It doesn't matter what hunting grounds will help you next season, or what logging zones will be ready in five years, because this will all be a barren wasteland. In less than a month, everything you know and love will be gone. Forever."

"What?" Lighter had stopped, and he was finally looking at me. "What're you talkin' about? I've lived my whole life in these parts, and there ain't been nothin' like that 'round here." His nostrils flared, and he started breathing heavier. "Don't you go droppin' threats like that for no reason. It ain't right to go 'round scarin' folks cause you think you can get away with it."

"I'm telling you the truth. Just because you don't want to believe it, doesn't change the reality of things." I tried opening my hands, spreading my stance to show how earnest I was. It didn't help.

"You can't fool me with your–" Lighter cocked his head to the side, stopping his own tirade in mid-shout. To give the old guy some credit, his situational awareness was top-notch. He looked around at the positioning of his hunters, and cursed under his breath. "They should know better! Hot chow don't mean 'abandon my post to get in line'. There ain't anyone watchin' our rear. If'n I was a gob, I'd hit us right now!"

Both of us sprinted down the rise, shouting for everyone to arm themselves. The cluster of sleds at the base of the hills was quickly a swarm of hunters scrambling to find cover and nock arrows to bowstrings. A few were even scrambling to get armor pieces back on, and Lighter was so furious with them I thought the old guy was going to give himself a stroke.

Jess had been quick to react, creating a low wall the hunters could duck behind for cover. Cross, Leedy, and Murphy were somewhere out on the flanks, and I didn't have eyes on them. Everyone else hunkered down in preparation for attack, splitting our focus on both the front and rear.

An attack that never came.

"False alarm!" Lighter slowly stood up from his place behind a sled, putting an arrow back in its quiver. "I guess I'm a little too jumpy with all the talk of gloom and doom goin' 'round."

Equal parts laughter and grumbling met his announcement. Everyone relaxed, and soon a cookpot was bubbling over a large fire next to the sleds. This time, the scouts stayed properly distributed.

While we waited for the resupply sleds to arrive, Cross and the others returned. They had seen more signs of cave openings further to our east, but we didn't see a point in exploring them. We divided up what was left on the sleds between the people going into the caves, stripping them bare of food and ammunition. The only thing we didn't take were spare parts for the sleds and the few kills the hunters had made on our way here. Unprocessed hides, claws, and bones weren't much use to us right now.

Lighter kept his distance from me while all that was going on. He seemed to have calmed down from our little spat, but he wasn't exactly looking to mend fences. It wasn't as if we were friends in the first place, so I guess he was just happy to get the concession that my people would lead the way into the caves.

About the same time that people started lining up to get a bowl of food, a scout came sprinting up from the south. They were waving their arms over their head and pointing behind them, and shouting something we couldn't hear due to the distance between us. The scout stopped and hunched over, catching their breath before standing up and running again. Whatever it was, they thought it was important. More than one person started to shuffle nervously toward cover, or setting aside bowls for bows.

"They're probably just telling us the resupply sleds are almost here." Jess planted the tip of her staff in the ground, flexing her mana through its length. "Right? That's what they're shouting about. We already had one false alarm about an attack."

Lighter started yelling at his people, staging them for another goblin ambush. He saw the desperation on the scout's face from here, the same as I did.

Jaeger was suddenly standing by my elbow, the giant of a man appearing out of nowhere. He'd been a member of the hunting team the whole trip, but I'd seldom seen him. Hillbilly ninjas were sneaky like that. "Hilda is leading the supply sleds. James, can you hear what she's shouting? I need to know if the sleds are okay."

"Hold on." I relaxed my hold on my senses. If I let them go at their full sensitivity all the time, I'd never get any peace. Being slowly driven insane by the sound of earthworms chewing their way through the dirt under my feet wasn't a great way to live my life, so I usually throttled them back a large amount.

Once I ramped them up, I could hear everything. Heartbeats were like thunder, pounding in my head. The sounds of everyone talking nearby were like the shouts of howler monkeys in my ears, nothing but individual sounds and too loud to understand. My brain screamed at me in pain, trying to decipher all the information that flooded in all at once.

The last time I tried this, my mind stat was thirty points smaller than what it was now. I was able to push through the cacophony and focus on the person running toward us in only a few seconds. Panting, pounding footsteps and racing heart, it was a woman who wasn't used to long-distance running. She was a hunter who sat in a tree and ambushed her prey, a burst predator that didn't need to sprint for extended periods of time.

As she paused to catch her breath again, I could hear what she said this time with no problem.

"Goblins… coming… thousands… of goblins."

## CHAPTER 22

"Everyone, into the caves!" I throttled back on my senses, returning them back to something I could handle as I started giving orders to everyone within earshot. "Grab what you can and get in the main cave. We're about to get overrun!"

Lighter didn't bother arguing with me. He must have heard something in my tone, or his danger sense was developed enough to understand the severity of the situation. He had his people up and moving in moments, and even had a few dragging the sleds behind them up the rise. I left him to it.

My group had gathered around me, waiting to see what to do next. I didn't know if the scout was exaggerating or not, or how organized the group might be. If it was an unorganized rabble, a few flashy spells might send them running, no matter how many of them there were. If they were an army, with leaders in secure positions to give orders, we were screwed six ways from Sunday. Either way, we needed a plan. I dropped to a knee and started drawing out positions in the snow, giving everyone a good idea of where they needed to be.

"Jess, I want you and Murphy to get in those caves and start leading the hunters deeper underground. We need a safe route through to the other side, and keep an eye out for places you can drop the cave ceiling on anything that follows us. We can't forget our true mission here."

Jess looked like she was about to argue until I mentioned collapsing parts of caves. She was primarily an earth mage, and she knew there was no one better for the job. Murphy could help protect her when she was casting.

"Cross and Leedy, you're going to help hold the entrance while we wait for the last of the scouts and the people on the resupply sleds to get inside. We'll buy them as much time as we can, but only range out as far as an average bow shot can reach if you need to help someone. Jaeger can support you from inside the cave, and run out when the sleds pull up to grab people and supplies when they arrive. Got it, Jaeger?" I looked up when he didn't answer. "Jaeger? Ah, damn it."

Sprinting full speed to the south, the big guy was already almost to the scout.

"Okay, new plan. Cross, you're with me. Everyone else, hold the cave entrance. Jess, prep it for collapse if you can. We'll be there as soon as we get everyone." I stood up, grabbing weapons off my belt. Knuckle duster for shield bash and starmetal mace in one hand, magic-eating ninjatō and triple-barreled wrist gun in the other, I was ready to go.

"Good luck you two. Fight well." Murphy gave both Cross and I a nod before sprinting for the caves. Jess and Leedy echoed his sentiments and were hot on his heels.

Both Cross and I didn't bother speaking. We both took off running to the south, using mana to boost our speed. Cross had a smile that made him seem more excited than anything. It was probably because he could use magic again without having to worry about losing himself to the curse.

We caught up to Jaeger as he finished talking to the scout. She looked ready to collapse, so I cast a quick healing spell on her, taking care of the lactic acid buildup in her body, as well as fixing a twisted knee that was slowing her down. She didn't bother to stop and say thank you, instead running with new energy for the caves.

"She told me Hilda was still alive the last time she saw her. The spider riders are toying with them, laughing as they make them bleed." Jaeger was already stomping his way south toward the edge of the tree line, where we could already hear the faint hoots and howls of goblins on the hunt. "They're herding them this way. Probably to kill them in front of us, to destroy our morale at the same time, before they attack our main group."

I didn't disagree with him. That sounded exactly like something a group of goblins would do. I cast a quick heal on Jaeger as well, making sure he was in the best shape possible before we fought.

"The priority is saving your people, so Cross and I are going to run interference while you get on a sled and get Hilda and the others out. Dump the supplies if you need to. Got it?" I made sure his head was in the game. I didn't need him running off in a blaze of glory and getting himself killed for no reason. "Okay. Let's do this."

161

We barely managed to make it to the trees when the first goblin arrows and spears started raining on our heads. Cross handled the left side, while I took the right and center. He used wind blades to cut down dozens of goblins mounted on cave spiders that were hiding amongst the trees, slicing through arachnid limbs and dropping them dozens of feet where they tumbled and splattered on the hard, frozen ground.

I used palm-sized disks of rock and ice, the instinctive casting abilities that earth mana gave me making the motions effortless. I only included the ice mana because I didn't want any accidental explosions wiping out half the forest with my friction mana. There wasn't anything that could stand in the way of the razor sharp stones, and they passed through goblins, spiders, and trees as if nothing but wet paper was in their path. It was overkill, and I felt a steady drain on my mana generator, but the shock and awe of our combined assault pushed the goblin scouts into full retreat on my side of the skirmish.

A scream had Jaeger sprinting through the trees so fast that Cross and I had to use mana to keep up with him. All around us we heard the sounds of goblins closing in–except the small area where I'd thinned them out a bit–but we couldn't blindly start blasting without knowing where the resupply sleds were.

"Hilda! Hilda, where are you?" Jaeger's shouting told the goblins exactly where we were, and their excited howls intensified. They weren't showing themselves yet, but they were closing the proverbial net around us. "Hilda, I'm coming for you!"

I couldn't help mentally kicking myself as we got closer to where we'd heard the scream. If I'd risked the airship, we wouldn't have run into all these goblins. Although I knew there was no way to guess the threat their numbers represented at the time, it was still my choice that put us here. Maybe the airship would have been the safer choice.

As a goblin fell out of a tree to drop on Jaeger's head, the mighty hunter turned and punched the little green monster so hard its head actually *exploded*. Chunks of brain and skull splattered across the snow as the body flopped to the ground bonelessly. Jaeger didn't miss a step, the entire interaction barely registering as he was focused on finding Hilda.

On second thought, we'd probably be okay.

"Jaeger!" Off to our right, on the other side of a dense area of trees, two sleds were fighting their way through the forest. Standing on top of a stack of crates was Hilda, furiously loosing arrows so fast her hands and arms were a blur. Another hunter was doing the same on the other sled, but not quite as effectively.

The people serving as 'rowers' on the sleds were all injured in some way, with more than one sprouting enough goblin arrows they could be confused for porcupines. That didn't mean they stopped trying. Despite their wounds, the hunters did their best to push their sleds onward.

Behind the sleds, the forest was blanketed in goblins. Some were riding cave spiders, but most were on foot. The scout guessing there were thousands of them was probably a tiny exaggeration, but not much of one. Closer to one thousand looked more accurate, but that was enough to drown us in sheer weight of numbers if we got caught out in the open like this. Considering the direction they were attacking from, they had to have come from the caves to the east our group had spotted earlier. At least they weren't from the same tunnels we were trying to retreat into.

Now that we knew where our people were, Cross and I didn't have to hold back. While Jaeger led the way to the sleds, the two of us started absolutely *hammering* the goblins.

Did I need to use my wrist gun to shoot two bolo rounds and one flechette round into the most dense cluster of goblins I could see? No. But did I want to? Most definitely, yes. Yes I did.

I was right about the accuracy being terrible with the new paper shells. It didn't matter so much when my point of aim needed to be 'southeast'. The bolo rounds scythed down rows of goblins in a screaming mess of tumbling limbs, and the flechette round hit the spiders and their riders in jumping around in the trees like a thunderbolt of supersonic wasps. They tumbled to the ground, screaming and chittering in pain. Reloading only took a few seconds, and I had so much fun the first time around, I decided to do it again. Yep, it was just as fun the second time.

While I was reloading, I saw Cross went a little more hands-on with his violence. He'd moved out to our flank, and was using the spear in his hands like it was a metronome. Swinging it back and forth in a steady cadence you could play piano by, Cross mowed goblins down without missing a beat. The rows in front were pushed into him from the rows behind, straight into a blender of death. When necessary, Cross still used the occasional wind blade spell to keep himself from being overrun, or boosted his speed and strength to superhuman levels.

Instead of using my wrist gun a third time, I decided it was time to start setting us up for a way to get out of this mess. I used earth magic to raise razor-thin sections of rock a few inches above the ground in random swirling designs between trees, and long rows that were dozens of feet across in more open areas. The goblins would shred their bare feet as they tried to walk through the forest, and it was impossible to see under the blanket of snow and wet leaves. I made sure to leave us a path out, but just about everywhere else was going to be a nightmare to walk through for some time. Covering that much surface area almost drained me, but my mana generator was already doing its best to refill itself already. The last upgrade had been a serious boost in power.

As the goblins' howls turned from predatory to surprised pain at my trap, we finally linked up with the sleds. They'd never stopped moving forward the whole time, but it wasn't looking good for the hunters on board. Even Hilda had taken a goblin spear to the shoulder at some point. Considering the poison I knew goblins liked to use, fixing her was an immediate priority. It could kill the baby before we even had a chance to get back to the caves.

"Jaeger, dump the supplies and get everyone on one sled. We're getting out of here right now." He opened his mouth to argue, but I was already jumping onto the pile of supplies to grab Hilda. "Don't worry, I'll heal her while you get us ready to move."

"Fine." Jaeger wasn't happy, however he didn't know how to cast a healing spell. "I'll make it fast."

"You have no idea how glad we are to see you." Hilda looked over to Jaeger. "How glad *I* am to see *you*."

"Romance each other later. Save lives now." I already had enough mana regenerated that I was over half my capacity, so I grabbed the spear sticking out of her shoulder and snapped off the barbed tip protruding from her back. Hilda cried out in pain, and I kept her from falling. "I'm going to take this out and heal you all in one shot, okay?" She gave me a shaky nod. "On three. Three."

I dumped healing mana into her shoulder as I ripped the spear out, ignoring her scream of protest. The wound closed almost immediately, and I was able to isolate the poison I knew was going to be there a few seconds later. Thankfully, it wasn't some kind of virulent or crazy poison I'd never seen before, only some organic-based mixture I burned out in one burst of fire mana. Another check of her body–and the baby–and I knew she was good to go.

Hilda didn't wait for me to give her a clean bill of health. She was back on her feet and taking shots at spider-mounted goblins in the blink of an eye. "That. Wasn't. Fun." Each word was accentuated by the snap of her bowstring, and a corresponding explosion from the impact of the arrows she was using. I caught a glimpse of the oversized flint arrowhead on the next arrow she nocked, and it was definitely made from the place of power.

I guess she decided it was time to unleash the big guns.

Cross and Jaeger had everyone on the other sled, so we jumped on and got moving. The goblin horde would eventually make it over the trap I'd set, but we had a little time before they did. With Cross and Jaeger serving as our rowers, we'd definitely make it back to the caves before the goblins caught up to us.

A large cluster of spider riders that were chasing us broke off and started rummaging through the supplies left on the ground and the back of the other sled.

I looked up from where I was trying to heal the other hunters, and pointed at the goblins. "What was in those crates? Anything the greenskins can use against us?"

Hilda was the only person able to stand guard, so she turned around and squinted. "Oh, this is perfect. I've got a few special arrows left. Watch this." She shouted for Jaeger to stop, which didn't make the injured hunters still conscious enough to understand what was going on around them very happy.

Jaeger listened, and our sled dragged to a halt. I didn't bother getting involved. There was enough room between us and the goblins now that we were out of goblin bow range, and most of my attention was taken up by trying to save the hunter with over thirty poisoned arrows in his body. However, it was an important distinction that we were out of *goblin* bow range. We were still well within *Hilda's* bow range.

Hilda took a few extra seconds to look over her available arrows, picking the one she liked best. Then, she pulled it back and let it go at a very sharp angle, intending to drop it down in an arc on top of the goblins' heads.

When the explosive arrow hit the stack of crates on top of the sled, for a single long moment nothing really happened beyond a small pop of smoke and light. Which changed when the resupply of 'special' arrows detonated all at once, ripping apart the goblins and their cave spiders into a fine mist. Most of the goblins we could see were knocked back on their backs, if they were even alive in the first place. The pressure wave might have killed them.

Hilda looked equal parts guilty and smug, clearly not expecting the size of the explosion, but happy she had done it. "Okay, we can go now."

## CHAPTER 23

Even with our head start, we only managed to beat the goblins to the cave entrance by a few minutes. I wasn't able to help while healing the injured we already had, and then we went and picked up more. There were several of our own scouts we saw still running for the caves as we got closer–the ones left out on our flanks as guards–so we were forced to zig-zag back and forth to grab them all. We managed it, but only barely.

The sled was standing room only by the time we were done, and the last few I couldn't even reach to see how bad their wounds were. All they could do was hold on until we got to the caves, where I could heal them.

While we were all scrunched together on the sled, I realized that I hadn't been paying close enough attention to the faces and numbers of hunters when we stopped at night, and Lighter had brought more people along than we'd agreed upon with the council. How and why, I didn't know. Most likely to hunt more game and scout a wider area, since I was moving faster than they'd initially expected. I guess it didn't really matter at this point. We were all team human right now anyway.

As the sled came to a skidding stop, the hunters holding the entrance gave out a cheer. They'd been busy, given the large numbers of dead goblins and spiders. Several of them came out to help the wounded off, and Lighter had the hunters not actively shooting at the spider riders who were hot on our tail to come and help tip the sled on its side and position it alongside the others to create more obstacles for the goblins.

"That's all our folks! Get to your spots!" Lighter waved his people back, while the mass of goblins crested the rise behind us. He took a step back and gulped in fear before catching himself, firming his shoulders and straightening his spine. He refused to back down in the face of overwhelming odds, and the respect I felt for the gray-haired hunter skyrocketed. "They're almost here. Give 'em a special hello!"

Even the injured hunters fell in a ragged line behind the tipped-up sleds, and as one they lifted their bows with the explosive flint arrowheads. By some unspoken command, they loosed almost as one. The heavy twang sound of nearly twenty bows releasing their tension all at once was quickly eclipsed by the rolling thunder that stretched across the front line of goblins. They were rocked hard, by stone shrapnel, choking dust, and the concussive blast. Many greenskins had dropped to the ground and didn't get up again, and even more were staggering about, clutching their heads in pain.

For a moment, it looked as if they would give up. The goblins would see sense, and realize the few humans standing across from them weren't worth the agony and death that would certainly result if they kept pushing forward. Then, the next line ran into the ones hesitating, and the flood of greenskins came for us.

Lighter motioned, and a second volley of arrows took flight. Explosions knocked down the goblins like bowling pins, but they'd gained ground. Enough that everyone, both human and greenskin, knew how this battle would eventually play out.

Backing away from the front line, I ran to the cave entrance. "Jess, how's the plan for collapsing the tunnel coming along?" I poked my head inside the cave entrance, looking for her. "We could really use it right now!"

"I need a few more minutes. If I drop the entrance, the whole thing could come down, so I'm reinforcing the rear portion where we're going to be standing first." Jess was sitting on the ground with her eyes closed, both hands holding her staff that was shoved into the dirt in front of her.

"Do you need help? We could try raising a wall in the tunnel to block it off instead of dropping it." I didn't want to bump her mental elbow while she was using her magic and accidentally create a cave-in while everyone was still outside, so I figured asking first was the better idea. "There's a whole bunch of goblins coming. We might be dealing with seconds, not minutes."

Jess shook her head, but didn't bother opening her eyes. "The dirt's so loose, raising a wall at the entrance would only make things worse. I'm doing my best. Now, quit distracting me, and get me what time you can!"

I backed out of the cave, being careful not to use my instinctive casting to accidentally reach out and destabilize what she was doing. In the few seconds I was talking to Jess, the horde had halved the distance between our two groups. Not wanting to waste time, I sprinted to where Lighter was standing with his hunters.

"Tell me you got good news." Lighter's eyes flicked down at the quivers of specialty arrows his hunters had on their belts. They were looking pretty thin. "I'm already spacing out our shots to slow 'em as best as I can. We're goin' to have to switch to regular arrows soon."

"Jess said she needs more time. My group and I will stay outside until the end, but we're armored for it. Your hunters aren't." I noticed the four or five hunters I hadn't gotten a chance to heal yet were having a hard time standing up straight, or pulling their bows back to full draw. "We can probably start shuffling injured people to the cave entrance, and they can pass off their arrows to the uninjured. Same with anyone who wants to get into cover. Maybe ask for volunteers to stay and help us, and the rest go back?"

Lighter nodded in agreement. "Good a plan as any I've heard. We'll cover a smaller front, but we can speed up the pace with more arrows in each quiver."

The orders were passed up and down the line, and I expected to see hunters starting to shift back into the cave. Not one of them backed down. Even Jaeger didn't bother to try and encourage Hilda to go. He just passed her a few extra explosive arrows from his own quiver to make sure she had enough.

Courage is a thing each man and woman must find within themselves at the most difficult of times. Facing overwhelming odds, knowing your chances of survival are next to nothing, that's an easy kind of courage. That's just choosing an honorable death. Choosing to stand and fight, to risk your life when escape and guaranteed survival are only steps away? That's a different kind of courage, the kind that very few have. That I was in the company of so many was humbling.

Now that I knew where the hunters stood, I looked for Leedy and Cross. They were each on opposite ends of the hunters' line of battle, making it difficult for me to coordinate with them. I decided that Cross had the most experience–and magic–so I'd leave him to figure out the plan for himself. Leedy was the one I needed to swap places with anyway.

As I ran up next to him, he was reloading his crossbow and trying to keep pace with the volley fire of the hunters. Since Leedy wasn't exactly an expert archer, and it had been awhile since we'd practiced with our crossbows, he was struggling a bit.

"You good? Need a hand? I think I saw a one-armed grandma back in the village that could probably give you some lessons or something." I smiled at the evil look he gave me. "What? I'm only trying to help."

"How about you open a crack in the ground and swallow up these nasty little greenskins so we can all relax?" Leedy finished cranking the string back and got a bolt in place. It was one of the acid versions we'd seen mixed results with against the undead. He loosed it into a cluster of goblin archers that were trying to get in range to start shooting back at us. Given the screams, the acid cloud it released was far more effective against the goblins than it was the bone knight ghouls we'd last tried it on. "Nice. Too bad I've only got three more of those."

"I can't use the ground to swallow up the goblins, because it could cause a cave-in. Jess said the tunnel entrance is unstable, so we're buying her time to fix it." I used my starmetal mace to help concentrate a mixture of fire, water, and air mana before blasting out a column of superheated steam that cut a line across the goblins trying to flank us.

The greenskins momentarily fell back, disoriented by the sudden flash of power, which gave our side time to take a drink of water and reorganize. I was once again amazed at how easy it was to control such a complicated spell, and how quickly my mana generator was already refilling my reserves. I looked back at my friend and started describing what I needed, using my hands to help show what I wanted to happen. "Leedy, I'm going to anchor this end of the line, and Cross is going to take the other. I need you to hold the center. When we fall back, your job is to hold the entrance of the cave while Cross and I make sure everyone gets inside. Like a 'V' shape, you'll lead the line in, and push them past you. Once the three of us meet, we'll know everyone's inside. Then, we let as many goblins as we can into the collapse zone and Jess can drop the cave roof on their heads."

"Got it." Leedy looked over at the Goblins, where they were already starting to push forward again. "When will I know to start pulling the line back?"

"Oh, you'll know. It won't be long. My guess is about the time you run out of those bolts you're using." My subconscious screamed at me, and I activated my shield bracelet a moment before a goblin arrow shattered against the crackling dome. It had been given a boost by some wind mana, meaning a goblin shaman was hiding somewhere in the horde. "Excuse me for a moment. I've got a twatwaffle to kill."

Leedy took off for his new spot in the line, and I concentrated on finding the enemy magic user. The faint glimmers of disturbed mana led back to the center of the horde, which was just now cresting the rise. We had only a minute, maybe less, before the goblins would be within their bow range and we would start seeing casualties.

I didn't know for sure how strong the goblin caster was, so I used my mace as a focus again to help build power for a long-distance spell. The most abundant mana type in my mana generator at the moment was earth, but I couldn't use it because of the cave. The next most abundant was the life and death lightning that made up the cage around my generator. Something told me using it right now was a bad idea, so I followed my instincts and went with the third most abundant.

Nature mana doesn't sound like it should be dangerous. On its surface, it really isn't one of the more deadly types of energy. But, if you really think about it, nature is one of the scariest things in existence. It just takes a while for it to sink in how lethal it can be. So, when I cast the bolt of concentrated nature mana at the center of the goblin horde, I wasn't surprised there was no reaction at first. I only raised a mild wall of wind and blew it back at the goblins, just in case.

Cross noticed what I had done, and mirrored my actions, creating a thin dome around us that blew a light breeze away from our line. It helped with the strain, and I was able to start regenerating power faster than what I was spending.

171

The high-pitched screams started when a spider-rider drunkenly stumbled its way from the middle of the horde, bleeding green from its eyes. Soon after, dozens of goblins were doing the same, coughing and crying blood as they staggered around, disrupting the attack.

"What's happening to them?" Jaeger had shifted to my end of the line at some point when I wasn't looking, and now he was holding back his next shot to stare at the goblins as they slowly died by the handful. "Did you curse them somehow?"

"You know how mushrooms are a type of fungus?" Jaeger nodded his head yes, so I continued. "And some mushrooms are poisonous." He nodded again. "Well, in one cubic yard of dirt, it can have millions of fungal spores, the stuff mushrooms give off so they can grow. Some kinds of fungus are really, really bad for you, and if somebody were to dump a ridiculous amount of nature mana intended to do nothing but stimulate fungal spores across dozens of yards to grow and spread incredibly fast, the odds that at least *some* of those spores are going to do nasty things are pretty high."

Jaeger took a step back as a goblin vomited so hard its eyeballs popped out of its head. "You mean to tell me, *mushrooms* did that?"

Shrugging, I gauged how long until the remaining goblins got things back under control and we'd have to fight it out again. Not long enough. "Basically, yes. Mushrooms did that."

Like I said, nature is scary.

## CHAPTER 24

The downside of the nature spell was how quickly it encouraged the fungal spores to grow. In less than a minute they were heavier than air, and the effects of my attack quickly died out. Still, almost a tenth of the goblin horde was killed outright, and it appeared at least a quarter of them were suffering from the spores in some way or another. Just like I'd learned on world ten, where I once had to fight a crazy druid. Never cluster up when fighting someone who knows nature magic, or you'll pay the price.

A goblin leader of some kind was still alive over there, because they were reorganized and ready to charge at us again in only a couple of minutes. It wasn't a good sign for us that the goblins did exactly what they should, and broke apart into smaller groups so I couldn't repeat my trick with the spores. Whoever was leading them must be really motivated to kill us, because we'd massacred over a third of their number by this point. Most goblins would have run screaming in fear long before now.

"Here they come! Let loose everything you have left, then run for it!" Lighter's command was the signal for both sides, and the shouts and screams began in earnest.

Both Cross and I held the ends of the line because we had to ensure our path to the tunnel entrance wasn't flanked by the swarm. If a major force of goblins got between us and the cave, we wouldn't be able to retreat. So, any greenskins that tried swinging around got the full effect of our magic.

Since I still couldn't use earth magic without risking the integrity of the tunnel itself, I mainly focused on air and fire spells. There weren't enough goblins in any one group to warrant a single large spell, so I went with quantity over quality. The mix of wind blades and fire bolts were enough to keep our line of retreat clear. I was more than ready to mix things up in melee, but none of the goblins pushed hard enough to get close enough.

As I looked across the front lines, I noticed a spider rider near the rear of the goblins that was mounted on something different from the regular cave spiders. Instead of being a reasonable size for the goblin to ride, the spider was bigger than a clydesdale. The coloration was different as well. It had a jet black, smooth exoskeleton, and glowing red eyes that seemed far too intelligent, and it was staring right at me from across the battlefield.

Whoever was riding that monster, *had* to be the goblin leader.

Now that it had made itself known, I needed to take the chance that targeting and destroying the driving force behind the goblins would break the will of the enemy. I tossed an empowered wind blade at it. As if mocking me, it bounced off some kind of shield. A firebolt did the same thing. It held strong, without showing any signs of weakening. For a goblin, it was impressive. My guess was some kind of item was causing the shield, or maybe shields were the only spells the goblin knew, allowing the creature to pour all of its mana into one spell, making it much stronger than normal. Of course, that was the exact moment the last ripple of explosions from the hunters' special arrows spread across the main front.

"That's it! Everyone's out! Swap to regular arrows, and fall back!" Leedy gave the command, his sword and shield in hand, ready to cover the hunters as they started their slow retreat.

As our line started collapsing inward, the goblin leader's spider reared back and let out a chittering screech, encouraging the greenskins to charge. It seemed to do the trick, because the tiny gap between our two sides closed in the blink of an eye.

Lighter had done a good job positioning the sleds, so it created only a few places where the goblins were forced to come at the hunters from the front. While they weren't exactly front-line fighters, the hunters had no qualms with getting up close and personal when the goblins finally broke through.

I had to stay focused on keeping our flank clear, so I wasn't able to help when a hunter got stabbed in the gut by a sharpened stick that a goblin was using as a spear. Another hunter was shot in the neck by an arrow, but they continued to calmly nock and loose their own arrows while blood steadily leaked down their front. Jaeger took two arrows to the back while he scooped up the man stabbed in the gut, but the heavily muscled man ignored them as if they were no more than wasp-squito bites. Lighter helped the hunter who was struck in the throat into the cave when their hands kept moving like they were shooting, but their quiver was empty. Hilda led a counter-charge back out of the cave to push back a trio of spider riders that threatened to overwhelm Leedy, crushing the skull of a goblin with a rock when her bow was knocked out of her hands.

More acts of bravery than I could keep track of followed, and somehow, despite being outnumbered by a ridiculous degree, the hunters managed to get everyone inside the tunnel. Only Cross, Leedy, and I remained standing at the entrance, covered in green goblin blood and blue spider guts. They continued to come at us, but we crushed them as soon as they came within melee range.

Cross looked exhausted, and he probably couldn't cast another spell if his life depended on it. Leedy was only a little better off, and he was bleeding from several places where goblin arrows had found gaps in his armor. I was more mentally tired than physically or magically spent, the long battle wearing me down in a way that my mana generator and stats couldn't quite fix.

"Ready to lure them in?" Leedy looked back, where streaks of human blood showed the path our people had taken. "Jess has *got* to be ready to collapse the roof by now."

"There's a crazy looking spider out there, and I think the goblin on its back is their leader." I pointed to the front, where the giant black spider with glowing red eyes was still staring at us menacingly. It was easy to spot, despite the mess of the battlefield. "It's got a shield against spells, but I want to try and kill it before we go in. Cover me for a moment, I have a plan."

"You got it." Leedy reset his shield, and got ready to push back whatever came his way. Cross only let out a weary sigh, but he held the spear in his hands without wavering.

My wrist gun was inaccurate at long range before making the paper shells. After making them, it only made the effective barrel length shorter, which made it even more inaccurate. Now that my Mind stat was so high, I thought I might be able to try a version of what the goblins had done with the arrow that had nearly hit me at long range, but adjusted for the type of weapon I was using.

I swapped out the paper cartridges I had loaded for the regular solid, heavy rounds. Then I lifted my arm and held the three barrels vertically, so when I fired all three at once they would hit in a line that went up and down. I concentrated as hard as I could on making three tubes of condensed air that connected at the ends of my existing barrels. Keeping them straight, perfect, and in line with one another was the most important part. Adding rifling to put a spin on the rounds briefly crossed my mind, but that was too much of a complication. I wasn't quite there yet.

Once the air tubes felt right, I let the flicker of a *Spark* spell ignite the powder in the three cartridges simultaneously. Even with my Strength stat being over one hundred and twenty five, the added recoil with the extra barrel length was intense. Despite the ache in my wrist and shoulder, I knew it was worth it the moment I fired. Somehow, without being able to see where the rounds went because of the smoke, I knew the goblin and the spider it was riding had been hit.

By keeping the three barrels vertical, the straight line of bullets were able to impact both targets. The goblin leader caught the top two, pretty much turning the goblin into little more than a pale green mist. The spider had been hit by the lowest round, and the lower half of its face was utterly destroyed. Only the glowing red eyes remained, and as the spider choked to death on its own viscera, I couldn't help but feel the hatred it felt for me from all the way across the battlefield.

As it was heaving its last, the black spider rubbed its two front legs together, creating a sound like nails on a chalkboard. Then it dropped, its hard shell seeming to collapse inward on itself as it melted with a burst of flames the same red as its eyes. The sound caused the three of us still outside the cave to wince in pain, while the goblins screamed in fury. They turned as one and charged us, determined to overwhelm us under their greater numbers.

"What in all the minor hells, James?" Cross looked on, wide-eyed, as the goblins went stark raving mad. "Was the goblin rider the leader, or the spider? Because I've never seen a spider cast spells before."

"I have no idea, but we need to go." I pulled the two men back into the tunnel as a flood of goblins followed us inside. We barely cleared the marked line in the ground before the whole ceiling dropped as a solid piece, crushing the greenskins with a crunching splat. Jess might have taken a while, but she did good work.

"That was a close one." Leedy leaned against the cave wall, coughing in all the dust. "Whatever that thing was, I've never seen anything like it before."

"Me either." Cross took a drink from a wineskin before passing it to me. "You really made them mad when you killed that thing. With all those side tunnels, they might know a way in here. We're going to have to keep moving if we want to stay in front of them."

"Guys, we need your help! Now!" Murphy's voice echoed from deeper within the tunnel. Now that the dust was starting to clear and my eyes had adjusted to the dim light of a few lanterns, I could see that injured hunters were spread out on the ground. Jess, Murphy, and whoever else was able to help were doing their best to save them. "This one's going to bleed out!"

We rushed over to try and assist the wounded. Cross found a second wind, and cast area healing spells that blanketed the tunnel in a green and yellow glow. It's probably what saved everyone, because it kept them alive long enough for either Jess or me to get to them. That was a huge relief to me, because I was still feeling a little guilt about choosing this path instead of the airship. I couldn't go back and change anything, but it still sucked that this is how it turned out.

Even the hunter who got shot in the neck managed to make it, but they wouldn't be singing and dancing about it anytime soon. I only healed people to the point they would be able to move. Getting them to perfect health would have taken too long, and we needed to get away from the area where the psycho goblins knew we had entered.

Once everyone was back on their feet, Lighter made sure the diminished supply of arrows was evenly distributed, and each hunter had a backup weapon ready to use in the tight confines of the caves. Most had daggers or long knives, but a few had swords or short spears.

While they were getting organized, Cross came over to talk with me.

"I've been thinking about the way things went with the goblins." He lowered his voice, looking around at the hunters that were within earshot. "It might sound crazy, but up until you killed that weird spider, I think they weren't really trying to kill anyone."

"What do you mean?" I replayed the events of the last few hours over in my head, trying to see everything from a different perspective. "You think they were holding back?"

"They could have rushed us at any time and most of the hunters would have been slaughtered. Sure, a lot of them would have been killed in the process, but that ended up happening anyway." Cross subtly lifted his chin toward Hilda. "Even the sleds that were bringing us supplies. The goblins were only herding them this way, not outright killing them."

"I don't know, some of those people would have died if we didn't have healing spells." I looked down the tunnel, thinking about how many had been wounded. "Maybe half of the people here would still be alive if it weren't for our healing spells."

"Yeah, but we *do* have healing spells, and we weren't exactly shy about using them in plain view of anyone that might be watching the whole way up here." Cross leaned in a little closer, lowering his voice. "I think the goblins wanted us in these caves. *All* of us. Not just the six or seven that would have gone on once we made it this far."

I thought about everything he was bringing up, and even though what he was saying might be more than a little paranoid, I was having a hard time disagreeing with it. "Let's say you're right. How does that change anything?"

"Nothing changes. Not right now, anyway." Cross rubbed his cursed, blackened hand. It was probably hurting from all the spellcasting he'd been doing. "It just means we need to be extra careful about what could be waiting for us deeper in these caves."

"We were going to do that anyway, but now I think our whole group needs to spread out amongst the hunters instead of us all being in the lead." I looked deeper into the caves, where no light could reach. "The hunters might need our protection more than we thought."

## CHAPTER 25

Travel by airship was nothing like Gleason had imagined. Rough winds, freezing temperatures, and an almost constant buzzing that made his molars ache had him nearly wishing for an opportunity to leap to the ground, no matter the height. Only the knowledge that the airship was eventually going to the place he wanted kept him from doing something… drastic.

When he'd woken up chained to a post on the open deck, Gleason was shocked that the crew hadn't bothered to search him, or even take away his armor and weapons. After two days of being exposed to the elements, he now understood. They didn't care enough about him to bother.

"Two degrees starboard!" The short woman–what Gleason had come to learn was something called a 'gray dwarf', a species that certainly wasn't native to his planet–had dressed herself in thick furs to combat the cold. Her ridiculous hat, with its long ear flaps and thick beaver fur, was so tall that it made her height seem nearly the same as the hulking ghoul that stood at the wheel that controlled the ship. She smacked the undead creature with the glowing rod in her hand, causing the ghoul to snarl. "Oy! Listen when your Captain speaks. I said two degrees starboard. That means turn the ship that way!"

She thumped the creature a second time, making the ghoul snap its jagged mouth at her, but it did as she commanded. Gleason had seen the same scene play out dozens of times over the last two days. He'd felt the power the rod held himself, and it was no mystery why the crew let a brute like the ghoul stand behind the wheel and bear the brunt of the woman's ire.

Every time Gleason had so much as moved too quickly, or even said a word above the volume of a whisper, the gray dwarf was suddenly behind him with the rod, beating him about the head and shoulders with it. The shocks it sent through his body completely ignored his armor, and the pain it left behind was enough to make him feel nauseated and weak for hours afterward. For a man like Gleason, there were few things worse than being tortured by a non-

179

human woman. If it weren't for the voices in his head telling him to bide his time, he probably would have done something that ended in his death within the first few hours of his captivity.

*Be strong. You come closer. Time draws near.*
*Prepare yourself. The ultimate trial awaits.*
*Prove you are worthy. Show the world.*
*Show them all. You are the true hero.*

As the ship completed its turn, Gleason couldn't hold back from shivering against the frozen winds that hit the ship from the rear. Its many black sails billowed outward, causing the deck to lurch forward as the airship caught a new burst of speed. The two rigid balloons overhead groaned at the strain, and the runes carved along the supports that kept their shape–and kept the balloons inflated–increased the buzzing that made his teeth hurt to compensate for the added stress.

Several members of the crew let out whoops of joy, while others scrambled to tighten down unsecured items that were jarred loose by the change in momentum. They were all excited about returning to their base of operations. Gleason was excited, too. His true test was coming.

"Well, human. It won't be much longer until you see how your story ends." The Captain was suddenly standing next to Gleason, her hand on his shoulder as she looked out over the mountains. Gleason suspected her incredibly fast movements were another ability bestowed by the rod she held. It wasn't like she moved quickly all the time, or had the kind of fluid grace a lethal warrior would normally exude. "Once the Destitute sees how weak you are, I'd put even odds on him adding you to his army of undead. He's always looking for more fodder to fight the demons that get by the dragon."

No matter how badly he wanted to ask questions, experience had taught him not to speak. She'd only use it as an excuse to beat him, and he'd never learn anything new while he was unconscious. Giving her the satisfaction wasn't something he wanted, no matter how badly the need to know more burned within him.

Another of the gray dwarves came over before she could continue with her torture. "Captain, the vamps want to know why we moved." This dwarf wasn't wearing nearly as many furs, but they had on a similar hat with the floppy ear flaps. It was only half the height of the Captain's hat, but Gleason still hated everything about it. It matched the beard on the sailor's face, which was a snarled mess that had grown out of control. Gleason bet himself that if the hairy mess had seen a comb or a bath in the last year, he would eat his own boot. His *metal* boot. "I told them you'd explain when you had the time."

"Useless, *stupid* undead." The Captain gave out a frustrated growl, then waved the glowing rod in her hand toward the front of the ship. "It's daylight outside. That means I'm in charge right now, not them. When it's night, they can decide where the ship goes. Those were the orders from the Destitute. That's how it works. It's not complicated."

"I know, Captain. It's the problem with the greater undead." The burly sailor shrugged his fur-covered shoulders before walking away. "They're all older than dirt. Parts of their memory are gone, brains probably eaten by worms and such. Most can remember what happened two, three centuries back, but they can't tell you what they did two or three days ago."

Grumbling to herself, the Captain followed behind her sailor, headed for the darkened hold below.

This was another thing Gleason had seen time and time again since he'd been captured. The tensions between the gray dwarves and the undead were rising the longer the airship stayed afloat. When the sun went down, the undead took over, and just before sunrise the gray dwarves would resume control. That didn't mean the undead liked having to hand over the power being in charge represented, but they had no choice. The sun would destroy the undead that were sensitive to its cleansing light. Now that Gleason knew they existed, he would serve as the sun, and sweep away the corruption they represented.

"Move, worm." A gray dwarf, this one with a beard that was much better groomed, kicked Gleason while he was distracted. Gleason hunched over to protect himself, and stayed curled in a ball as the dwarf kicked him again. "Some of us have work to do, and don't get to sit around all day. These airships don't fly themselves."

As the dwarf walked by, Gleason noticed this one looked much different than the others, and it wasn't only the neatness of the beard.

One of the things Gleason had learned by eavesdropping on the crew was that the airship he was on wasn't actually the Silver Star of legend. From the few conversations he'd overheard, this one was a smaller version only based on the designs of the older, more robust ship. He'd also heard they were working to restore the original, and most of the dwarven crew were hoping to move to it when it was up and running. They were waiting on their runesmiths to finish decoding the ancient security embedded in the ship, then it would join this one in the skies.

Gleason was pretty sure that was who had kicked him just now. One of the dwarven runesmiths. Given the lack of a ridiculous hat, and the bandoliers and belts of tools and crystals, he couldn't think of any other job the dwarf could be doing. He had seen two of them dressed like that so far, but he knew there could be more of them throughout the ship. However, he *was* sure the runesmith that kicked him was the highest-ranking of those available, because that particular dwarf was the one the Captain asked for when she had a question.

In the distance, the mountain with the crown was steadily growing closer. It was hard to tell from this far away, but Gleason thought he could see a hole near the base of the mountain large enough to fit the airship, surrounded by scaffolding that matched the craftsmanship of the airship he rode on. It had to be the goal they were aiming for, and if he knew anything about the mindset of the dwarven Captain, they wanted to reach it before nightfall. She'd most likely asked for the runesmith to see if he could help them get there faster. Since he was also a gray dwarf, he'd certainly be happy to help snub the undead in any way possible.

The runesmith was climbing a rope ladder that stretched high above the deck of the ship, trying to get to the rib-like frame of the balloons that were covered in glittering scrollwork, the runes like black diamonds flashing in the sun. He held out a stick with a green crystal on the end, completely focused on his task. There was no one paying attention to the runesmith, especially with all the other sailors still busy making sure the loose items were all tied down properly. If no one was paying attention to the runesmith, they most especially weren't paying attention to the prisoner chained up near the wheel.

Now was Gleason's chance.

He'd been planning a way for him to best disrupt the airship ever since they'd captured him. No matter what they claimed about fighting a war against demons, these were undead and non-human foreigners, and Gleason knew they needed to be cleansed just as much as the demons did. Turning them against one another was the best way he could manage it until he was free. Getting some revenge on the dwarf that just kicked him was only a bonus that made the corners of his mouth tighten in the ghost of a smile.

Gleason knew exactly what the rod felt like when it hit you, so he gathered mana for two quick spells that would mimic the shocking sensation. He'd stayed hunched over when the dwarf had kicked him, making it easy to hide the spells in his cupped hands. The overpowering buzz of the runes drowned out the weak amount of mana he gathered in each palm, and as soon as they were ready he launched the first bolt of energy at the steering ghoul's left elbow. After waiting for only a brief second, he used the second spell on the ghoul's right elbow.

The dumb undead's reaction time wasn't instant, but it was fast enough for the effect Gleason was hoping would happen. As the ghoul behind the wheel jerked the ship sharply to the left, everyone on the deck of the ship looked back at the ghoul to see why it was changing directions without orders. Sails lost tension from being perfectly aligned with the wind. Items that were still loose, or poorly tied, shifted once more. Then, the ghoul corrected itself and whipped the wheel back to the right, putting them back nearly on the original course. The ship leapt forward into the wind, and everyone stumbled at the sudden burst of speed. All the sailors saw the ghoul move without any direction, or interference from another. As if the undead was doing it on its own.

Shouts erupted from everywhere. Some sailors that hadn't finished tying down loose items had been injured by the sudden movement. One was screaming at the top of his lungs as a heavy crate was crushing his foot, causing a rush of sailors to come and help move it off.

No one had noticed the faint scream of a dangling runesmith that fell to their death as the rope ladder under him jostled unexpectedly. It would be almost an hour before anyone noticed he was missing, and at least twice that long until the ship was turned around for them to search for him. Gleason was surprised they didn't keep going, but from what he could understand, something about their culture required them to recover the body. The delay meant it would be the undead in charge of the airship when they made it back to their landing site, which infuriated the dwarves to no end.

The final result was that the ghoul behind the wheel had its skull crushed by the Captain. None of the undead were happy that one of their kind was killed without being consulted, and they universally denied ordering the ghoul to disrupt the Captain's orders. Of course, none of the dwarves that had seen the ghoul move on its own believed them.

So, tensions were at an all new high as anchors were dropped to search for the body of the runesmith, and none of the gray dwarves were willing to let the undead crew members help with the search. All it would take was a single spark to light the potential bonfire between the two sides. Fire was cleansing, and the two groups would purify the world of their stink with the help of Gleason's machinations.

Thinking Gleason wasn't a threat was a mistake.

He was happy to prove it to them.

## CHAPTER 26

Moving through the caves was harder than it should have been. There were dozens of side tunnels we had to worry about for potential ambushes, and even the main tunnel Lighter said we were supposed to take wasn't always the best choice. Cave spiders and goblins had been living here for a long time, and they had made obstacles and choke points everywhere we looked. Doubling back and searching for ways around took hours, and eventually, despite the risk, we had to take a break. As soon as we found a tunnel blocked at one end big enough to fit all of us, we stopped to rest.

"How long do you think we have?" Jess was sitting across from me with her staff across her legs. She looked exhausted, which is exactly how I was feeling. "It can't be long before those goblins outside catch up to us."

"I'm not sure they really *want* to catch up." I explained to her what Cross and I had discussed, about us being herded into the caves as a whole group. "Once their tempers have cooled, I don't know if we'll see them again. Their goal was to get all of us in here. Now that we are, I'm not sure what to expect. It can't be anything good."

"Who wants food?" Murphy interrupted us, dropping bowls of stew in our laps. How he was able to cook a quality meal in such a short period of time was a mystery only the type of people who are good at that kind of thing can understand. Since I was never a master chef, I would never know. "Better eat it while it's hot."

"Jess, you are one lucky lady. Don't let that guy get away." She murmured in agreement as I swallowed a spoonful of stew, both of us deciding food was more important than talking. The long stretch of fighting and non-stop action had seriously worn me down. The warm food was doing wonders to bring me the missing energy I needed to keep going. It wasn't the same as a good night's sleep, but I wasn't going to get one of those anytime soon.

After everyone got a chance to eat and catch their breath, we were back at it. I took the front with Jaeger and Hilda, Jess and Murphy were in the middle with Lighter, and Cross brought up the rear with Leedy. The rest of the hunters spread out between us, bows at the ready. With our three casters spread out along the line, it gave us the best chance to cover our group if there was an ambush. And somehow, we all knew there was going to be an ambush.

Deeper under the foothills we went, twisting and turning through a maze intended to disorient and distract. Old bloodstains and dirty spider webs littered the floors and walls, and the occasional scorch marks highlighted places where past travelers ventured through these cursed tunnels.

The tension in the air was thick enough I could've cut it with a knife. Everyone could feel the oppressive aura of something lurking down there with us, waiting for the right moment to strike. There weren't any more places for us to hunker down and rest, so we were forced to keep going.

Eventually, we found a juncture with several tunnels leading out of it. Cobwebs blocked several tunnels, so I quickly burned them away. Lighter sent a pair of his hunters down each of the tunnels to scout them out while the rest of us waited. It didn't take long for the first few pairs to come back with news of what they found.

"It's like they choked to death on poison, or maybe smoke." Lighter pointed at the tunnels that angled downward, deeper into the earth. "My people said there are entire goblin villages, including the young ones, completely wiped out down there. Probably hundreds of 'em, all dead."

"D-did they see what could have caused it?" Hilda couldn't help but overhear the report, and even though we were talking about the death of goblin younglings, she still reached for her lower abdomen in fear. "They didn't touch anything, did they?"

"As soon as they caught a glimpse of what it looked like down there, they turned right back. Don't you worry." Lighter motioned with his head at the pair who were standing off to the side. "Maybe you should check them out, just to be on the safe side."

"I was thinking the same thing." A quick scan with my mana showed they weren't carrying any kind of disease, and I even took a few extra seconds to take care of some strained muscles and a weak bladder issue one of them had. "They're good. No mystery diseases or anything. I'll go check it out with Leedy and see what could have caused such mass death and destruction while we wait on the others to come back."

Leedy got up from his place on the wall with a sigh. He was just as tired as everyone else, but the former corporal was good at hiding it. The two of us traveled down the narrow tunnel until it hit a sharp bend, where a broken gate lay in pieces on the floor.

"Does it look like our people did this?" Leedy knelt down and looked at the broken fragments of wood. He held up a smaller piece to better see it in the lantern light and answered his own question. "No, this wasn't us. It's at least a few days old. Maybe older. There's been heavy things walking over this, squishing the fibers flat even after it was broken."

"So, after the goblins were killed, something else besides us came down here." I could feel the hair on the back of my neck trying to stand on end, like something was watching me. "That can't be good."

"Normally I'd say some type of corpse-eating undead, like a ghoul or maybe even a white walker, but there haven't been any undead around here so far." Leedy swung his lantern around, looking for tracks of any kind. "There's no telling what it could be if it isn't an undead."

"A white walker?" I waved away the question, not caring about the answer right now. "Let's just get in there and see what killed all these goblins, and make sure it can't do the same thing to us."

We rounded the corner ready to fight, but there wasn't anything waiting for us. Instead, all we found were more broken timbers, and scraps of clothing laid out in the middle of the walkway. As if there were once shacks lining the sides of the tunnel, but something had knocked them all down to get at the juicy treats that were still inside.

Farther down the cave opened into a small cavern that was barely big enough to be considered anything more than a wide spot in the tunnel. That's where we found all the bodies.

The far side of the cavern was an artificial wall of stone and timber that must have served as a way to keep the goblins safe from whatever creatures lived deeper underground. It was also what got them killed.

I managed to inspect the bodies and the back wall without having to disturb much before I stumbled upon the culprit. Stains around their nostrils and mouths showed signs of smoke inhalation. The base of their back wall showed similar markings. A dense, heavy smoke had settled into their little cavern, and the wall had trapped it from going any deeper. None of the goblins had managed to get away before succumbing to the silent killer that came for them.

Given that most of the bodies were still inside their little huts, it was probably their night cycle when it happened. Most of them probably went to sleep and simply never woke up. They were stacked in this place like sardines, so the death toll was at least in the mid-hundreds. Given the fact it was just starting to smell especially putrid, I'd say it was only a few days ago. Three, maybe four at the most.

"James?" I pulled my head out of a goblin home to see Leedy holding up a piece of a broken hut. It had a very distinctive hole punched through the end of it, along with a shred of spider silk trailing from the bottom corner. "Does that remind you of anything?"

"The tip of a spider leg. A big spider." The trail of clothing scraps took on a whole new meaning. They were the clothes picked off the bodies the spiders had taken with them. "Leedy, we need to get out of here."

"You don't have to tell me twice." He tossed aside the scrap of wood and took a moment to pull out his sword. As if to answer the act of aggression, faint chittering sounds came from the other side of the wall, and the shadows around us appeared to grow darker. Suddenly, the goblin construction didn't seem to be nearly as sturdy as it did before, and the few gaps at the top were much more spider-sized than I first realized. Leedy held up his lantern as high as he could, but the light still didn't reach the very top of the cavern ceiling. "I don't like this."

"Me either." I pulled out my mace, and dumped enough mana into it to cause the starmetal to start glowing a bright blue. "Take the lead. I'll cover the rear."

The two of us made it out of the goblin cavern without seeing anything, but we could *hear* the steady clack of sharp legs coming up behind us. Lots and lots of legs. After passing the sharp turn where the broken gate was, we started running. Every time I looked back, I couldn't see anything, but I could feel something staring back at me. The shadows might hide them, but Leedy and I could sense them. These were no ordinary cave spiders. I tossed a few fireballs and wind blades behind us, and the shadows seemed to swallow them whole. Whether it was just a visual effect, or an actual spell nullification, it didn't matter. Now was not the time to stop and find out.

When we got back to the area with all the tunnel junctures, everyone was on their feet, alert and ready to fight. They had heard us coming and were waiting for whatever was making us run.

Lighter had his hunters stacked and ready to let loose a flight of arrows the moment we were clear, so Leedy and I dove to the side. The sound of so many arrows flashing by made a whooshing sound that was music to my ears.

Chittering screams came from farther back in the tunnel, and some of the grasping shadows seemed to retreat. I tossed a few more wind blades with my mace as a focus this time, adding to the projectiles headed down the cave. After a few more volleys, the hunters stopped, and we all waited to see if anything would come charging out after us. When nothing happened a few minutes later, we all breathed a sigh of relief.

"What was that thing?" Jess walked over holding out a canteen for us. It wasn't as nice as the wineskin Cross carried, but it was better than nothing. "It sounded awful."

"It was awful." Leedy took a drink before passing it over to me. "We never actually saw it, but it had to have been more of those crazy spiders. Only these could control shadows, and eat spells."

"No, I don't think they 'ate' my spells." I passed back the canteen after having a drink. "Their control over shadow is so complete that it includes mana and sound as well as light. Everything disappears when it goes into their shadow. There is no way to know what happens to it from the outside, one way or the other. I'm pretty sure my spells went through fine. They just dodged them, or they're tough enough to take the few unfocused hits that managed to hit them. That's why all those arrows did the trick. It was too many for them to dodge, and the hunters' bows pack enough punch to really cause some damage."

"Well, that's not quite as scary." Jess wiped her hands off on her pants, as if she'd touched something she didn't like. "Still, I'd rather not mess with spiders like that if I didn't have to."

"Agreed." Leedy nodded emphatically, clearly not happy about the thought of facing the spiders again. "Let's get out of here. They can have the dead goblins. I sure don't want them."

"I'll talk to Lighter. Hopefully, his people found where to go while we were playing tag with the eight-legged freaks so we can get moving again." I had a feeling we didn't want to be here in a room with all kinds of openings when those things came back, especially if they brought friends.

Because no matter what we wanted, I had a feeling we'd be seeing those things again.

Really, really soon.

## CHAPTER 27

"Two of my scout teams ain't come back yet." Lighter was obviously doing his best to not freak out. I couldn't blame the guy. It had been a rough day for everyone, and this was certainly not his usual kind of party. "Both of 'em have experience. They ain't lost."

"Which tunnels did they go down?" I moved to where he pointed, noting they were the two that had been covered with the thickest layers of webbing we'd burned away when we got there. Both tunnels angled upward, meaning either one could be the way out. "Any chance they might have found a way to the surface, and they're just scouting it a bit more before coming back?"

Lighter shook his head in the negative. "All of 'em had the same instructions. Go for a certain amount of time, then come on back. The way we always do it. That's why we know the other tunnels ain't no good. It's gotta be one of them two."

"Damn." I had a bad feeling I already knew what happened to them. "It would have taken more time, but I should have scouted all of these myself. Or at least split them up with Cross. Jess should have been enough to protect the room by herself."

"Scouts gotta scout." Lighter said it like he was some wise sage dropping a knowledge bomb on me. "That's what scouts do. Scout stuff. Sometimes, it don't go all that great. That's part of what scouts do, too. We can't let you folks do all the work." He looked down and scuffed his feet on the cave floor. "Was just supposed to be goblins down here, anyway. We can run faster'n they can any day, even in these caves."

"I understand, but now we know there's more than goblins to worry about. We still need to decide which of these to take." I took a few steps into one of the tunnels, trying to see if I could feel a hint of fresh air or any other kind of clue. Instead, I heard the faint echo of a familiar chittering sound. "Whelp, I don't think it's this one. Let's try the other one."

"What about our hunters?" Jaeger popped up out of nowhere, the big man somehow still able to camouflage himself in the caves. "Are we going to try and get them?"

191

"I hate to tell you this my friend, but there's no way they're still alive." I grabbed him by the shoulder to pull him back, and had to put a surprising amount of force behind it. Dude was swole. "I could hear the sounds of spiders, but no one was fighting them."

"They might be hiding from them, or injured too badly to fight." Jaeger said it matter-of-factly, as if it was a foregone conclusion the hunters were still alive somehow. "I'll go and save them. You'll see."

Once again, I was forcibly reminded of how young Jaeger truly was. His size made it easy to forget he was most likely barely pushing twenty, and life hadn't really punched him in the face yet. He'd almost lost his father, but I'd come by and saved him. Now he was under the impression that everyone would magically walk away from every conflict. If only things really worked like that.

"I'll go with you. In case you need some help."

Jaeger gave me a nod of thanks, and the two of us let Lighter know what we were doing before we went into the tunnel that I knew could only have a bad ending. From the look the older man gave me, he knew it too.

We stumbled upon two fresh blood stains after finding a series of web-encrusted side tunnels. The side tunnels were narrow enough that the only way Jaeger or I could get through them would be to crawl, and that wasn't something either of us wanted to do, even if it was to find the missing scouts. There were no signs of a struggle, and nothing to hint at which one the hunters could have gone down. I started burning out the webs I could see, causing an acrid smoke to cling to the ceiling. It wasn't generating a reaction from the spiders I thought were in the area, so I started increasing the air flow into each tunnel, forcing the flames to carry farther and get hotter.

Still, there was no reaction. Now I was thinking the chittering sounds I'd heard earlier were from the spiders leaving the area. "Jaeger, I think the spiders took them somewhere else. Unless you want to crawl up each of these tunnels one by one to double check and make sure, we can pretty much confirm they're gone."

"No." Jaeger started walking up the tunnel, farther than the point the hunters had ever made it. "I'll search more this way. Maybe they were wounded, and they're hiding–"

"Jaeger. They're gone." He froze at my statement, not wanting to face the reality staring right at him. "If they were wounded and ran, there would be a blood trail. At least a few drops. You know this, probably better than I do."

"Spiders… they don't always kill their prey, right? Sometimes, they wrap them up, and save them for later." Jaeger knelt next to the two splotches of blood. "There isn't enough blood here to be a lethal amount. If the spiders carried them off, we could still save them."

"That's true about some kinds of spiders, but we don't know if that's true for this kind, Jaeger. Don't get your hopes up. Focus on saving who you can save." A dozen memories of how I learned that lesson the hard way tried to flood my mind's eye, but I forced them back. Now wasn't the time. "We don't know where their nest could be, and we have to prioritize saving the people we know are still alive. People like Hilda." He jolted like I'd shocked him with a lightning bolt. It might have been a low blow to use her like that in this situation, but desperate times call for desperate measures. "Got it?"

"Yeah. I got it." Jaeger gave one last look down the tunnel and turned around, his features harder than the stone surrounding us. "Let's go."

Lighter didn't even bother coming up and asking if we'd found them when we returned. He could see it on our faces that things hadn't gone well. Instead, he started gathering his people and ensuring they were ready to leave. In less than five minutes we were moving out.

The second tunnel contained more rubble and debris than any of the others our group had traveled by an order of magnitude. Scraps of old webbing, shreds of clothing, broken armor remnants, and pieces of shattered weapons marked a trail of ruin that twisted through piles of shattered stone and trickling water. Most of what we saw looked like it came from orc origins, but there were plenty of goblin bits and bobs mixed in. The stench of old blood and layered stains across most of the surfaces only added to the ambiance of 'fun' and 'adventure' these caves were really giving off.

"I don't like the look of this." Leedy was walking next to me at the front of our line, his hand nervously clasped around the hilt of the sword sheathed on his belt. "Where did all of this come from? We haven't seen nearly enough orcs running around the rest of the foothills for there to be this much... *stuff* left by them."

"Remember how the ground was all torn up outside from a battle?" I kicked a broken spear tip out of the way. It had been bent completely sideways, almost like the orc using it had tried to stick the metal tip into a granite wall. "I think we're looking at what happened to the ones that got pushed into the caves."

"Like how *we* got pushed into the caves?" Leedy unsheathed his sword. "You know what? I'm starting to think waiting for you in Greendown might have been the better option."

"You're probably right." I stopped to shift a suspiciously placed pile of scrap out of the path with my foot, and uncovered another splotch of blood. Unlike the others, it was human. And fresh. "Damn it. That's not good."

"The other pair of scouts?" Leedy kept his voice down, trying to ensure the hunters behind us didn't overhear. "That looks like a lot of blood."

"It's too much blood for one person to lose and still be alive. If it's from two people, and they're still alive, neither one of them is in good shape." I used my mace to scrape the debris back over the blood. There was no need to destroy the hope and motivation of the whole line of hunters that were about to walk right by this point. Enough of them knew something bad had happened, so I didn't figure drawing attention to it was a good idea. "More than that, whoever–or *whatever*–took them down, tried to hide the evidence of where they attacked. That's a level of intelligence I don't like to see in my enemies. Especially if they're supposed to be giant spiders."

We both looked around, trying to see where the ambush could have come from. There were too many spots where shadows cast by piles of rubble could hide a spider, or three. Especially if you only had one or two lanterns, like the scout team had. We had far more than that with our group, so the chances of being ambushed in the same way were greatly diminished, but they were certainly still there.

I was especially worried about the last third of our group situated between Jess and Cross, where Lighter had put most of the hunters that'd been injured. They were healed enough to keep going and contribute in a fight, but they were obviously lagging more than anyone else. A predator would see them as the weak link, and target them first. It was also the group that had Hilda in it, so Jaeger was there as the only visibly strong spot.

"Leedy, I want you to go back to the group between Jess and Cross and link up with Jaeger. Between the two of you, I'm hoping we can keep any attacks from happening." I gave him one of the smoke grenades from my ruck, along with all the fancy crossbow bolts I still had bouncing around. I wasn't using mine, but he seemed to like shooting his recently. "These might help if things go sour." He wasn't happy about leaving me by myself, but Leedy didn't argue. I think he could recognize the weak spot in our line too.

As I started us off again, I focused on using instinctive casting with earth magic to try and feel for any hidden tunnels or hiding spots around us. Flexing the new kind of magic on purpose instead of by reflex was like exercising a new muscle you didn't know you had. Or, more like figuring out how to wiggle your ears. The muscles to do it were always there, but using them in such a specific way felt unnatural and stilted. Still, by practicing it now, I was hoping to have it mastered for when I needed it in a fight.

It was a good thing I was trying out my new abilities, because it tipped me off to the tiny tunnel hidden behind a pile of conveniently placed armor scraps. There was no way a spider large enough to be a genuine threat could be hiding inside such a small space. A house cat would have problems crawling inside, however it could certainly hide plenty of little spiders to spy on us. I knew all too well that a swarm of little bugs could overwhelm a group just the same as big bugs. It had been on world nine with centipedes in a jungle instead of spiders in a cave, but the lesson was the same. Don't underestimate the little guys.

Flexing my mana without having to use a gesture was definitely a freeing feeling, made all the sweeter by the results of my efforts. Instinctive casting allowed me to slam close the tunnel, like I was a teenager slamming the door on my parents after they took away my phone. It was dramatic, and it made a lot of noise. The column of mashed bug guts that shot out of the tunnel proved I was right to worry about what had been waiting for us. It would have taken a *lot* of spiders to make that much gunk volcano out of the cave wall. Whether they were spies or an ambush, it didn't matter now. They were goo.

A series of keening wails echoed down the tunnel, originating from the direction we needed to go. Apparently, the mommy and daddy spiders weren't happy about their little ones getting crushed. I didn't feel a shred of empathy for the murderous arachnids.

Lighter moved up next to me and looked over the smear left on the ground before he echoed my inner thoughts. "I think you went and made them mad." Then he looked back to where the blood from his scouts was barely covered by debris. "Good. I want 'em mad."

"Me too, Lighter." I pulled free my mace and started pumping mana into it. "And now we know where their nest is."

## CHAPTER 28

Rounding the corner into what had to be the nest chamber revealed a room straight out of a nightmare. Webbing coated nearly everything. Cocoons hung from the ceilings by the dozen. Tiny spiders with pin-prick red eyes crawled everywhere, dripping purple venom from needle fangs. Not-so-tiny spiders ranging between the size of a large dog to a horse, all with glowing coals for eyes, skittered in and out of the light, trying to position themselves to pounce as soon as the invaders to their lair dropped their guard. And in the back of the cave, hanging from the ceiling like a waiting portent of doom ready to slam down on any fool stupid enough to venture close, was the largest spider I had ever seen. It was big enough it could smack around a school bus for funzies, and then snack on anyone who fell out like they were meaty little treats. Snap into a slim-jim.

When faced with a hall of horrors stuffed to the gills with spiders, my knee-jerk reaction is to go with the classics. Kill it with fire.

So, that's what I did.

I started casting fireballs with my off hand as fast as I could, while simultaneously using my mace like it was a flamethrower. The relatively fresh webbing wasn't nearly as flammable as I was hoping for. It still burned with enough focused attention.

The chittering screams from the spiders created a chorus we used as our marching cadence while stomping into the cavern. Hunters spread out to either side of me while we advanced, picking targets of opportunity through the flames. Lighter and Jaeger did their best to keep them organized, but the bloodlust for revenge was in full swing. They wanted payback for their missing friends, and they were going to get it.

Jess had to focus on the little spiders that kept trying to drop from the ceiling onto our heads. We were all lucky she noticed them crawling around up there before they could bite someone. Their needle-like fangs would have easily pierced the thin armor the hunters wore, and the venom they carried sizzled and popped against anything it touched. Using her staff, Jess was able to turn the stone walls of the cave against the tiny hazards. She made the rock surface come to life, and it swallowed the creatures whole as they approached our group.

Murphy used his halberd to keep the spiders from overwhelming our left side. There were stone outcroppings that allowed dog-sized spiders to get close enough to be a threat, but he was too swift and strong to allow any of the monsters through. He worked like a machine, reaping limbs and heads as soon as they poked their way into the open.

Before anything else could develop in front, Leedy had to pair up with Cross to stop an ambush to our rear. A flood of man-sized black spiders came pouring in from the tunnel behind us, closing off any chances of retreat. Leedy was able to hold them at the chokepoint of the tunnel entrance, with Cross casting spells over his shoulder. Everyone else was pushed completely into the cavern just as I burned enough space for us to all stand in an area without webbing. It was an island of bare stone in a sea of webs that undulated from the movement of the creatures that made them.

"Circle up! Everyone, circle up and help defend one another! We've got to–" Lighter's shout was cut off by a giant blur of motion that flew past all of us fast enough to make our clothing ripple from its passage. When I looked over to see why he wasn't coordinating his hunters anymore, all I saw was a single boot on the ground to mark where he'd been standing. The boot wasn't empty. His severed foot was still inside.

Lighter was gone.

"Jaeger, you're gonna have to take over." I let loose an especially large flare of fire to give us some breathing room, and a few seconds to figure out what happened. The massive spider in the back of the cavern was gone too, which I took as a clue. "Something just took Lighter. I'll try and get him back."

"Huh? Took him? What do you mean?" Jaeger glanced over his shoulder and saw the boot on the ground and grimaced. "Okay, forget circling up! We're pushing forward! It's time to show these monsters who's boss!"

The hunters let loose a ragged cheer, and they started laying into the arachnids at twice the pace they were before. Hilda was at

Jaeger's side, dual-wielding torches to burn away webbing for him, the two of them taking over as the centerpiece of the assault.

While Jaeger was shouting, I used a nearby outcropping as a springboard and launched myself deeper into the cavern. I knew the bus-sized spider was the only outlier that could have taken Lighter. Considering it'd disappeared from the back of the cavern at the same time, I felt like it was the only viable option. If something that huge could move *that* insanely fast, it didn't bode well for our group. We'd be picked off one by one, with no chance to stop it.

Unless I put an end to the monster first.

There were only a few places the giant spider could have gone with Lighter, so I picked the closest tunnel big enough to fit its size and leapt for it. Playing jackrabbit was the only way to get through the web-covered room. The spider silk was sticky enough that an unenhanced person would struggle to pull themselves free if they touched it, and there were little ones with their needle fangs hiding in the layers that covered everything like a blanket of snow. I didn't have time to burn through it all, or act like a snowplow.

As soon as I landed in front of the tunnel opening, it erupted with a flood of tiny spiders intent on devouring me. A fireball at such close range wasn't normally good for the caster, but I didn't mind the burnt eyebrows. Once I had a split second to funnel the spell through my mace, I flamethrowered the tunnel entrance hard enough to slag the stone around the edges of the opening. Screw those creepy little bastards.

Several larger spiders tried to pounce on me while I was destroying the tunnel that must have held their young. Thank goodness the buckshot rounds I'd made for my wrist gun were so effective. The echoing booms of the shots going off stunned the monsters, and seeing their buddies get blown in half caused the other big ones to hesitate.

Instinctive casting helped with boosting my earth mana to slam close the slagged tunnel and not cave in anything else. As long as there were no exits on the other end, the heat would ensure if I missed something, it would get cooked nice and crispy. There wouldn't be a next generation of spiders from this hole in the ground. While I was reloading my wrist gun, I looked over to see how the others were doing.

Murphy had built himself a little fort of spider corpses, and he was using it to keep a couple of wounded people secure. His halberd was the perfect weapon for the job, giving him the reach to lean out over the wall of dead spiders and hack away at any arachnids dumb enough to try him.

Leedy and Cross had finished off what was left of the spider ambush and only Leedy had stayed to make sure a second wave of spiders didn't show up to repeat the maneuver. Cross had re-joined the hunters, and was helping them push further across the chamber. It had only been a minute or two, so they hadn't gotten very far. Jaeger and Hilda were pushing them hard, but they were only human.

Jess was still providing overhead cover, while also slowly shaping the roof of the cavern to make it harder for the spiders to get any closer. Smoothing it out and sending ripples along the surface made it impossible for the bugs to hang on, so they fell like rain before they could even get halfway across the chamber. Given enough time, she might turn the whole thing into an upside down bowl.

Once I was reloaded, I jumped to the next tunnel. I could tell right away it wasn't the right one, so I tossed in a fireball and hopped again. Right into the blurring claws of a spider-shaped freight train that came out of nowhere.

*"Killing the brood of a Demon Prince?! You will suffer a thousand deaths!"*

The screeching of the giant spider was like nails on a chalkboard, knife scraping on a plate, squealing truck brakes, and a dental drill digging away at a tooth all at the same time. If the volume was turned up to twenty on a scale of one to ten.

If it weren't for Cross and Jess, our entire group would have been overrun at that moment. Everyone was driven to their knees by the sound, some even knocked unconscious by the auditory assault. Our two magic casters somehow held it together long enough to keep everyone alive.

Jess raised a solid wall in front of the spiders that had charged while the hunters weren't killing them. She roared in rage, fighting to overcome some internal limit, and crystalline spikes erupted from the ground in front of the wall, piercing through the tough carapace of even the horse-sized spiders.

Cross had been affected much worse, and only managed to muster a great gust of wind that blew back the spiders trying to eat Murphy and the wounded he was defending. Still, it was enough to keep everyone alive, and it gave the stoic halberdier time to recover.

As for me, I was mostly concerned with the two spider limbs that had pierced my body. One had gone completely through my upper right thigh, barely missing my femur, and the other was lodged in my left shoulder. Somehow the tips of its legs carried a kind of paralyzing venom that was strong enough that in only a second it had made it hard to breathe, and I already couldn't feel my arm or leg. Both still twitched when I tried to move them, but the venom was fighting back against the healing spell I was already casting.

*"Come and learn why the name Demon Prince Makadee is feared throughout all the Hells, invader."* The giant talking spider, which was apparently a demon prince–yay me for finding a demon prince spider–lifted me up to stare at me with its rows of hateful, glowing red eyes. *"Perhaps I'll show you the sweet release of death after a hundred lifetimes of pain."*

Being this close to the thing, the stench of brimstone, ozone, and rot was nearly overwhelming. Everything about it was overwhelming. Its size, smells, sounds, speed, venom, this was one enemy that might be beyond me, if anything just because I couldn't even catch it.

Except, it had caught me. And I really appreciated it.

My starmetal mace flared as I dumped every bit of energy I could into it, using both my new and old mana channels. Not even the otherworldly metal of my mace could contain the myriad forms of power, and black and white lightning crackled along its length, charring the knuckles of my hand.

"Probably should have numbed the other arm, bug." I jacked him in the face with it so hard it cratered the whole side of the spider's head in. It reared back in a keening wail, dripping exploded eyeball juice and exposing its throat region.

So, I smashed that in too.

The demon flung me away from it, and I slammed face-first into the wall right next to where Leedy was still standing guard over the entrance. I could feel dozens of broken bones, along with the venom trying its best to kill me by paralyzing my heart and lungs. Both my left arm and right leg had nearly been torn off by the whipping motion of being thrown so hard, and there was no doubt I had a nasty concussion. Not to mention my poor armor was a wreck again.

"You need a hand? That looked like it hurt." Leedy peered into the new crater my body had made, wincing at what he saw. "I could get one of the others to help with something like this…"

"Just." I peeled my face off the stone, doing my best to hold in the groan of pain that tried to escape. "Give me a minute. I'll be okay."

"That big demon spider took off running. If you're going to catch it, you better hurry." Leedy reached in and grabbed the leg that was still mostly in one piece and started pulling me out. "Everybody else is starting to recover from its voice. I think the other spiders are scared you hurt the big one, so now's our chance for a counter-attack."

"You guys go on ahead. I'll catch up." I was healing myself as fast as I could, but it was a struggle to push out the demonic venom. "It's gonna take me a bit to fix all this."

Another wail of pain and rage echoed from somewhere in the distance, causing the whole cavern to shake. The shadows from the entrance tunnel suddenly seemed to deepen in response, and they started to stretch toward the light that was cast off from the lanterns Leedy had scattered around the opening.

Leedy shook his head and yanked me out even faster, which didn't feel very good. "I don't think we've got time for that. You'll have to heal on the move. The kind that can manipulate shadows are coming, and I don't think laying around is the best idea."

"Get Jess. Have her. Close the. Tunnel." Talking was getting harder for me. I couldn't catch my breath. It was a mix of both blood loss and the venom. "Stop them. Here."

"There's no time, James. I'm sorry, I know this is going to hurt." Leedy threw me over his shoulder and took off running.

He was right. It hurt. A lot.

Behind us, the shadows swallowed the lanterns.

The demon spiders' casters had arrived.

## CHAPTER 29

Leedy tossed my limp form to the ground next to the other wounded, which didn't feel very good. He ran off to talk with the others, while the cavern behind us slowly filled with darkness. I hoped whatever they were discussing was a really great plan, because things weren't looking very good for us.

The faint forms of hundreds of red-eyed spiders the size of large dogs were faintly visible as they phased in and out of the shadows. A few dozen bigger ones shimmered along the edges, pushing the magic of the demon spiders against the light cast by our lanterns and torches. Those must be the casters. Their control of dark mana was impressive, but they didn't seem to have any actual spells. It was the only good news I could see about them so far.

Either way, there were a *lot* of demons. Probably the remainder of what hid in the cave complex was now charging in to save the prince I'd smashed in the face. The giant spider was still occasionally wailing and cursing somewhere out of sight in some side chamber. That did cheer me up some. I had to fix myself if we had a chance to make it out of here, so I closed my eyes and got to work.

Damage was everywhere, so I had been spreading healing mana throughout my body in an attempt to stay awake and alive. Blood loss and venom were the two biggest issues, so I started focusing more of the healing energy on producing more blood, and burning out the venom. Still, the venom barely reacted, spreading further and deeper through my body. My mana generator even felt sluggish, meaning the venom was affecting me metaphysically as well.

Since I wasn't getting anywhere with the venom, I decided to focus on what I could fix. The rest of my body started to mend faster, and that's when things changed.

Healing myself finally turned a corner when the concussion I was suffering from cleared up. Brain damage always slowed me down, so when it was gone I managed to truly focus on the venom trying to stop my heart. Now that I could really see what was happening, I realized that attempting to *burn* the *demonic venom* out of my body was about as stupid as you could get. Of course fire wouldn't work.

Once I swapped to ice mana and froze the venom, I was able to push it out of my body and get to work finishing fixing everything else. It didn't take long before I was back to normal, ready to fight some demon spiders. Which was good, because they were almost on us.

I opened my eyes to see I was getting dragged on a makeshift stretcher by a hunter with an empty quiver. Behind me was Cross, who was the last person in line. He was using a mix of fireballs, wind blades, and spearpoint to keep the fast encroaching spiders off our back.

Leading the group was Jess, who had certainly reached a new threshold in her power as an earth mage. Her staff was a swirling blur as darts of crystal shot from the cave ceiling and floor, splattering any spider stupid enough to get in the way of our group as we made our way across the cavern toward the largest tunnel opening. It was also the only tunnel the spiders weren't retreating into. Hopefully, that meant it led to the surface.

On either side of Jess were Murphy and Leedy, who kept the few spiders dumb or brave enough to try and jump us away from the distracted earth mage. The rest of the hunters carried torches and lanterns, their only job to burn away the spider silk that was in the way. Jaeger and Hilda were the only exceptions, both of them ready with their bows to help support either the front or rear of the group if the demonic spiders decided to push their luck. They must have gathered all the remaining arrows to fill their quivers, because everyone else was empty.

"Finally! Took you long enough." Cross lunged forward and speared a shadow mage spider that tried taking advantage of him when he had turned to speak with me. "I was beginning to wonder if that big spider had actually managed to kill you off."

"Not likely. This isn't my first time facing demons." Memories from both my second and sixth worlds flashed through my mind. Fighting the demons on world six was why I had a Paladin class. I looked off to the side, where I knew the spider that called itself a demon prince had run to hide in a side chamber.

I could just leave. I could go with everyone else, and allow the filth to live another day. That meant it would rebuild its forces, and like a cancer, spread, killing everything it came in contact with. For the first time in a while, I felt the Mantle of a Judge settle over me. Even if I wanted to–which I didn't–my job as a Judge wouldn't let me leave something so abhorrent behind. The ancient forces that gave me its power were of the same mind. "Something for you to remember, Cross. Demons don't get Judged. They just get Executed."

With that, I leapt for the entrance to the chamber where the demon had retreated. The moment I crossed the threshold, I was hit by a wave of energy that had been contained by a set of hidden runes carved into the ceiling, walls, and ground. It was so strong, I had to lean into it to take a step forward. Then I got a ding from my system, and a screen popped up.

---

**Quest Update!**
**Unique Upgrade Quest: Find ten places of power - 4/10**
**-Absorb the power built up at the location to increase your level.**

**\*Note - This place of power has been claimed by a being from another plane. Defeat it to absorb the available energy. (Darkness Mana Aspect 50%/Earth Mana Aspect 35%/Water Mana Aspect 10%/Venom Mana Aspect 3%/Light Mana Aspect 1%/Demonic Mana Aspect 1%). Foreign Mana contamination present. Disturbing it may lead to unexpected consequences. Proceed with caution.**

---

The demonic mana must be the contamination it was warning about. It had surely come here to use the increased mana to help it heal the injuries I'd given it, and who knows how long it had been siphoning off the power in this area to grow stronger. Right now, it wasn't something I could focus on, because the demon spider had noticed the moment I entered.

It was hanging from the ceiling, all of its burning eyes focused on me. The chamber was littered with the bones of its past victims, and I could see the drained and shrunken bodies of Lighter and the four scouts we'd lost earlier stacked up like logs along the far wall.

Seeing them only made me angrier, the Mantle of Judge settled heavier on my shoulders, and the blue glow of my mace burned brighter than the orange flames of the torch I held over my head. "You die today, Prince Malarkey. Or whatever your name is."

*"Prince Makadee! Fool. You entered the place where I am most powerful, and now you will learn why my enemies never forget my name! It's whispered with fear across–"*

Whatever he was going to say was cut off by the three empowered bolo rounds that cut off most of the legs on his right side. The thin chain of the rounds cut through the spider's tough natural armor with surprisingly little resistance. Blue spider blood that stank of brimstone spurted from the stumps, tainted with streaks of demonic black and red. The severed limbs clattered to the ground, like they were a bunch of giant broom sticks dropped by a clumsy janitor the size of a giant.

Stupid demon didn't know it wasn't the time for monologuing. It was time for fighting.

Before the demon prince could emit a scream of pain or protest, I jumped and smashed it in the mouth with my mace, unleashing the pent-up mana held within like an invisible fist as it crushed the spider against the back wall of the cavern. The force of my hit held in place for a moment. Taking advantage, I used the unpowered mace to hit it over and over again as fast as I could, landing blows in places wherever it looked like it would hurt the most. Eyes, fangs, broken parts, leaking pieces, and any glowy bits that might be important, they all got a taste of my rage.

The image of Lighter and the other four hunters was a never-ending snapshot in my mind's eye, fueling my fury. Faces of children and wives left back at the village mingled amongst the withered corpses of the courageous warriors stacked behind me. My Judge's Mantle reveled in its role as an Executioner. This was what it was created for, what the foundational purpose of a Judge truly was. To right the wrongs the powerful commit against those who cannot defend themselves, and punish those who have gone beyond the limits of what the universe sees as acceptable. For the strong to kill the weak for nothing more than fun, or quick transitional power? Yes, the Mantle was *made* for this moment.

The demon spider finally started to tumble free from where I had it wedged against the wall, so I helped it along by using my *Shield Bash* skill combined with my knuckle dusters to super punch it straight down in the head. Prince Malarkey cracked the stone floor when he impacted, sending his diseased and rotting blood splattering across the cavern.

Recoil from the punch slammed me against the cave ceiling, so I kicked off and used the extra boost to my advantage. Pulling free my magic-eating ninjatō from its sheath, I buried it to the hilt at the base of the spider's head. The blade wasn't long enough to kill the demon in one blow, but whatever magical boost the demon prince was getting from being in the ley line nexus would certainly be negated by my sword. Checkmate, shitstick. Now it was just a matter of time.

I jumped down in front of the giant spider to start charging my mace and reload my wrist gun. A few more hits from the mace should be enough to finish it off.

*"You! What have you done?!"* The demon tried to stand, but could only drunkenly stagger to one side. It was missing too many limbs, so it had to lean forward onto its version of a shoulder to look at me. The glowing red eyes that still worked were flickering wildly, like a broken television screen. Mister Demon Prince was trying to draw power to heal himself, but it wasn't working. It looked at me, and I think for the first time it realized it might actually die. *"If you kill me, you won't know where to find my brother, or the dragon, or the gateway, or what the undead and their coalition with the other factions are truly doing with those–"*

That was a lot of interesting information. It was tempting to stop and ask what it was talking about. Then, in my peripheral vision, I saw Lighter and the other hunters again.

My mace crunched into the side of the demon's head, shutting it up. Since *Shield Bash* had come off cooldown, I used it to punch it in the face, snapping off a fang and sending more rotten blood flying. I didn't stop, continuously smashing the spider's head and face over and over again until it was nothing more than a caustic clump of organic matter. I knew the demon wouldn't be coming back when my system gave me a ding with a quest update.

---

**Quest Update!**
**Unique Upgrade Quest: Find ten places of power - 4/10**
**-This place of power is no longer claimed. Absorb the power built up at the location to increase your level.**

---

While it might have been a wiser choice to question the demon about the things it had been talking about, like more demon princes, dragons, and undead coalitions, I wasn't willing to give it any concessions for the information. It would have wanted to bargain for its life, and I wasn't willing to do so. Not only that, any information would have been suspect. Demons lie, and there was no reason to believe anything it said was the truth. And finally, I really, *really* wanted to kill that thing for Lighter and the hunters that had died at its whim. My Mantle demanded no less, and I was in full agreement with it.

After cleaning off the worst of the spider gore, it was time to absorb the place of power. I could tell this one wasn't nearly as powerful as the crater near the tree village, or the one under Greendown. It was about on par with the first one I'd found in the wilds of the forest, or the one the lich had subverted for its own use. I might actually have a chance at keeping this one under control, which was a good thing considering the contamination of demonic mana it had. There was absolutely no way I wanted to absorb that into my body or mana generator.

At first, I didn't see where I could connect with the place of power. Then I noticed a faint light emitting from under the body of the demon prince. I used a stream of fire to turn most of the remains to ash, and blew it away. Through the cracks in the ground, I saw where the light was coming from. A quick use of willpower reinforced by mana activated instinctive casting, and a section of stone crumbled out of the way.

Layers of fine crystals, like the inside of a geode, were everywhere. There was no specific focus point like I'd seen in other places of power. At a guess, it probably meant the ley lines that created this one weren't as thick, or maybe they weren't as clogged as the other intersections had been. Or, maybe they were deeper underground, and I was only seeing the very edge of what was visible. If it was the last option, I might have problems. If I tapped it and there was a flood of power hiding under a thin veneer, I wouldn't be able to control it.

Right now there wasn't time to hesitate. It was either take the risk, or leave. If the demon had been less cocky and more proactive, this fight would have been a lot harder for me. I still needed to get stronger.

I reached out with my hands, and my will, and grabbed for the power sitting in front of me.

## CHAPTER 30

Gleason sprinted through the trees, doing his best to get away from the wreckage and flames behind him. The chains binding his wrists and ankles together made it impossible for him to run. He could still manage a ground-eating shuffle that quickly put distance between himself and the crashed airship.

His plans had come to fruition much faster than he'd expected. Gleason had asked one of his undead jailers a few questions about the statements the dwarves had made regarding the 'weaknesses' of their undead crewmembers. Of course, the gray dwarves were off the airship looking for their missing crewmate, and couldn't refute anything he said. If the undead took the questions to be inflammatory and smacked him around a bit, it was a small price to pay for the seed of discord it had planted. Word had quickly spread amongst the more intelligent of the greater undead crew, and soon they were seething with anger over perceived slights from the airship's day shift.

While the dwarves are away, the mice will play.

Once the gray dwarves brought the body of their fallen runemaster back onboard, it was clear neither group was in a generous mood toward the other. All it took were a few snide comments from the undead about the frailty of the dwarves, and fighting had broken out.

Both the Captain and the senior vampire had broken up the skirmish, but the damage was already done. The leadership couldn't be everywhere, and tensions boiled over again and again until it culminated in an explosion below decks only miles from the landing site they were heading toward. The ship portion had managed to land without serious damage, but the bags and the enchanted frames that held them were left burning across a great swath of forest.

A section had fallen on the ship as well, setting several of the sails on fire, but a majority of the crew were intelligent enough to set aside their differences and put it out before the whole thing could burn them all to death. While Gleason was disappointed that it seemed most of them had survived, it had still provided him with a distraction to slip away into the night.

The further he got from the fires, the harder it was to see where he was going. Using his magic to light his way would be a beacon for any searchers looking for him, so his only choice was to struggle through the dark. Ever since a vampire had bitten him, his night vision had greatly improved, but the stark relief between shadow and starlight coming through the tree limbs somehow negated his ability. The contrast somehow made it harder for his eyes to focus.

Even worse, the chain dragging between his legs kept catching on every little snag and root along his path. It caused him to stumble and fall on his face in the snow more than once. Despite his exhaustion and the lack of proper food and water over the last several days, Gleason kept getting up and moving onward, time and time again.

In the confusion of everything going on, he had lost track of which direction he was supposed to be running. His goal was to sneak higher up the mountain and find an unguarded way inside. There had to be an entrance somewhere. All he had to do was find it.

Gleason was cold, lost, starving, dehydrated, and having difficulties breathing the higher he traveled. He wasn't sure how he was going to get the magical chains off of him, and while still surrounded by enemies. However, none of that was his biggest concern. From the moment his foot touched the ground in front of the mountain that was his ultimate goal, the voices in his head had fallen silent.

They had been his constant companion for so long now, their absence felt unnatural. The background noise of their babbling and humming had only stopped when he had touched certain enchanted items, like his whip. This was the first time they'd gone away on their own. Almost as if he was in a forest, and a predator was near. If the voices were the small creatures creating the constant sounds, what could have scared them away?

As if thinking it willed the creature into existence, a savage monstrosity Gleason had never seen before erupted from the side of the mountain far above and behind him. It let loose a roar that shook the snow from nearby tree limbs, covering him in white powder. An avalanche of rocks and snow tumbled down the mountain, thankfully nowhere near where Gleason was huddling in fear at the base of a tree.

While it was hard to tell from this distance, Gleason thought it looked like there might have been a man fighting the monster. They were both so high up that he didn't know how they could survive the lack of breathable air or lethally cold temperatures for any length of time. Enchanted items could only keep someone alive for so long, and fighting would burn through that time even faster. For a creature of any great size to be that high in elevation meant it must certainly be powerful in the extreme. The bigger the monster, the more air it needed to survive. Gleason didn't know of any monster that could get over that hurdle.

At least, he hadn't until recently. The giant demon spider had revealed the existence of more of its kind, including another demon prince, and a dragon. What he was looking at must be the other demon prince. While it didn't resemble any mole he'd ever seen before, it had certainly burrowed through the rock of the mountain with ease.

The battle unfolding above him quickly retreated back inside, leaving a long scar on the pristine side of the majestic King of the Mountains. Shouts echoed from behind him to his right, allowing Gleason to reorient himself. Now that he knew what direction the airship port was in, he could make sure not to walk right into their clutches and become their prisoner once again. While he was still suffering from all his other problems, at least he wasn't lost anymore.

Pure determination saw him through the rest of the night. He didn't stop to rest, not while the sun was still down. Greater undead would be able to hunt him during the night, and he had no way to cover or obscure his scent trail. While he didn't know all of the capabilities of the gray dwarves, he certainly understood how well a vampire or ghoul could hunt someone with warm blood and a beating heart across open ground. He liked his chances against the gray dwarves better.

It was simply a matter of time until they realized he was missing and there would be search parties covering the region. This was his best chance to find a way inside the mountain, before the area was saturated with groups he had to hide from. Gleason understood that fighting would end in his eventual capture. Even winning a few battles, or ambushing smaller search parties, would only narrow the zone they needed to concentrate their troops. As much as he hated it to his core, running away was his only option. So run he did, deep into the night, falling into almost a trance-like state to keep pushing himself past his limits.

The clink of the chain between his legs catching on a rock was the only warning Gleason had before he was yanked off his feet once more. He face-planted into a snowdrift, banging his elbow on a tree root that jutted awkwardly out of the rocky ground. He didn't know how many times he'd fallen, but it certainly felt like this was the thousandth time he had to pick his bruised and frozen body out of the snow.

As he sat up, the sun crested the horizon, crowning the King of the Mountain once more. Despite the inspiring sight, seeing the sunrise didn't make Gleason feel any better. He could see another entrance into the mountain up ahead, and it was exactly like the last two he'd bypassed. Heavily guarded, with fortifications both inside and out to keep away any invaders. Worst of all were the signal fires and alarm bells spread all throughout the miniature base. Even if he managed to kill the guards and get inside, they'd still most likely manage to call for reinforcements.

Gleason had a sinking feeling in his gut that every entrance he'd find would be like this, no matter how long he searched. The only way inside the mountain was as a captive, which meant he wouldn't be able to complete the mission the Trinity had given him. He didn't know how he knew that, but he somehow did.

Now that the sun was coming up, at least Gleason could get some sleep. He hadn't seen any animals to kill for meat, or plants that were edible, but he could melt some snow for water and get a few hours of rest before having to come up with a new plan. Perhaps, if he waited, the voices would come back and tell him what to do.

He carefully made his way past the entrance as he searched for a good campsite, this time staying hunched over so he could hold on to his chains. If the links were to clink together and make noise, or catch on something at the wrong time, the guards would certainly come out and investigate. Staying crouched for so long hurt his back and thighs, but he managed to get by them without drawing an alarm.

Unfortunately, there weren't many places suitable for hiding during daylight. The higher up the mountain someone went, the thinner and smaller the trees got. It forced Gleason to stay lower on the slopes, navigating through sections of snow-covered rocky and wooded terrain that seemed purpose-built for breaking ankles and twisting knees. Eventually, he managed to find a pair of trees that had fallen against a boulder long ago, their dead limbs creating a small hollow where he could hide without anyone seeing him from three directions.

It was as good as he was going to get, so Gleason quickly set up a small campsite to try and melt some snow for water. The branches above him broke up the smoke from his small fire, and his helmet did well enough as a pot to fill his canteen. He had to refill it four times before he stopped feeling thirsty. While it made him feel better, it certainly highlighted how long it had been since he'd had anything substantial to eat.

Of a much greater concern, the black veins that normally rose to the surface to fight back the frostbite in his limbs were acting sluggish and unresponsive. He was forced to waste time warming himself over the fire, slowly bringing back feeling to his fingers and toes. While the pins and needles sensation was uncomfortable, Gleason understood how important it was for him to fight the silent battle against the cold. It would kill him as surely as the undead, or one of the demons.

As he tried to get comfortable against the slowly warming boulder, Gleason closed his eyes and thought hard about what to do next. He understood how important it was to cleanse his world of the filth these interlopers represented. Demons, dragons, dwarves, they were all equally as bad as the undead. Or shifters. Or unbelievers. All should be wiped away by the burning flames of purity.

With that thought, the black veins that had struggled so hard to rise to the surface earlier were suddenly fighting to rip free of his skin, writhing and squirming in an orgy of frustrated tension that put pressure on Gleason's very soul, squeezing and straining him in a

215

way he'd never had to force strength from himself to envelop the sudden outburst.

Despite the struggle, it wasn't an unpleasant sensation. Gleason shuddered from the mixture of pleasure and pain that washed over him in waves that nearly consumed his consciousness in their intensity. He fought to control himself, unwilling to buckle against the sudden onslaught.

Gasping for breath, he opened his eyes to see he had stumbled out of his hiding place and fallen to his knees as if he was at prayer. All around him in a perfect circle the snow had melted, revealing an ancient road that was long overgrown. It was a straight line that led off into the distance, winding around the King of the Mountains. Now that it was pointed out to him, Gleason could see the faint indent in the snow where the old road traced its way up the nearly sheer side of the slopes.

The gods hadn't forsaken him. They might not be able to speak to him, but they could send him messages in other ways. Ways that he understood. His thoughts of righteous indignation had given them a pathway, a lifeline, to reach him, and he was ready to listen.

In the distance, he could see where the road ended. At an entrance into the mountain that was completely unguarded. Where the demon had erupted earlier from the side of the mountain.

Gleason got back to his feet, feeling energized and whole for the first time in weeks.

He had found his way inside.

## CHAPTER 31

When I tapped into the ley line nexus, it was a relief to find out they must have been minor flows of power compared to the more recent places of power I'd been dealing with. There were also three distinct mana currents, making this the first intersection of three ley lines I'd found. All three carried only a fraction of the power only a single ley line in the village's crater had, so their combined total was a manageable amount with my Mind stat above one hundred and forty.

Keeping tight control of what I allowed into my body, I managed to find and isolate the demonic mana before it could enter my system. Once I had it separated, I held the wisp of mana between my hands and the place of power. It acted like a lodestone for the corrupting mana contained within, drawing forth the infection in a dark swirl that somehow hurt my eyes to look at, while also stinging my nose with the stink of brimstone. The demonic mana quickly started to collect between my hands, changing from the size of a pea to a baseball in seconds. Then it swelled from a baseball to a basketball even faster, swirling in a dense swarm of angry power that nearly exuded a sense of sentient hatred. I was rapidly learning that one percent might seem like a small number, but it represented a very large amount of mana when spread across an entire place of power.

The rest of the mana seemed happy to release the taint hidden within its depths, helping to push the demonic corruption to the surface as it was drawn toward the growing orb I held in my hands. That only made it easier for me to take in the other elements. For the first time ever, I wasn't having any problems with my mana generator or channels dealing with the influx of the *regular* energy from the place of power. The mental strain of ensuring the scales in my mana generator stayed balanced, grew, or shifted into different positions based on the new power dynamics. The changes in mana percentages brought on were extreme, but I could handle it. Sure, it still felt like holding on to a live electrical wire while trying to solve long division. It was just long division with whole numbers. No decimal points.

Soon, I was holding an orb of demonic mana nearly the same size as myself. I had no idea what I was going to do with it, but there were no signs of it slowing down anytime soon. I probably would've been overwhelmed if I wasn't simultaneously also getting juiced up by the other mana. The secondary channel system combined with my mana generator almost ran everything on autopilot after I fell into a rhythm, which allowed me to focus more of my attention on the steadily growing ball of corruption in front of me.

Pushing the demonic mana back into the ley lines felt wrong. Not only did the Paladin class inside me want to blow a gasket at the thought, but the earth mana that I had an instinctive connection with trembled in anger at the idea as well. I could use the *Cleanse* spell my Paladin class gave me on the collected mass, but there were two big problems with that plan. Since I didn't draw on the power of a god for those spells, using any of my Paladin abilities drained something essential from me–most likely draining my own soul–and disconnecting me from the world. Right now wasn't the time for that. The other problem was, it could cause a massive explosion. The meeting of two diametrically opposed elements seldom ended well, especially in very concentrated forms. I didn't feel like causing a cave-in on top of myself right now.

The idea I kept coming back to was how big the orb was getting. It was about the size of a Buick at this point, and I was seriously straining just to hold it up. Real pain was starting to cut through my body from being in contact from such a large amount of such caustic, evil stuff. My only solution was to condense the giant ball of demonic mana into a size I *could* handle, and then, once it was more manageable, think about what to do next.

Containing the expanding ball was the first step, so I started building a framework of light, fire, and life mana around the growing orb. It didn't like that very much and started fighting back, proving the malevolent sentience I had felt earlier was, in fact, alive. Tentacles of smoky black mana that were sputtering flakes of sulfur lashed out at the grid I had snapped into place. Brimstone stink burned my skin, nose, and eyes, forcing me to use a bit of my concentration to cast a healing spell.

If it weren't for the constant stream of energy from the place of power supporting me, I might have lost in that moment. Instead, I somehow knew by instinct to use a blend of earth and nature mana to fill in the gaps of the grid I'd built, completely containing the overflowing corruption in a container reinforced by the power of the ley lines themselves.

Not a single square in the grid was left open. The density of so much demonic mana in one place caused the corruption still remaining in the nexus to be sucked through the walls of the orb I'd built as if it was a one-way mirror, where it joined the rest of its filthy rot. It was forced to grow denser and denser as more was added, turning a deeper black threaded through with smoky veins of red and green. The more there was, the stronger the suction force became, until soon enough there was nothing left in the nexus. It had been purified of corruption.

A series of dings went off from my system, but I had to ignore it for now. Dealing with the demonic mana was an emergency I needed to handle immediately. Now that it was all in one place, I could start to condense it into a size that would barely take up half the cavern. I had no doubt if it broke free, the place of power would be corrupted all over again.

Instinctive casting helped condense the grid much faster than if I'd done it before obtaining the earth mana boost it provided. Even with the bonus, it was a fight to continuously reinforce the grid and manage the balance between elements that kept the containment in place. No single thing was exceedingly difficult on its own, but considering I was still absorbing the place of power as well, I felt strained to my mental limits.

The malevolent sentience tried to fight being compressed. It fought hard, but the end result was inevitable once it became so dense that the colored smoke running through the black orb started to crystallize like veins of red and green marble. That was the turning point, and it started to collapse in on itself almost faster than I could squeeze the containment grid.

It went from filling half the cavern to the size of a marble in less than a minute. I couldn't even see the end result because of the intense brightness my own mana put off from also being shrunk

219

down so much. The corruption still fought, but it was weakening. A ding from my system tried to get my attention once again, but it wasn't important. Letting off the pressure for even a fraction of a second wasn't an option. I held it there until its struggles ceased. In many ways, it felt a whole lot like I was strangling a living being to death, even though I knew that was impossible.

Another pair of dings from my system alerted me to more accomplishments. It was as good a sign as I was going to get that the demonic mana was handled. A third ding followed right after, signifying I'd completed draining the place of power. Or, more accurately, cleared the ley line blockage, but either worked to my advantage.

With confirmation from the system, and the ability to put my full focus on the task now that the place of power was done, I started unraveling the grid. First I drained the earth and nature mana, pulling what I could back into my body so it didn't go to waste. That allowed me to see the shiny black marble with glowing veins of purple, green, and red. It wasn't perfectly smooth. It was more like the rough sheen that the demon spider had as its carapace. The ridges were nearly the same as a faint swirling fingerprint, barely visible unless you got close.

I held out my hand as I drained the grid of life, light, and fire mana. The marble dropped into my palm, and I nearly dropped it as the weight of such a tiny object almost jerked me off my feet. It was at *least* twice as heavy as I weighed, with all my gear on. That had to put it at close to five hundred pounds! I'd expected it to feel filthy or disgusting in some way, like it had when I was condensing the corruption, but it only felt like a piece of textured glass. There wasn't even a hint of power leaking from it at the moment.

Before I could cast *Inspect* on the demonic mana corruption marble, I had to clear out all the alerts from my system. First up was the updates about cleansing the place of power.

---

**Quest Update!**
**Unique Upgrade Quest: Find ten places of power - 4/10**
**-Foreign Mana contamination has been removed. Balance safely restored.**

**\*\*Warning!\*\***

---

> Your actions have angered a faction. This may lead to unintended consequences.
>
> **Warning!**
> Your actions have pleased a faction. This may lead to unintended consequences.
>
> **New Title Earned: Power Vacuum**
> -Your ability to suck in many different ways has gained the attention of the gods. Look at you go, proving that empty space in your head is a good thing!
> Skill Imparted: Your passive mana absorption rate and range is increased by 10%. During combat or meditation, an additional 10% will be applied to each if the ambient mana in the region is unclaimed. The original bonus applies regardless of the state of mana ownership.
> *Note - This bonus does not apply to internal mana generation, or provide any bonuses to mana storage abilities.

Overall, that was a very nice bonus to have. It helped explain why I was able to finish with the place of power so quickly, and why controlling the amount of power had gotten easier. The warnings about factions were more bullshit I didn't have any control over, and ultimately didn't really care about. If they wanted to judge me for my actions, I'd Judge them right back, regardless of who or what they were. It was a problem for a different time, if it even became a problem at all.

The next notifications were about collapsing the orb into a marble, and defeating the malevolent intelligence inside the mana.

> **Warning**
> You are harming an intelligent entity not native to this plane of reality. Beware the results of your actions.

That must have been when I started winning. Which meant the next two…

> **\*\*Warning\*\***
> You have killed an intelligent entity not native to this plane of reality. Your actions have angered a faction. This may lead to unintended consequences.

> **\*\*Warning\*\***
> You have killed an intelligent entity not native to this plane of reality. Your actions have pleased a faction. This may lead to unintended consequences.

Yep. More of the same. No new titles to give me a free boost, but it wasn't that big of a deal. One more to go, and then I could check the marble. I concentrated on condensing the stat screen to only show me what had changed so I didn't have to look over the whole thing, and thankfully it popped into my vision with only the new stuff showing.

> **Name: James Holden (Earth v7.6 → v7.7)**
> **Rank: 6 → 7/10**
> **Status:**
> **Strength- 126 → 147**
> **Flexibility- 125 → 148**
> **Vigor- 136 → 150**
> **Mind- 145 → 160**
> **Mission:**
> **Unique Upgrade Quest: Find ten places of power - 5/10**

The gains in my physical stats were much higher this time around, bringing me closer to a balanced state than I'd been in a long time. After some quick introspection, it felt like the Venom mana being introduced to my system might have been the cause. The strange new mana type forced a kind of cell growth and reinforcement for my body in a direction that hadn't been there before, which led to gains that were measurable on my stat sheet. It felt good to be closer to the balanced fighter that I was when I first arrived on this planet, and I couldn't hold in the stretch as I stood up to my full height.

Finally, I held up the black marble. It was time to see what all the struggles were about. Casting *Identify*, I waited to see what kind of monstrosity I was dealing with.

---

**Item: Artificial Refined Demon Core**
**Type: Demonic/Poison/Corruption Aspect**
**Grade: 9/10**
**Description: An artificially created core of condensed mana used to control or enhance interplanar beings from lower dimensions. Contains a portion of the segmented consciousness and crushed willpower of a deity, enhancing the innate effects. Can be used to empower enchantments, but mana types may cause unintended side effects. Demonic and Corruption Aspects make it unsuitable for use by those of the middle and higher dimensional zones.**

**\*\*Warning\*\***
**This is an Object of Power not native to this plane of reality. Handle with care. Using this item improperly may cause certain factions to view you unfavorably**

---

Well then. I guess that answers what malevolent intelligence I was dealing with inside the orb. Some demon god was poking its nose in where it didn't belong, and got its fingers caught in the cookie jar. And by caught in the cookie jar, I mean I severed them and crushed them into pulp. It was no wonder why it tried to use the system to warn me off. What a pansy-ass bitch.

The real question was, now that I had this thing, what was I supposed to do with it? I had the Enhancing Gem that could double the power of literally anything I pushed through it, and now this demon core that might be able to power a seriously strong enchantment. As long as it didn't blow up in my face, of course.

Combining the two would produce a majorly overpowered spell or ability that could potentially level mountains. I had no idea what mountain to level, though. With Lighter dead, maybe Jaeger could lead me to where I needed to go next.

With that thought, I realized how quiet it had gotten outside the chamber I was in. I needed to find out where the others were, and make sure everyone was okay. I didn't need to check my timer to know time had flown by.

Before I did anything else though, I used instinctive casting to open a hole in the ground, and gave Lighter and the others a proper burial. They had given their lives to help me try and save this planet. I wasn't going to forget that sacrifice.

Tucking away the bone necklaces I had gathered from them, I knelt before the bodies I had just buried. I was all too familiar with this. Burying good men and women. Placing my fist over my heart, I did the only thing I knew I could do. I promised them the justice that they and their families deserved, and were owed.

For only those brave enough to sacrifice their life for so just a cause as to protect and defend those who could not, required me to kneel before them. Not kings, not queens, not presidents, not emperors, but heroes who shed their blood for liberties, freedom, life, and loved ones. These were such warriors. As the Mantle of a Judge settled on my shoulders, I knew the next words to be true.

"This *will* end."

## CHAPTER 32

Leaving the chamber where I'd killed the giant spider demon was easy. Figuring out what to do with the stupid demon core wasn't.

It was ridiculously heavy, and putting it inside my ruck would only unbalance it, or rip off the pocket I put it in entirely. I had the same issue with putting it on my belt. The core would make it sag to one side dramatically, or possibly pull my pants down at entirely the wrong moment.

My only option right now was to use a strap of spare leather to make a sling, then reinforce it with wire and more leather so it didn't snap. Using runes to reinforce it wasn't an option, because they might interact with one another and create a demon-powered thermonuclear explosion or some other crazy shit I didn't have time to figure out.

The strap dug into my shoulder something fierce, but there wasn't anything I could do about it on short notice. Keeping my hands available was more important at the moment. A thick pouch of wire and leather held the marble for now, and all I could do was hope it didn't fall apart until I made something better. If I ever got the chance.

Once I had the heavy thing as settled as it was going to get, I carefully poked my head back into the main cave. It was a stinking, smoldering wreck, with fires dotting the larger cavern amid piles of dead spiders and fallen cocoons that had dropped from the ceiling and ruptured their rotting contents all over the place. Large patches of ground were still covered in spider silk, and curtains of webbing wafted from jagged sections of broken stone like forgotten ghosts fluttering in the wind. Nowhere did I see a spider that was still alive.

I followed the trail of destruction to the exit, and quickly got a faint hint of fresh air. It helped me put on a burst of speed, and soon I could smell the clean scent of freshly fallen snow.

The exit came upon me quicker than I expected. A sharp turn in the tunnel blocked the worst of the wind, and with it being night time during a blizzard, that meant it was barely brighter outside the caves than it was inside. I almost ran face-first into a snowdrift before I figured out I was free.

Looking back, the impassable deep canyons and sheer cliffs that separated the forested foothills from the mountainous north were barely visible from where I stood. Once again I thought about the choice I'd made to take the underground route. It had cost five people their lives so far, and the journey wasn't over yet.

On the other hand, getting rid of the threat the demon prince represented to the region was something I couldn't overlook. There was no telling how much damage it would have done if left unchecked, especially once its young ate their way through all the goblins in the region. A tide of demonic spiders washing over Greendown and working their way south along the Mighty Rekka would have been a disaster of epic proportions not even the Green Wardens could have stopped.

"James!" Jaeger's voice was muffled by the snow, but the overly large hunter was hard to miss when he wanted to be seen. He was waving his arms over his head a few hundred yards away, near a rocky overhang on a cliff above me. "James, we're up here! Follow the trail through the crack in the wall, I'll meet you on the other side!"

I waved to show I heard him, and started walking in his direction. There was no way for me to see what trail he was talking about through the fresh layer of snow, so I looked for the opening he was talking about instead. It didn't take long to find the carved and decorated opening that had clearly been ceremonial at one point in time.

Someone, in some long-ago time period, had really cared about this path. They had carved images of fanged serpents, vicious demons, ravenous vampires, wild dinosaurs, and I'm pretty sure I even saw a few wendigo running rampant up and down the stylized version of the trail. It reminded me of the ancient Mayan carvings from my world, but these had a hint of magic in them to keep the carvings from being worn away by time and the elements. At the end of the jagged line was a large triangle with a giant crown. A skinny, winged serpent sat perched on the tip of the crown, looking down over the length of the trail. I didn't know what it all meant, but the worn grooves of hundreds of thousands of footsteps meant it used to be really important.

The way forward was protected on three sides, so it only had a light dusting of snow. From what I'd heard, no one had lived in this region in a long, long time. Like, millenia timeframes. That meant this would have been old even to an elf, which was downright mind-boggling. I followed the path as it zig-zagged up and around another steep set of cliffs, and came out at a matching archway to what I'd seen below. This one's carvings didn't survive the test of time nearly as well, and were barely recognizable. It was most likely due to the much harsher winds from being higher off the ground. Winds that were blasting me in the face right this moment.

Jaeger was waiting for me with his hands cupped around a small hooded lantern, doing his best to keep his fingers warm. A strong gust of wind almost blew out the flame, and he shivered as he pulled his hood down tighter. Even the big guy was feeling the cold.

"Okay, I made it." I almost laughed as he jerked in surprise. It felt good to finally sneak up on him for once. "Where's everyone else, and how are they doing?"

"This way." Jaeger motioned me off to the side, where it looked like we'd be walking straight into the cliff face. "When you ran off and left us, a lot of people lost hope you'd ever walk out of those caves. Anyone who knows you told them they were fools, so we've been taking turns keeping watch while waiting for you to catch up."

"Well, I appreciate it. Killing that giant spider wasn't exactly a walk in the park, and then I had to fix what it left behind afterward." I held out the bone necklaces Lighter and the scouts had each been wearing. They were similar to the dog tags, or identification tags, the people in the military from my home world wore. I'd made sure to grab them before burying the bodies. "Here. I'm sorry I couldn't save them, the best I could do was avenge them."

"It's small comfort to their families, but a small comfort is better than no comfort." Jaeger put the necklaces over his own head, tucking them away and out of sight. "Thank you for doing what you could."

"Make sure their families know they died helping us rid this region of a threat that could have wiped out not just the village, but all life down to the capital." Jaeger looked at me with a skeptical eye, but I nodded my head sharply. "Think about it. If those things kept breeding over the winter, feeding on goblins, when spring came they would have swept across the land all the way south until the ocean stopped them."

We walked in silence a bit longer before he pulled me to a stop. "You might be underestimating the Wardens, but you're definitely not wrong about what would happen to the village. At the very least, we all would have died." Jaeger rubbed at where the bone necklaces sat against his chest. "Thank you again. I will tell their families the truth, and they will understand the sacrifice they made meant something *real*. This is a gift I don't know how to repay, James Holden."

"It's simply the truth. That's what a Judge is always on the hunt for." I waved my hand at the blank wall, obviously confused about where to go next. "Now, why don't you show me where everyone is camped?"

"The weather makes it easy to hide. Watch this." Jaeger grabbed what looked like a piece of snow and pulled it to the side, revealing a narrow crevasse that flickered merrily with firelight. They'd covered the entrance with a blanket painted to look exactly like the snow-covered cliff face. "Welcome to our new hideout. Be careful if you take your boots off, there's a lot of sharp rocks inside."

The crevasse was a very tight space to cram everyone. It reminded me of a long alley with a wide spot in the middle. Looking up I noticed it was open to the night sky. Snow fell on us, but thankfully the tight confines did a good job of containing the heat of the fire and all of those who were stuffed inside. Two, maybe three people could stand next to each other if they were willing to touch shoulders, and you might be able to add a fourth person at the widest point. The sides were a good thirty feet tall, meaning the smoke from our fire had time to break up a little before it rose above ground level. Hopefully, we'd be gone by the time the sun came up, so that wasn't an issue. As it was right now, someone would have to be directly above us to even know we were there, which was probably as good as we were going to get at the moment.

Jaeger's warning about stepping on sharp rocks wasn't really necessary. I wouldn't be able to step on the ground even if I wanted to. The whole area was covered by bandaged and sleeping hunters. Most were dead to the world, rolled up in their cloaks or sleeping rolls if they still had them. A few of the wounded were laid out on their stomachs, while friends treated cuts and burns on their backs. That's where I saw most of the untreated wounds. It made sense, since they were most recently running away from battle.

Almost everyone had at least one or two bandages on, but many had several more. Even the lightly wounded looked tired and beaten after the ordeal they'd been through. We'd left their village less than a week ago, and it had been pretty much non-stop ever since. The constant fighting over the last two days had sapped any remaining energy they might have kept in reserve.

Worse, the most telling problem was what my crew was doing. Or, more specifically, what they *weren't* doing. Cross and Jess were both asleep instead of trying to heal people. Given the number of hunters still actively bleeding, they were probably suffering from overusing their mana. For Cross, specifically, that was very concerning. I'd have to check on him when he woke up.

Leedy was one of the people standing guard near the entrance when I had walked in, but he was barely able to keep his eyes open. When he waved at me as I entered, I thought he was going to fall over. I knew the signs of someone who had received extensive magical healing, and he was a poster child for them. He must have lost a lot of blood, and either Cross or Jess had forced his body to replace it. The only way Leedy was going to be back to normal anytime soon was to get twelve hours of sleep and at least two, maybe three hearty meals filled with protein.

The single most concerning person was Murphy. He was tending a fire in the center of the open space, but he wasn't cooking anything. That could only mean one thing, and it was a seriously big deal.

"We're already out of food?" I tried to keep my voice down as I knelt next to him, but it was hard when we were packed so tightly in such a small space. "What happened to all the stuff we packed in with us?"

Murphy only gave me a bleary-eyed stare at first, his brain taking a moment to process what I said. "Oh, hi James. Glad you made it." Murphy was also suffering from post-healing problems. Possibly worse than Leedy. "Yeah, we had to prioritize what was in the packs when we were running. You must not have been there for that part." He pointed to the people around us before letting his arm flop back to his side. "Warm weather gear and medical stuff first, then weapons. We can't catch food if we freeze or bleed to death. That's what we were thinking at the time, anyway."

"I'm not going to second-guess a decision I wasn't there for, but we're going to need to get some calories in these people soon. Preferably some protein to help with the blood loss as well, but anything will help." I dug through my rucksack and pulled out a bundle of jerky. "Can you get this boiling in a pot? Even the broth will make people feel better."

The sight of food perked Murphy up, and he snatched it out of my hands. "Leave it with me, boss. I'll get something going that should help." He leaned over to dig through his bag and nearly fell into the fire.

I caught him and pulled out a large pot he had strapped over the top of his items from his bag. A goblin spearhead was stuck in the rim, so I pulled it out and bent it back into shape. "On second thought, why don't you let me handle this part? You wait here, eat one of those pieces, and get any spices you have squirreled away out and ready for when I get back with some water."

"Sounds like a yes." Murphy started gnawing on a strip of jerky while undoing buckles on the side pouches of his pack. Even getting a taste of food was already doing him some good.

Making my way back outside, I packed the pot with snow several times before using a quick burst of fire mana to melt it into water. It was wasteful, but I didn't want to make a dozen trips back and forth to fill the pot up all the way. Once it was topped off, I hurried back and passed it off to Murphy, who got a broth going for everyone.

The smell had everyone perking up, and I jumped in to start healing the people in order of those who were the least responsive. Cold like this could kill someone who was low on blood, and all the layers of clothing might hide how much bleeding a person had done.

Since just about everyone needed healing, I wasn't too picky about it. Eventually I'd get around to all of them.

About the same time I was finishing up with the last few people, someone shoved a hot cup in my hands. The blackened fingers were entirely too mobile to be frostbite, meaning it could only be one person who was interrupting me.

"You've been going non-stop for hours. It's almost sunrise, and if you don't take a break, you're going to burn yourself out." Cross peeled back his sleeve, showing me that his curse had grown back to his elbow. "Trust me, I'm the sage of burning yourself out."

"I appreciate it." I took a drink, savoring the flavors Murphy could bring out in something so simple. Cheap, plain jerky definitely didn't normally taste this good. "I'm actually doing better than you'd think. Killing that demon spider let me–"

"By the gods, what's that?!"

Shouts rang out all around us, and both Cross and I got to our feet. Everyone was looking straight up, where a shadow was blotting out the sky.

I could feel Cross pulling in as much mana as he could, causing the air around him to hum as he readied a spell to bring down whatever it was.

Pulling free my mace, I started doing the same, a throbbing blue glow highlighting our position.

Jess ran over, her staff already swirling with dust and pebbles.

"When it gets close enough, we hit it as one." Both of them gave me a sharp nod, flaring their nostrils in preparation. "Then Jess will focus on protecting everyone while I provide the distraction. Cross, you'll hit whatever weak points you see that open up. Nobody stops until it's dead, whatever it is. Got it?"

Before they could answer, an iron anchor dropped from the sky, shattering the walls, sending stone shrapnel everywhere, and completely blocking off our only exit.

If it weren't for Jess using the power of her staff to draw in all the sharp shards, half our number would have been cut down in an instant.

The heavy chain that trailed up into the clouds rattled as the shadow lowered itself, shifting into position to use the heavy ballista that I knew must be ready to fire on our position. Because I knew only one thing would be dropping anchors out of the sky.

"Ready yourselves! It's the airship!"

## CHAPTER 33

"I said I was sorry. It's not like we've had a lot of practice, you know. We basically got the airship off the ground, and came straight here. Plus it's dark outside, and the snowstorm didn't help with the aim." The werebear was gesturing wildly with a mop of all things, and I had no earthly idea why all of his crew seemed so terrified of it. "How are we supposed to be perfect with dropping our anchors already? Besides, it's not like anyone got hurt."

Maybe this planet had mop monsters I hadn't seen yet? Nah, that'd be too weird, even for this place.

"That's not the point! All you had to do was let us know you were there, and we could have been ready. Instead, we thought we were under attack! Do you have any idea how close you were to being massacred?!" Jess, who might not be aware her cat shifter claws were out, was swinging her staff around almost as much as the former mayor was his mop.

If I didn't know better, I'd say the two were related. Actually, I'd never asked. Maybe they were related. Small towns, limited number of lycans, the odds were actually pretty high.

The mayor swung his mop in a full three-sixty, almost knocking two men out of the rigging in the process. They managed to catch themselves before falling, and both men moved several feet higher to get out of range. "You think you could massacre us? Ha! You haven't seen what this baby can do! Why, you just wait until we–"

"That's probably enough shouting for right now. How about we get our guests settled, and make sure they have a proper meal. It looks like they could all use one." The raven-haired beauty that interrupted the werebear made it a point to stand as close to me as possible without crossing over into the realm of being improper. I hadn't even seen her approach, although I had seen her when we'd first boarded the airship a few minutes ago. Why she was here was still a mystery, but I wasn't going to look an alpacaoose in the teeth. Or whatever that saying was supposed to be.

Danika, the witch, was very possibly the most dangerous person I'd met on this planet, and not because she was especially lethal in a fight. It was because she was a survivor, and survivors had a knack for always finding a way to come out on top. No matter the circumstances. "And James, I have a special room prepared for you if you'd like me to show it to you."

Oh, and that. *That* was a different kind of dangerous.

"Let me check in with the captain before I worry about my own comforts." I gave her the ol' wink-and-smile technique, which works almost as well as the tip-o'-the-hat technique. "Afterward, we'll have to see what we'll see."

She tossed back a cocked eyebrow and a mildly confused look, which I took as a win. Keep 'em guessing, and you're still winning. The moment you get boring, you're automatically losing. One thing I know for sure, I'm seldom boring.

A couple of Greendown crewmembers started herding the hunters below, where the mess hall must be. Most of our group were still zonked out pretty hard, so they looked more like a herd of zombies than actual people as they stumbled down the stairs. I motioned for my quartet to go with them. They didn't act like it, but they could use a hot meal just as much as everyone else. A member of the Greendown Healer's Guild followed close behind to check everyone over.

"Thank you for doing this. Seriously." I turned to look over at the werebear mayor. The two of us had a complicated relationship given our past, but I most certainly didn't harbor any bad feelings after this. "Once we get dropped off, the very first thing I want you to do is take those hunters home. They've been through enough–sacrificed enough–and they deserve a break."

"Of course, Mister Holden. We'll keep them safe." The former mayor gave me a salute, his own mop handle almost poking him in the eye. Seriously, someone needed to take that thing away from him.

"Come, I'll show you where the captain is staying." Danika took me by the hand and led me to the front, where a glass-fronted room was built into the frame of the ship. It was an interesting design feature that didn't match what I remembered from the original blueprints, which more closely matched a galleon design from my home world. She must have noticed me looking things over as we walked. "When Greendown asked my Coven to consult on building this airship, we made some changes. Our first thought was, 'Why would you steer from the back where it's hard to see?' You need to see from the front, so we shifted the captain's quarters, steering, and the magical controls to this area, and put storage, crew, mess, and other non-essentials at the rear." As she opened the door, a wave of mana poured out, making the air practically sparkle with energy. "Not only did it improve power efficiency, but our balance became easier to maintain, and speed was boosted dramatically."

"Well, I can definitely say I'm impressed." I didn't know how this one would stack up against the other airship that was floating around out here, but it was certainly better than the Goodyear blimp. Or the Hindenburg. As we entered the ship's command center, I had to blink the spots out of my eyes from the bright lights they had inside. "In case we have to fight, how many crew are there onboard?"

"I can answer that one." One of the last people I expected to see stood up from a table covered with maps. He pulled back his green hood, showing off his gray hair. The emerald that decorated the hilt of the thick-bladed dagger on his hip gleamed in the lantern light. Tew, the Green Warden who was supposed to be dealing with a talking book, held out his hand for me to shake. "It's good to see you, James."

"Not that I'm upset, but why are you here? I thought you had to get rid of *The Oracle*, and convince the rest of the Wardens to try and stop killing me because of that talking book." I looked behind him and saw that Oriana, his apprentice Green Warden, was also here. Leedy would certainly be happy to see her, even if he didn't have a cold shot in hell. "Did that mission not work out?"

"Oh, it was a disaster!" Tew laughed, slapping me on the shoulder. It was a measure of how much I'd changed that I didn't get rocked by it this time around. The guy was stronger than an ox. "Oriana and I had to fight half the Order, and most of the temple got burned down in the process. But the tainted book burned along with it, meaning it was no longer connected to the Trinity. Simple fire destroying it proved we were telling the truth better than any testimony or evidence we could have brought forward, so it all worked out in the end."

"So you decided after burning down one of the Warden's most important buildings, beating up half the Green Wardens, and pissing off the other half, your best option was jumping on a flying ship and going to the most uninhabited region on the continent?" I gave him two thumbs up. "That's some seriously good planning right there. I couldn't have done it better myself."

He laughed, giving me another thump on the shoulder. I'd forgotten how often he liked to do that. "Anyway, when we got to Greendown, the Sailor's Guild was arguing over who would be the captain of the first airship, and had nearly come to a point where the Commandant was concerned people were going to die." Tew shrugged, and waved his hands around at all the complicated controls and consoles around us. Eight crew members were hard at work keeping everything running, while two more were running around helping to pass messages and coordinate between the various stations. "When he asked me to take command of all this, I decided it couldn't be that hard, so I said I'd be happy to take it for its maiden voyage. There's two more airships that are supposed to be ready to fly within a few days, so all those angry people won't have a reason to be upset soon enough, and they can take back this easy job when this mission is over."

Almost everyone within earshot, including Oriana, gave him a death stare when he said things like 'it couldn't be that hard' and 'easy job.' I had a feeling Tew wasn't destined to be an airship captain for very long–especially with that attitude–but he was certainly good enough for right now. Especially if we had to fight. Which reminded me, I still didn't know how many people were on the ship. I decided I'd try and help him out and changed the subject.

"So, about those crew numbers. If we had to fight right this second, how many people would be able to repel boarders?" I leaned in and lowered my voice so only Tew, Oriana, and Danika could hear me. "In case you haven't heard, there's another airship running around out here, and it was reported to be nearly twice the size of this one, with two balloons holding it aloft instead of the one you have."

"Oh, we've heard all about it." Tew waved me over to the table that was bolted to the floor and motioned for me to have a seat.

It was awkward squeezing myself in since the chair was also bolted down, but I understood why they wouldn't want loose furniture in the command center. "We were waved down by those tree people on our way up here, and they gave us this." He showed me a copy of the drawing the scouts had made of the enemy airship. "We have eighty crew members that can fight, and another twelve that would be useless in combat."

"That's… actually better than I expected." I guessed it was all kinds of cramped when you went below decks. "I'd rather not involve you at all if I can avoid it. Once the sun finishes coming up and the clouds clear out more, we can pick a good spot for you to drop us off and your ship can get out of here."

"We expected you'd say something like that, which is why I made these." Danika handed me several tubes of what felt like cardboard and tin. "These are markers that will shoot up into the sky and burn for hours. We'll be able to see and sense them, and come to pick you up, no matter where you are."

"Cool. Magic flare guns." I tucked them in my rucksack before turning back to the others. "You said there were going to be more airships ready soon. Is Greendown sending them north as well, or do they have some other tasks in mind?" I knew the Commandant and the Vice-Admiral of the Sailor's Guild understood how important this mission was, but they didn't control everything in Greendown. "It would change things if it was two against one, even if the enemy airship was nearly twice as big."

"It was still being discussed when we left." Oriana finally broke her silence, the Green Warden Apprentice still very distracted by the maps on the table. "Many in the city thought it was more important to send the airships south, where they could purchase vital supplies the city still needs. They're a long way from being whole after the undead attack they suffered." She very pointedly avoided looking at Danika, who was one of the leaders of the enemy army Oriana was talking about. Danika and her Coven were forced to use their witch abilities against the city defenses, but that didn't change the fact that they were part of the reason why the destruction was so widespread. "The Commandant argued that stopping another war before it could reach the city was more important than recovering from a past conflict, which understandably gained a lot of momentum from the public. We left before a consensus was reached."

"Which means there's a chance more airships could show up, and you could reasonably take the fight to the enemy instead of getting run over." I leaned forward in thought. "We can't put all our hopes on that chance. Taking the hunters back to their village is a priority as well, and I'm not willing to compromise on that. Lighter's sacrifice was enough." I tapped the map in front of me, trying to puzzle out where we should go next. "I wish we could figure out where the enemy was based out of. It would help us plan the next phase of–"

"Look at that!"

"Wow!"

"Have you ever seen such a thing?!"

Excited shouts interrupted me, and we all turned around to see what was going on.

Stretching in front of us was a mountain range that seemed to go on forever. Jagged tips of snow-capped stone covered the landscape, dotted with valleys of isolated pine forests and frozen lakes. Waterfalls and streams fed into a river that I knew eventually became the Rekka, which divided the continent in two. Some great cataclysm had created this desolation millenia ago, and it was a miracle this planet wasn't a barren wasteland.

There, in the distance, I saw exactly where we were supposed to go next. As the sun was burning away the clouds, it revealed a long dormant snow-capped volcano poking up higher than any of the mountains around it. The jagged rim of the volcano was perfectly shaped like the crown a king or queen would wear, and as the morning sun reflected off the snow, it looked exactly like a golden crown.

I remembered the old carvings preserved on the trail, with the triangle and a crown on the top marking the end. The ancient people that lived here before the Empire had traveled to that volcano for some reason, and they had carved the trail with images of monsters and demons of all types and varieties.

And at the peak, sitting on the crown, they'd carved a winged serpent overlooking everything. I remembered what the demon spider had said, and now I believed it. If ever there was a place a dragon made its lair, I was looking at it. I looked over at Tew and shrugged.

"Well, at least now you know where to drop me off."

## CHAPTER 34

Turbulence wasn't something I thought I'd have to deal with on a fantasy-fantastic world that thought things like indoor plumbing was advanced technology, but here I was, holding on to the railing like my life depended on it. Once we'd moved from the edge of the foothill region to over the mountain range proper, wind currents had started beating the crap out of our little ship like we owed them money. Unfortunately, safety harnesses hadn't been installed as a standard safety feature, so the only thing keeping someone on deck from flying off was a strong grip.

Almost everybody else was either below decks or inside the command center, but my group needed to tough it out. We were trying to get our bodies used to the lower oxygen levels, and get some idea of what the terrain was going to be like when we were dropped off. Sure, we knew where we would be on a map. That's not anything like understanding what the actual ground looks like when you have to walk around on it.

Hours went by, and we rotated in and out of the command center to warm up and take a break from time to time. As the day wore on, more clouds disappeared, and we had to rise in altitude to reduce the chances of being spotted. We wanted to time it so we arrived near our destination around sunset. Tew and Oriana thought they could hide their approach in the light of the setting sun, and then use the dark of night to slip away unnoticed. I thought it was a great idea on paper, but magic had a nasty way of ruining great ideas.

"Why. Is. The. Ship. Bouncing. So. Much." Jess was having the hardest time catching her breath with the reduced oxygen levels at the higher altitudes, probably because she was the smallest person in our team. She was forced to gasp between each word, and it wasn't helped by the heavy bouncing from the turbulence. "There. Isn't. Anything. To. Hit. Out. Here."

"You remember how the waves in water affect you when you're on a boat in a river?" I made a wave motion with my hand, immediately regretting letting go of the railing as I almost got flipped off the deck. "Well, the air has waves too, just like a river or an ocean. You just can't see them. We're getting hit by those waves in a very similar way." It was a simplified version of what was going on, but it was close enough to the truth that she could easily understand. "The waves are especially bad over the mountains, because all the wind comes up off the peaks. Like rapids in a river."

"I. Don't. Like. It." Jess winced as we hit a particularly nasty bump. Her staff was strapped across her back, so when the bouncing up and down motion made the lower half bang against the deck, the other end smacked her across the back of the head. "Oh. Kay." She pulled her staff free, letting go of the railing with one hand. "I'm. Done."

Mana came storming out of Jess in a torrent, enhanced and focused by her anger and the magical implement in her hand. A spiral of green and blue mana formed at the end of the airship, cutting through the rough winds that had been tossing us around.

"There. Much better." Jess was still breathing hard, but she wasn't gasping between each word anymore. "That should last for a while."

I could sense the effort and strain to cast the spell had drained a good portion of her mana, but Jess had learned not to drain herself down to nothing. She still looked a little pale, and I was a little frustrated that she used such a large amount of power when we were exposed like this. The only person still out on deck who wasn't on my team was more than willing to let her hear all about her mistake.

"You'd better hope there isn't a lookout somewhere close by who is sensitive to mana. Otherwise, we're going to have a fight on our hands." Danika pulled out a glass vial and a roughspun jute pouch that clattered as she shook it. A closer look revealed the pouch was filled with bones, and the vial looked like it had pickled frog eyeballs inside. That was one thing I knew that never changed, no matter what world I was on. Witches gonna witch. "I can cast a confusion curse, so that anyone who looks at the ship in the next few hours won't be sure of what they see. It should be enough to get us close to your destination, even if we've been spotted."

"Thank you, Danika." I passed over a few gemstones from my pouch, and she smiled as she pocketed them. Like I said, she was a survivor, and they seldom did their best work for free. I'd also gotten the sense that Greendown was footing the bill for her assistance, but they probably weren't paying one of the people that just attacked their city very well. "Any idea how long it will take until we get close enough for Tew to decide to drop us off?"

"While your teammate's spellcasting was foolish," Danika glared at Jess, who had the good sense to look at least a little embarrassed, "it did have the side effect of speeding us up quite a bit. With both Tew and Oriana feeding mana into the ship's runes, I'd expect us to get there in less than an hour."

I clapped my hands together one time, getting everyone's attention. "Alright everybody. In case you didn't hear, we've got less than an hour before we're dropping a few miles from the enemy stronghold. Any last-minute things you need to take care of, now's the time. There's only one chance to get this right, so let's get in there, get it done, and get back out in one piece. Just like we planned. Got it?"

Everyone gave me a thumbs up before they scattered to grab their bags and weapons. I already had my freshly repaired armor on, along with the rest of my gear. For some reason I didn't trust my health and safety while being alone in my room with Danika on the ship earlier. So, I did my best to stay in public areas as much as possible. Right now wasn't the time, or the place.

Once everyone got back on deck with their gear we positioned ourselves near the rear of the airship. The plan was to dip as low as safely as possible on the west side of the dormant volcano, where we would have plenty of trees to hide in case a search party saw us, and get dropped off by rappelling down ropes. We weren't supposed to use magic of any kind to slow our fall, in the hopes that anyone with mana senses wouldn't notice us getting dropped off. I was the only person with any real rappelling experience, so odds were we'd certainly have some mishaps on the way down.

My worry was someone would get seriously hurt, and we would have to wait hours, or even days, before we could heal them while we were hiding. If it was a life-threatening injury, I would have to create a pretty big distraction while one of the others used as little mana as possible to fix the problem. That would mean splitting the party, and in a place this hostile to human life, I really didn't like that idea.

All of my concerns went overboard the moment the enemy airship rounded a mountain peak right in front of us.

"Enemy to the front!"

"Sound the alert!"

"Activate the shield runes!"

"Why is that console on fire? They haven't even done anything to us yet!"

"Dive, dive, dive–"

"Get that power surge under control!"

"How do I activate the shield runes?!"

We could hear yelling from the command center all the way from where we were at the rear. I would have to say things didn't sound like they were going very well. The crew hadn't seen actual combat before, and it showed. We all looked at one another, and I could tell everyone had the same thought I did. If we didn't help, this was going to go really bad, really fast.

"Leedy and Murphy, as much as I hate to use them again so soon, go below and get the hunters. Make sure they've all got extra arrows in their quivers. They'll need them to help repel boarders." They both nodded at me and sprinted for the stairs. "Jess and Danika, go help Tew and Oriana in the command center. They sound like they need it. You can tell Tew that Cross and I will hold the deck until the hunters and the rest of the crew get up here. Knowing we've got security out here handled should take one worry off his plate."

"Be safe out here. We'll come through this in one piece, you wait and see." Danika went to reach for me, but a sudden jerk and bounce sent us stumbling in opposite directions. She gave up on the sentimental action, and yelled back at me over her shoulder as she ran for the doorway at the front of the ship instead. "I'll see you soon, James!"

Now that it was just Cross and I on deck, despite the situation a certain level of calm descended. We rode out the next series of maneuvers for over twenty minutes, hanging on to the railing as the two airships followed one another through a series of dips, zigs, zags, aborted barrel rolls, and riding dangerously close to the sharp tips of mountain peaks and forest trees. If we were martinis, we'd definitely be shaken, not stirred. The two of us used the occasional wind spell to knock away a ballista bolt or a shield spell to block an enemy fireball, but overall we were maintaining a stalemate. Since we used mana to power our forward momentum, and they used wind, it was a marathon we'd eventually lose.

As our shield array finally kicked in and started slowing us down a little, I was able to finally get a good look at the enemy airship, and I noticed it was actually looking kinda rough.

Entire sections of sails were missing from the masts it was supposed to use for propulsion, and the ones that were still in place looked to be more patch than sail. The two tandem balloons looked lumpy and deformed, no longer the sleek hunter of the skies I'd seen pictured before.

Bigger than any other sign the airship was barely afloat, not a single rune looked to be working correctly. Sparks shot out from cracks that ran along the hull reinforcement runes. Light flickered in and out in random places on the railing, causing the ship to list to one side. Broken ballista hung from their mountings in the front left quarter, neutering the offensive capabilities by a huge percentage.

Last, but not least, a whole-ass gigantic pine tree was sticking out of the bottom of their ship. I kid you not, the whole freaking thing. As in, The Grinch had raided Whoville and snatched the big Christmas tree out of the middle of the village square, and then used the power of his heart that was ten sizes too small to chuck that tree like it was a huge fuck-off spear into the bottom of a floating pirate ship. My life was all kinds of wild.

"Are you seeing what I'm seeing?" Cross had his non-cursed hand up to shade his eyes. "How is that thing even staying in the air? It looks like it was attacked by a bunch of angry honey badgers."

"Of all the things to have the same, you guys have honey badgers?" I shook my head. "Nevermind. I'll just thank my lucky stars I had to fight velociraptors instead." I fought off the shiver that tried to run down my spine. Honey badgers had been on world five, where I'd gained my Alchemist profession and successfully recreated napalm. The napalm hadn't helped against a single honey badger. It only made them more violent. And they were on fire. "I don't know what happened to it, but even damaged, that airship is more than a match for ours. We're going to have to jump off at some point while our ship makes a run for it. They need to sprint away, not keep up this slow jog they've been doing."

Cross and I spread out some to give us each room to fight. It would take time for the ship's quartermaster to resupply all the hunters with arrows and then bring them up on deck. Although, the regular crew should have been out here already.

"Hey, why do you think the boarding crew isn't already with us?" A more cynical person would think something nefarious was afoot, but I knew at the very least the werebear, Tew, and Oriana wouldn't betray us. I wasn't truly suspicious of the rest of the crew, either. Instead, I was wondering if we were being left out of the loop on some kind of important information when the shield had activated. "I haven't heard any announcements since the shield activated, have you?"

"No, I haven't. Now that you mention it, I don't think I've seen anyone shoot at the other side in a while, either." Cross looked over the side, where our own ballista had been shooting back at the enemy out of the weapon ports arrayed along the weapon deck. "Um, James? They closed up the weapon hatches." A low hum started from somewhere beneath our feet, throbbing with a quickly-growing intensity. "I have a bad feeling about this."

"They definitely forgot about us out here. I bet no one realized the shield is also noise canceling." We both looked at the closest way to get inside the ship. It was about the same distance to the stairs down as it was to the door to the command center. A heavy clunk of machinery shifting caused us to stumble, and the hum quickly cut off. I looked at Cross, who was as wide-eyed as I probably was. "Run."

It was too late.

Both of us went airborne as the ship shot out from beneath us, trailing plumes of smoke and fire as it rocketed away.

Luckily for me, a mountain broke my fall.

Technically, it broke my *falls*, since I bounced off of the solid rock face a good five or six times, but I eventually came to a stop when my pelvis shattered a bolder. It was a nice change of pace that it wasn't my pelvis that broke like a piece of cheap plate glass. The Vigor stat moving to one fifty had given me a qualitative jump in toughness.

Just because most of my bones didn't break, didn't mean I wasn't bruised half to death. I coughed up a ridiculous amount of blood before I managed to cast a focused healing spell powerful enough to put me back together. It turned out my only broken bone was my nose, and that was because the heavy-as-hell demon core I was carrying swung around in its pouch and smacked me across the face at some point. I was getting rid of that thing as soon as possible.

By the time I was healed up enough to walk, the shadows were getting pretty long. I had a decent idea of where I'd landed in relation to the big volcano we wanted to raid, but I had absolutely no idea where Cross ended up. He was a needle in a haystack, while the volcano was a mountain in the middle of a bunch of mountains. One was obviously easier to find than the other.

Shouting for him seemed like a bad idea. The enemy airship might have tried to follow our airship, or it could have given up and decided the two schmucks that fell off were a great consolation prize. Since I lost sight of it after using my face to sculpt new designs into the side of a mountain, I didn't know how sneaky I needed to be. Erring on the side of caution was usually the better idea.

"My, I didn't think I'd find anyone like you out here."

I spun around, my mace already in my hand. Barely out of reach, standing in the shade of a tree, was an exceedingly pale man dressed in fancy clothes that were about two centuries out of style. "Great. An elder vampire. You're the last *thing* I wanted to find out here." I thought about what I had loaded in my wrist gun at the moment. Buckshot, which had the explosive flint shards mixed inside. If my Titles activated, I could blow him to bits before he knew what hit him. Of course, everything within twenty miles would know I was here, but if he was standing across from me, they probably already did anyway. "Any chance you want to take a step forward into the sunlight and make things easy on me?"

"Oh, I think you misunderstand the situation. I don't want to fight you. I want to *help* you." The vampire tapped a well-manicured nail against one of the longest fangs I'd ever seen. The stronger the vamp, the longer the tooth. I suddenly got a lot more serious about this guy. "More specifically, I want the two of us to help each other."

"Really? I hope you don't take it personally if I don't believe you. If you knew all the places I've been, and all the vamps I've dealt with, you'd have a hard time believing you, too." I slid to my left a few inches, making sure the tree behind him was straight on. "Not a single undead I've ever met has been what I would call *trustworthy.*"

"Perhaps, but you've never met an undead like me. Allow me to introduce myself." He bowed, flourishing his cloak behind him. "I've been known by many names, but here, they call me by my title. The Destitute."

As soon as he looked down to finish his bow, all three barrels of my wrist gun roared, unleashing a storm of silver, iron, lead, flint, and fire. My Title, Send Them into Orbit, most definitely activated on several of the interactions between the flint and iron.

I was sent flying once again, bouncing off a couple of trees before I landed in a snow drift. This time, I only needed a quick healing spell to fix a few minor bruises. I wasn't in any rush to go check on the ashes of the dead vampire, especially since I figured it was ultimately the sunlight that killed him. There was absolutely no way he could have survived something like that, especially since I destroyed the thing protecting him from the sun.

Honestly, it was a little anticlimactic. I was feeling a little cheated as I reloaded, this time with a mix of flechette and bolo rounds. I'd been expecting more from the guy who'd caused so many problems for so long. If all it took was one blast from my wrist gun, I should have come up here and finished him off a long time ago.

"Now to find—"

My voice was cut off by a grip of solid iron around my throat. By reflex, I swung my mace at the threat, and it was like trying to hit a wall. One that I couldn't smash down.

"I see that it's going to take some convincing to get you to come around to my point of view, interloper." The Destitute–who was very much not dead–lifted me off the ground by the throat with only one hand. His other hand had caught my blessed starmetal mace by the handle–which should have been burning him, much like the sunlight should have been burning him–and he plucked it from my grip like I was a kid acting up at preschool. "Once you understand everything that's at stake, and all the forces in play, you'll be *begging* to help me finish my Quest."

Some might call me a dense man, but I was smart enough to notice the emphasis he put on the 'Q' word. Either he was all kinds of delusional, or he got quests from some kind of system like I did.

It wasn't extremely shocking to me, since I'd been on other worlds where people had systems, but I didn't think anyone here had them. Maybe it was an elder vampire thing, or he'd been cursed, or blessed, or some other tomfoolery.

Either way, none of that mattered, because I saw Cross poke his head out from behind a tree where the vampire couldn't see him. The explosions must have led him here, and now we were both about to get caught. I couldn't let that happen.

Him yanking away my mace freed up that hand–the one with the shield-shaped knuckle duster–so I made a fist and activated *Shield Bash*. Something about the Knight ability overcame his ridiculously powerful grip, and The Destitute was forced to drop me and stagger backward, grabbing his jaw in pain.

I looked straight at Cross and mouthed the word 'run' before drawing my magic-eating ninjatō. He was clearly frustrated, but when the elder vampire slapped the sword out of my hand and punched me on the top of the head so hard I turned into an accordion for two seconds, he got the message.

Apparently, I'd knocked a tooth loose when I'd punched The Destitute in the face, and he was upset about it. It was a good thing my Vigor stat was over one fifty, otherwise I don't think I would have survived when I used the ability a second time. He managed to strip the knuckle dusters off before I could use them a third time, but by then it was too late to save his molar.

The last thing I remembered before passing out was him digging through the snow, trying to find his missing tooth.

Totally worth it.

## CHAPTER 35

Climbing the icy trail would have been impossible for Gleason if he'd been wearing anything other than the spike-covered armor he'd ordered made while leading the Blood Wardens. It was surprisingly effective at stabbing through the thick layers of ice that coated the old paving stones, especially in the sections where it was nearly vertical. He was forced to scale walls almost as if he was a child who hadn't yet learned to walk, driving his elbows and knees into the ice so he could crawl higher and higher up the mountain.

It wasn't just his armor that aided him. If Gleason were to try this route during the warmer months, he would've spent most of his time slipping and sliding down layers of mud and grime that ultimately made this trail all but impassable without heavy expenditures of magic. Since he couldn't use any kind of mana this close to the nightly patrols of the undead, daytime patrols of dwarves, and the sporadic patrols of demons, it meant the weather was helping Gleason just as much as his armor.

The higher up the hidden trail Gleason climbed, the more demons he was forced to hide from. Most consisted of goat men like the one he'd seen get eaten by the giant spider. A few were mixed with all sorts of abominations, such as octopus-like demons that floated a few inches off the ground and changed the colors of their skin to match the terrain around them. Thankfully, that specific kind of demon smelled horribly strong, making it easy for Gleason to avoid them.

Of course, the familiar spider demons were prevalent, as were smaller versions of the huge mole creature he'd seen erupt from the side of the mountain. The one type of demon Gleason was most disgusted by was the kind that tried to closely imitate humans. They were easy to spot due to the complete lack of clothing in an environment that would have killed a normal person. The horns poking out of their heads helped as well, but they were less noticeable depending on how much hair the demon had, and how large the horns might be. Most had short, spiky stubs that looked similar to a goat, while a rare few had long, curling rams horns that swirled tightly along either side of their head. Someone who was weak-willed and prone to sins of the flesh might think them beautiful in an otherworldly way, but to Gleason that only made them more revolting.

All of the human-looking demons were clearly the lowest among the patrols' pecking order. Gleason couldn't determine any specific rank structure, like the undead and dwarves certainly had, but certain demons were treated with a kind of wariness by the others around them, while a few were universally seen as lower-caste, or in demon culture, non-threatening. Without the natural weapons or magical abilities of the other demons, they seemed all but useless.

When Gleason finally made his way up to the hole in the side of the mountain, he wasn't surprised to see it was guarded by a pair of the weak, human-like demons. Both were formed in the mockery of women, with the exception of thick, pointed nails and mouths full of shark-like teeth. They stood on either side of the roughly-made entrance, shifting impatiently from foot to foot on the frozen ground while they whispered back and forth to one another.

As Gleason huddled out of sight behind a boulder left behind by the battle that created the entrance, one of the goat man demons walked out and immediately backhanded one of the guards hard enough that she bounced off the rock wall behind her, dropping the demon to her knees.

"Useless succubus! I told you last time, if your vapid and hollow brain *must* gossip while you're on watch, keep your eyes looking *out*!" The goat man spun to look at the other demon, apparently called a succubus, and raised his hand to strike her as well. She cowered in fear, and he grinned an evil, goat-like smile before slowly lowering his hand. "You, I'll spare punishment. Visit my nest after your shift to show me your thanks as payment."

She nodded fiercely in agreement, looking down at the goat man's cloven feet in fear. He snorted, blowing a cloud of steam in her face before abruptly turning and disappearing back down the tunnel as quickly as he appeared. The uninjured succubus knelt down to try and help her fellow demon back to her feet, but she was still disoriented by the hit to her head.

Gleason didn't think he'd get a more opportune chance.

When the whip snapped around the demon's neck, the succubus did her best to rip it free. The built-in enchantments only made it tighten harder around her windpipe, making it impossible for her to scream for help. Her face slowly started turning purple as she dropped to her side, kicking in a circle as she struggled for breath.

While he waited for her efforts to cease, Gleason made sure the other succubus would never get to her feet again. He stomped on her throat, crushing her trachea and destroying her ability to live. He didn't want to cause any wounds that made them bleed. Leaving a pool of blood would let their replacements know they'd been killed, and an alarm would be raised. Two demons abandoning their post might also raise an alarm, but one Gleason wouldn't care about.

"Now I see why you're treated as the weakest of demon-kind. You're disgusting filth, and you're genuinely worthless." Gleason quickly started dragging them away, not even waiting for the first succubus to finish choking to death. He rolled both bodies off a nearby cliff, watching as they tumbled out of sight. He then let out a sigh, wishing the ravine was choked with the bodies of dead demons. "The stain of their existence is gone, but there's more of their filth to cleanse."

Striding back to the opening, Gleason didn't hesitate before plunging into the mountain. Now wasn't the time to second-guess his decision to come all this way. No matter what he found inside, he would push onward and complete the task the Trinity set before him.

At first, he didn't see anything but a dark tunnel and scorched rubble. To Gleason, it was glorious. Being out of the cutting winds and frigid temperatures meant he'd finally made progress. There were signs of the battle between the huge demon mole and the figure fighting it, but mostly Gleason's senses were assaulted by the sulfur stink of brimstone left behind by the demons that lived here. His nose and eyes burned, making it difficult to see or smell anything beyond a few feet. If another demon approached, he wouldn't know it until it was too late to do anything but fight.

Luck was with him, and Gleason managed to make it to the end of the tunnel without encountering a single demon. It wasn't

251

until he entered the next section that he truly understood how lucky he'd been. If the roving guard who'd beaten the succubus had come out only a few minutes later, Gleason was sure the alarm would've been sound and he would've drowned in demons before he even knew what had happened.

If the spider demons made a nest, then the demons in this mountain's cavern made a hive. Much like a beehive, hexagonal structures stacked on top of one another to form living areas, storage, and more. Thick support columns dotted the space, holding up half the mountain peak above. Organic glowing bulbs of various colors were stuck to the ceiling and walls, and they lit the whole place up like a diseased bruise. The odd light hurt his eyes in a different way than the stench of brimstone was making them water. It was more of a pulsing pain that forced him to feel his heartbeat pounding in his skull. Thousands of demons walked, flew, scurried, and crawled everywhere he looked. If anything was in his stomach, he would have vomited at the assault on his senses mixed with the most intense feeling of disgust he'd ever experienced. He hated these creatures with every fiber of his being, and he wanted all of them to die.

Gleason didn't know if anything existed here before the arrival of the demons, but now they had certainly made a home for themselves. Carving out a place like this in the mountain must have taken years, if not decades. Gleason was only guessing, but he thought possibly a full quarter of the upper central section of the mountain had been hollowed out for their hive.

At first, he didn't see any way for him to get by the snarled mess of demonic lifeforms. There were simply too many of them for him to sneak by, and the unwavering light and surprising lack of shadows everywhere except inside the actual hollow hexagons made stealth all but impossible.

Fleeting plans of going out in a literal blaze of glory flitted through his head until he quashed them. That wasn't how he completed his task from the Trinity. He needed to stay alive. There was a single, narrow, seemingly forgotten and unguarded tunnel a quarter of the way around the cavern from him, but there was no way for him to get there without being seen. Then, he saw his chance.

Several larger tunnels intersected the hive, and from one of them a great horde of demons erupted. They were being led by the Demon Prince Sunar. Now that Gleason was close enough to get a good look at it, he thought it closely resembled an amalgamation of mole and pangolin, but in all the worst ways.

Thick, ropy scar tissue ran down the length of the massive demon in ragged stripes that criss-crossed its body. Armored plates pitted with burns and cracks showed it had endured a lifetime of battle, and somehow managed to survive. Wide claws blunted from digging tipped each of its three toes, and a meaty tail ended in a heavy ball of bone meant to smash both rock and armor. Its face drooled enormous amounts of mucus and acidic spittle that sizzled as it splattered across the ground. Any demons too slow or unlucky to move out of range of the spray were burned horribly by the concoction.

A certain type of floating eyeball demon seemed to be immune to the terrible acid, and they swooped in with worm-like appendages to scoop up the mole's discharge and carry it away. Gleason watched in horrified fascination as they packed the slime against the cavern walls, creating new honeycombs for more demons to live. Their single-minded focus to expand the hive reminded Gleason of the way insects acted, and the image of the demon plague spreading across his homeland like an ant swarm filled his mind. It was horrifying.

Still, the arrival of the giant mole had given Gleason a way to continue deeper into the mountain. Demon Prince Sunar didn't communicate in a method Gleason could understand, but he must have given some kind of order to the masses around him. Demons flooded from the hive, filling the cavern with their buzzing, croaking, and screaming. Some unspoken order caused them all to rush en masse to a tunnel that was nearly hidden by a support column. The giant mole demon lumbered after them, trumpeting in rage.

All the commotion gave Gleason the opportunity to move from one empty honeycomb to the next, carefully shifting his way along the wall opposite the direction the horde of demons were swarming. The entire time, Gleason fervently wished he had the ability to turn off his sense of smell. To say that the demons lived in filth was an understatement that defied description. If there was food in his stomach, Gleason would have vomited a hundred times over by now.

In some ways, the heavy stench as a distraction turned out to be a blessing. Gleason focused on his immediate surroundings instead of the threats farther out, which meant he never even thought about using his magic to fight or protect himself. The mana around him didn't stir in the slightest, leaving his passage completely unnoticed by even the most magically sensitive of demons. Even though Gleason hadn't seen a bar of soap in weeks, and he smelled more like the inside of an old boot than a normal person, his stink wasn't anything like the hive. He managed to ghost through the cavern and make his way to his escape route in a shockingly short amount of time.

Once he was close, he saw why the tunnel was unguarded. It was a rubble-strewn and dust-filled tunnel that had obviously been abandoned by the demons long ago, probably due to a collapse, or the demons realizing the tunnel didn't go anywhere they wanted to travel. Unfortunately, it was still the only viable path forward for Gleason. He squeezed his way between piles of rocks, trash, and rotting refuse until he could no longer see, hear, or smell the demon hive behind him.

Collapsing on his knees, Gleason took a long series of deep breaths to calm his nerves. In many ways, that had been the worst experience of his life. He'd thought he'd known what it meant to be around the unclean, to see the need to wipe away the dirt and grime that made the world a lesser place. It had always been his job to root out the wrongdoers, the infection, the *rot* that settled where people thought none existed. He had taken pride in being the best at his job, at never flinching no matter how onerous the task. Be they elderly, women, or children, Gleason hadn't once stepped back from beating or burning out those he deemed unclean. Little did he understand– how naïve the version of Gleason all but one hour ago had been– everything he'd thought of as wrong in his universe was equal to the purity and cleanliness of freshly fallen snow.

Gleason had just seen the absolute worst spot of infection and rot *ever*. Possibly in the history of the planet, nothing had needed to be torn out by the roots more than this place, this mountain. He had never seen a more wretched hive of scum and villainy, and he would gladly give his life to burn it all to ash.

After giving himself some extra time to recover, Gleason continued deeper into the mountain. He wasn't quite sure what he was looking for anymore, not after the mental shock of what he'd just been through, but something inside him was pushing him forward. It had been several days since he'd eaten anything, and he hadn't found a clean water source since the last time he'd stopped and boiled some. If he stopped, he might not be able to get back up again.

When he came to a tunnel collapse, Gleason didn't let that slow him down. He climbed to the top of the loose pile of rock and started shoving it to the side. There were pieces too big to move by hand, so he went around. If he couldn't go around, Gleason risked small bursts of magic to help him burrow through. Time lost all meaning as he made his way deeper and deeper into the collapse, drawn forward by some unknown and unspoken power that was beyond him. All he could accept, all his brain could absorb at the moment, was if he wanted to complete his goals, this is what he had to do.

Cloying dust, a complete lack of light, and a growing sense of claustrophobia eventually started to slow him down. Like a candle being blown out, he lost the inner drive that allowed him to keep going. Gleason lay on his stomach in the dark, barely able to breathe through the thick dust, wishing he could just curl up into a ball and close his eyes and go to sleep. He couldn't even do that because the path he had carved was so narrow, forcing him to crawl like a worm.

Before waves of despair and self-doubt had a chance to wash over him, or a moment of self-reflection had a chance to settle into his brain, Gleason saw a faint hint of light coming through a crack in the rubble in front of his face. As the rock powder settled, he was able to see where the tunnel continued beyond the collapse. He'd made it.

Extracting himself the last few feet took more effort than Gleason expected, mostly because he didn't want the only way he knew he had out of the mountain collapsing behind him. A few small earth spells were necessary to reinforce the narrow path he'd created, and each one only highlighted how exhausted and close to the edge of his limits he had reached with this journey.

Once he was in the next section, Gleason stumbled his way toward the source of light. The distant glow wasn't anything like the dirty and diseased colors of the hive. It was clean, pure fire. The light of plain torches. In his mind, he imagined an oasis of humanity hidden within the fetid confines of the rotten caves the stark beauty of this mountain hid from the outside world. Deep down, he knew it was a fantasy, but that didn't make it hurt any less when the tunnel abruptly ended at a shadowed overhang overlooking another massive cavern, this one filled not with demons, but undead.

Below him were hundreds, maybe thousands, of vampires, ghouls, wraiths, and specters. They were the greater undead, herding the tens of thousands of lesser undead through the snarl of crates, supplies, and workstations that surrounded the two airships docked in the center of the open space. That many zombies and skeletons should have caused logjams and problems everywhere, but somehow they moved with a smooth precision on a level that frightened Gleason to his core. He had the experience to understand what it took to pull something like this off, and what it meant. Only a leader with a sharp mind and heavy hand could wield such a dull knife with lethal precision, and to date, he'd never seen their equal.

Mixed in with the undead were a surprisingly small number of dwarves. Most were congregated around the airships, and the rest were focused on manufacturing high quality arms and armor for the ridiculous number of undead soldiers. While they weren't as organized or regimented as the undead, Gleason didn't see a single dwarf stop to take a break the entire time he stood there, watching.

As he was surveying the second army he'd seen today that could easily wipe out most of the Wardens without much effort, Gleason saw something that made everything else fade away into background noise. A man in a stupid straw hat, with a very peculiar set of weapons and an oversized rucksack, had just been tossed over the side of one of the airships like a bag of rice. Several of the larger bone knight ghouls were ready for him when he hit the ground, and they stripped him of his things before he was tied tightly to a wooden post. As he was carried away, Gleason was sure of it. James Holden was *alive*.

"It can't be." Gleason started pacing back and forth, mumbling to himself out loud. "He can't be alive. He was in Greendown. I destroyed Greendown. Didn't I?"

Holding his head in his hands, Gleason did his best to force down the scream that tried to erupt from his parched throat. If Holden was alive, that meant he was a failure. Greendown might still stand. He wasn't worthy of the gods guidance, and he most assuredly wasn't worthy of the final task they'd assigned him here, under this mountain.

*Hero… soon.*
*Chance… comes.*
*Prepare.*

Doubts and fears washed away like shadows before the sun. The voices in his head sounded as if they were struggling to speak to him for some reason, but he knew he had heard them. They called him a hero, and they told him to prepare.

Gleason once again looked out over the cavern, seeing how massive the forces arrayed against him would be. He didn't understand how he was supposed to prepare for something like that, and this was only one side of the coin. The demons were just as bad, if not worse. And to make everything he'd seen so far seem like a trivial joke thrust upon him by unfeeling and uncaring gods instead of the benevolent and loving Trinity he knew them to be, Gleason knew there was supposed to be a dragon running around somewhere, too. There was absolutely no way he could do anything against a threat like a dragon.

*Enemy…*
*Of my enemy…*
*Is my tool…*

The voices in his head whispered their order, and he felt it settle into his soul. The black veins writhed under his skin once again, driving away the pain and exhaustion he'd been suffering from, healing everything but his mental fatigue.

With a feral grin, Gleason looked back at the tunnel he'd barely been able to make his way down. It would take a lot of work, and even more luck if he was going to stay undetected, but now he had a plan. The enemy of my enemy is my tool.

"No mistakes this time. I'm not going to fail. Ever again."

Gleason started digging.

## <u>CHAPTER 36</u>

It wasn't the first time I'd woken up in a dungeon with a headache, naked, tied to a wooden post. It wasn't even the second time. If you didn't count the times I had to use a safe word, this was the third. If you *did* count the times there was a safe word involved…

That wasn't really important right now. World three had been a weird time for me, and the Soldier Class could gain levels in a lot of different ways. My trainer, Eyide–which I later found out meant 'spiteful' in their language–had been a beautiful woman that maxed out the crazy scale. She wanted to find every possible exercise to get the class to its highest point in the fastest way. If I hadn't gained my healer class first, she most definitely would have killed me in the process. Some days, I still missed her. Most days, I wonder why we never ended up killing each other. Occasionally, I had nightmares about her.

At first, I didn't move, and kept my breathing pattern the same so any observers would think I was still unconscious. Barely cracking an eye, I looked around and saw that there wasn't anyone around me. That didn't mean I wasn't being watched. I just couldn't see them.

The room I was in didn't have any windows, and the only entrance was a narrow stone slab with thick iron hinges. Two small copper lanterns hung on either side of the doorway, each holding a single tallow candle that let out a thin stinking smoke trail from the flickering yellow flame.

Oddly enough, the stone room was perfectly clean and dry, and seemed to have been carved straight out of the bedrock as one solid piece. There was no drain or bucket, so if I had to do any bleeding, or other bodily functions, it wouldn't stay clean for long. The wooden post they'd tied me to was wedged horizontally in two matching grooves on opposite walls. Metal chains and ropes made from some kind of incredibly tough sinew had been used to tie my hands so my arms were bent at a forty-five degree angle. Shackles kept my feet locked in place with only a few inches of give. My cell was a little longer and taller than it was across, meaning I could probably lay flat on the ground without having to bend my knees, but just barely. Overall, it certainly could've been worse.

After what had to be two or three hours, nobody came to check on me. Normally, I'd be perfectly fine with playing the waiting game to see if their plan was to interrogate me, torture me, or play patty-cake, but something very serious was quickly developing. A problem I couldn't ignore for much longer.

My nose was starting to itch, and it was driving me nuts.

I pretended to jerk awake, and look around at the cell. In case they were listening to me instead of watching, I started talking out loud. "Third time's the charm, huh? Maybe this is the one that finally does me in. Fair warning though, the last two times somebody captured me they ended up regretting it more than a freshman's bank account regrets a spring break in Cancun." I tried to use my elbow to scratch my nose, but I couldn't quite reach it. "Hey, can somebody come in here? I've got a spot I can't reach that really needs to be scratched."

When nobody came in right away, I decided it was time to try to see what, if any, restrictions they had put on magic. There was absolutely no way they'd toss me in a dungeon that didn't have a way to block me from casting spells, but I was hoping I might manage something, especially with my instinctive casting.

Instead, when I went to cast a spell, I didn't have any problems or restrictions whatsoever. When the spellform started to take shape, it was yanked away from me with a bruising force, getting sucked into the ceiling above me. It definitely didn't feel good. While hard to describe, I'd say the sensation was similar to having all your eyelashes ripped out at the same time by electrified tweezers, and simultaneously getting kicked in the kidneys by an angry donkey. On the bright side, my nose didn't itch anymore.

"Well, I see you've discovered the little trick I installed when we built this place."

Somehow, The Destitute was standing in the open doorway. I hadn't seen or heard him, which told me more about how strong he was than even our fight did. I'd gotten cocky, thinking my stats being close to or over one fifty made me special. This guy put me to shame. He made me look like I was playing in the little leagues, while he was in the majors.

"Yeah, neat trick. What is it? Runes? An artifact? Oh, is it an artifact *empowered* by runes? I bet that's it." I tried to snap my fingers and point at him, but the ropes and chains were too tight. "If you tapped into a ley line or two, I bet you could expand the range on that a bunch. Let me out of here, and I'll show you how to–"

"Now that you're in a position to be a more… *active* listener, I think you and I have several important things to discuss." He cut me off, not willing to play into my banter. Instead, he pulled two familiar-looking objects out of a pouch on his belt. One looked like a large diamond, and the other looked like a black marble. "First, before I reveal anything about myself, I should tell you *why*. Why I haven't simply killed you, and taken these objects for my own."

Seeing the most powerful vampire I'd ever had the displeasure of meeting holding an item so powerful the system had warned me about it–including referencing interdimensional laws that carried death sentences for gods–was a sobering moment. Maybe now wasn't the time for fun and games.

"Okay, Vlad the Impaler's salty cousin, Desperate Dave. Let me go, and give me back my balls before something bad happens to you."

On second thought, this might be the perfect time.

"I'll release you and give you back your… balls… as soon as we've come to an agreement." The Destitute frowned, and took a step closer to me. "However, my name is not Dave, and I'm of no relation to someone called Vlad. Attempt to make fun of me again, and I *will* punish you." He flicked me between the eyes hard enough that my head bounced against the beam holding me in place. "Understand?"

"Understand? Oh, I get it, tall, dark, and sparkly." I dodged the next finger flick, and laughed in his face. "You get off on this kind of thing, don't you? Forcing others to do your bidding, keeping them prisoner until you've had time to warp their minds to your way of thinking. It's not going to work on me, Count *Count*. I'm on to your ways. One ball, ah-h-h. Two balls, Ah-Ah-Ah. Well, I've got news for you. I can do long division in my head!"

Every punch after his second one was entirely unnecessary. I couldn't even feel them, because he hit me in the gut so hard it broke my spine. I flopped around uselessly, like a broken muppet with half his strings cut. After five or six, he gave up, deciding it was enough.

I knew there had to be ruptured organs to go along with the broken bones, but all I could do was focus on breathing. I didn't have the option of casting a healing spell, so all I could do was hope my Vigor stat was high enough to keep me alive. My vision started fuzzing in and out, and I vomited blood all over the pristine floor. Yep, that wasn't a good sign.

The ringing in my ears was too loud for me to understand what he was saying, but when he pulled out a wand of some kind and tapped me on the chest with it, I knew instantly the burning sensation that flooded through my body was from the magic his device carried. Apparently, his enchantment didn't work on objects, only on spells cast by people.

"Now, are you quite finished? Or do we need to keep doing this?" The elder vampire tapped the wand against his thigh, staring impatiently at me. "I was very serious when I said I wanted to explain the *why* of things to you."

"Yeah, I think I got most of it out of my system. I'm almost out of famous vampires I know anyway. There's only the cereal guy left, and I can't think of anything funny with chocolate at the moment." I coughed up a little more blood before nodding. "Nope, I got nothing."

"Finally." The Destitute sighed, then tucked the wand back out of sight. "Now, back to this." He held up the Enhancement Gem, letting it catch the dim candlelight so it would sparkle. "As I'm sure you know, I can't use this. If I kill you, I could certainly bond with it, but then I'd be stuck with an object that certain powerful people and factions are *more* than willing to hunt down and kill for. As a member of the undead race, I can no longer generate offspring, and the bond doesn't extinguish until the permanent death of the current owner. For someone like me, that would be… *forever*."

I thought about it from his point of view for a moment. "Oh. Oh *dang*. You'd basically be carrying your own death warrant. It would only be a matter of time until somebody came looking for that thing, and they'd kill you in a heartbeat to get it." I smiled, this time being careful not to laugh in his face. He was a little sensitive about that kind of thing. "So, what you're saying is, you need me."

The Destitute grimaced, as if he'd eaten something sour. "I wouldn't go that far. There are plenty of minions in my forces I could pass this burden to, but none of them have the second thing you have."

I gave him a wink and looked down. "Really? I didn't think you'd go for–"

He backhanded me again, hitting me hard enough to crack the wooden beam. "Stop. We were making progress, and then you had to ruin it."

"Couldn't help myself." I blinked away the stars floating in my vision, fighting to stay awake. "Anyway, you mentioned a second reason for keeping me alive. Is it because I made the demon core?"

"This?" He held up the core in question between two fingers, obviously not having any problems with the weight. "No. These are common enough. Maybe not on this world, but common enough."

"Hold on." I felt a little fuzzy from the blow to the head earlier, but he definitely talked like he knew there were a lot of worlds out there. In fact, with the way he'd talked about the Enhancing Gem, it seemed like this vamp had a deeper understanding of the universal powers than I did. "You're not from around here either, are you?"

"If by that, you mean I'm an interdimensional traveler selected to represent my gods to perform various tasks they assign on select worlds spread throughout the cosmos in an attempt to control the spread of destructive forces intended to bring about chaos and the eventual destruction of all inhabitable planets, then yes, I'm not from around here either." The Destitute's lengthy canines gleamed in the candlelight as he grinned at the shocked look on my face. "Don't tell me you thought you were the only one?"

"Are you *kidding* me?" The fuzzy feeling had disappeared, but the room still felt like it was spinning. "Twenty years. For twenty *years* I've thought I was the only one. I've been stumbling around like an idiot, trying to figure things out on my own. Nobody *explained* anything to me, or *helped* with anything. Nobody *asked* me if I wanted this. One day I was trying to save someone getting attacked in a dark alley, and then the next thing I knew, I'm getting sucked through a portal, and I woke up on a different planet with a bunch of screens and messages in my face, telling me what to do!" I tried to slow my breathing. This wasn't the time to lose it, but damn it, how was I supposed to know there was more than one of us? Except, his actions didn't match with his words. "Wait. If you're like me, why are you going around killing innocent people, and sending armies of undead to wipe out whole cities full of women and children?"

"You must not have heard me. I'm a representative of *my* gods, not *your* gods. We probably have similar Quests. That doesn't mean we need to use the same methods to complete them." He waved a hand in front of his face, and poked at something I couldn't see. "You probably aren't at an ability level to manipulate your interface like this yet. Perhaps one day, you'll delve deep into the intricacies of what empowers our ilk and learn enough to do so."

Then, I could see it. Somehow, he'd made his system screen visible to me. It wasn't anything like mine, but I could certainly see the similarities. While mine was usually blue and silver, with the occasional gold highlights, his was red and gold, with shiny, obsidian-like black highlights. Exactly what I expected a gaudy vampire's system screen would look like. He spun the screen so I could read it, and for the first time I got to see what another person's system was like.

---

**Name: The Destitute (Current Alias)**
**Race: Ancient Elder Vampire**
**Age: 984 years (Local)**
**Evolution: Third**
**Level: 300/300**
**Class: Duelist/Mage/Bloodweaver (3/3)**
**Profession: Runesmith/Engineer/General (3/3)**

**Status:**
**Strength- 300**
**Flexibility- 300**
**Vigor- 300**
**Mind- 300**
**Quest List:**
**Quest One: Partner with Duergar Council**

> **Quest Two: Repair the Silver Star - [Time remaining: 19 moonfalls]**
> **Quest Three: Close the Demon Gate - [Time remaining: 19 moonfalls]**
> **Quest Four: Defeat remaining Demonic Forces**
> **Quest Five: Save Planet (79/100)**

There were a lot of similarities to my status page, and even more differences. Seeing his stats at literally double mine was a hefty punch in the gut, but it did explain why he manhandled me so easily. If I was almost a thousand years old, my stats would be way better. Just saying.

He hadn't been lying about the quests. We did have two that matched up almost perfectly. One thing I noticed was his 'Save Planet' seemed pretty close to my 'Deliver Justice', including the apparent world count. He just had his second number filled in, while mine was all question marks. Now that I'd seen his page, maybe mine would fill in, too.

"I was correct, yes? Our Quests are nearly identical, aren't they?" The Destitute waved his hand again, and I could feel his magic touch me momentarily before it was sucked away by the enchantment above us. His screen changed, to something similar to my *Identify* spell. He turned it to show me. "Don't lie to me. I know for sure at least one of them is."

> **Name: James Holden**
> **Level: 100**
> **Quest: Close the Demon Gate**
> **Threat Ranking: Moderate**
> **Description: Human male representing an unknown god, not native to this planet. Exact status points are unknown, but estimated to be close to his level. Actual age does not match physical age, increasing threat ranking. Chance of partnership to complete similar goals due to greater outside threat is moderate. Possibly irrational. Approach with caution.**

"Wow. I wouldn't say I'm irrational. That feels unfair, especially coming from a system that a goth kid would–" He raised his fist, preparing to punch me in the face again. "Okay, okay. Yes, we have two quests that are almost the same, and a third that's pretty close."

"So, you can see why it's important we join forces." The Destitute lowered his fist, relaxing his posture. "If the two of us work together, we can kill the dragon, steal the magical core in its immortal heart, you fly the Silver Star through the Demon Gate with the dragon's core, I toss it over the side, and we both escape before the power of the dragon core rips apart the connection with this world and it explodes."

I tried to follow everything he said, but I was getting hit with a whole lot of stuff, really, really fast. "Okay, lots to unpack there, but I'm not seeing a downside so far. What about–"

"It is a simple plan. Gateways are unstable connections between worlds. The best way to break those connections is to flood them with more power than they can maintain." The elder vampire started pacing back and forth, getting excited as he explained the details of his plan. "Dragons are the single most naturally magical creature in existence. Their core is what contains the majority of that power." He held up the black demon core again, rolling it between his fingers. "Unlike the unnatural abominations that created this, the power contained in a dragon core wants to return to the universe. That means we only have a few minutes once the dragon is killed to take it through the gate before it loses the level of power we need for it to work."

"And why is the Silver Star so important?" I had to admit, his idea had me hooked so far. It was far more developed than my current plan of 'find gate, figure it out'. "Why do we have to use that specific airship? Why not toss in the dragon core, or fly in one of the other airships?"

"Unfortunately, it all comes down to this." The Destitute tossed the Enhancing Gem up in the air before catching it again. "Although ancient, the builders that put the Silver Star together were far ahead of their time. In fact, I suspect there was one of us–an interloper–involved at some point in its design. The runescript they used during its creation is layered in every facet of the construction. When we toss the dragon core over the side, it's going to create the kinds of tears in reality that threaten the lives of deities. There's only one way to survive something like that, and the Silver Star has it everywhere. Protection, preservation, speed enhancement, there are some combinations I haven't seen before, in such elegant patterns, that it's more art than function. Even the nails holding the boards in place are covered in runes."

"Something that intricate would need an *insane* amount of power." I tried to shake my head, but the board stopped me. "With the gem, you might be able to power something like that for a few minutes at most. It sounds like a one-way trip to me."

"Normally, yes. The dwarves aren't sure how the creators did it in the past, either. It probably has something to do with the missing key." He held up the demon core and tapped it against the gem. I nearly winced before remembering he couldn't use the gem without me. "If we had a few more of these, we would have more than enough time to fly past the halfway point and back."

I thought about it. I thought about everything he'd said. To say it was a lot to take in was the understatement of the week. This guy dropped bombshell after bombshell on me, and I was having a hard time internalizing everything. Still, his plan was a good one, and it lined up with my Quests perfectly. I only had one sticking point he hadn't answered yet.

"What about the army you sent after Greendown? You never explained that." I noticed him tense up again in the shoulders. He'd been hoping I'd forgotten about that question. "Yeah, we're not following the same gods, but if we're both supposed to save everyone, how is that a—"

"You just answered your own question." The Destitute stepped closer, nearly touching his nose with mine. "You saw my Quest. It does not tell me to 'Save Everyone'. My Quest is to 'Save Planet'. That's what I've been doing for *years*. I used what tools I had available, at first. There isn't a graveyard, unmarked grave, ancient battlefield, or lost city within hundreds of miles that still has a body, bones, or restless spirit in it. I drained them *all*." His eyes were feverish, nearly glowing with passion. "To keep the demons contained, keep them *here*, I've made deals with the gray dwarves on *three planets*, brought every single powerful undead I could maintain control over to this mountain from across the *continent*, drained every prison I could find of their criminals of sound mind to be converted into vampirism, and leveraged it all so I could take the fight to the demons without a minute's break. For *years*."

The Destitute stood very still, waiting for me to say something in return. When I didn't, he let out a great sigh and took a step back, shaking his head. "The constant grind wears down even the endless endurance of the undead. When I needed more soldiers to fill my ranks, I sent a group to complete the task. Better one city lost, than an entire world."

I... I didn't know what to think.

On one hand, I agreed with him. Sacrificing one city was far better than giving up an entire world. It was a hard choice, but one any person with a brain would make every time, especially if they were in a position of leadership.

On the other hand, I'd been there. I'd seen the people of Greendown huddled in their homes as the undead ghouls pounded at the gates, yearning to feast on their flesh, and the vampires leading their version of platoons hooted and hollered in joy at the thought of draining their victims of blood.

This wasn't a simple Judgment. I tried pulling on my Mantle, to see what the ancient foundational power of the universe thought about the situation. When nothing happened, I didn't know if it was because the jail cell blocked it, or because even Justice didn't know the right answer.

One thing I did know, this entire planet owed The Destitute a debt of gratitude. He might have been an evil bloodsucking villain destined for damnation, but he was also kind of a hero. It certainly made me uncomfortable knowing that, and I think he could read it on my face.

"I'll leave you to think over everything we've discussed. If you have any questions, try casting another spell. It will draw my attention. My second will bring you some refreshments in a short time." He turned and walked away, closing the door silently behind him. Before it slammed shut, he poked his head back inside to leave me with some parting words. "Remember. I don't *need* you to complete my Quest. It would only make the situation slightly easier for me. So, the next time we meet, I expect an answer. We work together, or you die."

The candles fluttered as the stone door slid shut with a sense of finality.

"Yep. I called it. Third time's the charm."

## CHAPTER 37

After the vampire left, I stood there for longer than I probably should have, doing nothing but thinking over everything he told me. This wasn't the first time I'd been presented with a difficult situation as a Judge. Far from it. However, it might have been the first time I could remember that I didn't have the help of the Mantle to guide me.

Once I realized what I was really doing was moping, I got over myself and started getting busy trying to escape. No matter what my decision was going to be, I wasn't going to make it while I was a prisoner. After I got free, I could think more about everything I'd learned.

During our talk, I was sure one of the times The Destitute had whacked me I'd heard the beam make a cracking noise. Since I wasn't an owl, I couldn't turn my head all the way around to look at the damage. Hopefully, it had done enough structural damage to the wood that I had a chance to break it.

The beam definitely wasn't a normal piece of wood. I would've been able to easily snap it and get free otherwise. There weren't carvings visible anywhere, which meant it'd most likely been treated with some kind of alchemical mixture to make it stronger. Or, they had ridiculously strong trees somewhere I hadn't been yet.

Slamming the back of my head over and over against the beam only succeeded in giving me a headache. I decided to switch gears. The chains holding my feet in place gave great leverage, so I stood on my toes and shoved against the post as hard as I could. It groaned in protest, fighting me the whole way. Splinters dug into my shoulders like knives, making thin streams of blood run down my chest and back. Skin tore around my ankles where the chains pinched, making my footing slippery.

Before I could finish the job, I heard someone approaching from outside my cell. Heavy plodding footsteps were getting louder, and the scrape of metal on stone meant they were in armor. The moment they saw me, they would know what I'd done. The wooden post was splintered too badly to hide. More guards would come, and better restraints would be installed. This was my only chance at escape.

I dropped down, resting all the weight I could on my wrists, and took a deep breath. Then I drove my feet into the ground, putting everything I had into forcing my shoulders through the wooden beam. It finally gave way, snapping into two heavy chunks that both my arms were still tied and chained to. Several splinters tore free from my shoulders and neck, causing more blood to stream down and add to the slippery mess on the floor.

There wasn't time to try and free my feet. The door opened, and in stepped a heavily muscled gray dwarf wearing a full suit of plate mail armor. He was holding a loaf of bread in one hand and a wineskin in the other, which meant he couldn't immediately pull the heavy club free from his belt when he turned around and saw what had occurred. His eyes widened in surprise, and he tried to take a step back as I lifted the two heavy sections of wood over each shoulder.

"Ah, this is gonna hurt–"

I slammed the two halves together like they were cymbals, crashing them against his head. Our height disparity almost made it unfair, but I wasn't going to take it easy on him because he was shorter than me. He was in a full suit of armor, and I was naked. I think it balanced the scales a bit.

The dwarf crumpled to the ground, dropping the food and wine. At first, I thought the fight was over. I should've known, things never went that easily for me. He bounced back up quickly, trying to dodge to my left as he pulled his club out. It spoke to his sense of self-confidence that he didn't immediately try and run to get help. We'd have to see if it was a mistake or not.

Since I still had my feet chained to the ground, I couldn't let him get behind me. I flailed both halves of the heavy wooden post as hard as the tight space would allow, which unfortunately wasn't a full windup and swing unless I went with more vertical strikes. His armor absorbed the worst of the hits, but he definitely grunted in pain a few times.

He had to give up on getting behind me, however the two jabs he got in with his club on my ribs made me think I was the loser in the exchange. He hit *hard*, and I didn't have anything to help absorb the body blows.

"There's more polite ways to introduce yourself. Humans. I swear, your whole race is always so violent." The gray dwarf flicked his wrist, deftly spinning his club in his palm. It showed a deep familiarity with the weapon, and a greater understanding of its balance. That was definitely not a good sign for how this fight would go. If you were me. "The name's Shōen. Be sure you remember it when you tell your gods who sent you to meet them."

"Alright, Shōen. I'm man enough to admit it. That line was pretty badass." I got a better grip on the chains holding the wooden planks to my arms and lifted them above my head. "Too bad a sharp wit won't save you from this beating you're about to get."

He tilted his head to the side, trying to tell if my compliment was real or not. When he decided it was genuine, the burly dwarf gave his club another twirl and crouched, readying himself to attack. "Good. No fear, and you can compliment an opponent without damaging your own pride. Maybe I won't kill you, but don't count on it."

No other words were spoken. The two of us clashed, a fight of toughness and grit to see who would outlast the other. I had the advantage in height, strength, and leverage, while he had superior mobility, weapons, and armor. If my feet had been free, it would've been over in a matter of moments. I could've overpowered him with a few well-placed hits to the same spot, and he would have gone down. Instead, I was stuck in one place and it turned into a slog, with him focusing on body blows, while I was forced to concentrate on his arms and head.

What decided the fight ended up being my inability to heal myself. My fighting style, at its base, had always been built upon the foundation of my first profession of Healer. Under more normal circumstances, it's not as noticeable because I can utilize the skills of my classes and training. Basic stuff, like, I don't know… *dodging*. After that option was taken away, and I couldn't heal myself, the body blows quickly added up. Instead of attacking, I spent most of the time defending my ribs, liver, and kidneys from the punishing club that somehow seemed to hit me unless I used both arms to block.

Both of us knew he'd won when I hadn't swung at him in at least a good thirty seconds. That was a very long time in a serious fight for someone to not try and hurt the other guy.

"Ha! Never met a human I couldn't beat." Shōen took a step back, breathing hard from the exertion of thrashing me. "I'll give you one chance to give up. If you don't, I'll keep that promise to send you on to meet your gods."

I lowered my arms, letting out a sigh. If I'd only had a few extra minutes to get my feet free, this would have ended a whole lot differently. Instead, I'd gotten my ass kicked by a dude that would need help getting cookies from the top shelf at a grocery store. Before I could actually surrender, the stone door slammed open behind the dwarf.

"Whu–?" Shōen started to turn and see who was entering, a surprised look on his face. He wasn't expecting anyone, but he certainly didn't think an enemy would sneak their way into the middle of a base filled with undead. He never even thought it necessary to try and defend himself.

Cross took full advantage.

The Apprentice Judge stabbed the dwarf in the space between his shoulder and chest armor, perfectly fitting the lethally sharp blade of the spear I'd loaned him into the incredibly tight gap. Cross jerked the speartip free and thrust forward again, this time stabbing Shōen in the gap between his groin and thigh armor, but the blade pinched in place before it could dig too deep.

Shōen grunted in pain and twisted away, nearly jerking the spear out of Cross's hands in the process. Unfortunately for the dwarf, I hadn't given up yet.

Both halves of the wooden post slammed across his back, keeping him from being able to dodge the next hit from Cross. The speartip slashed diagonally toward the dwarf's neck, nicking him enough to cause a steady flow of blood without completely taking his head off. Shōen held his throat as he dropped to his knees, looking at the two of us with wide eyes. It wasn't instantly fatal, but he would soon be dead without any aid.

I held up a hand to stop Cross from finishing him off. He looked at me like I'd lost my mind, but I patted at the air in the universal symbol of 'hold on a sec, you'll see what I'm doing'. I bent down a bit and met Shōen's eyes. "You're an enemy, but an honorable one. You offered me a chance to surrender, with my life in exchange. I'm giving you the same offer. If you get me out of these shackles and clear of the magic-eating enchantment in time, I can heal you back to perfect health. If I do that, in return you won't try to escape, and you won't set off any alarms. Deal?"

The dwarf couldn't move fast enough. I had a feeling he knew what would happen to him if he died while working for a guy always on the hunt for bodies to fill the ranks of his undead armies. Ankle shackles fell away and Shōen literally dragged me out the door. Once we were a few steps away, he dropped to one knee and pointed with his free hand at his throat.

I felt a bit of resistance as I healed him, probably because he didn't trust me, but my magic wasn't sucked away by some crazy force and Shōen was kept from the jaws of death by only moments. With the amount of blood loss he was suffering from, I had no idea how he'd been able to walk out of the cell.

Since I'm not a complete idiot, while I had nominal control of Shōen's bodily systems, I sent a small jolt of electricity to the pineal gland in the middle of his brain. He spasmed for a bit, then passed out. I wasn't sure if a dwarf had a pineal gland like a human, but thankfully our brains were nearly the same. It was the gland that made the hormones meant to make people sleepy, like serotonin and melatonin. The exhaustion from extensive healing mixed with the sudden flood of sleepy chemicals in his brain were too much for the stout dwarf to handle. He passed out, collapsing onto his back, already snoring like a chainsaw. After searching him, I took a pouch off his belt that contained several tokens and artifacts meant to act similar to keys. Now we had access to all kinds of places, as long as they didn't require Shōen to also be present to activate.

"There, he's asleep. Now we don't have to worry if he was going to set off an alarm or not, and I don't have to feel bad about killing someone who might not deserve it." I turned to Cross, who was leaning heavily on the staff-spear. He was clutching his cursed arm, which had gotten worse while we'd been separated. The strands of the black stain now reached his elbow, with the majority of the curse still trapped in the middle of his forearm. "I gotta say, it's really good to see you. How did you manage to get down here?"

"I ran." Cross gave me a weak smile when I put my hands on my hips with an indignant glare. "Seriously. Once you were captured, I had to run to keep up with the airship that took you away. We were lucky it was damaged so badly." He motioned for me to follow him, so we started walking down a narrow stone hallway while we talked. "I saw them fly inside this base, so I started searching for a way inside. Everywhere I looked, it was guarded by both dwarves and intelligent undead, so I started tunneling. I'm not as developed in earth magic as you and Jess, but when I stop caring about the curse poisoning me, it actually made me stronger." Cross held up his blackened hand, which momentarily spasmed uncontrollably. "After I found the best place to dig, it didn't take long before I made it through."

"How did none of the enemy sense you casting magic?" I slowed down a bit, making sure I didn't outpace Cross. He was clearly exhausted, and moving stiffly down the hallway. "Not just that, how did the undead not detect you? I'd think at least a few vampires would notice you were around."

Cross shrugged and held up his hand again. "I think it's the lich curse. Since I didn't try holding it back, the curse must have tainted the mana my spells gave off. It probably felt like another undead casting spells and ignored me." He grimaced, thinking about what that meant for himself. "I guess it's the same reason why none of the undead noticed me. If their senses tell them I'm an undead, they don't bother looking my way. They're all so busy, I don't think they'd have time to run off and check on every little thing that doesn't perfectly match what's normally in their environment."

I let the matter drop, not wanting to worry him any more than necessary. It still didn't match up with what I knew about the olfactory abilities of a vampire, but right now that wasn't our biggest concern. I needed my gear, and some time to think.

Then, I wanted to get a look at the Silver Star with my own eyes.

I had a Quest to complete.

## CHAPTER 38

All of my stuff had been stacked neatly in a chest at the end of the hallway. Of course, the demon core and Enhancing Gem were still gone, but everything else was still there. While I got dressed Cross checked to see if anyone else was being held captive in the prison level. It felt good to get my gear back, and I even made sure to put fresh cartridges in my wrist gun. After making sure everything still worked, I joined Cross in searching the numerous cells spread haphazardly throughout the maze of hallways. It turned out to be a giant waste of time since none of the other cells were occupied, so we quickly left the area before anyone decided to check on Shōen.

"I don't think it's a good idea to go back the way I came down here. If we keep going straight down this hallway, it's going to lead out into the main chamber. The undead might ignore me because of the lich curse, but you, you're definitely going to draw some attention." Cross stopped at an intersection, craning his neck to look at a stairwell that spiraled upward into shadow. A thick layer of dust on the steps meant no one had used them in a long time. It was out of the way, and clearly forgotten. For some reason, I got the sense it was original, while everything else I'd seen so far had been remodeled. Cross gave up trying to see in the dark and shrugged. "This is a different path we could try."

"Right now you know your way around better than I do, so I'm happy to follow your lead." I tried to see how far up the stairs went, but it was too dark to see. "We should jump as far as we can before touching anything. No sense in disturbing the dust and letting anyone know somebody used these steps, especially since they haven't been touched in a long time."

Cross agreed, so I cupped my hands and tossed him as high as I could. He catapulted out of sight, and I waited for him to whisper down an all clear. Once he did, I jumped as high as I could, catching myself on a rusty iron railing that nearly gave way under my weight. I managed to scramble over the side before it could give way, and Cross came over holding a small lantern similar to the ones we'd used in the spider caverns.

"You threw me a full flight higher, otherwise I would've been here to help catch you." Cross handed the lantern over. "You get to carry this. Only one hand is cooperating for me right now."

"Fair enough." I took it from him and gently grabbed him by the arm. "You haven't asked me to yet, but if it's bothering you, we really should try and push the curse down again."

"No." Cross made a tight fist with his hand before shaking it out. "If we need someone to sneak around where there's undead, I'm the only option. We can't risk losing that advantage right now."

Reluctantly, I agreed with him. This wasn't exactly the time to give up any edge we might have over the enemy. "Alright, but the moment you feel it messing with your brain, you have to let me know."

With that settled, we made our way up the flight of stairs. They were heavily worn, and several places showed evidence of a long-ago battle. Sections of stone were melted like they'd been made of wax, and more than once the two of us had to jump across gaps where nothing but shadows and scorch marks remained.

"What do you think happened here?" Cross bent to look at a section of broken railing that was so rusted it would probably crumble to dust if he touched it. "For some reason, this stonework looks different from the kind in the cavern. No one bothered repairing the destroyed sections, or replacing the ironwork as it aged."

"The Destitute must have repurposed something that existed here a long time ago. He only refurbished the sections he cared about. This is an area he didn't care about. Remember the carvings on the path?" I waited for Cross to stop playing with the rusty railing and nod before continuing. "Those were *old*. Probably several thousands of years old, if I'm guessing right. This has to be from that time. Some ancient battle or cataclysm made people stop coming." I looked over the damage again. "Or, there was no one left who knew about it still around to come back and fix it."

"Must have been something really bad." Cross brushed his hand off on his pants and started up the stairwell again. "What are the odds we end up the same way?"

"Same as always. Every day you get out of bed, you either make it to the next day, or you don't. No other options." I shrugged, carefully hopping over a step that didn't look like it would take my weight. "The way I see it, that makes each day fifty-fifty."

Cross shook his head at me. "I'm not sure if that's profound, or stupid. Probably both."

I pushed his shoulder in mock anger, then immediately gave up pretending I was mad. "Yeah, I can agree with that. Probably both. Philosopher is the job I'm probably the least qualified for on this whole planet."

We both laughed a little, trying to lighten the mood, but any attempts were quashed by the oppressive atmosphere of the ancient battlefield we were ascending. Any blood or bones had long since disappeared, wiped away by time or scavengers. That didn't mean the heavy feeling of lives lost didn't linger, no matter how much time had gone by.

Eventually, after what felt like a good hour of walking, we reached the top of the spiral stairs. It had gotten punishingly cold again, meaning we had to be close to the surface. Long ago, there were four paths that branched off the landing at the top, but either the battle or time had collapsed two of them.

Given the fresh air and faint dusting of snow down one path, it obviously led to the outside. The other tunnel curved sharply out of sight, and had more than a little warmth coming from it. A thin skimming of ice where the two biomes met covered the floor and walls, which also showed the tunnel was being used. Cloven-hooved creatures had passed through recently, as well as several people wearing boots. All of them were headed toward the tunnel leading outside.

Cross kicked a few pieces of broken ice out of the way to better see the tracks, and then peeked around the corner before coming back to where I was waiting at the top of the stairs. "It's too dark. I don't see anything deeper in. The tracks look like a small patrol of demons being hunted by a mixed patrol of vampires and those ghouls covered in bone armor. With it being ice, there's no telling how old the tracks actually are, although they look relatively fresh."

"Bone knights." I frowned, thinking over our options. "We could follow the patrols and try to wipe both of them out so we know nothing will sneak up on us, or we ignore them and push deeper to look for the airships. Either option is a problem, especially since bone knights can be tough to kill. They might make enough noise to bring a mountain's worth of enemies down on us. Not to mention the demons. We don't know how tough they are at all."

"Sounds like we push on." Cross turned to leave, but I grabbed him before he could leave. "What? You want to risk it?"

"No. I want you to take these, just in case." I took off my ruck and rummaged around for a bit before pulling out the flares meant to call in our airship. I passed over all but one to Cross. "Keeping all of them for myself was dumb. Now, we both can get everyone else here quickly. I don't know about you, but I'd feel a lot better if we had our whole crew here to help."

He tucked them into a pouch on his belt and we took the tunnel that went deeper into the mountain. As we walked, the tight confines started to widen, and the natural look of a lava tube was slowly replaced by worked stone. Ancient carvings bordered the ceiling, somehow looking both unfinished and worn down to nearly nothing.

Whoever started this project had died before they could finish it, and there was no preservation magic in these to keep the ravages of time from stripping away the neat lines and fine details that would let us read the hidden messages the artists wanted to pass on to future generations. Still, there was enough remaining for me to see it was the same style as what we'd found on the trail farther south. It would have been nice to sit and study the ancient carvings to try and discover their secrets, but right now we didn't have the time.

The tunnel sloped down at a steady angle, undoing most of the upward travel we'd accomplished while going up the stairs. Just as I was thinking about calling for a short break to give Cross some time to recover–his breathing had gotten more and more labored the deeper we traveled, making me worry the curse was affecting him– the tunnel opened up onto a ledge that overlooked a great cavern.

I stood there, amazed at the scene below. Two airships were docked in giant bays, both being swarmed by an even mixture of gray dwarves and greater undead. One of the ships was familiar, since it still had a giant tree sticking out of the bottom. It had a much larger workforce trying to repair it, with ghouls serving as labor while dwarves directed them.

A ding from my system alerted me to the fact that I'd finally found the subject of my quest. The long-lost Silver Star was right in front of me, looking as pristine and beautiful as it probably had the day it first took flight all those centuries ago.

---

**Quest Update!**
**Rare Quest: Track down Silver Star - Complete**
**-You have found the Silver Star, an airship long thought to be forever lost. Two of the three required items to close the Demon Gate have been recovered. Find the Key before time runs out. [Time remaining: 24 days]**
**-Sub-quests:**
**-Find the Key to the Silver Star**
**-Close the Demon Gate [34,319 minutes remaining]**

---

I hadn't realized how much time had passed. Still, a little over three weeks felt like a lot of time when I had the ship I needed right below me. There were no hints about what the key might look like, or where I could find it, but I was hoping to get some hints if I snuck onto the ship. Which, right now, had dozens of dwarves running around on its deck. That probably meant there were even more below out of sight. I would worry about it after I figured out a way to get down from the ledge we were on.

Finding a route to the bottom of the cavern seemed impossible from where we were currently standing. There were plenty of other ledges surrounding the giant open space, like balconies overlooking an arena. None of them had a way that led directly to the ground. We were too high up to jump, and if I used magic to get down, I'd certainly be found immediately.

Thousands of undead marched around the area not taken up by the airships. Organized into rough rank and column platoon-sized elements, they seemed to have no end to their numbers as groups disappeared down one tunnel and more platoons came out from different tunnels. It was a swarm of undead unlike anything I'd seen before. Even the great Lich King on world nineteen wasn't this organized, and he'd had several millennia to get his armies arranged and in order.

"Crazy, right?" Cross looked over the ledge beside me, observing the sheer scope of the obstacle before us. "I still don't know how I made it through that rat's nest to get down to you. I should've been caught a thousand times over, but they ignored me the whole time."

I only nodded in agreement. Luck must have been on his side, because Cross definitely should've been caught. The sheer numbers alone made it next to impossible for someone to hide. "Take what wins you can get, and move on. Dwelling on the unknown will only leave you feeling crazy."

"Speaking of crazy, is that who I think it is?" Cross pointed down and to our right, where a very familiar figure was standing on a balcony overlooking the skunkworks repairing the airships. "Because if it is, I think that's someone we *really* need to call in backup before we fight."

"It's The Destitute." By saying his name, the Mantle of a Judge finally decided to come back to life. Either that, or now that I wasn't under the rune restrictions of the jail cell, it could finally activate.

Once it settled onto my shoulders, I started to replay the interactions I'd had with the elder vampire over and over again in my head. The thoughts I'd had before still held true. In many respects, the vampire was a hero. He'd sacrificed more than his fair share to keep this planet from being overrun. That didn't absolve him of one glaring issue.

Greendown.

The attempted murder of thousands of innocents, no matter the reason, wasn't okay. He hadn't even tried to approach the leadership of the city, or the Wardens, to try and get support against the demon threat. Would it have worked? Probably not, especially given the corruption of the guilds before my arrival, but we'd never know because he never even tried. That, more than anything, made him extremely guilty. The Mantle wasn't willing to bend on the issue, and I understood why. The Destitute hadn't asked, because he didn't care. He deserved Judgment.

Now that I had my answer–and it was one I wholeheartedly agreed with–I knew what I needed to do next. Get my Enhancement Gem and demon core back, Judge an elder vampire, kill a dragon, and close the Demon Gate.

Piece of cake.

"What do you want me to do?" Cross crouched down, making sure he couldn't be spotted by anyone below us. "I could help you fight him, but I don't know if the two of us will be enough."

"Now that I know what he's capable of, I think I have a better idea of what I need to do to beat him." I pointed a thumb back at the tunnel we'd just emerged from. "As much as it sucks, I think it would be best if you run back to the surface and call in our airship. Now that we have a confirmed way inside, it changes things to our advantage. I'll go too if you think you'll need help dealing with those patrols."

"I can handle something this easy." Cross gripped the spear-staff tightly in his unblemished hand before relaxing his grip. "Hand me the lantern. I'll need it to see on my way back. Make sure you stay in one piece before I get back."

"You know me. I'm really good at staying in one piece. Most of the time." I helped him hang the lantern from the end of the spear so he didn't have to worry about his cursed hand acting up. It was getting more and more twitchy the longer we stood around. "Good luck, and remember the priority is sending the signal flare, not killing random patrols."

Cross gave me a brief nod before taking off, the swaying lantern sending shadows dancing across the passageway. He didn't bother looking back at me, instead staying focused on what was in front of him.

Now that I was rolling solo again, I tried to figure out the best way to get to my appointment with The Destitute. He was overdue for an ass-kicking, and I was more than happy to deliver some karma.

The tunnel we'd been traveling down continued deeper into the mountain, but it doubled back the wrong direction. Instead, I saw another ledge at the midway point between where The Destitute and I were standing, poking out from the wall at a distance that only a crazy person would classify as barely within leaping distance. Today, I was feeling a little crazy.

I backed up as far as I could, and took a running leap for the distant platform. Using mana to help would announce my presence to any magic user in the cavern that looked even a little in my general direction, so I had to do this with nothing but sheer muscle power. Every bit of my one hundred and forty seven strength points went into the jump, and for a moment, it looked like I was going to make it. Then gravity took hold, and I started to fall.

Thinking fast, I pulled free my ninjatō and stabbed the wall next to me. The razor-sharp blade dug a furrow into the stone wall with a screeching echo, but it provided the momentary resistance I needed to be able to push off the wall and reach the stone balcony. I landed in a pile of loose debris and gravel that helped cushion the impact. It sent a shower of stones clattering down a dark tunnel that looked recently cleared.

I froze, waiting for a reaction from all the noise I'd made. When nothing happened, I let out a slow breath to help relieve the tension in my shoulders. I must have been too high up for the screeching sound to be noticed down below, especially with the ambient noise of all the workers hammering away at the airships, and the undead stomping around from tunnel to tunnel.

The balcony I landed on was larger than the one I'd jumped from, but stacked stones and loose gravel took up most of the space. There was a small cleared area that looked like a recently used campsite, and someone was even using a spiked helmet as a cookpot over the burned patch of stone in the middle. A single relatively flat rock sized for a single human had been placed next to it, meaning only one person was up here by themselves.

I picked up the soot-stained helmet and inspected it for a moment before putting the poor misused and abused thing back where I found it. Whoever owned it didn't do a good job of taking care of their equipment. It seemed familiar, but for some reason I just couldn't place it. Must not be all that important.

For a moment I thought I could hear shouts and screams of rage echoing from far down the tunnel, but when I got closer there was nothing. It was pitch black, and the noises coming from the chamber were too loud. If there were other sounds coming from deeper within, I couldn't hear them any more. Once again, right now it wasn't important.

What *was* important stood overlooking his army of gray dwarves and undead. The Destitute hadn't moved since I'd first spotted him, except now he was rolling both the gem and core that belonged to me around in his hand like they were stress balls. After gauging the distance between the balcony I was on and his as being much easier to manage this time–due to the drop in height helping–I decided to try and land on his head with as much force as I could muster.

This time, the leap across the gap went without a hitch. I pulled my mace free mid-jump, and waited until the last moment to shove as much lightning and fire mana into the weapon as I could to try and give the ancient vampire as little warning as possible. He started to turn his head to look up at me right before impact, but it was too little, too late.

Power flared from the blades of my mace as they impacted the side of the vampire's head. He flew off his feet, cratering head-first into the stone wall in a thunderous explosion of fire and light that banished the shadows from at least half of the giant cavern. Lingering bolts of lightning sparked from the head of my mace, tearing blackened furrows across the balcony floor.

I stood, gathering as much of the expended energy back into me as possible. Given the fact The Destitute hadn't dropped either the gem or the core, I had a feeling I'd need everything I could get. The dust cloud hid how much damage I'd done, but I wasn't holding my breath for an instant win. After all, he was almost double my stats in every category. Beating him would take more than one hit. It would take every step of my hairbrained plan going perfectly. And maybe a miracle.

"This must be your way of refusing my attempt to convince you to join forces." The elder vampire stepped out of the dust cloud, brushing off his clothes. A faint smear of blood marked where I'd hit him, but the injury had already healed. That wasn't a good sign. "It's too bad, really. I was hoping for you to truly understand your situation and conform to the reality placed in front of you. It was too much to ask from such an inexperienced human, I suppose."

"You almost had me for a moment." I pulled my magic-eating sword and held it ready in my other hand. Sparks jumped from the mace to the blade, its hunger always ready to devour any loose bits of power it might reach out and snatch from nearby. "There's just one mistake you made."

"Oh?" The Destitute leaned back a smidge and the faint red glow around his fingertips faded, pausing whatever plan to demolish me he was about to put into motion. "Do tell. Where exactly did I make an error?"

"There's no doubt your efforts to stop the demons were downright heroic." I motioned with the tip of my sword to the cavern behind me, where the undead troops below were still in an uproar trying to figure out what the flash of light from my earlier attack was from. "Even mostly containing the threat they pose to this world on this mountain is an absolute masterclass on tactics and command policy that plenty of people on other planets would kill to study."

Elder vampire or not, everyone has an ego, and The Destitute was certainly loving everything I was saying. He cleared his throat–something I was pretty sure an undead didn't need to do–and straightened out his clothing once more before speaking. "If you truly believe all of these things, why choose to defy me? Do you not understand the risks involved if my leadership were to disappear? Don't you also wish to save this planet?"

"Yes!" I slammed my mace on the ground, sending shards of stone flying everywhere. "That's where you messed up! Instead of *asking* for *help*, you *force* others to *serve*. You're so against even the *thought* of asking for help, you tried to extinguish an entire city so you could use their corpses as fodder. You couldn't stand the thought of another leader threatening your rule, or possibly presenting a good idea you didn't think of yourself. Nevermind the fact that you would neuter their most effective fighters, or destroy any innovative thinkers that might help you break the stalemate that's continued for years on end, you outright don't *care* about anything other than your own Quest. Even if it required sacrificing ninety percent of the planet, you wouldn't blink, or bother trying to find a different path."

The Destitute tried to interrupt me, but he was silenced as a power older than mortal reckoning, a power that existed during the founding of the universe made itself known.

Lights got brighter, and shadows deepened.

The grays of the world diminished.

I felt the Mantle of a Judge settle onto my shoulders, even though I hadn't called it forth. It came on its own. "And from how comfortable you are with it, I have a very strong feeling Greendown was far from the first time you made that decision. That's why you're wrong. Wrong for having an ego bigger than your wardrobe. And worse. That's why you're *guilty*. Guilty of murder, murder on a scale I have a problem even conceptualizing."

"You *dare* pass judgment on *me*?!" Mana flared as The Destitute pushed back against the powers of a Judge.

A red haze sparked against the dark blue aura that surrounded me, putting immense pressure on my body. I could feel blood leaking from my nose and ears as the red haze steadily deepened in color, and the smell of burnt hair filled my nose. I *might* have been smoking, but it was hard to tell through the tears of blood in my eyes. My plan to use instinctive earth magic at an opportune moment and drop the balcony with him still on it had gone right out the window. I hadn't even been able to really fight him at all.

"Now I know what god you serve, and the era of such petty and obstinate ideals has long gone extinct." He put a hand in his pocket and pulled out a small fist-shaped figurine that looked suspiciously like the symbol used by the Wardens. "I am beyond *asking* for anything. I give orders, and they are *followed*." He took a step forward, suppressing me further. I think he tried to take another, and found more resistance than he expected, but it could have been wishful thinking. Instead, he knelt down and held the figurine in front of my face. "You seem the type that likes to call out for help from others. Too bad for you that I hold the key to the lich curse afflicting your friend." He pushed flames so hot they went from red to blue into the small piece of glass, and a distant scream rang out across the cavern.

I turned my head achingly slow, and saw Cross. It was as if an invisible assailant dragging him by his blackened arm had yanked him out of the tunnel and onto the balcony. He was fighting it so hard his shoulder dislocated, but nothing could stop the inexorable presence of the curse taking over his body.

We made eye contact from halfway across the cavern, and I could see him mouth the words, 'I'm sorry'. I waved my hand, trying to tell him it wasn't his fault. There was no way either of us could have known this ancient piece of garbage had something that could control Cross.

The Destitute smiled, showing off his fangs. "Your other friend with the curse is fighting against my call. It feels as if something is helping to block my control, but he's coming here as well. Nothing, not even the *gods*, can deny me on the physical plane."

"What? What are you talking about?" I barely paid attention to what he was rambling about. I didn't know about anyone else cursed by the lich. All my focus was on what my next move needed to be to get out of this mess. I couldn't think of anything. So, I defaulted to the basics. Make them angry, and hope they make a mistake. "Did you use your vampire powers to suck off somebody with syphilis, and now the holes in your brain are making you feel funny? Actually, that would explain a whole lot about your decision-making process."

This time, when he punched me I activated every single shield rune I had in my armor, on top of my shield bracelet. It probably saved my life, because he didn't hold back. I went flying, with every rune overloaded beyond capacity.

In a fleeting sense of irony, I noticed I landed in the same crater The Destitute had created with his head only a few minutes ago. My broken collarbone and ribs kept me from appreciating any humor I might have found in seeing the distinct shape of his face permanently recorded in stone.

"At first, I was genuinely remorseful at the thought of ending your life, James Holden. You seemed a very capable opponent, and they always make the best underlings." The Destitute grabbed my ankle and yanked me out of the crater. "But now? Now, I think I'm going to enjoy ripping you apart far more than any benefits I would gain from keeping you around."

He lifted a hand, and his fingernails grew out like daggers. I was healing myself as fast as I could, while subtly shifting my wrist gun to blast his stupid face off. It wouldn't kill him, but it might buy me a few more seconds to get back on my feet.

287

Before he could spear me in the heart with his creepy hand, or I could shoot him in his stupid face, we both froze.

The entire chamber was shaking as if there was an earthquake. He looked down at me, and must have been able to tell by the look on my face it wasn't something I was doing. The Destitute let me go and ran over to the edge of the balcony, already shouting orders to those below.

"Something is coming! Protect the airships! Reinforce the runes with the–"

Anything further was cut off by a blood-curdling scream from the balcony where I'd seen the campsite with the spiked helmet. A human, so emaciated he looked nearly skeletal, was sprinting as hard as he could while a seething pack of diseased demonic flesh chased him down. The man was dwarfed by the swarm of demons chasing him out of the tunnel, and leading the swarm lumbered a giant mole-like creature covered in armored plates. The starving man dove to the side, nearly in the same place where I'd landed when jumping from one balcony to the other. The giant mole-thing couldn't stop in time, and went barreling off the side, taking half the balcony with it. The demons following their leader didn't seem to mind the huge drop to the cavern floor, and like a bunch of lemmings, they ran off the edge in an avalanche of epic proportions.

Most of the demons seemed to have some kind of magic ability, and those that survived the fall soon filled the cavern with storms of lava, lashing winds, burning acids, and whipping trails of tentacle-like smoke that tore through ranks of the undead as if they were made of porcelain and glass. The Destitute screamed out orders that were drowned out by explosions of stockpiled supplies, and as he tried to leap down and fight the giant mole demon, I shot him with all three barrels, shredding his legs with silver.

He spun, spitting mad, and claws extended into blades that could shred me to pieces. "Fool! You would side with the demons? At least I will leave this planet in peace, with survivors to continue the population! They will wipe out *everything*."

"No. I choose neither of you." I calmly reloaded my wrist gun, not even paying attention to the type of ammo. It didn't matter at this point. They were all just a distraction. "Right now, I think all

I need to do is weaken you enough, and then let the demons rip you apart. Then, I can clean up the rest."

"And the dragon, you idiot? What about the most powerful magical creature on this planet? What are you going to do about *that*?" The Destitute's legs finished healing, and he stood to his full height.

"I'll figure it out as I go along, like I always do. Without your tainted help." I pointed my wrist gun at him again, and got ready to shoot. He took a step forward, lifting a hand to flay me open.

Then the whole chamber shook again as invisible protection and support runes embedded in the walls suddenly became visible. The giant mole demon was slamming its head repeatedly against a pillar that both supported the vast underground chamber, and projected a shield to protect the airships. Vibrant sparks of green, blue, red, and yellow clashed against one another as the power contained within the individual glyphs was strained to their breaking point.

Even The Destitute seemed shocked at how many runes there were. From the designs and mana types, I got the impression he'd probably only known about the red and blue ones, which only accounted for a third of what I saw. They were also the cause of the cascading failure that started ripping apart the layers of protection that must have stood for millenia.

Rainbow lightning ripped across ranks of demons and undead alike, shredding and melting flesh and bone like an insane arc welder from the depths of hell had decided to wield a weapon designed by fairies and unicorns. The giant mole demon was lashed by the light over and over again, causing it to howl in an undulating reverberation that made my molars ache, and dust fell from the ceiling as the world around us vibrated and shook in sympathy.

A loud crack came from above, then the sound of shattering glass loud enough to rupture my eardrums. Every rune broke at once, and a great rent spread across the ceiling. Water rained down from above in a rapid torrent, turning the battlefield below into a morass of swirling whirlpools as the side tunnels tried to drain the mess that covered the cave floor. Demons, undead, dwarves, and the remains of the defeated were all swept away, some managing to hold on, but most screaming their last as they disappeared into the darkness of the unknown.

Both airships were torn free of their moorings, suddenly becoming actual ships in the surprise flood. The gray dwarves still onboard held on for dear life as they were dislodged, the mighty creations thrown about the huge cave like children's toys in a bathtub. The Destitute completely forgot about me as he screamed out instructions, both through some kind of speaking crystal and uselessly over the balcony edge. He was trying to save the ships, but both of them were quickly becoming more and more damaged as they were tossed around.

During all of the excitement, I saw Cross break free of the hold The Destitute held over him. I watched in amazement as he gripped the incredibly sharp spear I had loaned him long ago near the top, held his cursed arm out, and in an act of supreme willpower, chopped off the blackened flesh in one smooth motion. Blood spurted free for only a moment before he clamped it down. He didn't even take the time to look in my direction before sprinting for the tunnel that led outside.

Okay. Cross had officially leveled up to badass.

"You!" The Destitute spun, his red aura flaring around him in a dark haze. "This is your fault. Do you realize what you've done? How much you've cost me?"

"Look, you can get mad at me all you want, but I'm not the one who gave you the clap. Maybe some antibiotics and a few days –" I didn't see him move, but I certainly felt it when his hand speared me through the liver. Which hurt.

The Destitute leaned over me, his other hand ready to stab me in the neck. He was almost laying on top of me, our closeness making my skin crawl. "I wanted to draw this out, but now I have more important things to do. Die whimpering, James Holden."

I smiled, knowing there would be blood in my teeth. He didn't even feel the tug on his belt as I took off the pouch. The earth spell to collapse the balcony built inside me, and I got ready to release it.

"Fuck off, fang face."

It was about then that a really fat dragon fell through the ceiling.

## CHAPTER 39

The dragon was *huge*. Not just huge as in a large creature, but huge as in it was incredibly obese. If someone had given a silver and blue basketball a dragon head, wings, and a tail, then scaled it up to the size of a three-story house, you might get some idea of what it looked like. It couldn't even really fly. As the silvered dragon fell from the ceiling in an avalanche of stone, ice, and water, it managed more of a controlled glide than actual flight.

Of course, as dragons do, it let out a roar while still in midair loud enough to shake the mountain. Something primal and instinctive inside every creature's brain made them freeze when a predator made a sound like that, and nothing inside the cavern was immune to the effect. The dragon, still leisurely drifting downwards, zeroed in on the giant mole demon that lay prone in the rapidly draining water, and a one-sided clash started as it landed with a splash.

My freshly repaired eardrums burst a second time in only a few minutes, exacerbating the pain to a much higher level. The hand piercing my liver ripped free in a tearing motion that made me lose concentration on the earth spell I'd been holding ready. It dissipated into the stone beneath me, doing nothing but adding to the ambient mana in the area. Thankfully, I didn't lose the healing spell I'd been running since I'd started fighting. My ears popped as they healed again almost immediately, but the hole in my guts would take a little longer.

"No. No-no-no. Not now. We're not ready for this." Pure panic flashed across the vampire's face as the dragon began devouring the mole demon like a starving sumo wrestler released on an all-you-can-eat buffet. "The dragon should be guarding the portal, not running amok and risking an outbreak while my forces are scattered!"

Since he seemed to be going through a tough moment, I decided it was the perfect time to help take his mind off his problems. So, I shot him in the ass with all three barrels. I hadn't paid attention when reloading, but it turned out all three rounds were solid silver bullets. The heavy slugs caused him to stagger forward against the balcony railing with an audible crack of bone.

The Destitute stumbled as his broken pelvis had problems holding his weight. He glared back at me with a mixture of frustration and concern, pointing toward the stupidly fat dragon below. "This isn't the time for us to fight. I could have finished you a moment ago, but this isn't a threat we can ignore. Come, look at what's at risk."

When he didn't try to kill me again, I slowly got to my feet. My abdomen wound wasn't closed yet, but the bleeding had stopped, and I had most of a liver again. I gingerly made my way over to see what he was talking about, still doing my best to keep some distance between us.

He held onto the railing with both hands to take the weight off his legs to ensure his pelvis was aligned properly and nodded down toward the swarming mess below. "Do you see? If we band together, we might save it."

What he was talking about was the Silver Star. The other airship was already kindling, torn apart by the thrashing tail of the dragon as it subdued the mole demon. Enough water had drained from the cavern that the Silver Star had stopped floating, and now it had wedged itself between a support pillar and a pile of debris and dead bodies that had just enough combined mass to hold it mostly upright. The airship was on the opposite side of the cave from the dragon, but that didn't mean much when you were talking about a creature the size of a large building.

All around the dragon, most of the remaining demons and undead were still battling it out, with the occasional spell or severed limb inadvertently hitting the creature that was taking up a good portion of the far side of the cavern. The dragon barely seemed to notice, instead focused entirely on devouring the mole. It was having problems getting through the thick armor plates, until an arcane blast of reality-warping silver and blue fire melted the offending defense right off. The screams of the demon mole didn't last long after that.

"It looks to me like the Silver Star should be okay. It's not edible, and the universe's most gluttonous dragon only seems interested in things it can eat." I reloaded my wrist gun while holding my hand against my gut, trying to hide what I was doing from my evil counterpart. "Maybe if we ignore it, the dragon will go away."

"Are you stupid? We can't take that risk. Getting the dragon back into its chamber, where it was imprisoned and guarding the gateway, is our only true option. One stray burst of its breath attack would destroy any hope of either you or I successfully closing the Demon Gate. Gods above and below, how did two of my lieutenants die by your hand?" The Destitute shook his head in disgust before reaching for the pouch on his belt that contained the demon core and Enhancing Gem. Which I had stolen when he went medieval on my liver. He did the whole, 'oh-no-where-is-the-thing-I-just-had' full-body pat-down before looking at me with narrowed eyes. "Where are they?"

My guts had finished healing, so I pushed my focus back down into the ground below us. The mana I'd lost earlier was still there, ready and waiting to be used. It seemed more than happy to start moving into the spellform I needed. To keep the vampire from noticing what I was doing, I needed to distract him. Luckily, I knew how to do that. He'd already shown me exactly what to say to piss him off.

"I've heard memory loss is a common issue with men your age. In fact, it's probably made worse by all those blood-borne diseases I was talking about earlier, like syphilis. I wasn't joking before. It seriously does turn your brain into swiss cheese." I tapped my temple, insinuating his mind was slipping. "Healing a vampire isn't something I've tried before, but I'm willing to give it a go if you need help."

The actual flash of red in his eyes was my only warning that he planned on punching me again. Thankfully, the speed of thought beat even the ludicrous speed of The Destitute. When I asked for a row of long, thin spikes to rise at an angle in front of me, they barely erupted from the ground in time. Barely in time still means they managed to get between the charging vampire and my tender face. He speared himself at the belt line on four of the sharpened crystal quartz rods, his own momentum nearly tearing him in half. Black blood thicker than syrup slowly dribbled out of the wounds, and before he could escape I slammed over a dozen more spears through his body. I made sure to aim for soft tissue only, since his bones were too tough to break.

He grunted as he tried to pull himself free. When the stone rods held, mana flared from his hands as he tried to take control away from me. "This is a waste of time. Give me the demon core. I can tap into its power to trap the dragon." The Destitute's fangs grew a little longer when his first burst of power didn't push my mana out of the rods piercing his legs and abdomen. "You can even keep the gem, as long as you use it to move the ship to safety."

When I didn't answer, another burst of power from his upraised palms proved ineffective against my hold. He was really struggling to keep his anger in check, completely consumed with his own situation. I was scrambling to finish the spell under our feet before he noticed, or pushed for control of the rods again. He'd almost gotten me that time.

The Destitute's red aura boiled forth once again, this time staying tight against his body. It made the black blood oozing from his wounds harden and flake away, and the stench of old rotten blood nearly made me gag. "Human, I'm not going to ask you again. We both know I've been holding back in the forlorn hope you would see sense and join me. This is your last chance. Give me the core and assist me with the airship, or I'll rip your arms and legs off, force your friend to end your life, and they can serve as the holder of the Enhancing Gem. Do you understand?"

"Yep, totally get it." I nodded quickly, and held up a hand with my middle two fingers extended straight down, and the others pointed straight outward. Using the proper hand signals helped focus my magic, as the elves had taught me on world eight. I hadn't needed to use them in a while with my mind stat going so high above one hundred, but I wanted every extra bit I could get out of this spell. I held up my other hand, which had the demon core and Enhancing Gem in it. "I totally get that you're a twatwaffle."

The Destitute tried to tear free of the stone spears holding him in place, this time easily ripping free. I'd released control, because I needed everything I had for the spell woven through the stone of the balcony. As he got within arms reach of me, he let out an animalistic roar, letting loose the beast within himself.

I smiled, and activated the gem that doubles all spells with my mana.

He tried to stop his charge, sensing there was a trap. It was too late.

I snapped my fingers.

The first part of the spell under the balcony took over half of the mana, even though it wasn't flashy. All it did was reinforce the structure of the balcony, and help shape it a bit more into an arrowhead. It already roughly held a triangular-like shape, so giving the massive hunk of stone some encouragement to change into a more lethal form wasn't too hard.

Part two of the spell was a bit more… *spicy*. I'd layered what amounted to a giant version of the same stone spear I'd just used on The Destitute, spread across the entire area where the balcony connected to the wall. Then, at the connection of the wall and comically humongous spear, I combined an earthquake spell with the flint mana and spark spells that made the villager arrowheads go boom.

In my head, the balcony would project off of the wall as the head of a giant stone spear. Once formed, the base would snap free, and an explosion would project the spear forward into the dragon, killing it in one blow. Hopefully, the impact would kill The Destitute as well, but I wasn't betting on it. Maybe a good maiming was a reasonable goal to shoot toward.

Unfortunately, plans you make in your head don't always work out in real life. Namely, forgetting to calculate how a Title being doubled by the Enhancing Gem might work out.

---

**\*\*Title Synergy Attained!\*\***
**Titles Combined: Crack Kills and Send Them into Orbit**
**-Congratulations! Crack Kills II has been upgraded to Crack Kills III, allowing fusion with Send Them into Orbit III. Titles that have fused with synergistic potential will hold far more benefits for the Title Holder. Your hard work and dedication to nearly killing yourself in new and exciting ways has led to all new pathways you can now attempt to kill yourself and those around you!**

**Fused Title: I Smoke Rocks!**

---

-Your constant use of earth mana and dependence on explosions has led to this. A new and improved title! Now you can do all of those things even better!
Skill Imparted: Large-scale earth magic uses 15% → 40% less mana per minute. An additional 10% will be applied if the earth magic being used is outside of combat, including construction, training, and enchanting. All explosions are now 75% more powerful.
In addition, *all* magic will become easier to perform, and require less focus from the caster.

While the new Title was fantastic, especially getting instinctive casting for all mana types, it had come at the worst time. I'd already forgotten to account for the gem doubling the first Title which boosted explosions by sixty percent. When it went to seventy-five percent, and then doubled it? Yeah, there was no way in hell I'd be hitting my target.

Knowing I was going to be off, I tried to pull back as much mana as I could to reduce the damage. The giant spear didn't even finish forming before the earthquake spell triggered, and a very short and jagged pointy stone column was launched across the cave when the fully powered and gem enhanced explosion spells triggered. The Title that boosted explosion power was also gem enhanced, which of course turned the stone column into a stone cannonball.

So, The Destitute and I rode the former balcony—now the world's most ridiculous projectile—right over the top of a very confused dragon's head. We smashed into a support column, shattering it into rubble. I managed to create a bubble of stone and air to cushion my impact, while the vampire overlord of twatwaffles was too stunned by the rapid turn of events to do anything in time to save himself from being buried under most of the support column debris. It couldn't have happened to a more deserving person.

Getting slammed between a literal rock and a hard place inevitably caused some injuries. I had several broken bones, and a concussion that no one would ever describe as mild. Instinctive casting helped speed along the healing process, and in less than a minute I was aware enough again to understand what was happening around me. Namely, the dragon had lost its ever-loving mind.

My little magic trick must have scared it, or maybe made it think about something other than its stomach. The dragon was absolutely freaking out because it couldn't use its wings. It probably thought someone was holding it down, or some magic trick kept it from taking off. None of that was true.

Really, it was because the magic annihilation lizard weighed too much to achieve liftoff with such disproportionately sized wings. The thing was too fat to fly.

To show how upset it was, the silver and blue dragon had given up on finishing off its meal of the demon mole, and was now waddling around the cavern, roaring and blowing reality-warping silvered flames over anything that got in its way. I even saw the emaciated guy in the spiky armor that started the demon stampede running for his life at one point when the dragon thought he looked like an interesting snack, but the little guy managed to get away by darting under the crushed remains of a shed that held spare parts for the ships.

After toying with a few other things running around, the dragon became even more upset when it couldn't fit down any of the side tunnels some of its prey used to escape, and started using its claws to tear at the cave walls, making dust and rocks rain down on anyone still inside the mountain.

For some reason, the dragon didn't seem to notice the giant opening the airships used to come in and out of the underground chamber. Maybe because the escape route was on the opposite side of the cave, and it had bad eyesight. The longer I watched the dragon, I started to believe it was more likely because it was really, really dumb.

"Aim! Fire!"

Speaking of really dumb, now that The Destitute was buried under several tons of stone and couldn't give orders to his underlings, some surviving dwarves on the Silver Star had decided to try their luck at becoming dragonslayers. With absolutely *zero* chance of success.

They were dragging giant ballistas around on the airship's deck and shooting at the dragon, plinking what amounted to toothpicks off its back. Until one idiot got exceptionally lucky. Or, exceptionally unlucky, depending on your perspective.

"One more time! Ready! Aim! Fire!"

Seven bolts fired, and six were evaporated as the dragon turned its head while breathing out a gust of silver flame at a floating eyeball demon that was trying to get out of the blast radius. A single ballista bolt floated through the air an extra hundred feet, gently catching the updraft given off by the magic fire. The dragon opened its eyes in time to see its version of a splinter fly straight up a nostril. Which, given its reaction, I don't think the dragon appreciated very much.

There was nothing I could do but watch in a solid mix of bemusement and horror as the butterball turkey of dragons stomped its way over to the Silver Star–the thing I needed to save this planet–and breathed silver fire all over it.

For a moment, I thought the enchantments covering the ship would hold. They were able to stand up against the reality-warping effects of the dragon's flames for far longer than the stupid gray dwarves that pulled the dragon's attention to the airship in the first place. But, after a few seconds, the ship that had stood for over a thousand years melted as if it was made of snow.

A loud ding from my system, in a deep, unhappy tone told me something bad was about to happen. It wasn't often that I'd failed a Quest, but every time I did, it always ended in suffering and death.

---

**Quest Update!**
**Rare Quest: Track down Silver Star - Failed**
-You found the Silver Star, and watched while it was
destroyed by a morbidly obese dragon. This has allowed
**unintended consequences** to be taken advantage of by
hidden parties. The time to close the Demon Gate has been
reduced. [Time remaining: 15 minutes]
-Sub-quests:
-Close the Demon Gate [899 seconds remaining]

---

The seconds ticked away as I looked at my screen, stunned at the sudden time change. I hadn't ever seen something like this before, not in any of the nineteen worlds I'd fought on. This was absolute bullshit.

Stone erupted a few feet away from me, as my dark side counterpart finally decided to make an appearance. The Destitute punched his way out of the rubble that had buried him, and I couldn't help but be a little impressed as broken bones and gaping wounds rapidly healed themselves while he pulled himself free. Rage twisted his features as he looked over the destruction of the Silver Star. He must have gotten the same system update, which had woken him up, or provided the motivation to break out of his impromptu tomb.

"Idiots!" The elder vampire launched a blood-red orb of angry lightning at the dragon, which didn't seem to do much beyond make the fat lizard notice we existed. "Fools!" Another spell splashed across the dragon's chest, which convinced the creature to start lumbering in our direction. "All the hard work and time I've sunk into this pitiful, useless planet–*wasted*!"

"Don't be mad, honey boo-boo. We've still got fifteen minutes. That's plenty of time for you to finish. At least, that's what I've heard about you." I got ready for him to rush me. Instead, he ignored me and pulled out a folded handkerchief from an inner pocket. "What, you don't want to punch me anymore? Learn your lesson from the last time?"

"You aren't worth the effort, human. Nothing on this planet is worth the effort any more." With a sweeping motion, he cleared away a section of ground in front of him. "Soon, you'll reap what you've sown, and be forced to harvest the bitter fruits of your troublesome labor." He unfolded the piece of cloth and laid it out carefully on the ground, then placed four orbs at each corner to hold it in place. Four orbs that were nearly the same size and shape as the demon core I still had in my hand. "This will go down as a failure in my ledger, and I'll owe a few more planets to my god. Worse, I'll have to avoid the gray dwarves for a century or two because I broke the deals I bartered with their councils. But for you and your god? I think you'll find there is no ledger. You'll die here, drowning in an army of demons you could have avoided if you only would have bent your stubborn neck and served me."

While he talked, the dragon stomped its way closer. It probably saw us as two little morsels holding nice and still, just waiting for it to come and have a snack. While I wouldn't win a fight against the big lizard, I would definitely give it indigestion. Small victories matter too.

The Destitute activated some hidden marking on the handkerchief, and the sound of shattering glass filled the air as a tear in reality ripped open. He'd somehow managed to open a portal. "Good luck dealing with the dragon, James Holden. You might not have to worry about the army of demons after all." He started laughing as he turned away from me, tossing back a little wave. Beyond him, I could see a world of shadows and darkness. It actually looked a whole lot like my world eleven, which would make a whole lot of sense. "I'm sure I'll never see you again, but I'll certainly think of you the next time I send an army to wipe out a city."

"Oh, you'll think of me all right." As he started to step through the portal, I threw both the demon core and the Enhancing Gem as hard as I could at the portal while shoving every bit of mana I could inside them. Then, I dove for cover behind the nearest pile of rubble.

I was banking on one line in the demon core description being relevant, and the Enhancing Gem making whatever that effect was also being doubled. That line was very specific.

**Mana types may cause unintended side effects.**

With my new title leaning toward things being more explosive, and that tiny piece of cloth the vampire was using looking awfully susceptible to sabotage, it seemed like my best option. And sometimes... *sometimes*, things work out the way you hope.

The explosion was so massive, it blew up the mountain.

## CHAPTER 40

Gleason had a hard time remembering where he was for a few moments. He'd been digging for so long, with only the voices to keep him company. Hunger and thirst had nearly ended him, but the black veins always rose to the surface, urging him to push through. The voices helped remind him. Failure was not an option. He would prove himself the hero. He was the one found truly worthy.

After the digging was done, Gleason had created a landslide that killed dozens of the unclean demons. It had felt good to take them from the world. Then there was running, as the mob of demons chased him. A flood of freezing water out of nowhere dropped from the great cave's ceiling and washed away the unclean that nearly cornered him, proving the Trinity was looking out for Gleason.

He remembered more running. A dragon chased Gleason to exhaustion, and then the mountain had been ripped apart around him.

The explosion had been like nothing he'd ever experienced. It was so loud, he couldn't hear it. His bones had been crushed inside his body, and the black veins brought him back from the brink of true death. Light so bright it blistered his skin and made him raise his arms to protect his eyes, but it only provided more places for the light to burn. The world was torn asunder with the sound of a million glass windows shattering at once, and the mountain above him was ripped away by the hand of an invisible, angry god.

He saw a brief glimpse of the night sky, before the corpse of a fat dragon landed on top of him.

Gleason didn't know how long it had been since he'd been knocked out. All he knew was that right now, the tail of a dead dragon was crushing his chest and he couldn't breathe. He carefully unbuckled his chestplate and slipped out from under the tortuous weight. If he hadn't lost so much weight recently, there would have been no way for him to escape. Gleason would've certainly died under the unrelenting pressure, slowly suffocating while gasping for help from those that never even knew he was there.

He crawled on his hands and knees, barely able to move. A small black marble nearly made him slip and bounce his face off the floor, but Gleason barely managed to stop himself by hanging on to the jagged scales of the dead dragon next to him. Something inside him decided it was a good idea to pick up the very heavy marble, so Gleason put it in his only remaining belt pouch.

On the other side of the hulking corpse, Gleason could hear voices yelling at one another. Familiar voices. He slowly poked his head around the dragon's body, trying to stay hidden. He shouldn't have worried. The crystal orb erupting out of the dead dragon's chest was holding everyone's attention.

In the sky overhead floated an unfamiliar airship, with more people than he'd seen in weeks scrambling down ropes to the battle-scarred ground. They were forming teams to hunt down the few demons and undead that somehow managed to survive the flooding, dragonflames, and explosion.

For possibly the first time in his life, Gleason saw a Green Warden he didn't immediately want to kill in revenge for what they'd done to his father. The young woman wearing the unmistakable green cloak was leading the charge alongside a witch against the demons, wiping away the filth alongside teams of archers. A very big hunter worked in the opposite direction, chasing zombies through what remained of the mountain's tunnels.

Separating the ongoing battle from where the dragon corpse was stretched across the ground, was a jagged vertical line that reached high into the sky. It looked as if reality was as fragile as a sheet of glass, and the line was the first crack that signaled the end of it all. The pressure it exuded on his psyche was tangible, and nothing in the surrounding area dared get close. Deep down, somehow he knew the scar broke the laws of the physical world, and if it wasn't fixed soon, something very bad would happen.

Despite everything going on, Gleason was more focused on the group clustered around the rainbow of light erupting from the dragon's breastbone. A faceted crystal ball reflected a myriad of colors, turning night into day. Unlike the lights he'd seen in the demon's cave, this was pure. It brought a sense of soothing relief to his beleaguered soul, gently cleansing it of the crust and buildup caused by being in close proximity to the demons for so long. He didn't know what the crystal was, beyond a yearning ache to hold it in his hands.

Gleason recognized everyone that stood in his way. The shifter cat girl. Captain Cross–who was missing an arm–and his disgraced Blue Warden lackeys, Leedy and Murphy. The four of them were supposed to be dead, consumed in the destruction of Greendown. Since they were here, it was even more evidence the city still stood. More proof Gleason had failed in his last task from the gods.

Worst of all, his most hated foe stood in front of them all, his hands ready to pry the precious orb from the dragon's chest. James Holden. His enemy was pushing back the others, ordering them away from the orb.

"No, this is on me. I blew up the vampire's gateway without checking where the demon gateway was first. It was plain bad luck they were practically on top of one another. Now, the stupid vampire's portal combined with the demon's, and it's beyond enormous. There's less than three minutes left on my timer before it's too late to stop it. Our only chance is for one of us to carry the dragon core through the Demon Gate, and hope it holds long enough for the core to detonate in transit. Otherwise, this world is cooked." James tapped his chest, puffing himself up like an overproud suncock. "I'm the obvious choice to take the plunge. You four have too much to lose." It made Gleason sick to his stomach seeing someone like *him* thinking himself worthy of such an honor. "So step aside, guys. I got this."

"I don't think so." Cross tried to get in Holden's way, but his one arm made it difficult for him to do much of anything. "James, you're too important for the future. Jess still needs more training, and the leadership of Greendown will fall right back into old habits without the threat of a Judge to stop them. I'm the best choice to carry the dragon core. Let me take it."

Once again, Gleason was outright offended. The thought of the disgraced captain thinking he was capable enough to complete such a difficult task was laughable to him. The man couldn't even keep both arms attached. He'd probably lose the other one before getting halfway done with his mission.

"This is dumb." Leedy tried pushing both Cross and Holden aside, and only managed to make himself look foolish when he was the one that was moved back. "Both of you are important people. Guys that can do magic, lead people, all kinds of things. Murphy and Jess are in love, and have their whole life in front of them. I'm just a regular guy, with no family. Disposable. Let me do it. You've got to admit, it makes the most sense."

"Leedy, you can't do magic." Holden crossed his arms, making himself look superior. Oh, how Gleason hated him. "How are you supposed to overload the core, if that's what's needed instead for it to be activated? We don't know which one is needed until we get inside the tunnel, and you can only activate magic objects with willpower, not use mana to overload them." Holden then motioned to both Cross and himself before tapping the side of his nose like an idiot. "Besides, good leaders don't ask the ones they lead to do something like this. They lead from the front."

That did it. Gleason knew for sure Holden was the biggest dunce he'd ever laid eyes on. What general charged into the teeth of combat, instead of actually taking charge of the army in the rear? What king didn't allow his soldiers to lay down their lives in service of their king? Of them all, Leedy was the only one who seemed to know his place.

"One minute left. No more time to argue. I'm taking the core, and I'm saving this planet, one way or another." Holden held up his hand to wave goodbye, turning his back on the dragon for a brief moment. "I just want to say to all of you, it's been an honor. Be sure to tell Lighter's people about all of this as well. We couldn't have done it without his sacrifice."

All of them teared up, and gathered in for a hug. That was when the voices spoke to Gleason.

*Now is the time.*
*Prove yourself.*
*You are the chosen one.*

He somehow found the strength within to pick up his battered and bruised body off the ground.

*You cannot fail.*

*Close the gate.*
*Save the world.*

Gleason charged, sprinting faster than he'd ever moved in his life. Magic swirled around him as the black veins rose to the surface, giving him strength one last time. The black marble in his pouch somehow resonated with the power flowing around him, allowing his legs to become a blur.

More by instinct than conscious thought, Gleason ripped the dragon's core free from its chest as he ran by the cluster of his enemies. They could do nothing but stare at him in shock as he rushed by in a blaze of light that flared from the orb. He laughed, shouting back at the foes he'd finally bested. Gleason had finally shown he was the better man.

"You're not worthy! None of you are pure enough to cleanse this planet of the stain left by the unclean ones! I'm the true hero! I'm the one who saves everyone, not you! I'm the chosen one! Bask in my glory, you foolish–"

Gleason slipped through the crack in reality, and knew no more.

## CHAPTER 41

"Did that just happen?"

Jess stood gobsmacked, as confused as the rest of us.

Murphy smacked himself in the face. Then he did it again. "Yep, I think it did."

The tear in reality trembled, then shattered, tinkling to the ground in clear shards before fading away into nothing. A happy ding from my system told me something good was waiting for me when I checked it, but it could wait for a few seconds.

"Could anyone understand what he was saying?" I looked around, completely confused by the wild turn of events. "It sounded like a bunch of incoherent yelling to me. I seriously didn't hear a word he said."

"Me either." Leedy shook his head, just as flabbergasted as the rest of us. "I think I might have heard him say, 'Worthy ones, true heroes, save everyone, *glory*,' but there was other stuff mixed in there. Who knows what he really meant."

"Did anybody recognize him?" Cross was squinting, obviously trying to replay the events in his mind. "I could swear he looked just like Gleason, but much, *much* skinnier."

"There's no way it was Gleason." Murphy spat to the side in disgust. "That guy would never do something good. Saving the world? He'd rather help destroy it."

"Yeah." Jess nodded in agreement. "Gleason wouldn't say anything nice to us either. That guy called us true heroes, and told us to save everyone, all while he made the ultimate sacrifice. His life. It was like he was charging us with the mission to carry on in his stead, since he was going to be gone."

"Truly, a noble warrior's sacrifice." Murphy wrapped his arm around Jess to comfort her as she fought to hold back tears. "One who will forever be a mystery. The songs sung in his honor will be epic, even though we'll never know his name."

Leedy nodded. "We'll build a memorial in his honor, right here on the site of his great sacrifice. 'To the Unknown Hero', it'll read."

I shrugged, deciding it was a problem I wouldn't be able to solve. I wasn't a bard, or a sculptor. Really, I was still thanking my lucky stars I hadn't actually needed to carry the dragon core through the Demon Gate. Things had worked out in the end, but just barely. It definitely felt like some of those 'hidden factions' were running around getting involved in events. While it worked out in my favor this time, it only proved I needed to get far stronger if I wanted to stay alive in the future.

While everyone else continued to discuss the mysterious hero who sacrificed his life to save us all, I decided it was as good a time as any to check my system update.

---

**Quest Update!**
**Rare Quest: Quest Chain Completed.**
**-Demon Gate Closed.**
**-Planet Saved.**
**-Rewards held until Unique Upgrade Quest: Find ten places of power - 5/10 is completed.**

---

Having confirmation that the gate was officially closed felt like an invisible mountain lifted off my shoulders. My reward getting delayed for the Quest being completed kinda sucked goat balls, but there wasn't much I could do about it. There were several months before my scheduled jump to another world, so I had plenty of time to find more places of power. I'd get it done, and hopefully receive an even bigger bonus due to the wait.

A wave of exhaustion hit me, and I stumbled, nearly falling down. It had been a long couple of days.

The battle around us was far from winding down, so our group decided it might be time to get Cross and me back to the airship. Both of us could use some rest and healing, and the others wanted to jump in on the action. They felt like they'd missed out since the airship left without us, and plenty of undead and demons were scattered throughout the area. It would be days before we could scour the whole place clean, so they would have all kinds of chances to make up for lost time. I planned on sleeping for most of it.

"You sure you don't want anything before you go up?" Leedy had taken my pack, and was already holding the rope for me to climb up to the ship. "Plenty of loot lying around down here. It might not be here the next time you wake up."

I stopped, thinking about my future goals. Traveling to the next planet with only what I could carry limited my options, but there was one thing that could use a serious upgrade. My armor was barely better than cardboard nowadays, and right behind me was a dragon. Its scales, teeth, and claws might make some fantastic stuff.

"Give me a minute. I'll be right back." I jogged over to the body, carefully looking over what parts I wanted. Only the thickest, biggest scales would be useful, so the tail, chest, and spine sections looked best. When I reached out to grab one, a ding from my system sounded. A very specific ding.

It gave me a new Quest.

"Hydrogen bombs. I bet hydrogen bombs can kill gods. If I can find that *motherfu–*"

## EPILOGUE 1

The clink of metal against wood was the only sound as he shifted in his chair. The Duergar Council would lift the silencing enchantment that surrounded him when they were done talking amongst themselves, but until then The Destitute had been forced to live in a bubble no wider than the table he leaned against in despair. Shackles covered in runes held both his wrists and ankles, their black iron highlighting how pale the flesh of his bare arms and legs were in the stark light of the council chamber. The thick scars that covered his body would go away if he had access to blood or magic, but neither was likely.

Even the burnt clothing he'd been found in had been taken to help pay off the debts he owed. In an ultimate twist of irony, The Destitute's name had twisted in its purpose. His title no longer described how he made others feel in the depths of the night. It now described him perfectly. He genuinely was impoverished, a penniless creature on a planet obsessed with nothing but wealth.

All around him, gray dwarves shook their fists in anger, or waved scrolls at one another as if they were fighting duels to the death with swords, not rolls of parchment. Rings covered in precious gems, robes woven with actual gold, and even the occasional magical item covered in platinum dust determined rank more than where someone sat. Their wealth was also a good way to determine if they would win an argument, not if they were actually right or wrong. Gray dwarf society was always predictable, if nothing else.

The dwarf assigned as his barrister didn't bother to show up today, since sentencing had nothing to do with her or her law firm. She'd finished her closing arguments days ago, and left him to rot in debtor's prison. The fact she'd remembered how to say his name correctly by the end of the trial meant he'd gotten as good a representative as he could expect. Unless you had money to pay, there wasn't much effort involved.

His ears popped, and noise flooded in as if it was a physical wave, rocking him back in his chair. The show of weakness made him more angry than the rough treatment. If only he could heal himself, things would be so much different.

"Rise, vampire, and receive our decision."

Bright lights blinded him when he looked up, keeping The Destitute from being able to see which of the gray dwarves above him was speaking. Standing pulled at the scar tissue that covered most of his body, forcing out an involuntary wince. When the explosion caused by the damnable *human* had ripped apart his portal, it had nearly ripped *him* apart as well. Only sheer willpower held him together long enough for his spell to find a secondary connection point. Unfortunately, the nearest connection point had been the last world he wanted to visit. The world he'd made a lot of promises to.

"This council, in all its wisdom, has decided that ending your undeath would serve no greater purpose. Instead, you will work off what you owe with hard labor."

Despite promising himself he wouldn't show emotion, The Destitute sagged in relief. As long as he continued to exist, there was a chance. A chance he could change his current fate.

"Since you owe us the mining rights to an entire planet, our accountants have estimated your total debt at a number that has thirteen zeros." Gasps came from all around, and loud whispers sounded from behind the speaker. "I have been informed you owe the council approximately seven decillion gold bullion." More gasps and whispers came from those surrounding him, but The Destitute was having problems staying on his feet. "Current interest rates sit at four percent. Someone in your position will have to work very, *very* hard to pay us back. As an undead, you have all the time necessary to make sure each and every coin is returned to us. In full. Anyone in the future who wishes to double-cross the Duergar, or if they plan on dealing in bad faith, will have someone to look at as an example for many centuries to come."

Uproarious laughter filled the council chambers, making The Destitute wish he could curl up and hide. It had been a long time since anyone had dared to ridicule him, and it wounded him in a way he wasn't prepared to defend.

Papers were brought before him to sign, while a different pair of dwarves stood behind him. They exuded power, the magic in their runed items tangible from several steps away. The threat was clear. Agree to a lifetime of servitude, or die.

The Destitute–a destitute vampire–signed each paper in triplicate, cursing James Holden the entire time.

## EPILOGUE 2

Five figures rippled into place around a square table. Three stood on one side, one stood across from them, and the last walked up to his end slowly, looking the other four up and down as if they were to be his next meal.

Spread across the table were hundreds of colored marbles, some of them bright and sparkling, others dull and dark. Each one slowly tumbled and turned without the figures' interference, some faster than others.

"Is the other not coming?" The second to arrive, a skeletal figure, motioned to the empty spot at the table. "I thought they would want to play another round."

"Probably distracted by squirrel politics on some forgotten planet no one cares about. You know how Nature can get." The leader of the trio spoke, their human features a perfect match for the two standing beside him. None of the others knew which was which on any given turn the game was played, but it was unanimous they were sure it changed each time. "They lost this time anyway, so we don't need to wait."

"I still think it's unfair, Trinity." Usually the last to arrive, the goat-like demon pounded a fist on the table. "An extra player in the game made it unbalanced. This one should get a reroll in a few hundred years."

"We already did that once, Mammon." The human faction, Trinity, motioned to the undead figure across from him. "Remember when Vlad cheated? I won this one fair and square. My puppet closed the gate, just like I wanted. Don't act like it was easy, either. All of you saw how hard it was to maneuver that stooge. Getting him over the finish line was a task worthy of any god." Both figures behind the speaker gave the others an emotionless smile. Vlad and Mammon both growled in protest, but neither voiced an argument. "Better luck next time, boys. It looks like you lost this one."

The speaker for the Trinity reached out for one of the marbles that looked remarkably like a certain planet that barely escaped destruction. As he tried to pull it free, the marble refused to come off the table. Frowning, the other two parts of the Trinity came over to help. Even with all three of them tugging, the marble resembling the world didn't move.

A larger presence, more primal and ancient than the five, stepped sideways out of the void. Shadows and light rippled across the table, and all five gods took a hesitant step back.

The new arrival reached out and snatched the marble off the table. Any resistance the Trinity had seen disappeared under the overpowering presence of the dominant force. Its cloaked face turned to glare at the five smaller gods, any features hidden by the darkness of its presence.

"Do not claim credit for the work of my Warriors, lest you be Judged for your failures as gods."

As the dark presence turned to walk away, the Trinity could no longer hold back. All three portions of himself tried to block the god's path. "But, it was my champion that closed the gate! He carried through the core, not your warrior. You don't even have a place at the table. That world is mine to do with as I please!"

"I was there before these games were made to entertain yourselves, petty little gods, and I will still be here long after you are naught but dust. Your broken tools you sacrifice as pawns would never have accomplished anything by themselves, which is why the table gives you nothing. Now go play in other sandboxes, children, and leave my tools in peace. Adults have more important tasks than pandering to your complaints."

The weight of a primordial god's Mantle fell on all five of the smaller gods shoulders', and they dropped to their knees under the strain.

"Good. Remember your place if I ever have need to return."

The ancient god of Justice walked away, looking down at the physical manifestation of the planet where his current favorite was waiting for his next task. Now that he was getting stronger, it might be time to start sending him to more difficult worlds.

Justice smiled, tucking the marble away.

"I'll show you 'hydrogen bombs', little man. This should be fun."

## EPILOGUE 3

The portal opened with a tearing sound, ripping a hole into time and space that would take me to world twenty-one. It would drag me in if I didn't walk through in about fifteen minutes, so I needed to hurry. However, there were a few last-second things to finish up before I went through.

I was as ready for the next world as possible, with every bit of the supplies and upgraded armor and weapons a guy like me could ask for. Spread out in front of me were the last twenty recruits meant to join the Order of Judges. Once they swore the oath, my final Quest for this planet would be complete, and I would finally get my banked rewards.

The last several months had been spent mapping ley lines, searching for places of power, and building up the Order of Judges. Jess had been a huge help with the ley lines, and Murphy had ended up taking the lead on recruiting.

Since Murphy and I had to work so closely together, I'd told him my secret about hopping worlds. He knew he'd have to take over one day. which led to Murphy taking his job very seriously. He started developing a list of things every new recruit had to accomplish before they could swear the oath called 'Murphy's Laws'–which I certainly encouraged for no obvious reason–and an entire compound was built to help facilitate the process. It churned out Judges that met the standard like clockwork, which was exactly what I needed to meet the Quest I'd gotten from the system.

Cross went on a journey to find himself in the mountains for two months, and refused any kind of healing for his arm. When he came back looking like a one-armed viking, complete with fur clothes, braided beard, and long hair, I was afraid he was going to start another villain arc. Instead, Cross had taken over the Wardens in Greendown from the Commandant, and soon he would probably command the Wardens everywhere. He was still a Judge, but with a lot of additional duties.

Leedy was now in charge of the airship that the Order of Judges pieced together from the wreckage of the two broken airships. Really, the few surviving dwarves didn't want to get drawn and quartered, so they volunteered to build one from scraps for us, and Leedy was the obvious choice to take charge once they finished making it. He hadn't convinced a certain Green Warden to join his crew yet, but hope still lived in his heart.

I managed to avoid entangling myself with any witches that might or might not have been interested in me over the past few months. The memories of Sinthia on world nineteen were still too fresh, and I needed a bit more time before I could move on. It was probably for the best, anyway. Witches be crazy, yo.

Jaeger and Hilda had welcomed a baby girl only a week before. I'd managed to say goodbye, and the trio wished me well without knowing it would be the last time they saw me. It was better that way. I'd left them with a small mountain of gifts, and enough healing potions to ensure the three of them were all but immune to death for the next sixty years or so.

My wandering thoughts came back to the present when Murphy nudged me in the ribs. Twenty sets of eyes waited on me, while eighty more stood in ranks to either side.

"Raise your right hand." They snapped to attention, and moved as one. Murphy had really been drilling these people. "Repeat after me."

"I swear to uphold the tenets of righteousness and justice, to defend the weak and the oppressed, to show grace and mercy towards the innocent, to Judge their oppressors and the unrighteous, and to take up the heavy burdens of this responsibility. I take the Oath of a Judge."

Without prompting, they all drew their issued steel swords modeled after the ninjatō I had on my belt and cut a shallow gash on their palms. A heavy presence settled on the area, as if we were all being watched by a presence beyond what the human eye could see.

"I make this blood oath of my own free will. I swear to be a defender of the powerless, a guardian to those unable to defend themselves. I swear to be a warrior for good, a bulwark against those who wish darkness upon the innocent. I swear to punish the unjust, fairly and without bias. I swear to balance the scales. I swear to be a Judge."

The weight lifted, and the cuts healed without any magic I could sense. Something also took away the blood, leaving everyones' hands and blades spotless.

All the recruits seemed to hold their breath, amazed at what happened. I smiled, dropping my arm. "Congratulations. You're all the newest members of the Order of Judges."

The cheer from one hundred throats shook the foundations of the buildings around us. Murphy thumped me on the back before getting pulled away by a group of well-wishers. A cheerful ding from my system alerted me to the news I'd been waiting for. I'd finally completed the Quest.

---

**Quest Update!**
**Unique Quest: All Quest Chains Completed.**
**-One Hundred New Judges Created**
**-Ten places of power found**
**-Demon Gate Closed.**
**-Planet Saved.**
**-Rewards issued – Check status page for details**

---

Finally. My reward had been released by the stingy system. I'd been hoping for something tangible, like a rocket launcher, but maybe some epic stat upgrades were in store. I pulled up the new page, looking over the numbers. It had already changed a lot, especially since I'd absorbed five more places of power. If something new showed up, I hoped it would help me in my next world.

---

**Name: James Holden (Earth v20)**
**Title: Chief Justice/Arbiter/Justicar/Executioner/etc...**
**Level: 100/200**
**Rank: 10/20**
**Extra Life: +2**
**Age: 27 (Physical) 48 (Actual)**
**Class: Warrior/Soldier/Knight/Paladin/Mage (5/7)**
**Profession: Healer/Alchemist/Blacksmith/Runesmith/Judge (5/7)**

**Status:**

```
Strength- 221
Flexibility- 223
Vigor- 231
Mind- 245
Mission:
Mythical Quest: Deliver Justice - World Count 20/150
Legendary Quest: Return Home - Requirements not met
Epic Quest: Find out why - Requirements not met
```

Version twenty? New levels? More ranks? I could gain two more classes and professions? What in the hell did 'extra lives' mean? Most importantly, I now knew the world count for me to finish my Mythical Quest was *one hundred and fifty*! The stupid vampire only had one hundred, and he was almost a thousand years old. And he hadn't finished yet. This was total bullshit!

Before I could fully digest everything, the suction from the portal started getting stronger. My feet started getting pulled across the grass, and I had to lean forward and brace myself to stop it.

"James! Is it time?" Murphy rushed over, his eyes widened by what he'd seen. "I don't want you to leave. I'm not ready to lead all these people."

"You're in charge of them now. Remember, follow 'Murphy's Law', and everything will be fine." Sometimes it was hard to remember why I'd hated this planet so much in the beginning. World twenty was awesome. "Maybe I'll see you again someday, and remember to take care of everyone."

"I will. Don't you worry, I'll–"

Just like every world before this one, I was ripped away from every person I'd grown to care about in an instant. The portal refused to be denied any longer, and it yanked me away like I was a leaf in the wind.

Traveling from one world to another didn't take long. I barely had time to blink before being dumped onto the side of a steep hill. Loose scree shot out from under my feet, and I slid several feet before I managed to come to a stop. The dragonscale armor I was wearing under my loose robes protected me from the blistering heat that assaulted me, but it couldn't save me from the instant urge to

317

drink water. It was hot, and as I took stock of the landscape around me, I saw the nearby row of volcanoes that caused the punishing temperatures.

"Okay. World twenty-one isn't looking so good, but it's important to keep an open mind. Gotta give it a chance." I decided the first thing I was going to do was move away from the volcanoes, and try to find people. Then I'd figure out what I was on the planet to try and fix.

As I topped the first hill, I got spear-tackled by a minotaur covered in flames, holding two axes of molten fire and obsidian sharper than steel. We tumbled back down the rocky hill, bouncing head over heels all the way to the bottom. I managed to get on my feet first, and got some space between the two of us.

"What the hell, dude! I didn't do anything to you!" I tried backing up an extra step, just in case this was a person and not a monster. When the minotaur roared and charged, swinging his axes like a madman, I gave up on giving him a chance. My brand new dragonfang spear smoothly pierced his throat, completely ignoring the flame armor protecting his neck. A quick twist and shove made sure the big guy didn't have a spinal connection anymore, and the fight was over. "Stupid way to go out, but I guess I'll be your huckleberry."

Above me, a deafening series of roars made the loose rocks around me rattle and shake. "You've got to be kidding me." I looked up to see the hilltops around me were covered in nothing but monsters. Minotaurs, ogres, goblins, orcs, wolfmen, cyclops, lizardmen, griffins, a freaking *hydra*, and dozens more were all charging toward me, each with some kind of elemental affinity active. Fire was most prevalent, but earth, nature, water, ice, even metal auras surrounded them all, enhancing their lethal aspects beyond anything I'd seen before.

My system dinged as a series of Quests flooded my messages.

"That's it. World twenty-one is officially the *worst*."

# The End of Wandering Warrior.

# AUTHOR'S NOTE

Well, that's all, folks. It feels crazy to say goodbye to these characters. To me, they're friends I've lived with for a couple of years now, and I'm putting an end to that. Possibly forever. While I'm not the most emotional guy, it honestly kinda hurts my heart a bit. Even Gleason, the evil, crazy bastard I both loved and loathed to write. By the way, how nuts is it that he was indirectly right all along? Gleason kinda was the real hero, even though he really wasn't. Not only did he accidentally save Cross by splitting and diluting the power of the lich curse, *and* saved Greendown by creating the berserker potion, but he *actually* was the chosen one of the gods! Died with none of the glory, of course. That part couldn't have happened to a better person. Went out with a whimper instead of a bang, the way people of his ilk should all be remembered. Not at all. I hope you enjoyed that bit as much as I did.

Anyway, enough of that. This is supposed to be the part where I say thank you. Thank you to the editors and beta readers that helped make this mess somewhat readable. Thank you to my publishers for putting up with me. Thank you to my family for putting up with me more than anyone else I mentioned already has to deal with me. (I'm probably worth it, part of the time.)

Most of all, thank you, person reading these words. Without you, none of this matters. I'm just a guy writing into the void, talking to himself. I mean, I'm that guy anyway, but you make sure I'm not homeless while I do it. And I really do appreciate having a roof over my head while I get to do this absolutely awesome job. So seriously, from the bottom of my heart, thank you.

-Michael

P.S.- Almost forgot to ask you to please leave a review and stuff. It helps sell more books, which helps keep the roof over my head and also have things like food, and electricity. Those are things I also require to write more books, so it's a big circle of the two of us, helping each other. You get books, I get a house, food, and electricity. Win-win.

Also, check out my website, michaelheadauthor.com. It's got links to all my stuff, including merchandise, my other series (which I'm working on right now), and my facebook page and newsletter. All in one handy spot. You can even message me directly, and I personally reply to every email. It may take a couple of days depending on what I'm doing, but you'll get an answer.

P.P.S.- Oh! I nearly missed out on a golden opportunity to give all of you a tiny window into just how truly evil I *actually* can be. Some of you might have seen a few of the online interviews I've done, or even interacted with me in real life. Or, maybe you know me personally. For those of you that don't know anything about me, or haven't watched an interview or panel with me on it, you probably don't know I like to prank and/or mess with my friends. A great example would be in my Threads of Fate series, when I found out Travis Baldree *hates* the word 'dias'. There's a certain paragraph in one of the books where he has to read 'dias' about eighty times in less than thirty seconds, and the live stream of him recording it was absolutely hilarious. Well, lucky for Neil Hellegers–the narrator for this series–I also count him as a friend. We frequently play games together online, and like Travis, we see each other at a bunch of conferences every year. So, the idea of messing with him wouldn't leave my head. I just couldn't figure out how to do it. Then, in a stroke of absolute dumb luck, I thought of the perfect idea, and a character's name was changed. Lee became Lighter, but it's pronounced Lig-hit-er. That's right. Lig. Hit. Er. How many times do you think Neil had to go back and re-record a section when he was narrating this? I bet when you were reading, your brain automatically changed it to Lighter, not Lig-hit-er every single time you saw it. Every. Single. Time. Muahahahaha! I'm only a little evil, I swear. And Neil, if you're reading this, I love you, I swear. Please still call me in for reinforcements the next time we play together.

Okay, I'm finally done this time. Talk to you all soon.

## PATRONS AND PATREON

The people who support me directly every month deserve some extra credit, and a whole lot of extra love. Those who support at the higher tiers, get even more. Thank you all so much for helping me do what I do.

# **Jeff Williams**
# **Cromegas Flare**
# **Justin Novak Jackie Cornelius, Steve Horton, Dillon Kogod, Greg Mat, Nathan Scholl, and Kenneth Darlin**

If you would like to join their ranks, or check out my exclusive content you can go to:

**www.patreon.com/michael_head**

Thanks again, you legendary champions!

## FACEBOOK AND SOCIAL MEDIA

Want to see silly memes and occasionally relevant information about books and author stuff? Check out my Author page on Facebook!

**http://www.facebook.com/author.michael.head**

There's also the Legion Facebook group to check out. It's got a bunch of great people, and plenty of book recommendations to look into if you want to find your next great read.

Only rules for joining are to spread the word about great new books, and don't be an asshat. There are also plenty of author interviews, including a few featuring yours truly.

**http://www.facebook.com/groups/litrpglegion**

I'm on Discord, and I even have my own place. Fair warning, it's not the most active place, but maybe you can help change that! Here's the link:

**https://discord.gg/QSQHmSsGsx**

## ARC AND BETA READERS

ARC and Beta Readers are an integral part of turning a rough draft into a finished book, and the ones I had on this project were fantastic. If you see them out and about in the online community, be sure to poke them and say hello.
To each of you, all I can say is you are amazing.

**Brian Nordon**
**Shawn Weeks**
**Scott Reid**
**Ben Oliver**
**Richard Griffiths**
**Jay Beraz**

## QUEST ACADEMY

By Brian J. Nordon

**A world infested by demons. An Academy designed to train Heroes to save humanity from annihilation. A new student's power could make all the difference.**

Humans have been pushed to the brink of extinction by an ever-evolving demonic threat. Portals are opening faster than ever, Towers bursting into the skies and Dungeons being mined below the last safe havens of society. The demons are winning.

Quest Academy stands defiantly against them, as a place to train the next generation of Heroes. The Guild Association is holding the line, but are in dire need of new blood and the powerful abilities they could bring to the battlefront. To be the saviors that humanity needs, they need to surpass the limits of those that came before them.

In a war with everything on the line, every power matters. With an adaptive enemy, comes the need for a constant shift in tactics. A new age of strategy is emerging, with even the unlikeliest of Heroes making an impact.

**Salvatore Argento has never seen a demon. He has never aspired to become a Hero. Yet his power might be the one to tip the odds in humanity's favor.**

***Buy on Amazon***

## ARISE ALPHA

By Jez Cajiao

**When you steal a hundred grand from some very bad people, the best way to survive is to stay small and quiet...**

Possibly its not to save a pair of drowning girls, not go 'viral' on social media and certainly not to let the local police take your passport, trapping you on a small 'party' island in the middle of the Mediterranean Sea.
But Steve isn't the average guy, he's ex-military, ex-enforcer and ex-human. He's a one man nanite fueled nightmare for those that cross the line, and he's decided that it's time to clean up his act. He's going to make up for the things he's done, and save 'the little guys'.
It's a nice fantasy, but even he has to admit, it's really just a justification, because he's a very bad man, with horrifying abilities, and he's only just learning what he's capable of. He needs a reason to not go to the dark, and if that's hunting down the creatures of the night and beating them to death with their own femurs?
Well, he's just the man for the job.

**Stolen money. Greek Islands. Werewolves and Enforcers... What could possibly go wrong?**

***Buy on Amazon***

## KNIGHTS OF ETERNITY

By Rachel Ní Chuirc

**When Zara awoke in chains she thought she'd gone mad.**

She was Zara the Fury - mistress of flame and fear. Her name was whispered across the land, from ramshackle taverns to the royal court. Even the heroic Gilded Knights thought twice before crossing her path.
She was feared—*respected*
Now she was curled up on a dirt floor on her fiancé's orders. Valerius, leader of the Gilded, mocks her cries for help. And the kingdom is on the brink of war over the missing Lady Eternity…
But that wasn't why Zara thought she had gone mad.
The reason why is that the last thing she remembered was blood, an arcade screen, and the gun that changed everything.

**But no chains can hold the Fury, and when she gets out?**

**The world is going to *burn*.**

***Buy on Amazon***

# SCARLET CITADEL

By Jack Fields

Gormon Hughes is 19, thin as a broom, and has—not for the first time in his life—been swept into the path of trouble. Poor, recently heartbroken, and indebted to the sort of people who file their teeth into needle points and devour wriggling bloated spiders for fun, Hughes sets his sights on salvation.

That salvation is the Scarlet Citadel, a wealthy organization of pageant fighters, monster hunters, and secret keepers. With the aid of strange oracles, rare good fortune, and a unique power that bubbles like champagne in the core of Hughes' being, he must join the Citadel and advance himself.

But the ladder of progression is harsh and dark. The rungs are slippery.

*And falling means disaster…*

https://mybook.to/ScarletCitadel

## LITRPG!

To learn more about LitRPG, talk to other authors including myself, and to just have an awesome time, please join the LitRPG Group

**www.facebook.com/groups/LitRPGGroup**

## **<u>FACEBOOK</u>**

There's also a few really active Facebook groups I'd recommend you join, as you'll get to hear about great new books, new releases and interact with all your (new) favorite authors! (I may also be there, skulking at the back and enjoying the memes...)

**<u>www.facebook.com/groups/LitRPGsociety/</u>**

**<u>www.facebook.com/groups/LitRPG.books/</u>**

**<u>www.facebook.com/groups/LitRPGforum/</u>**

**<u>www.facebook.com/groups/gamelitsociety/</u>**

**<u>www.facebook.com/groups/litrpglegion</u>**

www.ingramcontent.com/pod-product-compliance
Ingram Content Group UK Ltd.
Pitfield, Milton Keynes, MK11 3LW, UK
UKHW030632010225
454425UK00016B/111/J

9 781916 729308